It was ⟨...⟩ olling down
until h ⟨...⟩ ed *Materializations* ⟨...⟩ crolling and
accesse ⟨...⟩ . . . .

A trickle of excitement rippled through Rydell . . . . There they were, one by one, the many reports of similar hauntings, linked together by a common theme: *all the reports had been submitted by professional pilots and every 'materialization' had occurred over Antarctica* . . . .

'The hole in the ozone layer over the Antarctic,' Rydell said, 'first appeared in 1979. The first report of this particular kind of materialization was made in 1979. In that report, as well as all the others since, the Antarctic was the location of the incident.'

'So that kind of materialization is directly linked to the ozone hole over the Antarctic.'

'Exactly,' Rydell said. 'There is another agent eating away at the ozone over the Antarctic and whatever it is, it's also causing materializations from the subconscious, *not* hallucinations, not apparitions, but materializations that have a physical reality. Those things are being *created*.'

'By what?' Polanski asked.

'You tell me,' Rydell replied.

Also by W.A. Harbinson and available in Sphere

**THE LODESTONE**

# DREAM MAKER

*W.A. Harbinson*

An Orbit Book

First published in Great Britain in 1991 by
Orbit Books, a Division of Macdonald & Co (Publishers) Ltd,
London & Sydney

Photoset in North Wales by
Derek Doyle & Associates, Mold, Clwyd
Printed and bound in Great Britain by
BPCC Hazell Books
Aylesbury, Bucks, England
Member of BPCC Ltd.

ISBN 0 7474 0542 5

Orbit Books
A Division of
Macdonald & Co (Publishers) Ltd
Orbit House
1 New Fetter Lane
London EC4A 1AR

A member of Maxwell Macmillan Pergamon Publishing Corporation

# PART ONE

# CHAPTER ONE

Rydell saw it coming. At first it was just a pinprick in a vast sheet of darkness, then a gleaming white eye, but then it expanded, flaring out in all directions, racing at him, exploding around him, obliterating the real world.

He was sucked through space and time, hurled into another dimension, spiralled down through the cascading voices of history and returned to his constant dream.

Space folded into itself. The sudden silence was stunning. He looked up from Europa, across the valleys and frozen mountains, and saw the great golden globe of Jupiter. It hung above the white mountains, which in fact were frozen ice, and it was streaked with yellow and gold, its Great Red Spot a bloody wound. Around it were the satellites, thirteen, maybe more, and all of them, the enormous apple and its seedlings, were drenched in stars.

Rydell knew where he was. Close to Jupiter ... in his dreams. He knew it as he emerged from his dream to the dawn's pearly light. ...

Suzy was sleeping beside him, snoring softly, her body warm. He wanted to stroke her blonde hair and roll gently into her.

'Goddammit!' he whispered.

He rubbed the sleep from his eyes, returning reluctantly to the real world. Glancing around the small bedroom, sparsely furnished, untidy, he wished that he could *really* fly to Jupiter or some other world.

No arguments there, he thought.

Suzy murmured in her sleep, curling up tighter, pressing against him. He felt a rush of heat, his helpless hardening, so groaning in despair at his mortal weakness, he pressed himself to her.

'Hon',' he whispered tentatively.

'Uh?' she grunted in reply.

'Come on, Hon',' he said hopefully, stroking the smooth arch of her raised hip and thigh. 'Let's get it on.'

She groaned and tugged at her raised nightdress. 'Gawd, Tony! What's the time?'

'It's dawn,' he told her, pressing even closer. 'I'll be leaving soon, Hon'.'

'Yeah,' she said. 'Right.'

'For four weeks.'

'You volunteered.'

'Four weeks is a long time, sweetheart, so come on, turn around.'

'I don't feel like it, Tony.'

'Jesus, Suzy, I'll be gone for four weeks!'

'You volunteered,' she repeated.

Her sleepy resentment dampened his ardour, brought him back to earth, and made him once more aware of the liquor on her breath, reminding him that she hadn't come home until the early hours, after leaving him and the kids alone for most of the evening.

She had done it, even knowing that he was leaving this morning to take part in a four-week National Ozone Expedition in Punta Arenas at the southern tip of Chile.

And she hadn't even done it to spite him.

She did it all the time these days.

Sighing in despair, he rolled away from her, gazed forlornly at the ceiling, then eventually slipped out of bed and hurried into the bathroom. He slammed the door behind him, letting her know what he felt.

By the time he had showered and returned to the

4

bedroom, she'd roused herself and could be heard in the kitchen, preparing breakfast and having words with the kids.

She didn't sound very happy.

'Here goes,' Rydell murmured.

He walked into the kitchen-diner and smiled brightly at his kids, Don and Ronnie – twelve and ten respectively – who were having their breakfast at the table. They both looked a bit scruffy, but Ronnie had the face of a golden-haired angel and his elder brother, Don, was listening to him with his familiar expression of grave concern.

'Spiders,' Ronnie was saying, tapping his spoon on the table and automatically scratching his ribcage. 'I dreamed about spiders again. I *always* dream about spiders these days. That's 'cause I hate 'em.'

'You shouldn't hate 'em,' Don said helpfully. 'They're just living things, that's all. I mean, spiders think they look perfectly natural, right? And to each other, they do. They probably think *we* look as ugly as we think *they* look. So, you know, you shouldn't worry about 'em. After all, they're not dangerous like snakes. *They* give me the shivers!'

'I still hate 'em,' Ronnie said.

'Just try not to think of them,' Don said, 'and you'll stop dreaming about them.'

'Stop talking about spiders,' Suzy said wearily, without looking away from the frying pan. She was making flapjacks and eggs. 'I can do without spiders at breakfast, so shut up and eat, kids.'

She was still slim and long-legged, her figure emphasized sexily by her figure-hugging denims, high-heeled boots and tight, open-necked checkered shirt. She was blonde and pretty, with oddly sensual, childish features, though this morning her cat-like green eyes were puffy and bloodshot.

'Morning, kids!' Rydell said. 'Morning, Suzy!'

'What's good about it?' Suzy replied automatically.

'I didn't say it was good, Suzy. I merely mentioned its existence. Not feeling well, darling?'

'Ha, ha. You want flapjacks?'

'With ham and eggs, sunny-side up. If it's not too much trouble ...'

'No trouble at all. That's why I'm here. I'm a good little housewife. It's all in a day's work.'

'I dream about rats, too ...' Ronnie began.

'Shut up!' Suzy warned him.

'I was just saying ...'

'Don't say anything, Ronnie. I don't like rats at breakfast either, so just finish your cornflakes.'

Rydell poured himself some coffee. 'Let him talk,' he said to Suzy. 'He just wants to express his subconscious fears, and that can't be a bad thing.'

'He should just try to forget 'em, like Don told him to,' she replied, breaking eggs into the pan. 'All this talk isn't good for him.'

*Nor for us*, Rydell thought, letting the coffee burn down inside him, smelling the frying ham and eggs, as he gazed out at the other houses of Greenbelt, Maryland, which this morning were bathed in bright sunshine.

'It's all psychology,' Don said helpfully. 'I read that in one of your books, Dad. All these things that scare us come to the surface when we're dreaming. That's why Don dreams of spiders and rats.'

'One more mention of those things at breakfast,' Suzy warned grimly, 'and you'll both end up starving. Why don't *you* make them stop, Tony? They're *your* kids as well!'

'OK, you two,' Rydell said, grinning broadly at them as Suzy placed his plate on the table. 'You're my kids as well, see? So stop all this talk about spiders, rats and

6

snakes and get on with your breakfast.'

Both boys laughed at that, but Suzy glared at him, and when he sat down to eat, he could feel her eyes boring like lasers into his spine.

'OK,' he said, tucking into his breakfast, 'let's call it a truce. I'm going away today, kids.'

'You're *always* going away,' they both said simultaneously.

'Right,' Suzy added.

She brought a cup of coffee to the table, sat down, lit a cigarette, then exhaled a thin stream of smoke.

'At breakfast?' Rydell asked sarcastically.

'At least I'm home,' she replied, then turned towards the kids. 'Are you finished?'

'Yeah,' Don said.

'As the sun's shining and it's Saturday morning, you can go out and play. Just keep the noise down, right?'

'You got a hangover?' Rydell asked.

'Yeah,' Suzy replied. 'I've got a hangover. What's that to you? OK, kids, get going.'

The boys hurried from the kitchen, forgetting spiders, snakes and rats. Rydell watched them disappearing through the door with a great deal of pleasure, but when he turned back to Suzy, she was staring accusingly at him, her face a haze in the cigarette smoke. At that moment Rydell wondered what had happened to the girl he'd once loved so much … and possibly still did.

They had both been born and raised in the high prairie plains of western Iowa, brought up by staunch Republican parents on neighbouring farms. They had met for the first time at high school in Des Moines, where almost immediately they plunged into a passionate, blind teenage romance which encouraged them to marry, probably too young, soon after leaving high school. Pregnant with Don, their first child, Suzy had remained in their small apartment in Ames, while Rydell went on to study physics at Iowa State University. Suzy had soon become dissatisfied with being a house-wife and mother, trapped at home all day. Her mood hadn't improved when Rydell, having passed his exams, was offered a job as a junior physicist with the Manned Spacecraft Centre in Houston, Texas, which meant leaving Iowa, which Suzy loved, and moving to a tract house in Seabrook, a small town located in the dry flatlands between Houston and Galveston.

It wasn't a particularly nice place to live. The winds from the Gulf of Galveston continually swept across the town, bringing with them the suffocating stench of natural gas, petroleum, sulphur and salt, from the many oilfields and plants producing cement, textiles, synthetic rubber and cotton. The region was hot and humid, prone to violent storms, and even the sleepy town they lived in seemed as mean as the weather.

Rydell hadn't liked it much, but at least he had loved his work, whereas Suzy, who'd had a busy social life in Iowa, was driven almost mad with boredom. They had another child, Ronnie, and she started drinking shortly after, and developed an itch for places like Gillie's bar and other noisy watering holes. She invariably went out with her girlfriends, some married, others single, and rarely returned until after midnight, usually red-eyed.

He kept waiting for her to stay out all night, but so far, to his surprise, she hadn't done that.

Still, things weren't too good between them. As Rydell's work-load at MSC had increased, he gradually became a workaholic like most of those at NASA, and he and Suzy had grown even more distant from one another. She had started going out more and the drink made her irritable and had begun to make visible inroads into her appearance.

Like him, she was twenty-eight, but unlike him (he

8

liked to think), she looked like someone in her early thirties – a hell of an age, really – a woman still sensual, even sexy, but no longer attractive.

At least, that's what he told himself.

Looking at her now, and convincing himself that she looked worn-out, he realized that he'd been hoping that their recent move would have changed her – but it hadn't. They had moved to Greenbelt in Maryland, where he was working in the space environmental physics department of NASA–Goddard's Space Flight Centre – work he loved. But Suzy hated Greenbelt as much as she had hated Seabrook and complained constantly that Rydell was away from home too much, which was true. She was drinking even more than ever and Rydell felt that his marriage was dying, but didn't know what to do.

'Look,' he tried, 'about this trip …'

'I don't wanna discuss it, Tony.'

'We *have* to discuss it. You're angry, I can tell, so let's get it out in the open. It's healthier that way.'

'What is there to discuss? It's your goddamned work, after all. I mean, the trip's already booked and as you said yesterday, it's part of the job and you couldn't get out of it if you tried. You have to travel a lot for your work, so why bother discussing it?'

In fact, he wanted to discuss it, but wasn't allowed to. He was going to the Antarctic, as his boss and neighbour Dwight Connors had informed him, because a USAF pilot had recently crashed there. Even now, Rydell got the shivers when he recalled the pilot's last transmission: 'Something's out there! It's above me! It's beside me! It's below me! Jesus Christ, oh my God, I don't believe … Please, no! No, no, no … *No, keep away from me!*' Then he'd started screaming dementedly and his aircraft had spun out of control, eventually crashing in the Antarctic ice, where it burst

9

into flames. … It was a mystery, all right, and one which Rydell wasn't allowed to discuss, which was no help with Suzy.

'You want me to give up my job? Is that what you want? You want me to leave NASA and take a job where the money's a lot less and the work not worth doing, but where at least I'll be at home all the time. Is that what you want?'

'At least we'd see each other now and then!'

'I'm not away that often, Suzy. I only make these trips four or five times a year and a month's the longest I've ever been away. I mean, I'd like to be at home a bit more, but what the hell can I do? The money's good and …'

'It's not the money and you know it. You stay there because you like it. You're fanatical about your goddamned work and you love making these trips and you don't give a damn that I'm rotting here while you have a good time.'

Rydell was outraged. 'While you *rot* here?' he shouted. 'At least I go away to *work*! And when I'm home, at least I'm home! I'm not out every evening, getting drunk and making eyes at the ladies, like you do with those cowboys. Goddammit, I …'

'Cowboys? What cowboys? We're not in Texas now, Tony. We're in Greenbelt, Maryland, in a dumb tract house in the boring suburbs, and our neighbours are pilots, astronauts, scientists and their god-awful wives. I don't make eyes at *cowboys*!'

'You know what I mean, Suzy.'

'Right, I know what you mean! But since you're married to your work, I don't know why my activities should concern you. And without them, without getting out at nights, I'd go mad in this place.'

'You said that in Texas, too. You'd say it wherever we moved to. Other women would take pride in raising their kids and running a decent home, but all you want is to have a good time with those tramps you call friends.'

'And why not?' she replied indignantly, blowing a cloud of smoke at him. 'You love your work, so *you're* having a good time. If you are, why not me?'

She had him there and he knew it. He loved his work and always had. Even as a kid he had dreamed about being a scientist involved with space research and since then, he had single-mindedly devoted himself to achieving his goal.

Not sure as an adolescent just what branch of science he wanted to enter, he'd had no doubts at all about his obsession with outer space and to that end had read voraciously about the great rocket pioneers – Konstantin Tsiolkovsky, Hermann Oberth, Robert Goddard, Wernher von Braun – and had built countless ingenious models of various aeroplanes and rockets, while most of his friends were out cruising or at the movies.

At one time, toying with the idea that he might become an astronaut, he had thought of joining the air force, but had changed his mind because he hadn't wanted to wear a uniform. Instead, he had taken flying lessons while studying physics in Iowa and eventually, given his academic brilliance and dedication, he had been accepted by NASA. Then he progressed to work with the Earth System Science programme of the NASA–Goddard Institute for Space Studies, created to study the increasing dangers of the greenhouse effect caused by the widening hole in the Earth's protective ozone layer.

Now, though still a physicist, he was more frequently called a climatologist and, on behalf of NASA, had worked with climate change models for a broad range of climatology organizations. He'd worked for the

National Centre for Atmospheric Research in Boulder, Colorado, the Geophysical Fluid Dynamics Laboratory at Princetown University, the Meteorological Office in Bracknell, Berkshire, England, the Beijer Institute in Stockholm, Sweden, the Centre for Applied Climatology and Environmental Studies in the University of Münster, West Germany, the TATA Energy Research Institute in New Delhi, India and numerous other similar organisations in Europe, England and the United States.

No wonder Suzy was mad at him. He did travel a lot. They both knew that he loved his work and couldn't give it up for anything – not even his marriage.

He felt guilty about that.

'Listen,' he said, as he had said too often, 'I've got to go now. We'll discuss this properly when I get back. We'll work something out.'

'No, we won't,' she replied. 'You always say that, but it never happens. You'll just go off for a month, leaving me alone with the kids, and when you come back, you'll be too busy writing your damned reports to have time to discuss our situation. Then, before you get time to do it, you'll be off on another trip.'

'It'll be different this time, Suzy.'

'No, it won't. Not at all. And I'm fed up of listening to your goddamned stories each time you take off. To hell with you and your work, Tony. I'm sick of being left alone here. This time, I'm warning you, if you go, I won't be here when you get back!'

Rydell sighed and stood up, glancing down at his suitcase. 'You're being melodramatic,' he said. 'I think I'll go while the going's good.'

'I won't stay here! I swear it!'

'You'll leave home?'

'Yes, I will.'

'Don't be stupid.'

'Just go to hell, Tony! I won't be here when you get back. You walk out that door and we're finished. Do you understand, damn you?'

Startled, he stared at her, hardly believing her vehemence, but gradually realizing that she meant what she had said.

'Christ,' he cried, 'this is crazy!'

'It's not crazy; it's the truth.'

'When I get back ...'

'I won't be here!'

'Will you *listen* to me?' Rydell shouted, raising his hands as if in prayer, already sweating, though he hadn't stepped outside to brave Maryland's morning heat. 'Will you just goddamn *listen*?'

'No!' Suzy snapped. 'Why should I? You *promised* you wouldn't go away again and yet you're going already. Damn you, Tony, I *hate* you!'

She had been saying that for months, but now he knew she was starting to mean it. He glanced through the window, trying to control his heavy breathing. Looking up at the brightening sky over Greenbelt, he yearned to be flying through it.

'I have to go and you know it,' he said, 'so I'm leaving right now.' He picked up his suitcase and stared at her, taking note of her flushed face, and convinced himself that he no longer cared for her, no matter how much he wanted to. 'You'll calm down as soon as I leave,' he said. 'You'll think more clearly then. Do I get a goodbye kiss?'

'No, damn you, you don't.'

He shrugged, trying to shake off the hurt. 'OK, Suzy, goodbye.'

She inhaled on her cigarette, stubbed it out in the ashtray, stood up and walked out.

That was her answer.

Rydell sighed then, not knowing what else to do, he

picked up his suitcase and left the house. He found Don and Ronnie on the front lawn. They stopped playing when they saw him and stared at his suitcase. Then each boy embraced him, stepping away to let him walk off.

Shaken by the fight with Suzy and deeply moved by the boys' impulsive display of emotion, he stopped before getting into his car and turned to look at them.

The boys smiled and waved. Then Suzy, smoking another cigarette, appeared in the doorway behind them and stared silently at him. Not knowing what to do, he simply shrugged his shoulders helplessly, climbed into his car and hurriedly drove off.

# CHAPTER TWO

Utilizing the will-power she had learned as one of the few female astronauts, Clare Holton slept like a log, awoke at nine without the aid of a room call, slipped out of bed, showered and dressed herself, then had the light breakfast she had ordered from room service. Then she sat down at the desk overlooking Montreal's Saint Lawrence River and proceeded to work.

As the scientific liaison officer between the United States Department of Defence, the National Aeronautics and Space Administration and its National Space Technological Laboratories, she had spent the past seven days attending a meeting of the representatives of the technologically developed countries, being held under the auspices of the United Nations. Now, while the representatives of over thirty countries were individually deciding whether or not they should sign the first global treaty aimed at reducing world-wide atmospheric pollution, she synthesized in her head the mass of detail she had soaked up over the past week. Later that afternoon, she was going to speak to the assembled delegates on behalf of NASA, which, in this instance, was representing the US government's official stance.

Three hours later, she finished her task, folded up the notes and put them into her bag, then left her room and went downstairs to join Jack Douglas for lunch in the hotel's restaurant.

'*Bonjour!*' Jack exclaimed, raising his glass of Scotch to her as she approached his table. '*Comment allez-vous?*'

he added, obviously trying to impress her with his limited command of French.

'I'm fine,' she replied, though her command of French was better than his. 'I'm actually feeling bright and healthy, which is more than you'll feel if you have another Scotch before the conference.'

He grinned wryly as she took the chair facing him.

'A mere medicinal,' he said. 'Of course we know that Miss Holton, physicist and former astronaut, is not in need of artificial stimulation like most other mere mortals. Can I tempt you at least?'

'I don't think so,' Clare replied. 'I'll have a Perrier water and the Caesar salad. And you should eat, too.'

'I could eat *you*,' he said.

'I didn't mean sex, I meant food. Have an omelette, at least.'

'You're so sensible, Clare.'

He called the waiter, ordered the food, then leaned over the table to ask: 'Have you prepared your speech?'

'I wrote it this morning.'

'Of course,' he said, sipping his Scotch and grinning at her. 'Your intellectual brilliance is renowned, your dedication much lauded. That's why you intimidate so many men; they can't be men in your presence.'

'You mean, they can't look after me, feed me sugar, pat my head. They can't have my blind adoration.'

'That's right,' Jack said. 'They're frightened by your intelligence and independence. They lose their balls in your presence.'

Clare couldn't help smiling. 'I don't seem to intimidate *you*, so what does that prove? That you're a man amongst men?'

'Not a man amongst men, but certainly more of a man than you are. Or, to be more precise, that I'm a man who's not frightened of women who don't fear

16

me. But you're so completely your own woman, most men can't get to grips with you.'

'And you?'

'Not being frightened of you, I can treat you as an equal and since that's such a rarity for you, you were attracted to me, though not as much as I'd like.'

'And how much is that?'

'As much as it takes to make you marry me.'

'That's too much,' she told him.

He didn't flinch, and she admired him for that; it was that kind of strength, so rare in a man, that had drawn her into his bed.

Just short of forty years of age, which made him ten years her senior, he possessed matinée-idol good looks, was too bright for his own good, and had cynicism welded to his intelligence and rampant ambition. An economic advisor on environmental issues, he worked, where she also worked, in the old executive office building next to the White House, reported directly to the President, and was widely rumoured to be a mean man to mix with where work was involved.

Clare enjoyed his cynicism, though she didn't actually share it, but was wary of him because of his rumoured mean-streak. Just occasionally, when she had teased him about something, she had sensed him suppress his anger ... and that, plus the fact that he'd been married, made her wary.

'*Why* won't you marry me?' he asked, as if reading her mind.

She sighed. 'I've told you before. I just don't want to be married.'

The waiter brought his omelette, her salad and Perrier water, placed them on the table and left.

'Why not? Were your parents unhappily married?'

'No, Jack, they weren't. They were very happily married. But they were also independent and gave

17

themselves the kind of personal freedom that's so rare in marriage. They gave that to me as well, and told me to hold it dear. I grew up aware of the sheer possessiveness of other people. Because they were both devoted to their work, they drilled that discipline into me and instilled the belief that since work takes up most of our time, we should work only at what we truly love and put nothing above it.'

'Not even personal relationships?'

'I doubt that I could get that seriously involved with a man who didn't share my beliefs.'

'Such a man,' Jack said, cutting his omelette with his fork and then raising a piece to his lips, 'would obviously have to love his work more than he loved you.'

Clare sighed. 'I suppose so.'

'Did your father love his work more than he loved your mother?'

'You're simplifying the issue,' Clare said. 'It wasn't as simple as that.'

She tried to explain it as they ate their meals. As she did so she smiled, thinking of her parents with all the love of a single, cherished child.

Born and raised in an elegant townhouse in Georgetown, Washington DC, she had nothing but loving memories of her childhood in a home that was always filled with people and, at least to her childish perception, with optimism, good humour and hard work. Her father had been, and remained, a Professor of Astronomy Space Sciences, formerly at NASA, presently at the Center for Radiophysics and Space Research; and her mother, when alive, had been a highly successful analytical chemist and distinguished author.

Clare, raised and guided by two singular personalities, influenced by their philosophy and experience,

18

had been filled forever, so she thought, with the absolute conviction that only people who first respected themselves, could offer true respect and freedom to their loved ones. Certainly she had learned that her father and mother, both dedicated to their individual careers, had each, by putting their work first, given the other the freedom to do the same. She would never forget that.

'So when, six months ago, my mother died,' she told Jack, 'my father and I were able to deal with it because we had what even my mother thought was the most important thing: the work we loved. A reason to be. Not too many have that, Jack.'

He stared at her, not with warmth, but in an oddly intense, curious manner, then said, 'And that's why you still haven't married?'

'Yes,' she replied without pause, 'I think so. I think I'm still single because I was taught to retain a strong sense of myself and haven't yet met a man so attractive to me that I'd surrender my emotional security for the dangers of a lasting relationship.' She smiled and murmured, 'Not even you, Jack.'

'My God, you're one hard, direct lady. No wonder I like you.'

'You like me because you think I'm just like you, but I'm not. I'm not that cold.'

'You think I'm cold?'

'Yes. You're hot in bed, but you're calculating. You know exactly how to please a woman sensually, but emotionally, you're not involved.'

'I am. I keep asking you to marry me but you refuse. Why would I take it if I didn't really want you?'

'If I'd said "yes" the first time, probably you'd have lost interest. You're a man who can't stand being refused.' Amused to have disconcerted him again, she smiled broadly and reached across the table to take his hand. 'Now let's pay the check and go to the conference.'

'I'll treat you,' he said. 'It's on the White House. They know how to waste money.'

'Money wasted,' she said, 'is money well spent. You can have me tonight for that.'

'You're so generous!'

When he paid the check, they caught a taxi to the conference centre, and took their places with the other delegates.

After seven days of often acrimonious debate, most of the delegates had clearly made up their minds and were merely enduring the closing summaries without any great interest. Nevertheless, under the glare of the spotlights and in front of the massed TV cameras, boom-mikes and photographers, Clare spoke on behalf of NASA.

Afterwards she summarized her speech for those who would see an edited version either on television or in the newspapers. In simple terms she explained that the ozone in the atmosphere protected the surface of the Earth from ultraviolet radiation produced by the Sun, which might otherwise destroy life on most of the planet.

'And ozone,' she said, 'is a form of oxygen, the active ingredient of the air we breathe, the gas that's essential for all forms of animal life on Earth.' She reminded them that the ozone layer was presently being destroyed at an ever-increasing rate by the fumes and gases emitted by spray cans, insecticides, paints, polishes, disinfectants, and car and aircraft exhausts; destroyed, indeed, to the degree where it had finally formed an invisible hole in the atmosphere – a hole as wide as the United States and as high as Mount Everest.

'The complete destruction of the remaining ozone

layer will cause an increase in skin cancer, cataracts and other diseases,' she told them. 'As well as blighting food crops, and harming animals, it will result in the upset of the world's climate and life-support systems. If the depletion of ozone isn't checked it will cause a shift in the global average temperature, which would plunge us back into a full Ice Age or melt the polar ice-caps and inundate major cities like New York, London and Leningrad.'

She paused to let her words sink in, then continued, 'In short, if we do not vote, here and now, to take specific steps to reduce world-wide atmospheric pollution and to protect the Earth's ozone layer, we will be accepting the eventual destruction of human life as we know it. Ladies and gentlemen, thank you.'

She stepped down to enthusiastic applause. Later that afternoon, when all the votes had been counted, nearly thirty nations had officially pledged to reduce the release of chlorofluorocarbons, or CFCS, by fifty per cent by the end of the twentieth century.

Clare was well pleased.

# CHAPTER THREE

'No,' Suzy insisted, wiping a tear from her eye, 'I won't listen, Maggie. I've had about as much as I can take, so this time I'm doing it.'

'For God's sake, calm down,' Maggie begged. 'You're just upset, that's all. Just give yourself time to think about it and I'm sure …'

'Are you gonna help me or not?' Suzy cried, hauling more clothes out of the chest of drawers in the bedroom and throwing them into a suitcase. 'If not, you can leave!'

Maggie was her neighbour and the wife of Rydell's best friend, Dwight Collins, and luckily she had seen a lot of life and did not easily take offence. Plump and blonde, she simply shrugged her shoulders and raised her hands 'OK! OK! I'm here to help, I'm gonna make you some coffee, give you a cigarette and try to calm you down and talk sense to you. That's what friends are for, right?'

'Wrong. I don't need that now. What I need is a friend who'll cut the crap and help me carry this stuff out to the car. Will you do that or not?'

Maggie sighed. 'Yeah, I'll do it. Dwight'll kill me when he gets back, but I'll do it. It's just I think you should sit down, have a drink and talk this thing through.'

'That's the best idea you've had,' Suzy said. 'At least pour me that drink. I can pack while I'm drinking it.'

She continued throwing clothes from the chest of drawers into suitcases as Maggie left the room, returning with two glasses of bourbon. Suzy sipped gratefully, then setting her glass on the table, she started zipping up the first suitcase.

'Why are you doing this?' Maggie asked.

'Because our marriage is finished.'

'It's not finished,' Maggie said. 'It's just going through a bad patch. Most marriages do, but they often recover. Just give it a chance.'

'Give *him* a chance, you mean.'

'Yeah, give Rydell a chance. I mean, the guy works for NASA. *All* those guys are workaholics. Even Dwight, for chrissakes, works all the time, but apart from that, he's OK. He is a good man, just like Tony Rydell. You're giving up a lot for a little, Suzy. It's all out of proportion.'

Suzy lit a cigarette, inhaled greedily and blew smoke-rings. She could hear the boys packing in the next room, which made her feel worse.

She'd told them only an hour ago that she wanted a break from their Dad, wanted to go live with her folks for a while and take them with her. For the boys it would mean a strange place and new school and if that had not shocked them enough, she told them that they were leaving immediately, with no time to say goodbye even to their friends, let alone their Dad. They'd asked why and she'd tried hard to tell them, but you couldn't explain it.

It was too grown-up for them.

'I don't care what you say, Maggie. I think I'm doing the right thing. You've been living like this for years and maybe you like it, but I can't stand being here all alone while Tony travels the globe and spends most of his time working when he *is* home. I'm not a scientist's wife, I never will be, and we don't love each other any more, which just makes it worse.'

'Love changes as you get older,' Maggie said. 'It's still

23

there. It's just not the same.'

'Oh, yeah? What does that mean?' Suzy could still remember the feelings she'd had for Rydell at high school: the blinding intensity and all-consuming passion, the radiance that lit you up inside and made you feel magical. She hadn't felt anything like that for years, only neglect and frustration, and the knowledge of what she had lost only made her feel worse.

'I mean, either it's there or it's not,' she said. 'If it's not the same, it's not there.'

'You're so romantic.' Maggie sighed. 'You still feel like an adolescent. But you're gonna have to learn to grow up, Suzy, and keep a check on your feelings.'

'I don't wanna be that way. It's not what I am, Maggie. I wanna live every day of my life and not get buried alive. He doesn't see me anymore. He only sees his goddamned work. I mean, even when I threatened to leave, he put his work first.' She shrugged, to hide her deep hurt. 'Well, to hell with him.'

She zipped up the second suitcase, hauled it off the bed, placed it on the floor and glanced around her.

She was looking for Rydell.

'You can't go home again,' said Maggie.

'What does that mean?'

'What the hell are you going to do in Iowa? I mean, what's there for you now?'

'My parents,' Suzy said. 'They still have the same farm. They live in the bread-basket of America and they have a good life. I'll stay with them. I might even help on the farm. The boys can attend a local school and breathe clean air for a change and maybe go to church once or twice. It'll work out fine, Maggie.'

'And that's it? You're set to go? You're just gonna leave a farewell note, get in the car and drive off to Iowa with the kids?'

'Yeah, Maggie, that's right. And I'm taking all my

albums and books with me, so come on, help me carry them.'

'Dear God,' Maggie murmured, but she did as she was told, picking up the box of books while Suzy resolutely took the suitcases and walked out of the bedroom. Glancing into the boys' bedroom, she saw that they'd practically finished as well, though they weren't looking happy.

'Are you set to go?' she asked.

'Yeah,' Don replied.

'Then bring your stuff out to the car.'

'OK,' Ronnie said.

She ignored his wounded look, though it hurt. She knew damned well that what she was doing was wrong, but wasn't able to stop herself. She was too emotional, was why, and she'd always been that way, and when she felt neglected, as she had this past few years, she just couldn't handle it.

She'd tried to, of course, but being here hadn't helped. She needed attention, was willing to give it, and so didn't feel comfortable in this scientific community, where everyone was so damned intellectual and obsessed with their work.

Tony was the same. He lived and breathed his god-damned work. And in doing that, he'd forgotten she existed, killed off the love they'd shared at high school, and almost turned her into one of those wives who quietly dwindle away each day. He'd never treated her badly or played around with other women, but he'd forgotten what had joined them together and she couldn't forgive that.

She still loved the scatter-brained bastard, but he was too dumb to notice.

More resolute, Suzy picked up the suitcases again and followed Maggie out to the car. Having just placed the box of books into the trunk, Maggie straightened up, breathing heavily. She looked near to tears.

'I can't believe …'

'Believe it,' Suzy said. 'I'm really doing it this time.'

Maggie glanced over her shoulder. 'The boys are coming,' she said. True enough, they came down the lawn, carrying their gear, Don, the eldest, grimly serious, Ronnie looking wounded. Both of them gave Suzy their suitcases to be placed in the trunk.

'Are you OK?' Suzy asked them.

'Sure,' Don replied.

'Look, I told you,' she lied again, 'it's not for a lifetime. We're just gonna give it a try. If you really don't like it after a time, I'll send you both home. OK?'

'OK,' Don said.

Ronnie didn't say a word, but he glanced up and down the street. He hadn't said goodbye to his friends and that was obviously bugging him … That and the shock of leaving so suddenly … Suzy choked up just seeing that.

'OK, kids. Get in the car. We'll be off in a minute.'

They did as they were told, climbing into the rear seats, then Suzy led Maggie up the lawn and back into the house. She checked all the windows, the gas and electricity, then sat down at the kitchen table to write Tony a short good-bye note.

Maggie started crying. Suzy simply glared at her. Maggie went into the bedroom, returned with the record-albums, said, 'I'll see you out at the car,' and hurried outside.

Suzy struggled with the note. She didn't know where to begin. She hardly ever had to write (like most people, she used the 'phone) and trying to put her feelings onto paper made her feel a bit threatened. She started a few times, tore the paper up, tried again, chewed her lower lip, sniffed back tears and remembered their better days.

God, he'd been so cute! He'd just charmed her immediately. A bit scatter-brained and most times dishevelled, but he'd had that little thing about him – a kind of childishness, or innocence – and strangely, an awful lot of girls had liked it.

He hadn't threatened them, was why. He was too distracted to be a threat. If you wanted him, you practically had to rape him, though he'd never complain. In fact, that's what *she'd* done – she'd come on real strong – and they'd done it in the car, not too well, but with lots of feeling, and after that, he could fill her up with such tenderness, she just couldn't believe it.

Then they'd married and eventually lost it and she couldn't forget it.

She'd tell him that in this note.

But she couldn't do it. You had to touch someone to say that. So, touching only pen and paper, she wrote carefully:

*Dear Tony,*

*I can't take any more, so I'm keeping my promise. I'm taking the kids with me to my folks in Iowa and I'm leaving you everything but my favourite records and books. Don't think you have to keep in touch. Goodbye and good luck.*

*Yours sincerely,*
*Suzy*

Leaving the note on the kitchen table, Suzy walked out of the house for the last time. After carefully locking the front door, she walked to the car.

Maggie, wiping tears from her eyes, said, 'Please, Suzy, just think about what you're doing. Just give it a ...'

27

'No,' Suzy said. Then she smiled, feeling light-headed, and suddenly brimming over with emotion, she embraced her good friend.

'You take care,' she said.

'And you.'

'Don't let Tony be stupid.'

'I won't,' Maggie promised.

They hugged emotionally again, then broke apart, embarrassed. Suzy climbed into the car, closed the door and turned on the ignition.

'Are you kids OK?' she asked.

'Sure,' Don said.

'Sure,' Ronnie said.

Suzy drove off as Maggie waved goodbye and both boys waved back.

Suzy kept driving, her vision blurred by tears, turned the corner at the bottom of the street and said, 'Here we go, kids.'

'Aw, Mom!' Ronnie murmured. There were tears in his eyes as well.

Suzy slowed down, eventually stopped the car, and just stared straight ahead.

'Iowa!' Don declared. 'What will *we* do in Iowa? We don't know a soul in Iowa! And what about Dad?'

'I told you; I'm leaving him.'

'It's not right,' Don said.

'I don't wanna leave home,' Ronnie said. '*Please*, Mom! Please don't go.'

'I've gotta go,' she told him. 'You don't understand, but I've got to. If you don't want to come, then don't come, but I've got to do this.'

'Would you be upset?' Don asked. Now he, too, was almost crying.

'No, Don,' she said. 'I understand. You two do what you have to do.'

The boys stared at one another, both with wet eyes.

28

Then Don nodded and they opened the rear doors and climbed out of the car.

Suzy opened the trunk from inside and the boys removed their suitcases. After slamming the lid of the trunk closed, they both walked back to her.

Don stuck his face close to the open window to show her his glistening eyes.

'Please don't go, Mom,' he said.

She smiled and kissed him. 'I have to.'

Don sniffed and sighed too loudly and stepped away as Ronnie raised his face close to her. She kissed the tears from his cheeks.

'We love you, Mom,' he said.

'I know,' she said. 'I love you too. I just can't help myself. I'll come and see you soon; I promise you that. In the meantime, you look after your Dad. Here,' she added, handing Don her set of doorkeys. 'Now get back to the house.'

Don took the keys and nodded, but this time he couldn't speak. Ronnie shuffled his feet uneasily, looked up at his elder brother, then tugged at his arm, made him pick up his suitcase and walked him away from the car, back towards their own street.

Suzy watched them turn the corner and disappear from sight. When they were gone, she just sat there, her heart beating like a drum, thinking of Rydell in the Antarctic – working, always working – and surrendering inevitably to a pain that threatened to tear her apart.

She wanted him to feel what she felt, to know what she was feeling now, and tried to send those feelings leaping over the vast distance between them, to explode all around him.

Failing and frustrated, she burst into tears, hammered the steering wheel with her clenched fists, then eventually stopped her crying and drove off ... all the way to Iowa.

# CHAPTER FOUR

Rydell felt sleepy and distracted as he entered the briefing room at the edge of the airstrip in Punta Arenas, Chile. Though this Airborne Antarctic Ozone Experiment had been organized and was managed by NASA, the National Science Foundation, the US National Oceanic and Atmospheric Administration and the US Chemical Manufacturers Association were also involved. The briefing room, Rydell noted instantly, was filled with their representatives, as well as members of university and government research establishments in the United States, Britain, France, Argentina, Chile and New Zealand. Most of these men, like Rydell, looked bulky in their flying suits, but none of them seemed as distracted as he felt.

Taking a seat near the back of the crowded room, he felt hungover and looked forward to taking some oxygen. He had only vague memories of the previous evening which he'd spent in a bar in downtown Punta Arenas, thinking long and hard about Suzy, before getting drunk with a vengeance. He did remember that at some point in the evening, he'd left the hotel bar and staggered down to the shore to observe the sunset over the Strait of Magellan, with its spectacular view of Tierra del Fuego, the Land of Fire. He'd fallen asleep on the beach, was drenched by a rainstorm, and had awakened shivering, ashamed of himself.

He had never acted like that before.

Still ashamed of himself, he tried to concentrate as his good friend Dwight Collins, the Energy and

Environment Programme Director of the NASA–Goddard Institute for Space Studies, took his place on the stage. Behind him was an enlarged image of the ozone layer over the South Pole, computer-processed from last year's Total Ozone Mapping Spectrometer (TOMS) data. It looked like a surrealistic painting of a globe, the different coloured circles representing atmospheric readings, the ragged black hole in its centre, disturbingly clear.

Dwight, who would not be flying with the Airborne Expedition, grinned laconically as he picked up a pointer and tapped the black hole in the computer-processed, aerial view of the South Pole.

'Good morning, gentlemen. This,' he continued, tapping the black hole again with his pointer, 'is where you'll be spending the next six or seven hours. Flying through the hole in the ozone layer over the Antarctic, you'll make what we hope will be, in combination with our unmanned balloon, satellite and land-based observations, the most complete examination yet of the growing hole in the ozone layer. The hole is presently the length and breadth of the United States and the depth of Mount Everest, and is getting bigger all the time. We must ascertain what's causing it and find a way to stop its growth. That's your mission, gentlemen.'

Putting the pointer down and leaning his hands on the table he carried on. 'The hole was first noticed by members of the British Antarctic Survey team, working at Halley Bay, Antarctica, in 1982. Although those ozone readings were taken with a fairly primitive spectrophotometer, the data collected was later supported by the findings of our own satellite, Nimbus 7. Its Total Ozone Mapping Spectrometer, or TOMS, and Solar Backscatter Ultraviolet, or SBUV experiment, between them confirmed that the depletion of ozone over Halley Bay amounted to more than thirty percent, that it wasn't happening just over Halley Bay, and that the loss of ozone from the stratosphere was increasing rapidly, both upwards and outwards, at a dangerous rate.'

He paused dramatically, to let the full import of his words sink in, then glanced around the room, caught Rydell's eye, and nodded, smiling slightly.

'By 1986,' he continued, 'we'd discovered a definite link between high altitude clouds over Antarctica and the formation of the ozone hole. These clouds, called Polar Stratospheric Clouds, or PSCs, form in the lower stratosphere over Antarctica in the winter months, then dissipate in the spring. It's believed that a series of chemical reactions within the clouds releases chlorine in an active form, which leads to drastic destruction of the ozone. We know that a link exists between extreme cold, the formation of Polar Stratospheric Clouds, chemical reactions on the surfaces of those cloud particles and the destruction of the ozone layer, which has led to the great hole in the atmosphere over the South Pole. The purpose of this expedition is to find out everything we can about this phenomena.'

Rydell usually enjoyed his friend's scientific talks, but couldn't concentrate as normal. Sitting in a hut on the edge of an airstrip in the southernmost city in the world, he wished he was in a briefing room in the Goddard Space Flight Centre, Greenbelt, Maryland, ten minutes drive from his home. He kept thinking of home and of his problems with Suzy. With grief and self-pity he recalled how he and Suzy had changed over the years, drifting further apart, until they hardly recognized each other as the people they had been. He thought about his kids, whom, in his view, Suzy had started to neglect and about her threat to leave before he got back. He didn't want to believe that she would do that, but you never could tell.

He almost groaned aloud, but checked himself just in time, and tried to concentrate on what Dwight Collins was saying.

'For this particular expedition,' Dwight continued, 'we'll make about twenty flights over the next month, using two aircraft filled with our instruments. One of the aircraft is a converted DC-8 airliner, which will hold up to forty passengers and their equipment and fly at an altitude of about twelve kilometres at the bottom of the ozone layer. The other aircraft is the ER-2, an updated, research version of Lockheed's U-2 spy plane, one of the best of its kind for high-altitude flights. However, since it's a single-seater aircraft, with its scientific payload packaged in two pods, one under each wing, those of you who can fly can take turns with the ER-2 while the rest of you will be together in the DC-8. Since Tony Rydell was instrumental in initiating this whole project, I think he should be the one to have the pleasure of the first flight in the ER-2 today. Any others who want to have a go, put your name down, and we'll go in strict rotation. OK?'

There was a general murmur of agreement and much shaking of heads. Rydell, realizing he was to go first, felt even worse. At least I'll get my oxygen, he thought, without being seen.

'Right,' Dwight said. 'You've all got your separate instructions. Any queries during the flight you can put direct to me in the control tower. Now get going, and good luck. Rydell, you wait here.'

Rydell climbed to his feet with the others, but waited until most of them had left the room before walking up to Dwight. Over six-foot tall, Dwight looked down at him with a broad grin.

'You like your birthday present?' he asked.

'You mean the ER-2?'

'Right.'

'Yeah, thanks,' Rydell said without conviction. 'I really appreciate it, Dwight. I can't wait to get up there.'

Dwight's brow furrowed thoughtfully. 'You don't look so keen,' he said. 'In fact, you've been a bit distracted since you got here. What's going on?'

Rydell shrugged. 'Nothing.'

'Don't bullshit me,' Dwight said, forthright as usual. 'Something's wrong. I can tell. Is it Suzy again?'

'Yeah,' Rydell confessed. 'It's Suzy. She's threatened to leave me.'

Dwight sighed. Living in Greenbelt, he and his wife socialized a lot with their neighbours and knew them better than most. Certainly, Dwight had observed Suzy and Rydell growing apart over the years. He had flirted innocently with Suzy because he knew she liked the attention, but privately he disapproved of her and had said so to Rydell.

'She's not the NASA kind,' he said, repeating what he had told Rydell before. 'She's never understood the fact that we're dedicated to what we do, that we have to work all hours and that a NASA wife has to support that, even if she doesn't like it. Suzy comes from a small town – from a bunch of Iowa farmers – and she's more inclined to live for the moment, than to think of the future. She can't see that *we* live for the future; it's what our work's all about. She just can't get to grips with that.'

'Yeah,' Rydell said, 'I agree. But what the hell, she's my wife. We've shared a lot together and she's the mother of my kids. What the hell can I do?'

'For a start, you can stop worrying. You've got a job to do here. She's gonna be there when you get back. She's just angry, that's all.'

'I think she meant it this time.'

34

'They *always* mean it,' Dwight retorted. 'Well, at least while they say it, but that doesn't mean too much. How many times have you heard it before? How many times were you breaking up?'

'A lot, I suppose.'

'Damn right, so forget it this time. You'd do better to concentrate on your work, because this flight could be dangerous. You'll be flying at an altitude of roughly twenty kilometres, which is, as you know, about as high as you can go without a rocket-propelled spaceship. You're going right into the area where the unmanned balloon flights have shown the most ozone depletion. It's gonna be damned cold and the air's so thin up there that one fault in that single-engined baby could prove to be fatal, so forget Suzy, concentrate on the job and be careful as hell, OK?'

'OK.'

'Good. Let's get going.'

They left the hut and stepped into the wind which was blowing forcefully across the airstrip, lined mostly with the planes of the Chilean air force. The single-engined, single-seater aircraft with the payload pods beneath each wing had been prepared for take-off and was surrounded by wind-whipped engineers. Still not happy, but now able to concentrate, Rydell climbed up into the aircraft's cockpit, strapped himself in, then gave the thumbs-up to Dwight and watched him hurrying away. He called the control tower to request permission to take-off, received it, quickly checked the windspeed and direction, and the length of runway, then manœuvred out of the parking bay and prepared for take-off.

With the plane roaring in his ears, Rydell covered his face with the oxygen mask, took a deep breath and instantly felt better. Removing the mask, he checked the flying controls and instruments, then ran through

35

the appropriate take-off drills. Finally, when clearance came, he pushed the throttle forward with his right hand, controlling the nose-wheel tiller with his other. He repeatedly called out his speed as he taxied along the runway, the white central markings rushing at him ever more quickly. When the plane reached the decision speed, Velocity One, Rydell saw the nose rise and the ground fall away and was filled with irresistible, childish exhilaration as the landing gears moved back into their wells and the plane climbed steeply into silvery light.

The airport disappeared and was replaced with a widening landscape: the fjords, lakes, lagoons and great mountains of Patagonia suddenly sweeping out on all sides to the Earth's curved horizon. Rydell felt better then, losing his cares in the joy of flight. He watched the land retreat and the rivers run into the sea, which stippled with light and shadow, was like a great sunlit, reflecting bowl. Rydell flew on in a trance of delight, hardly aware of passing time, until he saw a boot of land, the Antarctic Peninsula. Crossing the Antarctic Circle, over the Bellingshausen Sea, he finally saw, emerging out of a striated, silver haze, the vast, overwhelming expanse of the Antarctic continent. The sight took his breath away.

The ozone hole covered an area even greater than the whole Antarctic, so he realized that he was inside the hole when he saw the white wilderness.

Since the scientific instruments packed in the two pods, one under each wing, operated manually, he switched them on as soon as he crossed over the snowy wastes of Ellsworth Land and began his careful ascent to an altitude of twenty kilometres.

The instruments in the pods beneath his wings automatically measured what the thirty-odd scientists in the DC-8 were also measuring at a lower altitude with individual instruments: ozone concentrations, chlorine and bromine monoxides, nitrogen oxides and nitric acid, aerosol particles and water.

Looking down, Rydell was fascinated by the spectacle, almost drunk on the awesome beauty of that most fabulous of Earth's continents, with its dry valleys of moss and lichens, flecked with snow, gleaming white ice-shelves, frozen mountain ranges and lakes. It was a wilderness of pack- and sheet-ice, alluvial ice-falls and glaciated earthen ridges between polar plateaux, where mountain peaks towered majestically over glittering ice-caps. The icebergs and snow banks appeared jade-green because of the algae and plankton which survived on the rocky knolls between the plains of virgin snow. Piles of whalebones also lent their surrealistic contours to the otherwise immaculate sheen of the whiteflowing wilderness.

It seemed to go on forever.

Rydell flew high above it, farther into it as he ascended, taking the ER-2 to the very limit of its 5,500 kilometre range, and there, in the polar vortex, where the circumpolar winds isolated the air inside from the rest of the atmosphere, he flew into the dangerous haze of Polar Stratospheric Clouds, or PSCs.

He ignored them and stayed on course, trusting his automatic pilot. Glancing down, he saw nothing beneath him but deepening haze.

Then he saw the UFO.

He blinked and looked down again. He couldn't believe what he was seeing. The Antarctic had disappeared, there was only a silvery haze, and pacing his aircraft, almost directly below him, but gradually ascending, was what looked like an immense, glowing, disc-shaped craft.

Rydell suddenly felt the cold – not the atmosphere, but something else, an unnatural, numbing cold, so

real it seemed almost palpable, like a definite ...
*presence*.

*The cold!* he thought. *It's alive!* Then he glanced
down again, saw the dazzling, disc-shaped craft
growing larger as it ascended – a silvery island
surrounded by light – and his heart raced as he turned
on the radio and tried to contact the base camp.

He couldn't even hear himself talking.

There was nothing but static.

Frantic, he tried again. The static simply increased in
volume. It was filling his head with a demented
crackling and ghostly voices. Glancing out of the
cockpit, he saw that the silvery haze was spreading
around him. He felt that he was being swallowed by the
thing beneath him, and then ...

Nothing.

He blacked out.


Had he blacked out? Rydell wasn't sure, but he
thought that he had. Recovering, he was filled with an
unholy terror and felt the cold increasing ... then, in
the ghastly light of another world, he felt a weight on
his legs.

Someone was sitting on his lap.

Opening his eyes, he saw Suzy.

Rydell almost screamed, but he managed to choke it
back. Suzy's arms were around his neck and she was
staring accusingly at him. He saw her and felt her – in
fact, he even smelt her – and looked at her and *through*
her, saw her face and the clouds behind her, was filled
with a dreadful guilt and a shocking feeling of his own
mortality, loved her and denied her and was terrified
by her presence, and heard the static, or the voices of
his history, all around him, *inside* him.

His fear squeezed all sense out of him.

The plane started descending and he regained his

senses. Taking hold of the controls, his hands passing *through* Suzy, and she smiled with a slight trace of mockery and gradually disappeared.

*Lack of oxygen!* he thought. *Hallucination! It was no more than that!*

But he couldn't believe it.

He was cold but bathed in sweat, his hands too numb to grip properly, but he clawed at the controls, saw the silvery haze vanishing, then, thank God, the frozen wilderness beneath him spinning wildly, as the plane raced towards the earth for a final, fatal embrace.

His aeroplane, hurtling down through the ozone hole, was going to crash.

He was numbed by the cold, with fear and disbelief, but he recalled that glowing UFO, his ghostly Suzy, the static's voices, then felt the warmth of Earth rush back around him, giving touch to his fingertips.

The white wilderness stopped its spinning, levelled out, came much closer, and he took control again – of the plane and his pounding heart – and went winging back up towards the sky and its promise of life.

Still shaken by fear and disbelief, he gratefully flew back to Chile.

# CHAPTER FIVE

The informality of the meeting took Clare by surprise. After a thirty-minute wait in the adjoining federal building, she was collected by a presidential aide, who led her through the North Entrance, along the marble floors of the Cross Hall, to the Oval Office in the southeast corner of the West Wing. When the aide opened the door and waved her inside, she found the President of the United States seated behind the ornate oak desk that Queen Victoria had presented to President Rutherford B Hayes in 1880. He was having a relaxed conversation with Jack Douglas, who had arranged this unofficial meeting for her.

Both men stood up when she entered, smiling as Jack introduced her to the President.

'Hi,' he said, 'nice to meet you at last, Miss Holton. I've heard so much about you from various sources – not only Jack here – and all of it good.'

'Thank you, Mr President,' she replied, shaking his hand, instantly charmed that he could be so natural. 'And thanks, also, for seeing me about this matter. It really is urgent.'

'So Jack's told me,' the President said. 'Here, take a seat.'

He indicated an antique velvet chair resting to one side of the Victorian desk on the turquoise and pale gold, oval rug. He even pulled the chair out for her to sit down. Jack took the chair at the other side of the desk as the President sat down facing them. He was framed by the Presidential flag and the flag of the

United States, which flanked a smaller desk upon which were displayed numerous photographs of the President's family. There were potted plants in Chinese vases on either side of the French windows, which overlooked a rose garden. The Presidential seal in low relief was set into the ceiling.

Clare lowered her gaze as the President sank back into his chair, clasped his hands on his lap, and gave her another easy-going smile.

'Do you like the office?' he asked her.

'I love it,' she replied sincerely. 'It's surprisingly cosy, as befits a democracy.'

He chuckled warmly, glancing appreciatively at Jack. 'Yes,' he said, returning his attention to her, 'that's the point.' Then he glanced at his wrist-watch – the first sign of informality – and said, 'Jack says you want to discuss this problem with the ozone layer on behalf of NASA. I'm not sure why you should come to me for this, but I'm willing to listen. Jack's filled me in on your background and on the details of NASA's involvement, so feel free to get right to the point.'

'Thank you, Mr President,' She glanced at Jack, who smiled reassuringly at her, then turned to the President.

'Can I remind you, Mr President,' he said, 'that Miss Holton is officially the scientific liaison officer between NASA, its National Space Technology Laboratories and the Department of Defence, and that while defence is not the major issue in this case, the economic considerations raised by NASA's discoveries could have great bearing on matters of defence.'

'OK, Miss Holton, let me hear it.'

Realizing that the President was not as soft as he seemed, and aware that the baby-faced White House aide breathing evenly behind her was probably armed, Clare leaned forward in her chair and said, 'As you

41

know, Mr President, earlier this month the first global treaty aimed at reducing pollution was agreed between twenty-seven nations in Montreal.'

'Yes, and I know that you represented us most effectively. I also know from Jack here, that you wanted this off-the-record meeting to reassure me that the countries who signed the agreement really *can* take the necessary steps to reduce the pollution that's causing the hole in the ozone layer.'

'I confess, that's why I've come, Mr President.'

'Well, you can try convincing me otherwise, but certainly based on what I know so far, the problem seems to be atmospheric, rather than environmental. And if that's the case, we simply have to pray that the winds will blow it away.'

'Unfortunately, Mr President, that *isn't* the case. Initial reports that the hole in the ozone layer is being caused by natural chemical changes in the atmosphere were wrong. Chemical changes in the atmosphere *are* depleting the ozone layer, but the problem *is* environmental which is caused by human intervention and can be solved if we take the appropriate action.'

The President stared thoughtfully at her, rubbed his chin, then smiled slightly.

'What you say contradicts what I've been told, so you'd better explain yourself.'

'At the time of the Montreal meeting,' Clare told him, 'it was widely believed that man-made pollution of the atmosphere was having an effect on the hole in the ozone layer. However, since that meeting, a combined satellite, balloon, and a land-based and airborne Antarctic Ozone Experiment, organized and managed by NASA with the support of the National Science Foundation, the National Oceanic and Atmospheric Administration, the US Chemical Manufacturers Association *and* scientists of many other nationalities, have come up with conclusive evidence that the hole in the ozone layer is being caused almost *exclusively* by man-made pollution of the stratosphere.'

'*Man-made?*'

'Yes. Put simply, the depletion of the ozone layer is being caused by the increasing release of chemicals called chlorofluorocarbons, or CFCs, into the ozone layer around the Earth. Those CFCs are caused by the fumes and gases of spray cans, insecticides, paints, polishes, disinfectants, and car and aircraft exhausts. Unless we can dramatically reduce the use of such products on a world-wide basis, that great hole over the Antarctic will get deeper and wider, until eventually the ozone layer will be destroyed altogether, exposing the Earth to extremely harmful solar ultraviolet radiation. This isn't science fiction Mr President, it's fact and what it means is one of two equally frightening scenarios.'

The President smiled, then glanced again at his wrist-watch. 'Please continue,' he said, returning his gaze to her.

'In both scenarios,' she said, staring deliberately at him, 'the destruction of the ozone layer will result in increased skin cancer, cataracts, hepatitis, the herpes virus, and other infections of the skin caused by parasites. It will also cause a dramatic shift in the global average temperature. Given regional differences in the prevailing temperature, a shift in the global average temperature could, in the one direction, plunge us into another Ice Age, or, in the other, cause widespread famine through the destruction of agriculture, while the simultaneous melting of the polar ice caps will lead to the flooding of many major cities, including New York, London, and even Leningrad. In short, either way we'd be in for an unprecedented global disaster.'

The President glanced at Jack Douglas, whose

expression was neutral, then sank back into his chair and gazed up at the Presidential seal set into the ceiling. Having gathered his thoughts, he smiled slightly, then sighed and lowered his gaze, giving Clare his charming smile.

'It sounds serious,' he said. 'I've no doubt that it *is* serious. But I'm still not too sure that here, in the United States, the most technologically advanced nation on Earth, we can take the steps that were recommended in Montreal. If what you're saying is true, motorized transport, aircraft, agricultural insecticides, chemical plants and oil fields are all contributing to the destruction of the ozone layer and it would require enormous sacrifices, both agriculturally and industrially, to save it. I'm not sure that we can afford such sacrifices, let alone get support for them. What you're asking, in effect, is that we use less of the products that produce the CFCs, as you call them, and that means – until we find other ways of doing without them – cutting down drastically on our industrial, chemical and agricultural growth. That's not what I see as the function of this Presidency. Since our function is to *create* growth, not limit it, what you ask isn't feasible.'

'Because the Presidency can't make unpopular decisions?'

'That's insulting, Miss Holton.'

She saw the steel in him then and was briefly frightened by it, but remembered what her parents had taught her and said what she believed – irrespective of the warning glance that Jack Douglas was trying to give her.

'I don't think it's insulting,' she said. 'I think it's a fact. You believe what I'm telling you – that the whole world is under threat – but since you think it won't happen during your own term in office, you're going to put off the problem in the hope that it will resolve itself eventually without undue embarrassment.'

The President's face remained kindly, but his eyes became cool.

'No,' he said. 'You're wrong. You're misinterpreting my reasoning, which isn't based entirely on self-interest as you seem to think. My reasoning, Miss Holton, is based *very much* on the present; on my belief that some of the countries who've signed your precious ozone-reduction agreement, particularly the Soviet Union, might be doing so simply because they know that the only way the United States can make its contribution would be through dramatic reductions in its industrial, chemical, technological and agricultural growth, which would be of significant value to those countries, notably Russia.'

'I'm sorry, Mr President, but I don't see how . . .'

'What the President is trying to explain to you,' Jack Douglas contributed, 'is that the economic realities of international politics can't be ignored.'

'Precisely,' the President added. 'The Cold War is thankfully dead and *Perestroika* is welcomed, but unfortunately the whole world is now at war; a war in which industrial, chemical, technological and agricultural growth will decide who wins and who loses. And what you propose, Miss Holton – the drastic reduction of the very output that makes us strong – could threaten the economic superiority of the United States. It isn't purely self-interest that decrees what I can and can't risk.'

She understood his reasoning, but didn't admire it.

'And the hole in the ozone layer?' she asked, ignoring Jack's chastizing look. 'Do you intend to let that grow and grow, until there's no ozone left and the world either freezes or succumbs to a combination of famine and flood?'

The President managed to remain charming. 'No,'

he said, 'I don't. But I think your sense of urgency is unwarranted. While I accept that the hole in the ozone is a serious problem – and one that can't be ignored – I also think we have time to make more careful considerations about what should be done. I *have* taken note of what you've just told me. I also have the very thorough briefs on the subject written by Mr Douglas, whom I respect and trust, and I'll ensure that the matter is placed on the agenda for immediate attention, but I will *not* guarantee a reduction in our use of CFCs. However I *will* guarantee that the matter will not be forgotten.'

Clare began to feel angry and was just about to say something when the baby-faced aide behind her stepped forward, placed a hand lightly on her shoulder, as if by accident and said, 'I'm sorry, Mr President, but I'm afraid you have another appointment and you're already running late.'

'Of course,' the President said, as if surprised. Then he shrugged apologetically, raised his hands in the air, and said, 'I'm sorry Miss Holton, but my time's so limited. Maybe another time . . .'

Before she could reply, he'd stood up, walked around the desk, and even as his aide had subtly encouraged her to rise to her feet, he was shaking her hand. 'Believe me,' he said, 'your contribution's been invaluable. I'm sure we'll meet again real soon.'

'I hope so, Mr President.'

Stifling her anger, she forced a smile, then walked through the door opened by the aide. Jack fell in beside her, taking hold of her elbow, guiding her back through the West Wing and eventually out of the White House. She didn't speak until she was outside, when her suppressed anger exploded.

'God!' she exclaimed. 'I'm so mad I could spit! I think I need a strong drink.'

'It's lunchtime anyway,' Jack replied, unperturbed,

46

'so let's go to Maison Blanche where you can have something to eat while you drink, and hopefully calm down.'

'No thanks,' she replied. 'Certainly not Maison Blanche. I've had enough of politicians for one day. And besides, I don't want a real meal. A snack would be fine. Can you take the afternoon off?'

'Of course.'

'Then let's go back to your place.'

Clearly amused, he grinned at her. 'I'll have to thank the President,' he said, glancing up and down Pennsylvania Avenue in search of a cab. 'I'm benefitting from the anger he caused. He should get an award.'

'He should get a psychiatrist,' she retorted. 'He's obviously paranoid.'

A cab pulled up beside them and Jack held the door open for her. 'Get in,' he said, even more amused, and slipped in beside her. 'Dupont Circle,' he told the driver and let his hand rest on her thigh as the cab pulled away. 'No,' he said, 'he's not paranoid. And he's not stupid, either. He just pulls that good ol' boy act for the folks. Don't under-estimate him, Clare. He's a match for you anyday.'

'I'm not in competition with him. I just want some action taken. I want his support for what we're doing, not his paranoid politics.'

'What's paranoid about what he said?'

'All that crap about the Soviets. On the one hand he says that the Cold War's long gone and on the other he says we're fighting a war with the whole world, but one in which the Russians are still the main enemy. It's nonsense!'

'No,' Jack replied, 'it's not. He just phrased it a bit dramatically.' He squeezed her thigh as she gazed out the window at the Renwick Gallery, which made her feel a lot less angry and increasingly sensual.

'But what he said was essentially sound and can't be ignored,' Jack continued. 'The world *is* at war – a war of economics – and we can't ask our citizens to reduce their production of oil, automobiles, chemical products, corn and wheat, while other countries, notably Russia, quietly continue to gain economic strength. That's the President's major concern, Clare, and it's one that I share.'

He guided the cab-driver to his apartment-block in a leafy street off Dupont Circle, paid him, then led her into the apartment. Though not particularly large, it was certainly elegant. The afternoon sunlight fell through velvet curtains, onto antique English furniture and deep white pile carpet.

Presently in the middle of an acrimonious divorce from his wife of fifteen years, Jack had rented the apartment only three months before, having moved out of his family home in Georgetown, not far from where Clare lived with her father. In fact, she had first met him at a party in her own home, given by her father and mother, and had later been invited to his house, where she had met his wife and teenage children. She had been impressed by their decency and intrigued by his calculating charm, intelligence and urbanity, but had not, thank God, become involved with him until after his wife had sued for divorce and he had actually moved out into this expensive bachelor's apartment.

Shortly after the break-up of his marriage, Jack had become the President's financial advisor on government scientific research expenditure, so Clare had come into more regular contact with him, through her liaison work between NASA and the White House. Still attracted to him, she had learnt of his separation from his wife, and had accepted his invitation to dinner, ending up in his bed.

Though she enjoyed him in bed she didn't take him too seriously and was wary of his obvious need to manipulate people, as well as events.

Some people, she knew, would call her attitude cold, but she thought it was sensible.

'Why did your wife file for divorce?' she asked him.

'Incompatibility,' he said. 'Which translated, means we'd been married too long and could no longer share things. It also means we'd both turned to other partners with increasing frequency.'

'In other words, a pretty normal marriage that had gone past its prime.'

'Yeah, you might say that.'

'She seemed such a nice woman.'

'She was and is,' he said honestly. 'But niceness has little to do with marriage when it starts turning sour. We just lost whatever we had. We were moving in different directions. And then, when the kids became old enough to be self-sufficient, the discipline that had held us together just slipped away.'

'Any regrets?'

'Not so far. I've never been too emotional. Like you, I've usually placed my work first. I'd like to feel nostalgia for our shared past, but I simply can't do it. I feel only relief.'

'You're a selfish bastard, Jack.'

'That's why you like me,' he said, grinning. 'It makes you feel safe. You think I won't get too close to you.'

Which was true enough, she realized. It was his self-interest, his invincible pragmatism, that made her feel secure with him, since she didn't want involvement with the kind of man who would be hurt by her refusal to commit herself. Jack was intrigued by her refusals, even aroused by them, but he certainly wouldn't be hurt by them which made her feel at ease.

'Anyway,' he said, 'I'm not as selfish as the President.

I'm just more *open* about my selfishness. Now that old bastard, he has theatrical talents and can charm the birds from the trees when he wants to.'

'He's a politician to his fingertips.'

'Like little ol' me, right?'

'Right.'

'You're so honest, it destroys me.'

'I doubt that you'd be destroyed by honesty Jack, since you wouldn't see it if it stared you in the face.'

She thought she might have pushed him too far then, but he just grinned laconically.

'So,' he said, as he removed his jacket and slung it over an armchair, 'let's have a drink and a snack. What would you like?'

'I'd like you to take your clothes off,' she said. 'We can have the snack later.'

He was amused more than surprised, being used to her by now. 'A woman who knows what she wants,' he said. 'How could I refuse?'

He started taking off his clothes, without batting an eyelid, and she watched him, saying nothing, appreciating his lean physique and tight muscles, his hard masculinity. When he was naked, she made him undress her, arousing him with her touch as he did so. She sank to her knees, kissing his burning body. Trembling he followed her down, then fell carefully on top of her.

She wanted to lose herself, to have no control for a while, and it happened when he played his tricks on her and then burned up inside her. She heard her own sighs and moans, a distant sound, a receding plea, then felt herself tumbling backwards, as if out of her own skin, and plunging into a deep well of pure sensual feeling.

Not her, someone else; not the scientist, the woman. And that woman, wanting freedom, clinging always to

50

her pride, lost the latter and surrendered the former for what seemed like an eternity.

When she returned to herself a few minutes later, she felt breathless, exhausted and dazed, yet strong and triumphant.

'Very good,' she whispered into Jack's ear. 'You did really well. I'll have a tuna salad and white wine – and I'll have it in bed.'

'Yes, Madam,' he gasped.

And as he walked into the kitchen to prepare her light lunch, she climbed into his bed, covering her lower half with the quilt and thought of that great hole in the ozone layer, growing larger each day. She imagined the light of death burning through it while she burned with the lust for life.

She wanted life in a dying world.

# CHAPTER SIX

'She's gone!' Rydell blurted despairingly into the phone to Dwight, who had also returned that day from Punta Arenas. 'She really did it, this time! When I got back, I found this letter she'd left on the kitchen table, telling me she was going back to Iowa and taking the kids. The kids are still here – they wouldn't go – but goddammit, she's *gone*, Dwight!'

He could hardly believe what he was saying. He had only been back an hour. Even now, though he managed to control himself, he felt confused and deeply hurt.

'Yeah, I know,' Dwight responded, sounding embarrassed. 'Maggie's just told me.'

Rydell was astonished. 'What? *Maggie* told you?'

'Yeah, Tony, that's right. She didn't *know*, you understand – it wasn't planned or anything – but when Suzy decided to go, she asked Maggie to help her.'

Now Rydell was outraged. 'And Maggie did? She actually helped her?'

'Come *on*, Tony! They're friends. I mean, what do you *do*, you know? The situation is difficult.'

'What you do,' Rydell said, not believing what he was hearing, 'is refuse to help your best friend's wife walk out on him without warning. You don't actually *help* her!'

'Maggie tried to stop her,' Dwight replied. 'She just couldn't do it. What did she say in the letter, Tony?'

Rydell glanced down at the letter crumpled up in his free hand, then looking through the window he saw that his two sons, playing on the front lawn, had suddenly started fighting one another. They didn't often fight one another, so it was a bad sign, and he realized that they would soon need a firmer hand than his.

He finally answered his friend in a distracted voice: 'She wrote that she couldn't take it any longer, by which I assume she meant my work and this house and Maryland. She also said that I needn't keep in touch, but I certainly don't intend to!'

Dwight chuckled over the phone.

'This isn't funny, Dwight! How the hell am I gonna handle this situation, look after the kids and get on with my work?'

'Take some time off,' Dwight said. 'I think you need a rest anyway. As I told you, that hallucination during your flight was a sure sign of stress. That's why I grounded you.'

'It wasn't stress!' Rydell nearly shouted, remembering his experience with a chill of fear. 'Goddammit, Dwight, I've told you a thousand times, it was a genuine experience!'

'It was stress.'

'It was a phenomenon! It was caused by something in the ozone hole. I didn't imagine it.'

Dwight sighed in despair. 'It was imagination, Tony. If, as you say, it was a phenomenon caused by the ozone hole, how come none of the pilots who replaced you experienced the same thing?'

'How the hell do I know? And besides, they might have. Since you grounded *me* for reporting the goddamned thing, they wouldn't be likely to tell you if they experienced the same thing.'

'I've said it before and I'll say it again, Tony, you were worried sick about Suzy, you were thinking about her when you made that flight, and then, in the thin atmosphere near the top of the ozone hole, your anxiety made you imagine you saw her.'

Rydell felt insulted. 'Oh, yeah? And what about the UFO? What the hell had *that* got to do with Suzy? Answer that one, wise guy!'

There was another long silence. 'Let's talk about it some other time,' Dwight said finally. 'Let's deal with this problem first. I think you should take some time off until you sort this mess out.'

'I *can't* take time off. I've got too much work to do. I want to help analyze that data. I want a few answers, Dwight. So how the hell can I do it and sort this mess out?'

'Call your mother,' Dwight suggested. 'Tell her to come right over. She'd probably be thrilled if you asked her to look after the kids. She'd be there in a flash.'

'Christ, Dwight, that's brilliant! Why didn't I think of that? I'll give her some work to do. She'll think she's in heaven.'

'Right,' Dwight said. 'And I'll try to call in and see you later. OK?'

'OK, buddy.'

Feeling less isolated, Rydell put down the phone. Then he glanced through the window at his kids and felt distinctly depressed.

Things hadn't been working out but he sure as hell hadn't expected her to pack up and leave. Now, he felt bewildered, outraged and anguished.

He picked up the phone again, dialled the retirement home where his mother was staying and asked to speak to her.

'Hi, Mom,' he said. 'It's me.'

'Tony?'

'Yes.'

'I thought you were away.'

54

'I'm back. So how are things in Menopause Manor?' he asked, using the name which she had given to the retirement home.

'Oh,' she said, 'the same as always. They're all mad and getting worse.'

'Well,' he told her, 'you're gonna have to come home Mom. Suzy's just left me for good and I'm gonna need help.'

'What did you say? She's left you! I know she's threatened to before but I never thought she really would!'

'Well, this time she went and did it. She left this morning and she said it was for good and now I'm here with the kids. You have to come home, Mom.'

He heard his mother coughing. 'I always knew that Suzy was a bad one,' she said.

'No, Mom, she isn't really. She just got bored because I was away so much, and she finally blew out. And now I'm here alone with the kids and too much work on my plate. I need you. I really do.'

'Well, if you really *need* me . . .'

'I do. I'm goddamned desperate.'

'It's nice to know I get these invites when you're desperate. It makes me feel really wanted.'

'I *always* wanted you here, Mom.'

'That Suzy of yours didn't.'

'Suzy isn't here anymore and the kids and I really do need you.'

'Those kids need a firm hand. Suzy never raised them proper. If I told her once, I told her a thousand times: those kids need more discipline.'

'You're right Mom. Now are you coming or not?'

She sighed, as if martyring herself. 'Oh, all right. I'll get this sadist of a nurse to pack my suitcase and call for a cab. I'll be there this afternoon.'

'Great, Mom. I love you.'

55

'Bye son.'

'Bye Mom.'

Intensely relieved, Rydell put down the phone and glanced once more at the crumpled letter in his hand. He folded it neatly and, recalling his vision in the plane over the Antarctic, shivered with fearful incomprehension.

Returning to the present, he stuck his head through the open window and bawled at the boys to come inside. They stopped fighting and stared at him resentfully but before they could protest he waved them inside. They did as they were told but with great reluctance, dragging their feet. Rydell made them sit together on the settee while he gave them his pep talk. He hardly knew where to start.

'Look, kids,' he said to them, 'I want you to listen very carefully, 'cause I've got something to say to you. Although your Mom's left me temporarily I'm really glad you decided to stay. I mean, it must have been hard on you.'

'I just did what Don decided we should do,' Ronnie said.

Rydell heard the pain in his voice and it made his cheeks burn. 'Say, hey!' he said, observing Don's hurt look. 'Your big brother had to make a decision and it must have been hard, so stop fighting him over this. OK?'

'OK,' Ronnie said in an unconvinced manner, his golden locks falling over lowered eyes.

'Anyway, your Mom's gonna come back soon, so stop worrying about it. I mean, when women get mad, which they do a lot, they then do these crazy things. But they get over things fast and I think your Mom will too and when she does, we'll have a little chat and I'm sure she'll come back. In the meantime, your grandma's coming over to look after us all, so there's nothing to worry about.'

56

The boys glanced at one another at the mention of Grandma. Her arrival was a sign that things were worse than they'd thought.

'Any questions?' Rydell asked.

'Why Grandma?' Don responded.

'Because she'll look after you better than I can.' Rydell coughed loudly into his clenched fist and asked, 'Any *more* questions?'

'We can look after ourselves,' Ronnie said.

'Right,' Don said. 'We're not kids.'

'You *are* kids,' Rydell informed them, 'and you need looking after, and right now, before Grandma gets here, I want you to tidy up your filthy bedroom.'

'Gee,' Ronnie said, 'it's startin' already. We're gonna get worked to death.'

'You'll get the back of my hand as well,' Rydell told him, 'if you don't clean that bedroom. Now go in and get started.'

They went into their bedroom, but they didn't do much work – instead distracting themselves with a pillow fight, television and some arguments. Rydell hadn't the heart to stop them. He poured himself a beer instead. Feeling better, he had another, which exacerbated his jet lag, so he lay down on the sofa and fell asleep. His sleep wasn't restful though, as he had bad dreams about Suzy and was finally shaken awake by his mother.

'What a welcome home!' she whined. 'You asleep in front of the TV with empty beercans beside you and your children going wild in the bedroom! I got here just in time, I see.'

'Good to see you, Ma. Real good. Here, give me a kiss.'

'Oh, all right then.'

He kissed her cheek as she sniffed and wiped a tear from her eye.

'I don't know where to start,' she said. 'This place is such a mess. And those kids – just listen to the noise – they've gone to hell and highwater. I'm not criticizing, I'm not casting stones, but that Suzy had an awful lot to learn about being a mother. I definitely got here just in time. The Lord works in mysterious ways.'

Rydell sat up and rubbed the sleep from his eyes. 'Listen, Mom,' he said, 'I've gotta get to work. I won't be long, but I've gotta get there urgently. Do you mind if I go now?'

A self-made martyr, she sighed loudly. 'You do what you have to do, son. Suzy never understood you like I do. I tried to tell her, but she never listened. "Suzy," I said, "that boy of mine has to work for those greenback dollars and that's why he's away all the time. It's not pleasure to him," I said. Of course, she never listened. Thought she knew it all, that girl. And now here we are, in a pretty mess, with two motherless boys and a man weighed down by responsibilities. Suzy never understood that son, but I do and always did. You go to work and I'll sort the kids out, clean the house and prepare a good meal. That's what mothers are for, son.'

'Thanks, Mom, you're a doll.'

He kissed her again, then went to get his jacket, impatient to check the data from the expedition that had caused him such trauma.

He felt guilty because his need to examine that data was as great, if not greater, than his concern over Suzy's departure. What had happened to him in that aircraft over the Antarctic was something he couldn't forget or ignore even for one day. No, he had to get to the NASA–Goddard Space Flight Center and check out the data. He wouldn't sleep if he didn't.

'Right, Mom,' he said, 'I'm going now, but I'll be back by six, OK?'

'Back for dinner,' she repeated, knowing his clever

ways. Then she sighed. 'All right, son.'

He hurried out of the house as she turned towards the boys' bedroom. Rydell heard her shouting instructions as he climbed into his car. He drove away from the tract-houses and blandness of Greenbelt, straight to NASA–Goddard.

Once there, he went urgently to the data-processing unit of the Institute for Space Studies, where he found Mike Esposito, fat and flabby and brilliant, surrounded by his banks of computer monitors and reams of folded print-out sheets. Esposito, who smoked like a chimney, was coughing more than he should.

'I didn't expect to see you until tomorrow,' he said, 'or maybe even next week. You must be really steamed up my friend.'

'What makes you say that?'

'I had a talk with Dwight Collins.'

'And?'

'He said you had a funny experience over the Antarctic.'

'Did he tell you about Suzy?'

'Yeah,' Esposito said sheepishly, 'I'm real sorry she's left you.'

'Thanks. 'Did he tell you anything else?'

'No.'

'I'm amazed,' Rydell said sarcastically. 'Anyway, let's get on with our work. What have we got?'

Esposito surprised him by shaking his head in bewilderment, pointing at the tiered banks of computer monitors and their trailing reams of print-outs. 'You tell *me* old buddy.'

While the payload pods on Rydell's ER-2 had been taking their measurements, a mass of other data had been accumulated by the forty scientists in the DC-8 flying through the lower area of the same hole, TOMs on Nimbus 7, and other American and European satellites and balloons, as well as from the numerous land-based information-gathering stations around the globe. Now, as he studied the data and tried to make sense of it, Rydell felt dazed and disbelieving.

'Jesus Christ!' he said softly.

# CHAPTER SEVEN

Suzy had forgotten just how beautiful Iowa was. She arrived at her old home in the evening, just as the sun was sinking, and the pink light bled into the deepening azure sky, to bring out the stars as she had not seen them for years. It made her think that she was in a fairytale world, where magical events might occur.

The cornfields went for miles, all the way to the flat horizon, a yellow sea turning deep gold in the twilight's soft darkening.

Even the breeze was soft.

As he had done each evening for as long as she could remember, her father was sitting out on the porch of the house, in that same old rocking chair, wearing his dungarees, his face hidden in the shadow of the overhang, his feet close to the railings. It was a lovely old house, bright white in the sea of gold, and the lights inside it were burning and beaming onto the porch.

The house was quite a long way from the road, but Suzy saw all that clearly.

She sat on in the car, wondering if her father had seen her. He wouldn't know the car if he had, but he wouldn't be worried. Her father was a calm man, at one with the seasons, and the faith by which he abided included trust in his fellow man.

Life was different in Iowa.

Feeling like a kid again, Suzy glanced about her, taking in the fields of maize undulating and whispering, glorious under a vast, subtly changing sky

61

in which the stars were emerging like crystals twinkling on velvet.

It was so beautiful it seemed artificial, like nature's own theatre. She'd forgotten that view of things.

Starting the car, she turned off the road, driving between white-painted fences and up to park in the driveway in front of the house. She turned off the engine, then glanced up at her father, still rocking in his chair, and saw that he was gazing in her direction. She smiled, even though he couldn't see her, and opened the door and climbed out. The air was so clean, you could practically taste it. The breeze brushed her like feathers.

'Hi, Dad!' she called out, just loud enough for him to hear. She closed the car door as he stopped rocking, removed his feet from the wooden railing of the porch, and leaned forward, out of the shadow of the overhang, to get a good look at her.

'Suzy?'

'Yes, Dad.'

He didn't get out of his chair when she walked to the house, but as she mounted the steps onto the porch, she saw his welcoming smile. He didn't even look surprised, just delighted to see her, and it made her feel a lot better after what she'd been through.

Leaning over him, she saw his thick grey hair and lined face, his eyes as blue as the Iowa sky at the height of summer. Without embarrassment, she kissed him full on the lips, then straightened up again.

'You look real good,' she said.

'So do you, Suzy. You could probably do with a change of clothes, but otherwise you look fine.'

'I drove all the way, Dad.'

'From Virginia?'

'Right.'

His gaze shrewdly took in the empty car, then he

looked up again. 'No husband, no kids,' he said. 'So what is it, darlin'?'

'I've left home,' she told him.

He didn't bat an eyelid but just stared steadily at her, giving her time to catch her breath, letting her know that whatever she had to say, he'd be willing to listen.

'Where's Mom?' she asked.

He tilted his head towards the house behind him. 'In the kitchen,' he said. 'You got here just in time for dinner. There's enough food for you as well.'

His grin was so damned warm, it made her feel good again.

She'd driven a long time to get here, drained by guilt and confusion: through West Virginia to Ohio, in tears half of the time, thinking of Tony and the kids and what she was running from. Cried again in Cincinnati, in a motel just outside of town, then back on the road at the break of dawn, right across Indiana, spending her second night in Peoria, Illinois, in another lonely motel. She hadn't cried that night; instead, she'd practised self-justification. She'd spent the night condemning Tony (as his judge and jury, his hangman), and only cried when she hung him in her mind and got back in her car.

After that it was easier, another two or three hundred miles, past farms producing oats and hay and barley and soya beans, through a landscape that hourly became more familiar, with names that took her back to her adolescence and childhood – Galeburg, Rock Island, Davenport, Iowa City, then the final run through the cornbelt of Montezuma and Brooklyn and Little Red Rock – then across the river of Des Moines and right on to this rich, rolling farmland, where the working farms, including this one, were now on the tourist routes.

All the way from Maryland, Virginia, to the home of

her childhood, near a place called Indianola, Ohio . . .
She felt like a pioneer.

'I'll go in and say hello to Mom,' she said.

'No, don't,' her father replied. He pointed at the
wooden chair beside him and said, 'Sit right here. Let
her get on with the dinner. She'll come out to get me
and to check how much beer I've drank and the
expression on her face when she sees you will be worth
the seein'. Come on, honey, sit down. And I always
keep those extra glasses on the table in case someone
visits, so quench your thirst with a beer. A long drive
from Virginia to Iowa. You musta had a strong
reason.'

He was too polite to ask, but was opening a doorway
to the subject. Suzy sat down and poured herself a beer
and felt a great weight fall off her. She looked across
the land, a sea of yellow husks turned golden, and saw
the crimson lava of the sun pouring along the horizon.
As the sun sank with majestic ease, the stars became
brighter.

'God,' Suzy said, 'I love coming back here. Nothing's
changed at all, Dad.'

'How long's it bin?' he asked.

'About six years, I think. Ronnie was only four at the
time, so it must've been six years.'

'Things don't change here that quick.' He'd always
cut his words off short. 'The rain falls and the sun
climbs high in the sky and then the rain falls again. It
just goes on and on.'

'The farm's doing well, right?'

'Why not? We do our work. If a man does his work,
he gets rewarded, an' the land understands that.'

'Not always, Dad.'

'This is Iowa, the heartland of America.'

'The bread-basket of America.'

'Right,' he said with a grin. 'The richest agricultural

64

land in the world. If you work it, it works for you. You just have to respect it.'

'But the land can turn on people.'

'Not this land. It goes on forever.'

The sun had almost disappeared, setting the whole world on fire. It was not a fire to scourge, but one that beautified all it touched: the flowing gold of the seas of corn, the odd silhouetted tree, the geometry of the fences crisscrossed on swells of land, the horizon which, though flat, seemed slightly curved, the sky now drenched with stars. It made Suzy remember the dreams that had enriched her childhood.

'It's so romantic,' she said.

'Yeah,' her father replied. 'I guess so. That's why I like to sit in this old rockin' chair and drink beer and just look at it. What the hell, it's done me proud all my life, *and* my Dad, and *his* Dad. You think of that and you know you've got an anchor that no one can steal. Not too many can say that.'

Suzy raised her hand. She held the pale moon in her fingers. She'd wanted to give that moon to her kids, but she'd left them instead. Decent folk didn't do that.

'I won't stay too long,' she said.

'As long as you like, Suzy.'

'I'll tell you all about it.'

'If you want to.'

'I wanna tell you. I need to.'

'That's important,' he said.

Suzy sighed and poured more beer, filling her father's glass as well, then she sat back in the chair and looked up at the brightening stars. She felt choked with love and grief.

'What'dya think of Tony, Dad?'

'I kinda like him. He amuses me. Not a practical man, by any means, and not too good on the manners, but he doesn't have a nasty streak in him; just a tongue that's too quick. I think he got that from his mother. She was one sharp-tongued critter. That woman, she could make the devil grovel, though she did have her charms.'

'What charms?' Suzy asked.

'That was quick, darlin' girl.'

'Tony's mother never liked me at all. I could always tell that.'

Her father shrugged and grinned. 'They were dirt poor, you know? Farmed a bit of land about forty miles from here. Nothing much to talk about – just a coupla acres – and they just struggled along, probably working themselves to the bone, but managed to send Rydell to university, which was something to boast about.'

'You mean that?'

'Yeah. I respected them. I thought they had lotsa guts.' He had a swig of beer, licked his lips, and watched the sun going down. 'Mostly her guts,' he said as his face sank into shadow. 'Rydell's father was an honest man, but that don't buy bread and butter, and she was the one who did the pushin' and shovin' when it got down to business. He died early, of course – I think she exhausted him – but that woman, she did what she said she'd do and got her boy off to college. That was part of her charm for me.'

Suzy watched the darkness building, shifting east and west, rising, as if painting itself quietly on the daylight, taking over the canvas. The beer tasted real good, as well.

'And Tony?'

'I told you. Not a farmer, but I like 'im. I shook his hand when you introduced him, looked into his eyes, and knew he didn't belong in this world, but had a clean, kindly nature. Not a man to be organized. More than bright, but dizzy with it. You could tell he wouldn't wanna hurt a fly, though he might aggravate it. A good kid, I thought. Drive you crazy, but OK. I always thought you coulda done a lot worse and maybe never done better. You gotta problem? It's up to you.'

'I walked out on him, Dad.'

'And the kids?'

'Them as well. I mean, I wanted them to come, but they wouldn't, and I had to respect that.'

'Sure,' he said. 'You did.'

'But you don't approve?'

'No. I think a woman stays with her kids, come hell or high water.'

Suzy put her glass down, closed her eyes, sank to her knees, then wearily laid her head on her father's knees.

'You think right and you always did,' she said. 'I feel godawful, Dad.'

He placed his hand on her head and stroked her hair with unbearable tenderness.

'You did wrong,' he said, 'but you're not alone in that. What you did has been done, but that ain't the end of things. Let's find out exactly why you did it and maybe try fixing it.'

'That might take some time.'

'Sure,' he said. 'These things do. Everything worth doin' takes time and the sun is slow sinkin'. Look there! There she goes!'

Suzy looked up. Her father's hand was like a warm hat. The last slice of the sun was being eaten by darkness and stars. Then the stars filled the velvet sky.

'I love him,' she said. 'I know that. But he just drives me crazy.'

'That sounds normal,' her father said. 'If it's something else, tell me. I can take it. Does he beat you, or what?'

'No, he doesn't beat me.'

'I didn't think he would.'

'He's just forgotten what we meant to each other. It's his work he loves, not me.'

'Men love their work,' her father said. 'If they don't, they shouldn't be doin' it. If they do it, but they don't love it, they die, though they're still on their feet. Say your thanks that it's his work and not a woman. You always were a demanding child.'

'But you still love me, right?'

'Yes, Suzy, you know that.'

'You still love me and you've still got your work, but Tony just loves his work.'

'That can't be too bad.'

'Yes, it is. I'm locked out.'

'A man's work is what he *is*, child. It's *him*. You just got to accept that.'

'I can't. It's just not in my nature, Dad. I need his attention and I'm willing to give him mine, but he thinks that if he's *nice* he's giving enough and otherwise I'm demanding. He's crazy. You know that? He's the pits! He'll wear the same clothes for days, hates socializing, forgets the kids, can't bear to look at paperwork, never checks the car, but has the house wired up like a laboratory and keeps blowing the fuses. Our anniversary? Forget it! Birthdays? Forget them! I swear, I sometimes think he even forgets my name, though he always wants breakfast. I can't live with it anymore. I can't take not being noticed. I need magic in my life – what I had as a kid – and if I can't have my dreams in the flesh, then I don't want to know. Do you understand that?'

'I have to think about it,' her father said, 'and that might take some time. But we got lots of that in Iowa. Here comes your mother.'

The door creaked on rusty hinges and Suzy's mother walked out, wearing an old shirt and slacks and a gleaming white apron. 'I'm gonna let you finish off that beer,' she said, 'and then you have to . . .'

Suzy stood up and saw her mother's dark eyes widen – dark eyes and dark hair and an ageing, still lovely face – then that smile, which had warmed her all her life, not failing her now.

'Lord have mercy, I do not believe . . .'

'Aw, God, Mom, I'm a mess!'

She felt her mother's arms around her, a soft kiss, all that love, and collapsed into tears of relief and the spasms of grief and guilt.

'Let's have dinner,' her mother said.

# CHAPTER EIGHT

Clare wet her parched throat with more water before squinting into the hot glare of the TV lamps and flashbulbs that were turned on the members of the American Geophysical Union. She hated press conferences in general, and this one, being held in Baltimore, was more crowded than any she had attended for a long time.

'Sorry,' she said. 'I didn't mean to . . .'

'What you're saying,' said Art Tabori, a particularly aggressive reporter from the *Washington Post*, 'is that while just about every other technologically developed country has signed the first global treaty designed to reduce the pollution of the atmosphere, the United States, though having signed the agreement, is expressing certain doubts about its feasibility.'

'Well, yes, I suppose . . .'

'Suppositions aren't answers Miss Holton. Is it true or not?'

Clare felt like a crooked lawyer, but was trapped by her official position. Though she didn't want to protect the President's stance she *did* represent NASA.

'I apologize for my supposition,' she answered more confidently than she felt, 'but the issue isn't as simple as you'd like it to be.'

There was a ripple of laughter at that, and Art Tabori changed his line of questioning to a less daunting subject.

'According to the official White House statement – by which I mean the press release from NASA – the recent Antarctic Polar Expedition revealed that the hole in the ozone layer is growing bigger at an alarming rate. Is it true that it will eventually leave the Earth unprotected from ultraviolet radiation, and that this will in turn lead either to a new Ice Age or widespread destruction through famine or flood?'

'I wrote that press release,' Clare said, 'and I stand by its content.'

'I'm glad you do, Miss Holton. Would you also stand by your statement that the nations of the world must unite to drastically reduce the use of CFCs? Which means, of course, a possibly dangerous reduction in most of the products that support the US economy.'

Clare saw the trap, but could not avoid it. 'It's my personal belief,' she ventured without hope, 'that a limited restriction on the use or production of anything involving CFCs could be counteracted with other kinds of production. It is also my . . .'

'It may be your belief, Miss Holton, but it's certainly *not* the belief of either the President or his scientific financial advisor, Jack Douglas, so the country *is* interested in the conflicts aroused by the recent ozone expedition. Are you willing to discuss the rumoured disagreements?'

And so it went on. Clare was greatly relieved when the press conference finally ended. She intended to head back to her room and have a stiff, soothing drink, but was waylaid before she reached the elevator.

'Excuse me. Miss Holton? I . . .'

'The press conference is over,' Clare said. 'I have no more to say.'

She started to brush past him, but he grabbed her shoulder, practically dragging her back, making her turn towards him.

He was a short man, slightly overweight, his blue eyes bright but darkly shadowed, his features hidden by an untidy beard under dishevelled brown hair. He was wearing dirty denims, unpolished high-heeled boots, a tasteless checkered shirt unbuttoned at the neck, and an awful, old-fashioned, black leather jacket.

Marlon Brando with a beard, but without his charisma, and definitely worse for wear. A small-town journalist, obviously.

'Hey, hold on a minute!' he exclaimed, a hint of anger in his voice. 'Gimme a break, here!'

'The press conference is over. I . . .'

'I'm not a goddamned journalist,' he said. 'I'm a physicist; a climatologist. I work for NASA. I was part of the Airborne Antarctic Ozone Experiment. I've just sat through our ridiculous press conference and now I want to talk to you, OK, lady?'

She could hardly believe her ears. '*You* work for NASA?' she asked him.

'OK, lady. True I'm no fancy dresser, but I'm a good scientist. Now can we sit down and talk?'

She couldn't believe his cheek. 'The fact that you work for NASA doesn't mean I have to . . .'

'No Miss Holton, it doesn't. Not under normal circumstances. You'd be too far above me to even look down at me, too distant to even hear what I say. That's exactly the way it would be lady, at least under *normal* circumstances.'

She caught his inflection, his uncommon intensity, and stepped back, releasing her shoulder from his grasp, staring at him more closely.

'*Normal* circumstances?' she asked.

'You don't know me personally,' he said, his gaze very direct, 'but I'm one of your best physicists. When I flew through the hole in the ozone layer, I had a very strange experience, returned to NASA–Goddard, where I work, and analyzed most of the data. Came up with something that's even stranger than what I experienced,

72

Miss Holton. Now will you listen or not?'

'I was going for a drink,' she said.

'I won't argue with that,' he said.

'Sorry, but what did you say your name was?'

'Rydell. Tony Rydell.'

'OK, Tony, I apologize for being rude. I've been under a bit of pressure over this business. Please let me make amends with lunch. You do eat, I take it?'

'I'll accept your apology *and* the lunch.'

She had to smile. 'I really need some air. Do you mind going to the harbour? It'll only take five minutes in a cab.'

'That's fine with me, Miss Holton.'

'Clare. Please call me Clare.'

'No sweat,' he said.

They had mussels and beer at Bertha's on Fell's Point, overlooking the Inner Harbour of the Patapsco river. The sun beamed in on their table and that, together with the light food and cold beer, soon made Clare feel refreshed.

Rydell also ate with relish, and clearly enjoyed his beer. Though he looked uncouth and sometimes talked like a cowboy, it soon became apparent to her that he was bright, if possibly eccentric.

He told her in detail about the Airborne Antarctic Expedition, which she found fascinating, then about his computer analysis of the scientific data collected by his ER-2, the DC-8, and the numerous payload-carrying satellites and balloons.

She found it unbelievable.

'What I'm trying to tell you,' he summarized grimly, 'is that nothing that anyone can do will stop the depletion and ultimate destruction of the ozone layer.'

'Rubbish!' she replied abruptly.

'No Clare, it's not rubbish. Your problem isn't the President of these here United States; it's that a reduction in your dreaded CFCs won't make the slightest difference to the rate of ozone depletion, since an immense disparity exists between how fast the ozone *should* be disappearing, according to our calculations, and how fast it actually *is* disappearing, according to the computer analyses of NASA–Goddard.'

'There can't be such a gap. It's impossible.'

'It's impossible, but it's happening. There's no question about it. I didn't check only my own ER-2 data, Clare. I also called in the data collected by the forty scientists in the DC-8 that flew through the ozone hole at low altitude at the same time. I wasn't willing to believe my own computer analysis, so I called in the TOMS data received from Nimbus 7, as well as the data received from the other satellites and balloons of every damned tracking station being used – Carnarvon Station and Honeysuckle in Australia; Goldstone in California; Corpus Christi in the Bermudas; Tananarive Station in the Indian Ocean; Hawaii, Madrid, Mexico, the Bahamas – you name it, I got it. Finally, when I *still* couldn't believe what I was getting, I had my results cross-checked by Mission Control, Houston, as the same data had been relayed there by the tracking stations. The answer was always the same, Clare. The ozone over the Antarctic is definitely disappearing much faster than the CFCs can account for. In other words, another agent, *something unknown*, is now destroying the ozone layer much faster than the man-made substances that originally began the process.'

'Something . . . *unknown?*'

'You heard what I said, Clare.'

Her first impulse was to laugh, but his intensity stopped her doing so; instead, she studied his face, trying to place him in her thoughts, aware that his name was familiar for some reason.

He was a physicist for NASA, on the Earth System

Science programme, and that meant he had to be good, even one of the best. It also meant that she had almost certainly come across his name at one time or another, in one NASA file or another. She had heard about him and she didn't know why, but she wished that she did.

'I'm afraid I remain sceptical,' she said. 'There must be some kind of mistake. It just doesn't make sense.'

'I've just told you, I cross-referenced everything and there's definitely *no* mistake. Something *unknown* is eating away the ozone layer even faster than the CFCs. And I'll tell you something even more scary . . .'

'Please don't,' she said with a smile, trying to make a joke of it.

'My analysis of the data received from around the globe reveals that the hole growing over the Antarctic isn't doing so all alone. The TOMS data, and all other cross-referenced measurements, show conclusively that another hole is forming over the Arctic . . .'

'Oh Christ!'

'. . . and recently the depletion in the ozone layer has been as widely spread as forty-five degrees south, to the southern tips of South America, New Zealand and Australia. In fact, measurements from the SBUV instruments on Nimbus 7 have shown a rapidly increasing depletion in the concentration of stratospheric ozone right around the globe.'

He pushed his empty beer glass aside in order to lean across the table and stare even more intently at her.

'You hear me? I said a *rapid* increase – too rapid for CFCs. Something's up there, and it isn't just exhaust fumes, insecticides or the gases from spray cans . . . It's something else altogether.'

Clare glanced at his empty beer glass because she couldn't meet his gaze. 'Let's be rational,' she said. 'The only thing that can possibly be up there is man-made pollution.'

'No,' he insisted, 'it's something else. When I flew through the hole, I saw an unidentified flying object. It was right below me, pacing me, then it ascended and seemed to surround me. It was blindingly bright, filled with noise and seemed incorporeal. I passed out for a short while, and when I awoke, I found what appeared to be my wife sitting on my lap. An apparition, right? Yeah, that's what I thought. But then I realized that I could *feel* her and even *smell* her, that her presence was palpable, almost physical, but when the light and noise of the UFO faded away, she faded away with it. There's something up there, Miss Holton.'

She couldn't believe what she was hearing, could hardly accept that he was serious, but his blue eyes displayed no sign of mischief.

'Let me get this straight,' she said, when she had gathered her wits again. 'You saw a flying saucer . . .'

'I didn't say it was a flying saucer. I said it was a UFO.'

'OK. First you saw an unidentified flying object – which may or may not have been a physical entity – and then it ascended towards your aircraft, seemed to dissolve around it, briefly rendered you unconscious, and then made you hallucinate that your wife was in the cabin with you.'

'It wasn't an hallucination,' Rydell insisted. 'I could actually *feel* her and *smell* her.'

'You could have hallucinated all that as well.'

'I could, but I didn't.'

God, he was serious. Maybe he was having a nervous breakdown or had already gone mad. . . . And to think that he worked for NASA. She had better have him checked out. . . . But even as she thought of doing that, she remembered why she had heard of him. She didn't know whether to laugh or cry.

'Excuse my scepticism, but aren't you the same Tony Rydell who caused NASA some embarrassment a few years back, with your publicly stated belief in the existence of flying saucers?'

He clenched his fists and pursed his lips before speaking, stifling his anger.

'Right and wrong,' he said. 'Before you start sniggering, let me remind you that it was my investigations of the environmental impacts of super-sonic transport aircraft, or SSTs, that led to the whole damned ozone debate in the first place . . .'

'I'm aware of that,' Clare interjected, ashamed at being reminded of it.

'And it was shortly after my discovery of the link between SST operations and a reduction in the concentration of ozone in the stratosphere, and a further link between that ozone depletion and cancer, that I stated, perhaps naïvely, that UFOs, or unidentified flying objects – *not* flying saucers, as you so crudely put it – should be treated as unexplained phenomena and scientifically investigated without prejudice. Since my innocent remark was blown out of all proportion and nearly destroyed my career, I think it's safe to say that my negative comments about supersonic transport aircraft had hurt the vested interests of the airline companies. In short, I'm not a crank, Miss Holton, so don't try it on.'

Embarrassed because Rydell had had to remind her of his revolutionary work with ozone depletion, but still unable to accept that what he was saying made sense, she tried to wriggle out of her discomfort by keeping up her attack.

Sighing loudly, as if weary, she said, 'Nevertheless, you have expressed a belief or interest in UFOs and that certainly makes your experience suspect. I'm afraid I can't . . .'

'And the data?' he said angrily, his face flushed. 'Does that lie as well?'

'I didn't say you were lying. I merely suggested that your obsession with UFOs had some bearing on . . .'

He cut her off in mid-sentence, noisily pushing back his chair and standing up.

'It wasn't a goddamned *obsession*.' He spat the words out loudly, making some of the other diners turn and stare at them. 'It was scientific curiosity, and at least I wasn't just sticking my head in the sand out of fear of what my colleagues might think of me, as *you're* doing right now!'

She was outraged. 'I resent . . .' she began.

'You resent being faced with something you can't comprehend and you haven't the guts to admit that the facts I've presented you with, have you baffled. That's probably why you got moved up from the laboratory to administration – you're more of a politician than a scientist. I should have guessed that immediately.'

'How dare you!'

'Goodbye, Miss Holton. And thanks for a lousy lunch!'

He turned away and walked out without looking back. She watched him depart in shock, not having met his kind before and intrigued to have done so. For someone so bright, he sure was dishevelled and ill-mannered . . . though oddly attractive with it.

It surprised her to think that.

# CHAPTER NINE

*Phoenix, Arizona*, Rydell thought, sleepy from his flight from Washington DC, and now driving from the airport to Scottsdale. *I need it like a hole in the head.*

In fact, he was about to have what promised to be a pleasurable meeting with an old friend. The anger he was directing towards this fair city was really an expression of his guilt and shame because a few days after installing his mother at home, he'd had to bid the kids goodbye again.

They hadn't been very happy and he couldn't really blame them. He was hardly ever at home these days, he hadn't improved since Suzy's departure, and he knew they weren't keen on his mother, though she sometimes amused them. His mother wasn't all that bad – you just had to get used to her – but the boys were clearly hurting over Suzy's departure and recently, to disguise the fact, had started behaving badly, which they'd not done before. They were sullen and resentful, fought each other all the time, and in general were behaving like little horrors. Not like his kids at all.

Rydell felt ashamed of himself and had driven away from the house in sour humour. His mood hadn't improved during the flight to Phoenix, during which he had spent most of his time gazing intently out of the window, thinking of UFOs and brooding on his run-in with Clare Holton.

He had thought her an arrogant bitch, but a damned attractive one.

Thankfully, it didn't take him long to reach his destination, which was what looked like a large saloon bar on Pinnacle Peak Road in the recreated western community of Scottsdale. Pulling into a parking space beside some hitching posts, thinking that perhaps he was on the lot of the movie *Westworld*, he climbed out of the car, into the scorching mid-day heat and hurried back along the street. He entered the saloon bar which was a restaurant owned by his friend Rick Polanski, frequented by a great many tourists.

The place was already frantic. Sexily dressed, pistol-packin' waitresses were serving a noisy bunch of tourists and locals wearing stetsons and high-heeled boots. The cowgirl behind the desk asked him if he had a booking. He told her he'd come to see Polanski and she smiled prettily and jerked her thumb back over her shoulder, indicating the bar. He saw Polanski behind the counter, face flushed and beaming under a white stetson as he helped the two barmaids serve the many customers who wanted drinks, while they waited for a table in the restaurant. Polanski saw Rydell when he was half-way across the room and waved and boomed out his name.

'Rydell! You sonofabitch!' he hollered. 'Good to see you, old buddy!' Then he leaned across the counter, pushing two customers aside, to pump Rydell's hand. 'You just off the plane?' he asked.

'Yeah,' Rydell replied, flexing his crushed fingers.

'Feel like lunch?'

'Terrific,' Rydell said.

'Good. I kept us a table. Over there,' he said, jabbing his index finger at the only empty table in the restaurant. 'You sit down, I'll bring us some beers and we'll talk about old times. Go on, take a seat!'

Rydell did as he was told, and Polanski soon joined him, carrying a large pitcher of beer in one hand, two glasses in the other, and holding them well out in front of him, away from his great belly, which flopped generously over his belt. It crossed Rydell's mind that he probably ran a successful restaurant because he looked like someone who enjoyed his food and drink. He did not look like someone who had once been an astrophysicist for NASA. Polanski had retired because of their refusal to finance his planned Instrumented UFO Research programme, and now, in his spare time, was the head of what Rydell thought was the most reliable UFO organization in the country.

'Here,' he said taking a seat and filling a glass with beer from the giant pitcher. 'Slake your thirst, Rydell. So,' he added, touching Rydell's raised glass with his own, 'what's been happening in Washington D.C., apart from rape, mugging and murder? Home and family in one piece?'

'Not quite,' Rydell said. 'The home's still there, but Suzy's packed up and gone.'

'*That's* why you look so rested!' Polanski cracked. 'So what else is new?'

'I have an interesting little mystery,' Rydell said. 'You want to hear about it?'

'Are you talking about the sky?'

'Right.'

'It sounds more interesting than marital discord. But let's order first and then talk while we eat. Since I own the joint, I recommend the food. As you can see, I eat a lot of it!'

He called a sexy cowgirl over and squeezed her rump playfully while ordering the food. She didn't seem to mind, in fact giggled and winked at Rydell, then flounced back towards the kitchen with her tightly-clad hips swinging like a metronome. Polanski changed his mind and enquired about Suzy's reasons for leaving home. When Rydell told him about his many trips and her boredom, Polanski, divorced, chuckled understandingly.

'Sounds like the same old story. It's what working for NASA does to marriages. Well, now you can get on with your work without being hassled. Can't be *all* bad buddy.'

Rydell wasn't so sure, and was glad to change the subject to what had happened to him in the aeroplane over the Antarctic. Lunch consisted of a broiled two-pound Porterhouse steak, served with sour-dough-bread and pinto beans. While they ate Rydell finished his story. Finally Polanski put down his knife and fork and looked thoughtful.

'You say you could actually *feel* and *smell* the . . . apparition? That it was practically . . . *physical?*'

'That's right,' Rydell said.

Polanski gave a low whistle. 'Weird!' he said. 'Really far out!' He drank more beer, wiped his lips with his hands and looked thoughtful again. 'And you're sure it wasn't just the high altitude and cold? A sort of . . .'

'I'm sure,' Rydell said firmly. 'I blacked out – I know that – but it was only for a few seconds, and when I recovered I was in command of my senses. That UFO was there – Rick, it wasn't imagined, and if Suzy, that apparition – was some form of hallucination, it was certainly no ordinary one. She *was* practically physical, dammit, and the smell of her lingered in the cabin long after she'd vanished.'

'And she vanished as the UFO disappeared?'

'Yeah, Rick, that's it. I think that Suzy, though not real, was some kind of entity. I think she was produced by that UFO, though don't ask me how or why.'

Polanski gave another low whistle and shook his head in bewilderment. 'Oh boy,' he said, 'ain't that something? You've got my interest, for sure. So how can I help?'

'I want you to check your records. I want to find out if there were other cases like this and if so, if there's a pattern to them.'

'I'm a man who loves his work,' Polanski replied, 'so let's get up and go.'

'Is it far?'

'Just a five-minute drive to the outskirts of town. Five minutes through hell,' he said.

He meant the heat. It clamped around Rydell as soon as they left the restaurant, suffocating him, and by the time he climbed into Polanski's car, his clothes were soaked with sweat. As they made the short drive to the eastern edge of Scottsdale, Rydell tried to distract himself by recalling Polanski's work with SETI – the US government's attempt to locate extraterrestrial civilizations through the use of radio astronomy.

Polanski was initially involved with NASA's Project Cyclops, which would have consisted of a circular array of about fifteen hundred antennae, each larger than a football field, covering about twenty-five square miles. When the project was aborted Polanski had helped to initiate a more successful project called SETI, or the Search for Extraterrestrial Intelligence. Involved in the programme were the Caltech Jet Propulsion Laboratory in Pasadena, California, NASA's Ames Research Centre at Moffett Field, and the existing antennae at the Deep Space Network in Goldstone, California, which between them had conducted a targeted study of selected stars within one thousand light years of Earth – an immense undertaking.

'You never found anything through SETI, did you?' Rydell asked, feeling hot and groggy. 'Not a damned thing.'

'No,' Polanski replied, slipping on his sunglasses as he drove into the blinding sun. 'It was real damned

83

frustrating. But of course that doesn't mean they're not out there. In fact, given that there are three-hundred thousand stars in one such group of stars, for instance, Messier 13 in the Great Cluster of Hercules, the possibility of no intelligent life-forms existing there is extremely unlikely. On the other hand, you have to bear in mind that even if intelligent beings *did* intercept our communications in that area, the distance of twenty-four thousand light years from Earth means that it'd be at least forty-eight thousand years before we'd get an answer. So, they're almost certainly out there – but contact with them, if it's to be made in our life-time, isn't going to happen through radio astronomy.'

'What about the so-called UFOs?'

Polanski shrugged, then pulled into the parking lot of a large, prefabricated building in the parched flatlands just outside of town. The building was covered with glittering bowl-shaped antennae and numerous aerials.

'Who the hell knows?' he asked rhetorically. 'We can only assess them with our own technology, and if the UFOs *are* from a highly advanced extraterrestrial civilization, it would hardly be up to the task. Already Einstein's Theory of Relativity is under attack and if it falls, a lot of things thought to be impossible will suddenly be possible.'

'Such as the need to actually travel those twenty-four thousand light years.'

'Right,' Polanski agreed, switching off the engine and applying the handbrake. 'It might be possible to go *through* that space or somehow avoid it. If quantum physics replaces our present understanding, *all* things become possible. So, here we are.'

When they were both out of the car, Rydell let Polanski lead him from the scorching sunlight into air-conditioned coolness. Above the main door of the building, a sign announced 'Project Skywatch International.'

A non-profit organization financed by the tax-deductible contributions of those who believed in the value of instrumented UFO tracking and monitoring, Project Skywatch was housed in two laboratory buildings and many smaller facility houses, filled with state-of-the-art instruments, scattered widely about the surrounding hills and plains, from where they constantly monitored the sky to detect and record UFO activity.

Polanski, like a proud schoolboy, gave Rydell a guided tour of the two main buildings, introducing him to the many volunteer scientists and technicians and showing him the vast array of technical equipment needed to monitor the sky: radar, a laser system, magnometers, a gravimeter, a microcomputer, ambient and parabolic microphones, an eight-channel sensor-activated chart recorder, video equipment, motion-picture cameras and thirty-three millimetre still cameras.

'If a UFO's located,' Polanski explained, stopping in front of a simulated UFO tracking programme on a computer monitor, 'the data from the instruments in the facility stations is fed in binary format into the computer, which then calculates and displays the distance, altitude and size of the object. The UFO is then shown on a video picture superimposed over an image of the area beneath it. We can also display a three-dimensional model of the magnetic field around the UFO, which shows each component of it in a different colour. And by using the latest helium neon laser we can even receive the UFO's voice, code or television signals, should such be present.'

'Which they haven't been so far.'

Polanski sighed. 'No.'

Leading Rydell away from the banks of computer monitors and into his office, equipped with its own complex computer system, he added more hopefully, 'But we're not wasting our time. So far we've managed to obtain UFO light pulsation measurements by photographic analysis, instrumented recordings of UFO plasma emissions, shock-wave emissions and propagation, magnetic field-effect Faraday-rotation rings, and instrumented data of precise UFO size determinations. We're getting *somewhere*, at least. Here, take a pew, pal.'

There were two swivel chairs in front of the working shelf along one wall of the office, facing three separate computer monitors. Polanski settled his large bulk into the chair facing the central monitor, meanwhile indicating that Rydell take the chair beside him. Polanski turned on the central computer and while waiting for it to load, Rydell studied the large charts pinned on the walls.

One was an illustrated chart of the most commonly reported UFO shapes, grouped into flat discs, domed discs, Saturn-like shapes, double-domed discs, spheres, hemispherical discs, flattened spheres, and elliptical, triangular and cylindrical shapes. Another chart was broken into two illustrated sections, one showing the most commonly reported UFO formations, the other showing UFO manœuvres, both singly and in formation. Other charts showed the world-wide locations and flight directions of the major UFO waves from 1896 to the present; major UFO events in the United States and overseas; the major areas of alleged magnetic deviation around the world including, as Rydell noted, the north and south poles; and the names, addresses and telephone numbers of the world's major UFO organizations.

'OK,' Polanski said, starting to move the flickering

cursor down the list of files that was being displayed on the computer monitor, 'just what are we looking for? After-images? No. Aliens? Not quite. Contactees? No. Close encounters of the third or fourth kind? No. Electromagnetic effects? Well, you *did* have those, didn't you?'

'Right,' Rydell replied. 'Fading and loss of radio reception, static, odd noises, possibly even the brief stalling of the aircraft's engine when that UFO practically swallowed it, but we won't learn anything new there, so keep searching the files.'

Polanski started moving the cursor down again, then stopped and moved back a bit, until the cursor was illuminating *Ethereans*.

'Hold on,' he said. 'This could be interesting.'

He accessed the file and Rydell leaned forward to read it.

'*Ethereans*. Hypothetical, invisible creatures who in-habit *Etherea*.

'*Etherea*. Name given to the hypothetical world composed of ether, an invisible substance that, as postulated by physicists, pervades space and functions as the medium for the transmission of radiant energy. UFOlogists who support the etheric hypothesis claim that UFOs are both inanimate craft and living aeroforms, propelled and sustained by orgone energy, which exists in the etheric realms. Inhabitants of *Etherea* are known as *Ethereans*.

Rydell studied the screen for some time, reading and rereading the short article, and thinking with a shiver of the eerily real Suzy he had found in the aircraft with him.

When he noticed Polanski was staring at him in a questioning manner, he said, 'It's worth thinking about. An invisible substance pervading space and functioning as the medium for the transmission of radiant energy, which could be orgone energy. Remember Wilhelm Reich? He used the term to describe what he believed was the universal life-force that acts through the medium of magnetic current. He was convinced that the Earth, as well as all its living creatures, was surrounded by an aura of such energy, and he also believed that energy to be the power source of Etherean craft, or UFOs. And UFOs, as we now know, are definitely related to magnetic current. That chart on the wall shows the world's areas of alleged magnetic deviation – all areas with a high incidence of UFO activity.'

'Right,' Polanski agreed. 'And accepting this hypothesis, we could then assume that the apparition of Suzy could have been created out of some form of etherea, an invisible substance briefly rendered visible by that UFO, which also appeared to dematerialize. Maybe another form of Etherea?'

'Shit,' Rydell said, 'I don't know. Go back to the files.'

Polanski exited the file and again ran the cursor down the screen, stopping again when he came to *Hallucinations*.

'OK,' Rydell said, 'retrieve that.'

The summary told him what he already knew; amongst the numerous causes of hallucinations were physical and emotional deprivation or emotional disturbance ('That was you!' Polanski said with a chuckle) and a great many UFO sightings had been encouraged by the use of hallucinogenic drugs. However, Rydell perked up when he read that a certain number of UFO sightings had been assessed as hallucinations 'induced by some unknown force or some unknown intelligence'.

'We seem to be getting warm, Polanski, so keep scrolling down.'

It was a thick file, but Polanski kept scrolling down until he came to the heading: *UFO Related Materializations from the Subconscious*. He stopped scrolling and accessed the file. They both read in silence.

*UFO related materializations from the subconscious have offered a novel addition to the UFO phenomenon, particularly since the first such report was recorded as late as 1979. In that report* (Flying Saucer Gazette, *Vol 3, No. 9, September 1979), New Zealand Air Force Captain Harold Falke, claimed to have almost crashed his C 130 cargo plane on August 4, 1979, during a flight from McMurdo Sound on Ross Island, Antarctica, to Christchurch International Airport, New Zealand. While in mid-flight an apparition of his wife materialized inexplicably in the cabin. During his subsequent debriefing by the authorities at Christchurch, the subject insisted that he had not been hallucinating, that he had been aware at all times of where he was and what he was doing, and that the so-called "apparition" had been, quote, "almost physical", unquote. He had, he said, been able to touch and smell it. Since the subject had recently been through a traumatic divorce from his wife, his experience was felt to be an extremely vivid hallucination brought on by stress.*

A trickle of excitement rippled through Rydell. He glanced at Polanski, who was grinning triumphantly at him, then nodded to let his friend scroll on down through the text.

There they were, one by one, the many reports of similar hauntings, beginning in 1979 and running up to the previous year, linked together by a common theme: *all the reports had been submitted by professional pilots and every 'materialization' had occurred over Antarctica.*

'Jesus Christ!' Polanski cried. 'Ain't this something? One: there was no report of this kind of incident until 1979, two: all reports since then confirm that the hallucinations, or apparitions, had an almost *physical* presence as well as smell, and three: every report was made by a professional pilot who had his experience when flying over the Antarctic.'

'Right.' Rydell nodded excitedly. 'And what does that suggest, Polanski?'

His friend shrugged. 'Fucked if I know.'

'The hole in the ozone layer over the Antarctic,' Rydell said, 'first appeared in 1979. The first report of this particular kind of materialization was made in 1979. In that report, as well as all the others since, the Antarctic was the location of the incident.'

'So that kind of materialization is directly linked to the ozone hole over the Antarctic.'

'Exactly,' Rydell said. 'There *is* another agent eating away at the ozone over the Antarctic and whatever it is, it's also causing materializations from the subconscious: *not* hallucinations, *not* apparitions, but materializations that have a physical reality. Those things are being *created*.'

'By what?' Polanski asked.

'You tell me,' Rydell replied.

# CHAPTER TEN

Suzy started to unwind with her folks on the farm in Iowa. She'd almost forgotten what it was like to be looked after – cooked for, talked to, given some attention – and although she was still guilty over the kids, she felt something come back to her. It was like being a child again, secure again, taken in, and she surrendered to the routine of the household and let her heartbeat slow down.

'I just wish the kids were here,' she told her mother. 'That would make it all perfect.'

'You think so?'

'Sure.'

'And what about your husband, Suzy?'

'I feel better without him.'

'Do you?'

'I do.'

'How long will that last, I wonder. You've bin with Rydell a long time, practically since you were teenagers, and to try and cut that out of your life could leave a big hole.'

'I can live without him Mom. I've *been* living without him. That man, he was never at home, so I don't see the loss.'

'He was only working, Suzy.'

'I don't see the difference.'

'A man isn't away from home if he's out there doin' work. He's always there, right beside you, in spirit, if he's not with a woman.'

'There wasn't another woman.'

'It's good that you can say that.'

'Thing is, Mom, I just became invisible and that's hard to take.'

'You want too much attention.'

'I'm too emotional, I know.'

'You're gonna have an awful big hole to fill and I don't think you'll do it. You need the kids, Suzy, and your home and that man. Lord knows, he may be a bit distracted, but he's better than most.'

'He never beat me, that's true.'

'Never cheated on you, either.'

'You're just trying to make me feel bad, Mom, but I did what I had to do.'

'Tell that to your kids.'

Her mother could talk that way without causing offence. She spoke out of a love that lent resonance to her voice, but she also had a fine wedge of honesty that could not be dislodged. Like her husband, she did not believe in saying what didn't come naturally.

'Some day I might,' Suzy said.

They got up real early, when the sun was still rising, and had breakfast together in the big kitchen, around the big table. Then Suzy's father would go off to work, wearing his dungarees and battered hat, and Suzy and her mother would talk for hours while doing the chores. It was like life in the previous century, much slower, more orderly, and it helped her feel less hemmed in by the world, more in control of things.

'He's so brilliant,' she told her mother, still talking about Rydell, 'but he just doesn't look where he's going or think about what he's saying. He's like a horse wearing blinkers – he always stares straight ahead – and if you don't happen to be right in front of him, he's blind to your presence. That's why he forgot me. I wasn't involved with his work. I shared his bed and cooked his food and washed and ironed his damned clothes but like a rich man with his servant, he forgot that I was actually there every hour, every day. He just ploughed his straight furrow.'

She helped around the house, did the shopping with her mother, and often went for long drives in the car, exploring what she had left behind. She took the long, straight roads, past fields drenched in gold and yellow, into the silvery haze of noon, under the vast, azure sky. It was where she'd grown up, blooming just like the flowers, and she recaptured her childhood during those journeys, filling up with old memories. She visited the old schoolhouse, the church and general store; went to Indianola to retrace her childhood footsteps, and even to Des Moines, where so many places reminded her of her adolescence with Rydell – the high school, the university, the movie houses, the ice-cream parlour, and the streets they had cruised in his old car.

She often choked up when she saw those places, which just made her resent him more.

'He's so creative,' she told her mother, 'but he destroys things so easily. He knows all about things, but he doesn't understand people. Oh, he doesn't mean any harm, there's no malice in him, but he gets up their noses, rides roughshod over them, and never stops to think about what he's saying or who he's saying it to.'

'I kinda like that aspect of him,' her mother said while beating dough on the table. 'At least it shows that he's honest.'

'But dumb with it, Mom. Never knows when to shut up. Like that flying saucer business last year which almost cost him his job. I mean, he said he believed in 'em, that the government should investigate, and NASA caught the flak from the media. Gawd, the

93

humiliation! It was even on TV! They treated his off-hand remarks like an official NASA statement and the big boys at NASA and other places went out of their minds. They wanted to kick him out, to get rid of him for good, and if it hadn'ta been for Dwight Collins, they'd've probably done it. That's the kind of thing he *always* does, Mom. He just can't keep his mouth shut.'

'Some men, they're just impulsive,' her mother said.

'Some men are just nuts.'

She even went to church, which she hadn't done for years. She'd forgotten what it was like to get up to the sound of church bells, say prayers over breakfast, and take the car along an empty road to a white-painted, packed church. She felt real fine and dandy dressing up for the occasion, filing into the pew, smiling at the congregation, then opening her hymnbook and letting loose with all the power of her lungs.

There were men in that church as old as she was, but they still gave her glances.

She was worshipped, as well.

'It's so hot,' her mother said.

'I love it,' Suzy replied.

'It's the hottest summer we've had for years. We'll have to be pretty careful. Are those from the kids?'

Suzy kissed the two letters, one from Don, the other from Ronnie. She had written to them and asked them to write back and they'd done so immediately.

Don's was real grown-up serious, the sentiment held in check, but Ronnie's was almost heartbreaking in its transparent grief. They both wanted her back, but they said it in different ways: Don saying that he missed her, but knew she must have her reasons; Ronnie saying that the house seemed too big, now that she wasn't there.

She read both letters repeatedly and soaked them with her tears, rubbing them ragged with the tips of

94

her fingers, trying to touch the boys; to feel them. Then she put the letters under her pillow and had vivid dreams.

That's what love could do to you.

Suzy loved the comfort of her bedroom because it hadn't changed at all; her folks had kept it exactly as she'd left it, not removing a thing. It was a small room with big windows, overlooking the back lawn, and between the lawn and starry sky were dark fields that seemed endless. The room itself was a cozy mess, filled with teddy bears and toys, and she liked cuddling up in there, taking a teddy bear to bed, as she had before she got married and cuddled Rydell instead. Now, not having him, and yearning more and more for the kids, she went back to her teddy bears, sometimes even giggling guiltily, lying there in the darkness, looking out at the moon and stars, thinking about how wonderful life could be when things didn't press in on you.

It was heavenly being home.

'We should never've left here,' she said. Her mother stared at her, amused. 'We were neither of us cut out for the big time in Texas or Maryland. Of course, Tony didn't notice. He'd be happy in an igloo. Just give him a notebook and pencils and tell him he's working! But *I* noticed, yeah. I always knew I didn't belong there. Those people, they were like Tony – they all lived for goddamned NASA – but me, I had too many emotions and needed folk who *felt* things. I lost all that in Greenbelt.'

'Surely not,' her mother said. She sounded so English sometimes.

'Well, not *completely*,' Suzy confessed. 'I mean, they weren't *all* workaholics. There was Maggie, my next-door-neighbour, Tony's best friend's wife, and . . . and . . . ' She could see the faces clearly, though she

95

couldn't quite remember their names. ' . . . and . . .
What I mean is, most folk stayed well clear because
Tony was . . . '

'What?'

'Pardon, Mom?'

'Unpredictable?'

'Yeah, Mom, that's right. I mean, he treated the kids
swell and always tried to make me laugh, but – you know
– like, he'd *die* if you suggested a dinner-party or drinks
or a barbecue. It'd always be next week, next month,
next year, and if you *did* get something going, he'd blow
it by turning up late, or having a fight with someone, or
saying something like, "Jesus! Where'd you get this
steak? It crawls faster than I do!" You know? A real *wise*
guy!'

'He could always make me laugh,' her mother responded. 'I guess that's why I liked him.'

Suzy couldn't believe that at first. Then she did,
though she didn't want to. She wrote to the kids, telling
them how much she missed them. She missed them
even more in the telling and made a mess of her
pillowcase. Still, she had the stars, that great moon, the
silky dawns, and could soak in the sun of each new day
and let the golden fields dazzle her.

She loved the long, lazy, loping hours.

'It was so frantic there,' she said, telling her mother
about Maryland. 'It was folks coming and going and
the telephone ringing and driving the kids to school,
going shopping and collecting the kids and then
making dinner. It was cleaning up after Tony – his
computer diskettes and CDs and books and discarded
clothes – and it was traffic jams and being home alone
with the TV until Tony turned up, which wasn't that
often. But here? It's completely different. Now I know
what I missed. What I missed was the feeling of family
and things that abide. I missed my man coming home

96

at nights.'

Her father usually returned home in the early evening, swinging the front door open and entering with an explosion of striated, incoming sunlight, his broad shoulders covered in golden-coloured corn husks, looking like some great tree that couldn't possibly die.

He'd done that throughout her childhood, always filling her with faith in life, saying things like, 'The land will endure. You have land and you're safe.' He didn't say that any more though; instead, he said, 'It's just too damned hot. It ain't natural, honey.'

That night, they watched TV; a programme about the weather. Great Britain was being devastated by terrible storms, the river Ganges, in India, was flooding her banks, sunny Spain was a sodden mess denuded of tourists, and Florida, though not yet like Siberia, was unusually cold.

'It's all them chemicals,' her father said distractedly. 'They're changing the weather.'

'*We* use chemicals,' Suzy's mother pointed out.

'We *need* 'em, honey. This hot weather breeds things. We need to keep the land healthy. Without that, we'd be finished.'

Suzy loved the land, too. It was all she possessed now. She'd left her old life behind – her husband and kids; her hopes and disappointments – and now she was taking refuge in the soil that had formed her in childhood.

The corn was yellow in the daylight. In the twilight it turned golden. At night, bathed in the light of the moon, it was a dark, murmuring sea. There was no land at night – only dark sea and starry sky – and Suzy lay in her bed looking out, and knew those stars fell on Maryland.

They covered her whole life.

There was nowhere to hide. You had to admit that was true. She did, but didn't know what to do, since she'd burned all her bridges. So she slept and dreamed about her family, awoke and blessed the new day. She tried distracting herself by spending more time with her father, standing side by side with him, shoulder-deep in corn stalk, looking out across a golden sea of food, a great bread-basket, and into the iridescent light of a voluptuous summer.

'It's too hot,' her father said, sounding anxious.

'Yeah,' Suzy agreed. 'Hot as hell.'

# CHAPTER ELEVEN

The sun was shining over Greenbelt when Clare drove through the guarded gates of the NASA–Goddard Space Flight Centre, making her way through the maze of right-angled roads, past featureless office-blocks and laboratories, and eventually stopped outside the building housing the Goddard Institute for Space Studies. Leaving the car in the parking lot, she entered the building, told the receptionist that she had an appointment with Dwight Collins, the Institute's Energy and Environment Programme Director, and was escorted to his office in the environmental physics department.

The office was windowless, the walls covered with a mass of charts and graphs relating to atmospheric phenomena and world-wide pollution.

Dwight Collins, who had been informed that she was coming, stepped forward as soon as she walked in.

'Hi, Clare,' he said, shaking her hand. 'It's good to see you again. I just hope you're not bringing me money problems or some God-awful paperwork.'

She smiled at his suspicions, but shook her head and said, 'No. I haven't come to see you on Department-of-Defence business. It's something else altogether, and for the moment it's private, a purely personal interest.'

'Well, *that's* a relief,' Collins said with a pleased grin. 'You're a beautiful lady and I love to see you, but since you became a liaison officer between the Department of Defence and NASA–Goddard, your appearances here are usually the sign of bad news, most notably budget cuts. Now you tell me you're not here on official business, you look even more beautiful than ever.'

'If I were that beautiful, you'd offer me a seat.'

'Whoops!' he said. 'Please allow me!' He pulled a chair up for her, and returned to his swivel chair. 'Cup of coffee?' he asked her.

'No, thanks, Dwight.'

'Tea? Whiskey?'

'Whiskey at *this* time in the morning?'

'Now you know where my budget goes. So, what's your problem?'

'One of your physicists, Tony Rydell.'

Surprized, Collins rested his chin on his clasped hands and stared quizzically at her.

'Right,' he said. 'A physicist. A climatologist. Why is *he* bothering *you*?'

'He waylaid me at the American Geophysical Union in Baltimore and told me about a fairly extraordinary theory he's developed since returning from that Airborne Antarctic Ozone Experiment you headed earlier this year. Recalling that infamous UFO scandal he'd been involved in, I treated him like a crank which made him fairly angry. Since then, I've done a thorough check on his career, and realize that he is one of our brightest physicists. I've been feeling increasingly guilty about the way I treated him, and have started to wonder if his theory *could* be plausible. So,' she shrugged, feeling oddly embarrassed, 'I thought I'd have a quiet talk with you and sound you out about Rydell and his damned theory.'

Collins sat back in his chair and studied her suspiciously.

'It must have been some theory,' he said carefully, 'if he went to see *you* about it. What did he tell you?'

Clare recounted Rydell's story of his bizarre

encounter, then outlined his theory that something unknown was gobbling up the ozone at a much quicker pace than the CFCs produced by man-made pollution of the stratosphere possibly could.

'And he therefore believes,' she concluded, 'that the Montreal agreement is irrelevant because nothing we can do will halt the ozone depletion; it's being depleted by an unknown agent. It sounds crazy, but that's what he believes, and since meeting him, despite my scepticism, I keep wondering about it. You were on that expedition with him. You're also his neighbour and good friend, so what do you think?'

Collins leaned on the desk, now smiling slightly at her. 'Well,' he said, 'you've been through his records, so I don't have to tell you how bright he is.'

'Academically bright, yes, but also eccentric, so how far can we actually trust his judgement? He's already caused NASA embarrassment over that UFO business . . .'

'He was widely misinterpreted. He didn't say he believed in flying saucers, but that's how the papers reported it. What he *was* in fact trying to say is that if hypersonic vehicles were destroying great quantities of ozone, which was true, then unidentified flying objects could be doing the same and should be investigated officially and not just by amateur UFO groups. The media were more interested in a good scare story and turned him into some kind of UFO freak. There's also no doubt in my mind that the media were encouraged in their activities by certain members of the commercial airlines, who were none too pleased with Rydell's revelation that aeroplanes were responsible for a lot of our stratospheric problems. True, it embarrassed us and damaged him, but it wasn't his fault.'

'It was his fault for not choosing his words more

carefully,' Clare said. As she spoke she wondered if she was deliberately doing him down because she couldn't get him out of her mind and resented him for that.

'That may be so,' Collins said, 'but Rydell is a physicist, not a politician, and he's always been a bit loose with his tongue.'

'So I gathered,' Clare said.

Collins grinned broadly. 'Can I take it from that remark that you had a few problems with him?'

'Just a few, Dwight. He got annoyed when I didn't show too much patience with his ozone-hole theory.'

'That's m'boy,' Collins said.

Unsure of her reasons for asking, Clare persisted, 'But tell me what this guy's *really* like.'

Collins shrugged. 'You've read his reports, Clare. You already know he's a damned good physicist. He's also dedicated, independent, and very outspoken. But then you've gathered that, too.'

'Wipe that grin off your face. I want to know what he's like as a human being. Is he emotionally stable? Does he drink? Does he beat his wife? Is he unusually imaginative?'

'He's pretty normal,' Collins laughed. 'He's a decent husband and father, though because he lives for his work, he has a disorderly house and a dissatisfied wife. But does he drink? Only normally. Does he beat his wife? Never! He's emotionally stable, at his very best when working, and though he's highly imaginative, I've never known him to let it impinge on his work. In fact, he's one of the best men I've got, and I don't say that lightly.'

'Do *you* believe what he says?'

'You mean regarding the ozone hole?'

'Yes.'

'Rydell's my friend, but I have to confess that I view his interpretation of what happened to him with some scepticism. I know for a fact that before he left on the expedition, his wife told him that she would leave him if he went. In other words, he was under a certain amount of stress during the expedition and that, combined with the thin atmosphere and cold he would have experienced during the flight, could have led to that particular hallucination. I think that's what it was.'

'*Did* his wife leave him?' Clare asked before she could stop herself.

'As a matter of fact, she did. She was gone when he got back. I don't think that helped his temper. It happened only a few days before you met him.'

'Oh, God,' Clare said sympathetically, though she also felt hot with shame at the feeling of relief slithering through her.

*I don't believe this!* she thought.

'Rydell insists,' she continued, to distract herself from her own confusion, 'that his aircraft was surrounded by some kind of unknown light, or even a craft, and that he could actually *feel* and *smell* his wife.'

Collins shook his head from side to side. 'Makes no difference, Clare. Hallucinations can possess a powerful reality, so I still think my explanation fits the facts.'

'What about his belief that something other than CFCs is depleting the ozone layer?'

'He didn't tell me about that. He must have come to that conclusion very recently. He probably didn't tell me because I was so sceptical about his experience.'

'Do you believe it's possible?'

'All things are possible, but it strikes me as being unlikely. Certainly the ozone is being destroyed much faster than we'd first anticipated, but we don't have *all* the facts and figures at hand. Here at NASA we know exactly how much our SSTs and shuttle flights are destroying the ozone in the stratosphere, but we can't be too sure of how much is being contributed by

European and Russian hypersonic vehicles and prototypes.'

'But Rydell claims that his calculations are based on computer analyses of the data collected world-wide by the Airborne Antarctic Ozone Expedition.'

'He actually said that?'

'Yes.'

'Then we'd better have a talk with him,' Collins said, sounding concerned. 'He wouldn't lie about that. I'm not saying his findings are sound – he *could* have misinterpreted the data – but he certainly wouldn't lie about his source, which is what disturbs me. Let's call him in now.'

Clare's heart started to race. She knew that she wasn't ready to see Rydell walking through that door, to be trapped in this uncomfortably small room with him. The very thought made her burn, her emotions in turmoil.

'Let's wait,' she said, trying to sound as casual as possible. 'I'd like to discuss this with a colleague before taking it further. It goes beyond your department, maybe touches on national security, so I might have to talk to Rydell alone, on behalf of the Department of Defence, rather than NASA. What do you think?'

'I think you're right,' Collins replied. 'Rydell went directly to you without consulting me, which could make for certain embarrassment in our working relationship. So, it might be better if officially I know nothing about this.'

'Right,' Clare said. 'Thank you.'

She shook Collins's hand and gratefully left his office, more disturbed by her growing feelings for Rydell than by the terrible future he had forced her to contemplate.

# CHAPTER TWELVE

The sun was sinking when Clare arrived in Washington DC. She decided to stop off at Jack Douglas' apartment near Dupont Circle. Pleased to see his car in the driveway, she parked just behind it and rang the bell.

'Yes?' he said.

'It's me, Clare.'

'Do you have an appointment?'

'Let me in, damn you, before I get mugged.'

She heard his soft, sardonic chuckle, then the buzzing of the intercom, pushed the door and let it close behind her. She walked up to the third floor, and found Jack standing by the open door of his apartment with a grin on his face.

'You can come without an appointment anytime,' he said. 'This *is* a pleasant surprise.'

They embraced in the hallway, then entered the apartment. Jack removed her coat and hung it up for her, while she sat on his leather sofa, facing his collection of modern art.

Tony Rydell, she thought, wouldn't have an apartment like this. His home would be cluttered, as untidy as his appearance, whereas Jack's apartment resembled *his* personality – cool and detached.

Just like she had been before meeting . . .

Rydell . . . She kept thinking about him . . . even here, with her lover.

'I've just been to Goddard,' she explained to Jack, 'and thought I'd drop in for a quick drink on my way back to Georgetown.'

'Only a drink?' he asked hopefully.

She smiled. 'Only a drink. That and a little talk. I'm feeling a bit unsettled at the moment, not too sure of my bearings. A neat bourbon would help.'

Jack looked down at her, surprised. 'A bit unsettled? *You*? I can't believe my own ears!'

'Just get me the bourbon.'

He fetched her the drink, then sat beside her with his glass of beer. They touched glasses and Clare sipped some bourbon. When Jack placed his hand on her thigh, she felt oddly uncomfortable.

'Well,' Jack said, 'this *is* a surprise! The coolest, most pragmatic woman I know isn't sure of her bearings. So, what's the problem?'

'It's work,' she replied.

'I'm glad to hear *that*, Clare!'

'It's to do with what we discussed with the President – the hole in the ozone layer over the Antarctic.'

He sighed. 'Christ, not *that* again. I've already told you that these things always take time. The President agrees with you in principle – he knows what needs to be done – but even he can't change the world overnight. He can't suddenly cut our country's use of insecticides, chemicals, oil, automobiles and aircraft by half. You're losing sleep over *that*?'

'Not just that,' she said. 'Something else entirely. It's possible that the ozone layer is being eaten away a lot faster than we've calculated, and by something other than CFCs.'

'It's no use trying this on, Clare. It's not going to work. Our own people have all the facts and figures, and what *you* say won't budge them, or at least won't make them hurry. The depletion of the ozone layer is an officially recognised problem; but it requires world-wide co-ordination, and that could take years.

106

Nothing you say, no trick you can play, is going to change that.'

'It's not a trick,' she said. 'It's something I've been told since having my talk with you and the President. Have you ever heard of a NASA physicist called Tony Rydell?'

Jack thought about it for a moment. 'No,' he decided, 'but then my concern is with NASA's accounts, not their personnel, and they have a lot of physicists on the payroll.'

'OK,' she said, 'listen to this.' She told Jack about her meeting with Rydell, about what he had told her. 'That's why I went to see his boss today – to sound him out on the matter.'

'I hope he kicked you out of his office.'

'No, he didn't. He simply confirmed what the records had revealed: that this guy isn't a fool.'

Jack grinned wryly. 'No, of course not. He just sees flying saucers and ghosts. No fool at all.'

'Jack, if what he says is true we're in worse trouble than I'd thought.'

'Don't even whisper that,' Jack said. 'You'll just unsettle *me*.'

'This has started already, Jack. Already, most of the United States have been devastated by the fiercest heat wave and drought we've experienced for fifty years. In Minnesota, animals died in their hundreds while corn and soy-bean production was only a fraction of what it should have been. On the West Coast and in the Rockies there were the worst forest fires in living memory. The Mississippi river is now at its lowest level since records began in 1872 – and severe water restrictions have been in force from Chicago to San Francisco.' She stared steadily at him, trying to drill some of her intensity into him. 'And that was just *this* country, Jack! Russia was also devastated by unprecedented drought. China was devastated by simultaneous drought *and* floods. More floods in Bangladesh and Brazil, and, in other countries, hurricanes and cyclones and typhoons, killing millions and shattering whole economies. That great hole in the ozone layer is *already* changing the climate, with the results I've just mentioned; and if, as Rydell thinks, it's changing even faster than we've calculated, then we have to find out what's causing it and do something about it. And I mean *now*, Jack!'

But Jack remained unconvinced.

'So a guy with an eccentric reputation has come up with a theory based on *his* reading of the data. The data would have to be analysed by an awful lot more people before the Department of Defence, let alone the White House, would make a move on it. And I'm surprised that *you're* taking it so seriously at this early stage. What's convinced the great realist?'

It was a good question, one she had asked herself.

'I'm not sure,' she confessed. 'There's just something about this guy. He's impressive – a bit cocky, but convincing – and he's made me think over this whole situation.'

'Yeah,' Jack said, 'I can see that.'

Something in the tone of his voice made her look at him.

He was gazing at her questioningly.

'I'd planned to ring Rydell,' she continued nervously, 'and arrange to analyze the data with him and see what I come up with.'

'Oh, you had, had you?' Jack's voice was cool, his tone slightly mocking. Then he took his hand off her thigh and leaned closer to her. 'And is that a necessity?' he asked her. 'Or just an excuse?'

She suddenly felt embarrassed and childish. 'What the hell does *that* mean, Jack?'

'It means that you're showing unusual faith in a man you've just met. It means you're confused between the theory and the man, but don't want to admit it . . . What's this guy like, Clare?'

'For Christ's sake,' she said, feeling more confused.

'You're intrigued by him, Clare. That much I can tell. You already believe his story, though you haven't checked his data, and you're using that data as an excuse to see him again.'

'That's nonsense, Jack!'

'I don't think so. I've never seen you like this before. I've never known you to accept *anyone's* theories before checking them out. Why this time, Clare?'

'Because it could make sense.'

'Because *what* makes sense? This guy tells you that something else, something *unknown*, is destroying the ozone and you actually *believe* him!'

Feeling humiliated and angry, aware of the truth in his remarks, she stood up and hurried towards the door, saying, 'Dammit, Jack, I won't listen to this nonsense! You sound just like a . . . '

She couldn't complete the sentence, so he did the job for her. '*Juvenile*?' he said. 'I sound just like a kid? How the hell do you think you're behaving, Clare, coming here with this nonsense?'

'Goodnight, Jack,' she said firmly, opening the door.

'Whether or not Rydell's theory has any validity, your interest in it is more than purely scientific. Don't kid yourself otherwise.'

'Go to hell, Jack!'

She walked out and slammed the door, then hurried back down the stairs. Though shocked at her outburst and burning with shame, she was unable to return and apologize. She just wanted to escape.

Darkness had fallen and the domes and spires of the capital looked eerily beautiful under moonlit clouds, as

109

she drove to Washington Circle, turned into Pennsylvania Avenue, then crossed Rock Creek and entered M Street. She hardly knew where she was going, driving instinctively, thinking only of what Jack had said, ashamed of the truth in it.

She had inherited from her parents a strong, independent nature and respect for the mind, rather than matters of the heart, which she had always viewed with grave suspicion. Romantic or sexual love, which she had experienced only in adolescence, had always left her feeling helpless, distraught and foolish. After adolescence, she had devoted herself to her education and work. The sex she had accepted – it was a therapeutic necessity – but the messiness of other human emotions she had left well behind her. That's why she was comfortable with Jack Douglas – his pragmatism presented no threat. It was also why she felt so confused when she thought of Rydell.

She couldn't think rationally about him. That was the first shock. When she forced herself to do so, she thought of him as a mess – a dishevelled, undisciplined, ill-mannered, arrogant man – but despite that she knew, without rhyme or reason, that she had to see him again.

Turning down one of the narrow streets off Wisconsin Avenue lined with Federal-period homes, she soon came to her father's house. Letting herself in, she hung her coat up in the hallway, then went into the lounge where she expected to find her father. He wasn't there, which meant he was in bed, so she decided to ring Rydell and get this thing over with.

To her shame, she had to pour herself a drink before she could do it. Sipping her bourbon while she dialled, she forced herself to think in a rational manner.

Someone lifted up the phone and yawned and said, 'Yeah?'

'Mr Rydell?'

'Yeah.'

'Mr Rydell, this is Clare Holton. We . . .'

'*Who*?'

'Clare Holton. You came to see me at the American Geophysical Union in Baltimore, Maryland. I'm the scientific liaison officer between NASA and the Department of Defence, and you spoke to me about . . .'

'Dammit, lady, do you know what *time* it is? It's nearly *midnight*, for chrissakes, and I've got two kids and an old lady trying to sleep here. What *is* this? An *emergency*?'

Horrified that she had forgotten the time, Clare muttered, 'I'm sorry. I didn't realize. I was so immersed in my . . .'

'Work. Yeah, right. I understand.' He sighed at the other end of the line. 'So what is it, Miss God-Almighty Holton?'

'You don't have to be offensive. I *said* I was sorry. And I'm calling because I'm concerned about what you told me and want to go over the data with you.'

There was a brief tormenting silence, then he said, 'Am I hearing right, lady?'

'Please don't call me lady. I think it's demeaning. Either call me Clare or Miss Holton. Yes you *did* hear correctly.'

'So what changed your mind . . . *Clare*?'

She closed her eyes, wanting to strangle him. 'I just thought it over and decided that I should at least have offered to double-check your data. It's my way of apologizing for my rudeness, so I hope you'll accept.'

'When can you come over?'

'Well, let's see . . . I'm a bit busy this week. What if we make it . . .'

'The weekend. Let's do it at the weekend. The other

111

guys will all be at home and can't look over our shoulders. Unless of course, you think that being *alone* with me wouldn't be kosher.'

God, he was impossible! Where the hell had he been brought up? Probably in some God-awful Western town.

'Since I'm not Jewish, I'm not concerned with being kosher,' she told him. 'Will Saturday morning do?'

'We don't *all* have servants! I do the shopping on Saturday mornings. What about Sunday?'

'What time?'

'Ten.'

'Fine. Goodnight, Rydell.'

She dropped the phone before he could answer, almost slamming it down, and immediately went to pour herself another drink. Crossing the old-fashioned room, she noticed the note left on the writing desk. The note was from her father. Puzzled, she opened it and thoughts of Rydell left her mind as she read:

*My dearest daughter, my Clare,*

*When you read this letter I will already be gone. I know that what I have done may be morally indefensible and will certainly wound you deeply, but I beg you to understand that it was done out of love and respect. I love you as I write this, and that love helps me to do what I know I must.*

*A few weeks ago I was informed that I had incurable cancer. If I had my left leg amputated I would buy myself another six months, perhaps even a year, but I would not wish to survive this way. I wouldn't want to become an invalid, with you as my nurse. I do not wish to deprive you of the life you so richly deserve.*

*I did not die with your mother because she asked*

*me to live for you. Now that I can no longer live*
*for you without becoming a burden I do not wish to*
*live at all.*

*My suicide is my act of love.*

*I have taken some tablets. I will suffer no pain at*
*all. It is the best way, the only decent way out. I love*
*you.*

*Farewell, dearest one.*

*Your loving father, Walter*

Clare's hand was shaking. She was blinded by her tears.
Her heart was racing when she gently laid the letter
back on the desk, then walked towards the light in her
father's bedroom.

She stopped just outside the door. She could hardly
bear to walk in. It was only the thought of her father's
courage that gave her the strength to do so.

The room was well lit. He had not wanted to
frighten her. He lay, stretched out under the sheets,
with his hands folded across his chest. He had died
quietly, with dignity. At some point, just before death's
long sleep, he had opened his eyes again. Now he
seemed to be smiling.

Clare was no longer frightened, but her grief knew
no bounds. She walked slowly to the bed, looked down
at her dead father, sat beside him, gently stroked his
cold forehead, then closed his eyes.

She lay upon him, her cheek resting on his stilled
heart, listening to his great silence.

Her tears fell for a long time.

# CHAPTER THIRTEEN

The colours of her childhood were disappearing, bleached out by the sun. Suzy saw that it was happening, but she wasn't sure just why; she didn't know if it was actually the weather or her changing view of things.

The weather certainly was unusual, too hot even for summer, and her father was complaining all the time that it was ruining the crops. That had something to do with the colours – the fabulous yellows and golds drying out and becoming brownish – but she also sensed that it was the way she was seeing things, which was not so romantically. She still loved being home, talking to her mom, helping her dad, but even for her it was too hot, and now their talk was anxious, and she found herself thinking more of Maryland and shedding tears for her kids.

She really needed to see them.

She'd received a letter from Rydell, asking her to come back. If not for his sake, he'd said, for the sake of the kids. It burned her up to read it, since it was so typical of him: she'd thought he'd at least write to say he loved her and missed her, but, no, he only mentioned the kids, as if nothing else mattered.

God, she could kill him!

She started going out in the evenings, mostly wandering about Des Moines, looking in on the old places where she and Rydell used to fraternize, but mostly just hopping in and out of bars, hoping to find some friends. Of course she didn't see a soul – all her old girlfriends had moved away – and so she found herself drinking more and more, brooding on Rydell and lost dreams.

He hadn't even said he wanted her back. He only mentioned the kids. What a sonofabitch he was!

'You're staying out a lot these days,' her mother said. 'What do you do all night?'

'It's not all night, Mom. It's just the evenings. And I just walk around.'

'Looking for what?'

'Old faces, I suppose.'

'The younger folk are moving out,' her mother confirmed. 'I never see your old friends.'

'I like to have a drink and think.'

'About Tony and the kids?'

'Yeah.'

'You miss them?'

'I want my kids, at least, but I've got too much pride.'

'They didn't want to come, you said.'

'But they want me back, Mom.'

'Then go.'

'I'm not ready for that yet. Phew! It's real hot in here!'

She often went out to avoid the heat. It was hot even in the evenings. It was cooler in the streets of Des Moines than it was on the farm, and the bars, thank the Lord, had air-conditioning, unlike the farmhouse.

She drank alone in the bars, out of sight of the stars, thinking of Maryland and her kids in their beds. She started to convince herself that she couldn't go back because she didn't deserve them. She'd deserted them and any woman who did that, didn't deserve her kids. Thinking that, she had to take out her kerchief and wipe tears from her eyes.

'Anything wrong?' someone asked her.

He was over six-foot tall and had twinkling blue eyes

and thick brown hair. His muscles were bursting out of his short-sleeved shirt and he wore a white apron. He worked the bar and cleaned tables.

'No,' she replied, feeling a bit flustered. 'Just got a bit of dirt in my eye.'

'Oh, yeah?'

'Yeah,' she said.

He nodded thoughtfully. 'Don't I know you?' he asked. 'Didn't you used to go to . . . ?'

'High school!' She almost screamed it. 'You're Joe Wheeler! You and me used to . . . Lord!' She giggled softly.

'Yeah,' he said, 'we made eyes. Then you married . . . ?'

'Rydell. Tony Rydell.'

'That's right. The bright spark.'

'Yeah,' she said. 'Real bright.'

He lifted her glass and wiped the table. 'You just visiting?' he asked.

'Yeah,' she said. 'Just visiting.'

'You bin gone for years, right? Since you got married. You went to . . . '

'Texas.'

'Yeah, right.'

'Then to Greenbelt in Maryland.'

'Kids?'

'Two.'

'I never got married,' he said. 'Don't know why. It just never happened. Now it's too late to think of it.'

'Don't know why. You're an attractive guy.'

'Sounds like poetry, Suzy. You here with your husband and kids?'

'No. All alone this time.'

'Really?'

'Yeah.'

'Just here seein' the folks?'

'Right.'

'I sometimes see your mother in town, though I don't think she knows me. One helluva fine dame, that woman. You oughta be proud.'

'I am.'

'You look good.'

'You think so?'

'Yeah. No kidding. You look like a goddamned million dollars.'

'Stop it. You're making me blush.'

'That just makes you look prettier.'

Suzy laughed. She could never resist a compliment. Men could make you feel good in a way women couldn't; they could reach in and pull out that part of you that too often stayed hidden. Without a man, she didn't feel right, not whole, missing something, and she guessed that it came from her happy childhood, then marrying so young. First her Dad, then Rydell – the two pillars of her life – her Dad as solid as a rock, Rydell always able to make her laugh; never boring. Yeah, she'd liked him for that. She liked a man who could make her laugh. But somewhere along the line she'd stopped laughing, which is why she was here now, laughing with this old flame, Joe Wheeler, and feeling good for it.

'You wan' another drink?' he asked.

'Sure,' she said. 'Why not?'

The place was practically empty, so when he brought her the fresh drink, he also brought himself a beer and took the seat facing her.

'Do you mind?'

'Not at all,' she said. It was good to have a man about her own age sitting right there in front of her. He had a nice, easy smile.

'You been running this place long?' she asked him.

'*Too* long. About ten years. I took it over when my

117

Dad died. As a favour to my Mom. She died about five years ago and now, here I am still; the sole owner and only member of staff. It beats some jobs I know.'

'You see many of our old friends?'

'Naw. They mostly got married and had kids. Scattered and went away. Those were some days, eh?'

Suzy smiled, remembering being a teenager; maybe wanting to be one again, without all these problems. 'Yeah,' she said. 'You used to give me that heavy-lidded look; obviously thought you were Richard Gere.'

'You used to like 'im. I remember that.'

'I still do,' she told him. 'You look a bit like him, you know that? Same lips, the same long-lashed eyes.'

'Gee, now you're making *me* blush.'

'It makes you look younger.'

'Why don't I close up and we'll go eat?'

'Yeah,' she said. 'I'd like that.'

But, when he closed the doors, they went upstairs instead, somehow undressed and climbed into bed. It seemed a natural thing to do, no embarrassment at all. He was very gentle, very considerate, and everything blocked up in her poured out in a great wave of relief. She stayed there all night, letting him stroke her and lick her all over, making her purr like a cat. And what was nicer was when they weren't making love, he continued to talk to her. She really liked him for that.

'Smoking in bed,' he said, 'is a dangerous habit, but I really like doin' it.'

'And having bourbon in bed, too.'

'Yeah, at four in the mornin'. Makes you feel that you're on an all-night party, gettin' higher each minute.'

'Makes you feel young, right?'

'Yeah, Suzy, I guess.'

'Marriage takes that away from you,' she told him. 'It just slips away quietly.'

'It's not been working out?'

'We had something, but we lost it. He just doesn't see me anymore. It's like I'm there, but I'm not.'

'You left home? Is that it?'

'Yeah,' she confessed. 'I did. I asked the kids to come along, but they didn't want to, so I left them as well. That's what makes me feel bad.'

'You think you'll go back?'

'I dunno. I don't think so. I'm too proud to go back. I also think that a woman who leaves her kids, deserves all she gets. I don't deserve them, no more.'

'That's bullshit, Suzy.'

'It's kind of you to say so. An' it's nice to be with a man who knows how to look at me.'

'And how's that?'

'With greed.'

'Come here, honey. Let me hold you again. I wanna show you what greed is. You sure are some handful!'

'Godalmighty, that's good! That's *so* good! Don't stop, Joe. Take as long as you want. Keep me locked up in chains.'

'Don't tempt me,' he said.

He asked her what she liked and tried to please her and made her smile, and when dawn broke, when she finally walked out of there, she felt like a new woman. She got back to the farm in Indianola just in time to miss breakfast.

'Where you bin all night?' her mother asked, as she cleaned up the table.

'With an old friend,' Suzy said.

'A girlfriend?'

'No, Mom,' Suzy confessed. 'It wasn't a girlfriend.'

'I don't think your Dad was pleased.'

'No, I don't suppose he was. You got any coffee in that pot?'

'Sure, help yourself.' Suzy poured some coffee. 'Who is he?' her mother asked.

119

'Joe Wheeler. I don't know if you remember him. He went to my high school.'

'I remember him,' her mother said. 'A nice kid, but never married. I hear he runs his Dad's bar in town and has an eye for the ladies.'

'He enjoys being a bachelor, Mom.'

'And you're on his list, right?'

'I need someone in my life right now, Mom, and he's kind and considerate.'

'You be careful, child. Remember you're still married. You've got things to work out.'

'Thanks, Mom. I'll remember that.'

'OK, then, let's drop it.'

And that was that. They didn't like it, but accepted it. Suzy saw Joe again, then it became a regular thing, and she soon spent more time in his bedroom than she did in her own.

She'd gone off her own room. It now seemed small and confining. She'd sit there on the bed and look out through the window, noticing that the golden sea of corn had turned a dark, dried-out brown. She saw her father standing shoulder-high in the ruined crop, his eyes crawling all over it. He'd pull husks off and drop them on the ground and then glance anxiously about him, looking unreal in that silvery light; a man no longer sure if the earth would abide and always sustain him.

Suzy knew he was frightened.

# CHAPTER FOURTEEN

Coming out of sleep, Rydell had his familiar dream. At first all he saw was a pinprick of light in a vast sheet of darkness, then a gleaming white eye, but then it expanded, flaring out in all directions and raced at him, exploding around him, obliterating the real world.

He was sucked through space and time, then cast forth into silence. He looked up from Europa, across the valleys and frozen mountains, and saw the great golden globe of Jupiter, its Great Red Spot a bloody wound. Around it were the satellites, thirteen, maybe more, and all of them, the enormous apple and its seedlings, were drenched in stars.

He usually woke up then, but this time it was different. This time the enormous apple somehow drew him towards it, changed shape as it did so and gradually became a human face in a dazzling white haze. He was sucked in, surrounded, ingested, and then he saw the face again – the teasing smile, the mocking green eyes – and recognized it as Suzy's.

She was very close to him, giving off heat and light, at once extraordinarily sensual and frightening. Her smile chilled his blood.

His lust for her dissolved into terror and he screamed and . . .

Awakened.

'Goddammit!' he whispered, rubbing the sleep from his eyes, naked and sweating beneath the sheets, his heart racing. He glanced around the bedroom, taking in the real world, still caught in the web of his dream.

For years he had been dreaming about flying to Jupiter – it was a simple yearning for escape – but the recent addition of Suzy to the dream was extremely disturbing. She was so vivid in it that it reminded him, with a shudder of dread, of what had happened when he had flown through the hole in the ozone layer.

Had that creature been an hallucination, a ghost, or some other form of life disguised as his Suzy? He was convinced that it had been the latter.

Why her?

Because she had left him. Because the thought of her had filled him with guilt and recrimination, shame and rage and frustration, all of which had obviously been preying on his subconscious. Yes, that had been part of it, but it didn't wholly explain his experience. Nor did it explain why, ever since that fateful day, his dreams of Suzy had made her seem different from the Suzy he knew. In his dreams, though she certainly *looked* like Suzy, she was inexplicably frightening. Not Suzy at all.

Bewildered, he sighed as he swung his legs out of bed, rubbing his face with his hands. He stopped to listen to his kids shouting and his mother barking at them, then wandered into the bathroom to wake up with a shower. He took it cold, feeling brave and triumphant, and emerged feeling far more alive, then dried himself and got dressed.

'Groaning in your sleep again,' his mother said when he entered the kitchen. 'It's not a good sign, son.'

'All right, Ma, no analysis.'

'You've been sick ever since that Suzy left you. You've hardly had a good night's sleep since then – all that moaning and groaning.'

'I have bad dreams, Ma.'

'So do I,' said Don, looking up from the dining table

where he was sitting with his Grandma and Ronnie. 'I have terrible dreams all the time. It's 'cause I'm neglected.'

'*I'm* neglected,' Ronnie added, staring pugnaciously at his brother in that way he'd developed lately. 'I bet I have more bad dreams than you do – and *real* bad as well!'

'Crap!' Don replied.

'Watch your tongue!' Grandma snapped.

'OK, cool it!' Rydell said as he sat down with them. 'I want no fights this morning. How are you, Mrs Gomez?'

The question was directed at the portly Mexican woman standing at the cooker, dressed in a plain dress and apron, sweating as she fried eggs and flapjacks.

'I feel real bad,' she said as the toast popped out of the electric toaster and the coffee boiled noisily. 'I don't feel good since I get here. I only been here for five days and already I'm done for. This place is a zoo, Senõr!'

'And we all know who the animals are!' Grandma said clearly, looking at the boys.

'And all the time she criticizes!' Mrs Gomez continued, pointing at Rydell's mother. 'I don't clean the house proper. I don't do the food proper. She shows me dust on her finger and moans that the meat is under-cooked and complains that my chilli is too hot and my coffee too cold. She follows me everywhere, sniffing at me like a dog and she holds the dishes up to the light to find invisible dirt. And these kids, they do the same. She encourages them to do so. They play stupid tricks, they try to frighten and confuse me. I can't take any more, Senõr!'

Mrs Gomez threw more flapjacks onto the plates, shaking with outrage.

'She also takes her time serving us,' Grandma noted. 'That's why the food's always cold.'

'Mother!' Rydell snapped.

123

Mrs Gomez let out a wail. 'Aye! Aye! Aye! That's enough! This is the last abuse I take!' She threw down the spatula, breaking a plate, then hastily untied her apron and threw it to the ground. Rydell kicked his chair back and stood up to talk to her, but was distracted by his mother's snort of mirth.

'Goddammit,' he snapped, 'shut up! Mrs Gomez, please wait a minute . . .'

'No!' she said with magisterial dignity. 'I leave this madhouse right now!'

'*Please*, Mrs Gomez! I just want you to try . . .'

But Mrs Gomez cut him short by pointing a finger at his frail, silvery-haired, smirking mother. 'That woman,' she said, jabbing her finger to her temple and twisting it like a corkscrew, 'is as mad as a starving coyote, and just as unpleasant. And these,' she continued, removing her finger from her temple and pointing at Rydell's two boys, 'are more delinquent than the wetbacks *she* says are ruining this country. Adios, Mr Rydell. You are a good man, but your family is terrible. You can mail me my money.'

Having regained her lost pride, she glared at Rydell's mother, stuck her tongue out at his giggling boys, then marched from the house.

The boys fell about laughing, Rydell's mother smiled at the wall, and Rydell, who hadn't as yet had a coffee, lunged across the table at the boys, his hands slapping them wildly. They both kicked their chairs back and rushed out of the room, their footsteps making a shocking racket in the hallway, leaving Rydell alone with his mother.

She was nodding at an invisible friend across the room, her smile one of triumph.

Rydell loved her, but she wasn't herself these days, which had made for some trying times.

'Happy, are you?' he asked her.

124

'What *do* you mean, Tony?'

'You know damn well what I mean. Mrs Gomez was a really good housekeeper, and you've driven her out.'

'*I* didn't drive her out. I didn't do a thing, dear. The woman was just a bit hysterical, as most Mexicans are.'

'You *made* her hysterical.'

'What an awful thing to say. 'Specially knowing that foreigners, *her* kind, aren't like us at all.'

'She's an American, just like you.'

'She's *Mexican*, not American.'

'She's an American citizen, born and bred, but let's forget that for now. The point is that she's gone, she certainly won't come back, and that puts the ball in your court. I mean, I got her to get all this off *your* back and *now* look where we are. Again, there's no one to look after the house and kids, just you and me, Ma.'

His mother stopped smiling. 'You and *me*?' she said. 'Oh, no, I don't think I can do that. I'm exhausted already.'

'Exhausted?'

'Yes, exhausted. Those two boys are so trying. You left Suzy to look after them, but Suzy was inadequate, and now they're like a pair of juvenile delinquents. I *always* said that Suzy was useless. I said it a lot, but no-one listened. That Suzy, I said, she's as pretty as a little bird, but she doesn't have the sense of a rabbit and just isn't a housewife. And now the proof, God help us, is in the pudding and those two boys need discipline.'

'That's why I asked you to come back. I need someone to impose a little discipline – and you can do that.'

'I couldn't with you,' she reminded him. 'Just look at the state of you. *You're* as unruly as your children and that's saying a lot, Son.'

Rydell couldn't believe his ears. But when he

thought about it, he realized, with a shock, that what his mother said was true. He *had* been an unruly child, and still was. He knew only the disciplines of his work, which didn't help much in daily life. It certainly hadn't been good for his wife and children – that much was clear.

'It's all your fault,' he told his mother. 'I mean, I'm *your* son, after all. *You* brought me up! *You* made me what I am.'

'Don't blame *me*,' she replied. 'You've blamed me all your life for all your problems, but I wasn't responsible. But I'm too old and feeble for this. I wanna go back to the home.'

'Dammit, Ma, you can't leave me now!'

'I have to. I have a migraine. In fact, I think I'm going to faint.' She placed her hand on her head, swaying a little on her chair. 'I think I'll have to lie down.' She stood up. 'Please ring the home . . . '

'Menopause Manor,' he said sarcastically.

'Tell them to come and fetch me this evening. I should feel better by then.' She started to leave the room, holding her hand to her head, but stopped when she reached the kitchen door. 'Don't worry about me, dear. You go on to work. I know you have to. Just make sure the children stay outside. At least tell them to be quiet. When I wake up, I'll make lunch.'

'You don't have to.'

'And after that, I'll pack my suitcase and wait for the ambulance.'

'I'll be home by then, Ma.'

'You don't have to be.'

'I will be.'

'OK, Son. I have to lie down now. Have a good day, dear.'

'You have a good sleep, Ma.'

She sighed. 'I'll try, Son.'

He grinned when she'd walked out, amused despite himself. Then he thought of Mrs Gomez's departure and knew he had problems. Still, he rang the rest home, not having much choice, and arranged to have his mother collected that evening. He thought of his forthcoming meeting with Clare Holton, and was about to get his jacket when a car-horn honked repeatedly outside.

Don and Ronnie called out excited greetings . . . then Rydell heard Suzy's voice.

'Jesus H Christ!' Rydell murmured, though he didn't move straight away. Instead, he went to the window, pulled the curtain back and looked out furtively to see a dusty red Ford parked by the road. Suzy was hugging the boys on the front lawn, all three of them so excited, it made him resentful.

Eventually Suzy straightened up, patting her blonde hair into place and adjusting her sunglasses as she glanced at the house. She was wearing a tightly belted, open-necked shirt and high-heeled leather boots which, combined with her skin-tight denims, emphasized her long legs. She sure as hell didn't look like the mother of two. She looked too damned attractive.

'OK Tony,' she shouted, lowering her sunglasses. 'You might as well come on out.'

'Why not come in?' he responded, feeling embarrassment.

'I don't want to,' she said.

Letting the curtains drop back into place, and cursing softly at his own stupidity, Rydell walked out onto the porch, closing the front door quietly behind him. Suzy slid her sunglasses back up her nose and stared solemnly at him, looking too sexy for her own good, flanked by their sons, each one holding a hand of hers.

'Hi, Tony,' she said.

'Hi, Suzy.' He glanced over her shoulder, at the car by the kerb, and saw that a man was sitting in it, smoking a cigarette, his fingers drumming lightly on the steering-wheel, his face hidden in shadow.

'Who's that in the car?'

'Just a friend,' Suzy replied.

'It's not your car,' Rydell noted.

'It's a rented car. We've just come from the airport.'

'You flew here from Ohio?'

'Yeah.'

'Your folks pay for it?'

'I know what you're implying,' Suzy said, 'and you're totally wrong. My folks paid for me; Joe paid for himself.'

'Joe! You've got a boyfriend named Joe. Did you know him before you left?'

'I *knew* him, but not the way you mean. I didn't leave you for that.'

'You know him that way now, right?'

Her grin was defensive. 'Yeah, Tony. Right. Nothing lasts forever. You know. We have to move on.'

That was like a slap in the face.

'Hey, kids,' he said, 'go inside for a minute. I have to talk with your Mom.'

'Aw, gee!' Ronnie exclaimed.

'She's just got here!' Don complained.

'It's OK, kids,' Suzy said, pushing them towards the house. 'I'll see you before I leave. Go inside and let your Dad and I talk for a bit.'

'You promise?' Don asked, looking grave.

'Yeah, I promise. *I promise!*' She grinned and stomped her boot on the lawn and the kids reluctantly ran off. When they'd gone, she stopped grinning.

'You're obviously not coming back,' Rydell said, 'so what the hell are you doing here?'

Suzy shrugged, an oddly forlorn gesture. 'I just wanted to see you and the kids. You know? Just a visit.'

'Are you here to make trouble?'

'What ya mean, Tony?'

'If you want to see the kids, you must miss them. Do you want them back, Suzy?'

She lowered her head, kicked distractedly at the lawn, then looked up again, chewing her gum. 'No,' she said, 'I don't. I mean I do, but I know I can't. I mean, I miss them, you know, I really do, but . . . '

'They need a mother, Suzy.'

'More than you need me, right?'

'I needed you, dammit, in my way. I just had my work, that's all.'

'Yeah,' Suzy said. 'Work.'

'Why not come back?' he said.

'For you,' she asked, 'or the kids?'

'Goddammit, Suzy, for *all* of us. We all need each other.'

'You don't need me, Tony.'

'OK, dammit, for the kids.'

'No,' she said. 'For you. You want someone to do the housework and cooking while you get on with your work. Isn't that true, Professor?'

'Just stop this shit, right?'

'Still foul-mouthed, I note.'

'Given the kind of company you keep, it shouldn't shock you too much.'

He couldn't resist looking at the guy she had picked up. He couldn't see his face; just the shoulder and arm that were framed by the car's window, suntanned muscles, fingers drumming the steering wheel.

'That's some ape you've got there in the car,' he said spitefully. 'Where did you pick him up? On the farm or in some honky-tonk?'

'He's no ape,' Suzy said. 'He owns his own bar in Des Moines, and he makes more than you do.'

'Gee, whiz, I'm impressed. He owns a bar and earns

more than me. That sure makes him something, right?'

'You used to know him Tony. His name's Joe Wheeler. He went to our high school and . . . '

'Yeah, yeah, I remember. The one whose eyes you thought were soulful and I thought were dumb. Don't let's have a class reunion on the lawn – my stomach's churning already.'

Suzy sighed. 'Let me say goodbye to the kids.'

'What the hell did you come here for?'

'I came to say hello to my kids, but now I want to leave.'

'Aw shucks, I've hurt your feelings!'

'I'm immune to your sarcasm. Now do I get to say goodbye or not? Just let me know where I stand.'

'What's the matter? You got a *conscience* or something? You wanna pretend you still care? Go to hell, Suzy! Clear off!'

'You're a shit, you know that?'

'I didn't leave my kids, Suzy. I didn't leave them, then turn up at the house with some stud in my car, like you've done with Joe Wheeler.'

'He loves me!'

'He loves your sweet ass. Now waltz it back to him.'

Suzy sniffed back her tears. 'I don't deserve that,' she said.

'Don't bring your boyfriends back here again. Now goodbye, Suzy. Adios.'

Before she could respond, he turned away and walked back into the house, slamming the door, his heart beating fast. Don and Ronnie rushed up to him, but froze when they saw the look on his face. They glanced at the closed door, then at one another, and only when the car outside roared off did they rush to the window.

They watched the car departing and that made Rydell feel worse. He knew that he'd behaved badly and that the boys knew that too. He couldn't move, was paralysed by shame, and just leaned against the door, letting his racing heart settle down, as the sound of the car faded away.

The boys turned away from the window, towards him, Ronnie more bewildered than hurt. Don placed his hand on Rydell's arm, trying to be understanding.

'You fought again, didn't you?'

'Yes,' Rydell confessed, 'we did.'

'It's OK, Dad,' Don said, his eyes wounded. 'We know you didn't want that. We understand. It's OK.'

Rydell couldn't believe it. The generosity was too much. He pulled both boys against him, hugged them passionately, kissed their heads, then let them go and hurriedly left the room.

He was still wiping tears from his eyes when he walked out of the house, aware that he was going to be late for his meeting with that hard-case, Clare Holton.

# CHAPTER FIFTEEN

Even though Rydell was late, Clare Holton didn't act like a hard-case when he met her this time. In fact, she seemed unusually subdued and merely smiled wanly when he walked into the reception lobby of the NASA–Goddard Centre.

'Sorry I'm late,' he said.

'It's OK. It doesn't matter.'

'No, really,' he said, taken aback by her manner, 'there's no excuse for . . .'

'I wasn't checking the time,' she said, 'so really, it's OK.'

'That's decent of you, Miss Holton.'

'Clare, please call me Clare. Now shall we get down to business?'

'Yeah, Clare, let's do that.'

He took her straight to his office in the environmental physics department. Since this was a Sunday morning, most of the offices were deserted and Rydell felt oddly intimate with her. More aware of her, he found himself glancing frequently at her, though he tried not to.

'Would you like a coffee?' he asked, as he switched on half-a-dozen computer monitors that were on a shelf along the wall facing his desk.

'No, thanks,' she replied. 'I'm fine. If I want a drink, I'll help myself to water.'

'Very healthy,' he said, then pulled up another chair, placing it beside his own for her. 'OK, here we go. What I'll do first is show you the climate-model figures on which we calculated what the ozone-depletion rate *should* be. Then I'll show you the comparative figures between the climate-model summaries and the actual ozone depletion over the Antarctic, as assessed from that last land-and-airborne Antarctic expedition. As you'll then be able to see for yourself, there's a hell of a difference between how fast the ozone layer *should* be disappearing and how fast it's *actually* disappearing. And the difference, believe me, is dramatic and, so far, inexplicable. OK?'

She nodded.

He accessed the required file on each of the computer-monitors.

'What you're seeing are the computer enhancements and analyses of the Earth's atmosphere, taken from the principal climate-modelling centres, namely, our own Goddard Institute for Space Studies in New York, the Geophysical Fluid Dynamics Laboratory at Princetown University, the National Centre for Atmospheric Research in Boulder, Colorado, the British Meteorological Office in Berkshire and even the Soviet Hydro-Meteorology Centre in Moscow. Do you know what climate models are?'

'Yes,' she replied. 'Since it's impossible to represent the Earth's atmosphere, in its entirety, in the detail necessary for atmospheric analysis, the climate or greenhouse models are a way of dividing Earth's surface and atmosphere into so-called numeric "boxes". Each box covers a surface area of up to one thousand kilometres square and the atmosphere ten or twenty layers deep. By doing this, you can mathematically reproduce the changes that are presently taking place in the atmosphere, as well as calculate more accurately the expected changes for the next hundred years approximately. Am I right?'

'Yeah, you're right.' He was impressed by her

knowledge. 'And the data in those windows on the computer screens corresponds to the visual representations of the Earth's changing atmosphere on the same screens. As you can see, according to the calculations, there should be a depletion of about fifteen to twenty-percent in the ozone layer over the next ten years alone.'

'I know that already. I also know it's too much. That's why I've been trying to get the White House to sit up and take notice.'

'Right,' Rydell said, 'it's already too much – and yet those figures don't match up to the figures gained from that last expedition. According to *those* figures, the speed of depletion is twice what it should be.'

'Dear God,' Clare murmured.

Pleased that she was taking it seriously this time, Rydell accessed the files obtained from the Antarctic Airborne Expedition.

He noted that Clare was jotting down notes. That further impressed him. She examined each monitor screen in turn, scribbling in her notebook, cross-checking the TOMS and SBUV readings that had been taken during the last expedition and relayed back to the numerous tracking stations, then on to here, via NASA, Houston. When she had finished, she checked her results against the figures she had taken from the climate-model analyses. Having studied them at length, she finally looked up, shaken by what she had concluded.

'I apologize,' she said.

'There's no need,' he replied, pleased. 'But are you willing to take a stand on what you've seen?'

'Yes Rydell, I am.'

'Call me 'Tony,' he said.

She sighed nervously and glanced around her. 'Yes, Tony.' 'But what *is* it? What's causing such rapid ozone depletion and where did it come from?'

'That's what we've got to find out.'

Rydell felt more excited and had forgotten his domestic problems in the thrill of exploration. He picked up another diskette and slotted it into one of the monitors.

'My prized possession,' he said. 'I had this information transferred from the analysis system of Project Skywatch International, in Phoenix. It's the most reliable UFO tracking organization in existence – No, don't say a word! – and it's run by Rick Polanski, the former NASA physicist who worked on the SETI project. He left NASA disgusted by their lack of commitment.'

'I've read about him,' Clare said. 'It was before my time.'

'Lucky you,' Rydell replied, then accessed the file named *UFO Related Materializations from the Subconscious*. Scrolling down the list of case histories, he said, 'Have a good look.'

Clare did. He watched her as she read the screen. She had a very fine profile, a high forehead, and full lips. The dark hair falling over her shoulder matched her luminous brown eyes. She was serious, too sophisticated for him, but he was secretly drawn to her.

When she had finished reading, she sat back in her chair and smiled at him.

'OK,' she said, 'other people have had experiences like the one you had over the Antarctic. What does that prove?'

'You missed something,' he replied, unable to prevent a grin of pleasure as he jabbed his finger at the list on the monitor-screen. 'You should have checked the dates. Hallucinations are common, but *palpable*, or even *physical* manifestations of the kind all those people experienced are a relatively new phenomenon . . . and it started in 1979.'

She was quick on the uptake. 'Which was the year that the hole in the ozone layer appeared and that the greenhouse effect began.'

'Exactly,' he said.

'Which you're taking as proof that the physical manifestations are being caused by the unknown something that's gobbling up the ozone over the Antarctic.'

'It sure seems to be that way.'

She gazed thoughtfully at him, but with that odd, slightly stunned look that he'd noticed before. Then stood up and restlessly paced the office. He saw how slim and shapely she was, her legs long in the high-heeled shoes. Eventually, as if the silence was unbearable, she stopped and looked down at him.

'So *what* is it?' she asked.

Rydell shrugged. 'There's only one way to find out.'

'To make another flight through the hole over the Antarctic?'

'Right,' Rydell said.

She smiled at him, but he could still detect the pain in her eyes. 'Very clever, Tony,' she said. 'I *wondered* what you were after. And now I can't say no, can I?'

'Not if you face the facts.'

She smiled again. 'You've hooked me,' she said, 'but what you're asking for won't be that simple. Jack Douglas, the president's advisor in these matters, is already concerned about the money being spent on the ozone problem and the President himself is more concerned with his own period in office than he is with anything that might happen in the future. I should also point out that Jack Douglas is extremely sceptical about you and has been ever since the media had a field day with your UFO theories. Given that, it's not

136

going to be easy to persuade them to finance another expedition.'

'You've got to try, Clare.'

'I will – on one condition.'

'What?'

'That if I manage to pull it off, I go with you as part of the team.'

'I don't think . . .'

'Wait a minute,' she said, raising her right hand to silence him. 'I'm not just an executive. I *was* an astronaut, I *am* an experienced pilot, and my particular branch of astrophysics is biotechnology. I'm just what you need.'

'I'm not sure I understand.'

Now Clare was looking excited. 'What's up there?' she asked. 'What's eating the ozone layer even faster than the CFCs? Whatever it is, it's invisible to the naked eye and hasn't been picked up by our scientific instruments. Whatever it is, then, it's not something real in any sense that we know.'

'I'm with you so far,' Rydell said, caught up in her growing excitement.

'Since 1968,' she continued, 'many of the molecules basic to chemical evolution – water, carbon dioxide, ammonia and hydrogen cyanide – have been found spectroscopically in outer space. Organic molecules, including amino acids, have also been found in meteorites. Because of this, a lot of physicists, including myself, believe that alien life doesn't have to be carbon-based and organic, and that space could in fact hold two other forms of life – plasmodes and radiobes – the former evolving within suns, the latter in inter-stellar space. And that, Tony, is what we could have up there at the top of the ozone hole – either a plasmode or radiobe form of life.'

'The fourth state of matter,' Rydell said to himself

with excitement. 'An electrically neutral gaseous mixture of positive and negative ions, or charged particles.'

Clare smiled again. 'You're showing off,' she said, 'but you've certainly got the message. That unknown factor feeding off the ozone layer could be a plasmode or radiobe form of life, possibly brought to Earth's stratosphere by some passing meteorite or in the tail of something like Halley's comet.'

'Not Halley's comet. That passed over in 1986 and the hole in the pole was first observed well before that.'

'Damn!' Clare exclaimed in frustration. She paced the room, then stopped, excitedly snapping her fingers. 'No!' she said, arguing with herself. 'The journey that brought Halley's Comet back into the path of Earth was the one in 1910. In 1910, the Earth actually passed through part of the tail of Halley's Comet, and that tail contained the cosmic dust of the Orionid and Eta Aquarid meteor showers that travel in Halley's orbit, so our assumed plasmode or radiobe life form could have attached itself to that cosmic dust, then spread itself around the globe of the Earth, with most of it settling over the Antarctic.'

Rydell was so excited he couldn't stay seated. Standing directly in front of Clare, he stared into the brightening depths of her lovely eyes.

'Could be,' he said, '*could* be . . .' And then faltered, disappointed. 'But that still doesn't explain why the ozone didn't start disappearing until 1979 – sixty-nine years *after* the Earth passed through the tail of Halley's Comet.'

Clare didn't miss a beat. 'According to the panspermic hypothesis,' she said, 'the seeds of life are in the form of spores, which can survive prolonged intervals in a vacuum – outer space – as well as conditions of extreme cold. However, on return to more favourable conditions, such as a warm climate, they return to their particular form of life again. The same could be true of a plasmode or radiobe form of life contained in the cosmic dust of, say, Halley's Comet. It survives in a kind of sleep throughout its cold journey through space, is cast off in the Earth's stratosphere, and is gradually revived by Earth's warm climate.'

'A climate growing even warmer as the alien life form feeds off the ozone layer.'

'Yes, and the more it devours the ozone layer, the warmer the Earth becomes and the stronger the alien life form becomes. In short, the Earth dies to feed it.'

Rydell suddenly felt unreal as all his senses focused on Clare's brown eyes. He was looking into her soul and he wasn't too sure what it was that he'd eventually find there.

'You've got to get that Antarctic flight arranged,' he told her.

'I'll try my damnest,' she said.

She glanced vaguely around the room. As she did so, she changed, the excitement fading from her eyes, giving way to an oddly stunned look he had noticed before.

'I'd better get going,' she said. 'I'm going to have a lot to do.'

'Are you OK?' he asked.

'Yes,' she said and shrugged. 'Sure. Why do you ask? Do I look any different?'

'As a matter of fact, you do. At least, you *seem* different. You're not as high-stepping as when we first met. You seem slightly . . . *exhausted*?'

She smiled in a weary manner. 'Yes,' she said, reluctant to tell him the truth, 'maybe that's it. You're an exhausting man, Tony.'

He led her back out of the building and across to the

parking lot, aware as she unlocked her car that she had him in a state of agitation. He placed his hand on her shoulder and stopped her as she was about to slip into the driver's seat.

Her brown eyes seemed opaque.

'You haven't been an astronaut for years,' he said, 'and haven't practised astrophysics for a long time either. Why do you want to go back to basics by flying into that hole?'

She stared steadily at him, though her gaze seemed focused inward. Eventually, she took a deep breath and said with quiet simplicity, 'I buried my father last week and now I need an escape. You've just given me that. Thanks. I'll be seeing you.'

Then she slipped into the car and drove off in a cloud of dust, leaving him alone in a silence broken only by the church bells pealing out over Greenbelt.

# CHAPTER SIXTEEN

Still in a state of shock, grieving over her father's suicide, Clare was now in emotional turmoil over her growing feelings for Tony Rydell. He wasn't her kind at all, yet only he could crowd out of her mind the awful events of the past few days. The discovery of her father's body, the reluctant acceptance of his death, the awful business of arranging the funeral and the ceremony itself – she had endured it automatically and only escaped her growing depression when thinking about Rydell.

'I don't understand it,' she confessed to her best friend, Nicola Williams. They were having lunch in the baroque splendour of Clyde's, at Tyson's Corner in Virginia. 'I can't get him out of my mind and keep wanting to see him.'

'Your problem is you insist on trusting to your commonsense. Then, when commonsense decides to elude you, you don't know how to handle it. Put it down to infatuation, honey.'

'More likely I'm just compensating for the loss of my father. I need someone – some excitement – in my life. I think that explains it.'

Nicola's laughter was raucous. '*That's* a good one!' she exclaimed. 'If you can't find one reason, you'll find another. So why not Jack Douglas? Why didn't the death of your father push you closer to *him*?'

'Because he isn't *new*,' Clare responded, feeling distinctly foolish. 'Because he's part of the life I was living before the death of my father. Rydell represents something *different*, for sure, and I think that's why, even if he's not my type, I've let myself become obsessed with him.'

Nicola grinned, shaking her head, and said, 'Mind if I smoke?'

'Of course not.'

Nicola lit a cigarette, exhaled a cloud of smoke, and smiled winningly at a couple of the well-dressed men in the expensive restaurant. She was big boned, twice divorced and very rich.

'Why don't you just admit you've got the hots for him?' she asked.

'I don't believe in having the hots, as you crassly put it, and although I need sex, I don't think of him that way.'

'Oh, no?'

'No.'

But Clare couldn't help but remember her meeting with Rydell at NASA–Goddard. He had convinced her of his theory – and if it was true, it was history's greatest story – but it was *him*, more than his work, that she was constantly dwelling upon.

'Talking about the hots,' Nicola said, 'it's a real relief to be in this air-conditioning after being outside. This is one hell of a summer!'

'Yes,' Clare said, brooding on her meeting with Rydell and what he had told her. 'Too hot for comfort.'

'But not too hot for love. So what's this new man of yours like?'

'A bit rough,' Clare said without thinking, then ashamed, she added, 'Well, more like a brilliant schoolboy. He's one of our best physicists, but says too much too loudly. He's certainly not the most *sophisticated* guy you're likely to meet.'

'But cute, eh?'

Clare sighed helplessly. 'Yes, sort of.' She avoided

Nicola's knowing grin by glancing around the large restaurant and nodding at the friends and acquaintances who were sitting at other tables. Most of the people Clare recognized were agents from the Central Intelligence Agency headquarters at Langley, with a smattering of Pentagon and Capitol-Hill politicians and some wealthy Georgetown residents out for the day.

The cool and sophisticated ambiance had always appealed to Clare, but when she tried to imagine being here with Tony Rydell, she came to a blank wall. Likewise, when she thought of her home in Georgetown – that lovely Federal-period house that now seemed so large, empty and haunting – she could not imagine entertaining Rydell there. He wouldn't feel comfortable.

She and Rydell came from very different worlds and that was all there was to it.

'You'd probably like him,' she told Nicola. 'You'd probably find him unpredictable and entertaining.'

'Are you accusing me of liking rough trade, Clare?'

'You know what I mean.'

Nicola laughed again and glanced around the restaurant, trying to pick out her old flames or set her eyes on a new one. Born and bred in Georgetown to wealthy, party-loving parents, she had inherited their lust for pleasure and devoted most of her days to having a good time. Though overweight from eating and drinking, she was a natural seductress, and had led a life of what seemed, at least to Clare, to be good-natured, life-affirming chaos. Inheriting her wealth, she had only married wealthy men, but she had always gone for the rougher kind – self-made tycoons and entrepreneurs – which had guaranteed violent quarrels, emotional reconciliations, and eventual divorce. Currently between husbands (she would certainly find another), she was socializing widely and having a good time; she looked younger, if heavier, every month. Clare was appalled by her friend's emotional chaos, amused by her conversation, and increasingly envious of her ability to throw herself wholeheartedly into life. In comparison with Nicola she felt dead inside.

As if sensing what Clare was feeling, Nicola leaned across the table to take hold of her wrist and squeeze it affectionately.

'So how *are* you faring?' she asked with genuine concern. 'Are you able to deal with it?'

'You mean my father's death?'

'Yes.'

Clare shrugged, feeling helpless. 'I'm OK,' she said. 'Not great, but OK. I find the silence in the house oppressive and I have trouble sleeping at nights, but the worst thing is that sometimes I'm haunted by the feeling that he's still in the house.'

'That's natural,' Nicola said.

'Yes, I suppose so, but I hate it; that and the constant recollections of last week, which seems like a bad dream. I felt better once he was buried – at least the worst of it was over – and I went straight back to work to help me forget it. So, I'm OK. A bit shakey, but surviving. There's just this sudden, shocking awareness of being totally alone for the first time, an awful feeling of isolation, and that's what I have to learn to deal with, one way or the other.'

'Make it the other,' Nicola said. 'This new man you have the hots for. You *do* need something different in your life and he sounds like the ticket.'

'I think he's *too* different,' Clare said.

'That difference could give you new life,' Nicola told her, 'so why not give it a try?'

'It's not my style, Nicola. Anyway,' she said, cutting

her friend short, 'I've got to get back to work now, so do you mind if we go?'

They paid the bill and left immediately, walking around the fountain, to wave and smile at friends before making their escape through the crowded bar.

Outside it was hot and humid, definitely more so than usual, and as they walked to their parked cars, Clare thought of the greenhouse effect and what it was doing. It was like a bad dream, not quite real . . . yet the world seemed so normal.

'So what about Jack Douglas?' Nicola asked her, as they were opening the doors of their respective cars, parked side by side. 'Are you still seeing him?'

'Yes, I am. As a matter of fact, I'm going to see him right now, though this time about work.'

'Don't tell him about the other guy,' Nicola said with a broad, wicked smile as she slipped into her car. 'He might react pretty badly.'

'There's nothing to tell him,' Clare insisted. 'I'm not *involved* with Rydell.'

Nicola slammed her door shut and rolled down her window. 'Oh, yes, you are,' she said firmly. 'You may not want to accept it, but you are. You've hardly talked about anyone else throughout the lunch and that's not usual for you. You're infatuated, whether or not you accept it, and I'm delighted to see it.'

'I'm not listening,' Clare said, then impulsively leaned down to kiss Nicola's forehead. 'Drive carefully,' she said, straightening up. 'And let's meet again soon.'

Before she could walk away, Nicola reached out to grab her by the wrist and pull her back down again.

'Will you take a word of advice from an old friend?' she asked.

'Sure,' Clare replied, surprised at how serious Nicola sounded.

'Be careful of Jack Douglas,' Nicola said. 'I've been hearing talk for months now, and I don't think the man is what he seems.'

'He's always had a reputation for being tough,' Clare began, 'but that doesn't bother . . .'

'No, Clare, it's more than that. Rumour has it that his marriage actually broke up because of his relentless domination of his wife; apparently he slapped her around a few times. Finally, she'd had enough and got out, though Jack never tells the tale that way. According to Capitol Hill gossip, his politics are very extreme and have caused some concern amongst the doves in the White House and Pentagon. He is, reportedly, so virulently anti-Soviet that he views *Glasnost* and *Perestroika* as a desperate Russian attempt at a different kind of war against the West, a more subtle war of economics.'

'He's mentioned that to me,' Clare said, 'but I didn't take it too seriously.'

'Believe me, Clare, he's serious. He's convinced that the Soviets are simply using *Glasnost* and *Perestroika* to gain the confidence of the West. According to Douglas, once the Soviet Union is as wealthy as the West, it'll become another Japan and lay siege to our already endangered economy.'

'Oh, God,' Clare exclaimed, 'that sounds so paranoid! I knew the President was thinking along those lines, but I didn't believe that Jack . . .'

'Jack has the President's ear,' Nicola said, 'and whispers into it day and night.' She tugged at Clare's hand, demanding her full attention. 'What I'm trying to say is that Douglas isn't what he seems. He's a violent man who likes to control and manipulate, and he's also more virulently right wing than you would care to imagine.'

'Christ!' Clare whispered.

'You be careful, Clare, not to cross him over Rydell because Douglas, if he decides to go for you, will go all the way. You understand?'

'Yes, Nicola, and thanks.'

'My pleasure, Clare.'

With those parting words Nicola reversed out of her parking space and drove off. Clare followed Nicola out of the parking lot and headed for Capitol Hill and the Old Executive Office Building, west of the White House.

The closer she got to Washington DC, the more nervous she became. She still found what Nicola had told her hard to accept, but was worried because she knew that Douglas wouldn't be pleased when he heard what she wanted: to set up, and take part in, another Airborne Antarctic Expedition, this time to ascertain whether or not some alien life form was devouring the ozone layer around the Earth.

He would think she'd gone mad.

As she parked under the massive edifice that had formerly been the State, War, and Navy Department building, but now housed a presidential 'hideaway' suite and most of the President's White House staff, Clare tried to conquer her nervousness. Walking resolutely to the Department of Management and Budget she marched into Douglas's surprisingly spartan office.

He was sitting behind his expansive desk, leaning back in his chair, moodily tapping his perfect teeth with a pencil.

'Where have *you* been?' he asked her.

'Pardon?' she asked, glancing automatically at her wrist-watch to check if she was late.

'I don't mean this morning,' Douglas clarified. 'I mean for the past two weeks.'

She knew then what he meant and felt embarrassed.

Then, recalling what Nicola had told her, she felt a spasm of resentment at his attempt to stake his claim on her.

'Are you going to ask me to sit down?'

'Sorry,' he said. 'Pull up a chair, Clare. I haven't seen you since the funeral and it's bothered me greatly, particularly since I've left messages on your answerphone and haven't had one call back.'

'I thought you'd have understood,' she replied. 'Some things you have to face alone, and this was one of them.'

It was a lie of course. Or at least half a lie. She had wanted to be alone, to adjust to her father's death, but she had deliberately avoided Jack because of Tony Rydell.

'And that's it?' Douglas asked, staring searchingly at her.

'Yes, Jack, that's it. And I don't think you should even have raised the question. After all, you've no claims on me.'

'No,' he said, grinning sardonically, 'no claims at all. It's just that I expected you to lean on me during this bad time.'

'I'm not the sort to depend on anyone, as you know.'

He sighed and leant over the desk. 'So why am I blessed today?' he asked her. 'You did say it was business.'

Clare took a deep breath. As calmly as she could manage she began: 'It's about Tony Rydell's theory concerning the depletion of the ozone over the Antarctic.'

Jack's face hardened immediately. 'Yes,' he said. 'I remember. The theory you were willing to believe on his word alone. I *should* remember, since that's when I last saw you, except for the funeral. We had a fight, did we not?'

'Please, Jack, let's stick to business.'

'OK. You were going to visit him and cross-check his data. I take it you did.'

'Yes.'

'And?'

'I'm forced to conclude that what he suggests is substantially correct – that something unknown, something alien, is devouring the ozone even faster than our CFCs.'

Jack wasn't thrilled, but he sat up straight in his chair.

'And the data's in that file on your lap?'

'Yes.' She handed the file to him. 'You can have it cross-checked again,' she told him, 'but I'm willing to stand by my findings. Rydell's not talking nonsense. The ozone is being depleted at a terrifying rate, and unless we find out what's doing it and somehow stop it we're going to have a major global crisis within the next five years.'

Jack looked at the closed file as if it contained a bomb, then gently placed it on his desk without opening it.

'I'll certainly have it cross-checked,' he said. 'I'm sure we'll find a rational explanation. But on the unlikely assumption that you're correct, what do you want?'

'Since it's vital that we find out what's devouring the ozone in the stratosphere, I want you to finance another Antarctic Airborne Expedition,' Clare began to explain nervously. 'And since, as the report reveals, the mostly likely cause of the problem is a plasmode or radiobe form of life, the solution can only be found through biotechnology, which is my special field . . .'

'You want to go with him.'

'Yes,' Clare confessed.

As if trying to control his temper, Douglas covered his face with his hands. When he withdrew them, Clare was confronted by his most unyielding face. Or was she, given what Nicola had told her, simply imagining that?

'Are you losing your mind?' he cried. 'You *know* that's not possible. NASA's already overdrawn on its credit and is no longer popular with the administration. As for this extraordinary theory, how can I take *that* to the President? He's already wary of you and now you want me to go back to him with the possibility of an *alien entity* up there. I can't do this, Clare, and probably wouldn't if I could. I think the whole thing's cock-eyed! I'm convinced your judgement is askew, and I'm not sure if it's because of your father's death or something to do with you and Rydell. Is this *personal*, Clare?'

She felt that he had slapped her face, so shocked was she by the truth. Humiliated, she spat out, 'Of course it's not personal! How dare you even imply it! We're faced with the possibility of alien contact and you're saying it's *personal!*'

'Contact with *what*? With some kind of cosmic dust? Do you want me to take *that* to the President?'

'Yes, dammit, I do!'

'Well, I won't do it Clare. I won't encourage your foolishness. What we have here is some theory by a physicist noted for controversy . . .'

'Examine that file, damn you!'

'Your research is probably biased because you *want* to believe this theory! A lot of scientists do it, Clare, when they become too emotionally involved with their work. And in my view, given my knowledge of you, this is just what you're doing. You *want* to believe Rydell. That alone will distort your judgement. And since you're so brilliant, you'll be able to present a case that would take us months to break. Yes, I'll have your file cross-checked, but I'll ensure that it's done properly, and in the meantime, you'll just have to wait and hope we find in your favour. This should take at least three months.'

'We can't wait three months!'

'Nothing is that urgent, Clare, and you damn well know it. Now is there anything else?'

She was shocked into silence and stared at him, feeling helpless. Then her anger forced her to her feet. She made her way to the door, where she stopped to glare at him and say, 'Damn you! This is just irresponsible!'

'*I'm* not irresponsible, Clare. *You're* the irresponsible one. You didn't want to get married because you didn't want to be enslaved by your emotions or demeaned by dependence. You took pride in your emotional health, in your scientific objectivity. I admired you for that Clare. It was something rare in a woman. But now you're making a fool of yourself because you've let your personal interests interfere with your work. You're obviously besotted with Rydell and you're behaving irrationally.'

'Go to hell,' Clare replied, blind with rage, slamming his office door behind her, and hurrying out of the building.

She had to call Rydell.

# CHAPTER SEVENTEEN

Unfortunately, Rydell was in the middle of a domestic crisis when Clare called him.

With his mother and the Mexican housekeeper gone, he had to deal with the boys on his own and he wasn't really cut out for the job. To make matters worse, ever since Suzy's brief visit the boys had become more resentful and had sometimes blamed him for her departure. They wanted her back. Rydell told them it wasn't possible, that Suzy didn't want to come back, but that only made them more resentful and increasingly rebellious.

Don took to sulking in his room, refusing to eat, and bullying Ronnie, who began wetting his bed, complaining constantly of various illnesses, and often playing truant from school.

The school complained about Ronnie's truancy and the cops brought Don in twice after catching him vandalizing the flower beds in Greenbelt Park. Soon Rydell's neighbours began hammering irately on his door with complaints of the scandalous behaviour.

Rydell tried to find another housekeeper, failed repeatedly and gave up. He even begged his mother to return but was flatly refused.

When not fighting each other, the boys quarrelled with their harassed father, and it was in the middle of such a quarrel that Clare rang with her bad news.

'You're going to school!' Rydell was bawling at Ronnie who was sobbing melodramatically while the sullen-faced Don played with a yo-yo and studied the

TV. 'Don't tell me you've got pains in your goddamned stomach! You've pulled that one too often.'

'It's *true* this time! My stomach hurts!'

'Crap!' Don exclaimed.

'Shut up, Don!' Rydell shouted as the telephone started ringing. 'This is none of your business. *You* can switch off that TV, pick up your schoolbooks and leave right now while I sort this kid out.' With that, he picked up the telephone.

'I've got a *headache*,' Don said.

'You're a liar!' Ronnie shouted. 'You're just saying that 'cause I've got stomach pains. You always copy what *I* do!'

'Shut up both of you! Yes?' he said into the telephone.

'Rydell?'

'Yeah, right. Don, turn off that TV!'

'This is Clare.'

'Clare?'

'Yes, Clare Holton.'

'Sorry, Clare. Hold on a moment. Let me fix something up here.' He grabbed a telephone directory and hurled it across the room at Don. It bounced off his shoulder and hit the TV set, frightening him into action. Don jumped up and switched the set off, grabbing his schoolbooks from the table. He hurried out of the house, followed closely by the galvanized Ronnie, who was not without common sense.

'OK, Clare,' Rydell said into the telephone, 'I'm with you. I'm all ears. How did it go?'

'He didn't buy it,' she told him.

'Who?' he asked, still agitated because of the boys' behaviour. Observing them through the front window, he could see them quarrelling violently as they waited for the school bus.

'Jack Douglas. At the Department of Management and Budget. He refused flatly to mount another airborne Antarctic Ozone Expedition. He was adamant, Tony.'

Outside, little Ronnie lunged at the bigger Don and started swinging wild punches at him while Don held him off. Rydell's instinct was to bawl abuse at them, but the windows were closed.

'What the hell do you mean, he was adamant? Didn't you show him the file?'

'Of *course* I showed him the file! I gave him the file, I told him what was in it, and he said he would have it thoroughly checked, but that it would take at least three months.'

'Three months!'

'He also insisted that there had to be a more rational explanation than the one we'd suggested, and that I was letting my scientific objectivity be distorted by some kind of wishful thinking. I had a terrible time there.'

The bus pulled up outside. Don pushed Ronnie away from it. Then Ronnie rolled on the lawn and jumped back up, screaming something. It was too much for Rydell.

'So what?' he shouted at Clare. 'So you had a terrible time! You shouldn't have walked out of that goddamned office until he'd agreed! You *know* how important this is! You should have impressed that upon him. How the hell do you have the nerve to ring me and say he just didn't buy it?'

'Hey, hold *on* a minute, Tony!'

'You should have told him he *has* to buy it! You're supposed to know how to talk to those guys.'

'I tried my best, damn you!'

'Then go back and try again!'

'There's no point. The President will be against it! What can *I* do against that?'

154

'Go back and *argue*, for chrissakes!'

'I *did* argue! He was adamant! And your involvement in this matter didn't help me, since he thinks you're a dreamer.'

'That goddamned UFO business.'

'Your scandal, not mine.'

'So you let him use that against our case and didn't kick back.'

'I did!'

'Not enough.'

'Damn you, Rydell . . .'

'I won't accept this.'

'You can't fight Jack Douglas *and* the White House – I can't and neither can you.'

'You can't, but I can.'

Rydell slammed the phone down. He watched the schoolbus moving off and sighed with relief, then poured himself a cup of coffee and turned on the TV. What he saw didn't register. He simply wanted the flickering image. He could hardly believe what he'd said to Clare and felt ashamed of himself.

It was because of the kids. It was because of all the hassle. It was because he was obsessed with what was devouring the ozone layer and, to his astonishment, also increasingly obsessed with Clare Holton. He couldn't accept that he'd fallen for her, felt confused and out of his depth, so had flown off the handle at her.

She had tried to help, and he'd slapped her face in return.

Very neat, Mr Rydell.

Yet he had meant one thing; he wouldn't accept their refusal. Politicians only cared for the present, for their own term in office, and were ruthless in turning their backs on anything that posed a threat to it. That's what was going down here with that bastard,

Jack Douglas. He was supporting a President whose sole concern was to keep the US economy healthy during his own term in office, irrespective of the long-term cost to the country, let alone the whole world. For that reason he could ignore the increasing use of products that released CFCs into the atmosphere . . . and for that reason he would no doubt suppress the knowledge that an unknown factor was feeding off the ozone in the stratosphere. On behalf of the President, Jack Douglas would ruthlessly bury what could be the most important discovery in history.

If Rydell didn't do something to stop him.

Rydell stared at the TV thinking of what he had said to Clare. He felt deeply ashamed, knowing that what he was about to do would give her even more trouble . . . but he had to do it.

Ashamed but determined, he picked up the telephone.

# CHAPTER EIGHTEEN

Suzy couldn't sleep at nights without Joe Wheeler beside her. She wasn't in love with him, at least not as she recalled the feeling; it was more that she needed to be filled up to help her forget. She wished she'd never gone back to Maryland to see Rydell and the kids, to be humiliated and hurt and forced to hurry away in shame, and now she needed to be filled up by Joe Wheeler in order to forget it, at least for a while. You could do that with sex.

She liked Joe. He was kind and considerate and filled her up beautifully.

She just didn't love him.

'Thing is,' she told her mother, 'that he gives me what Rydell didn't: a little love and a lot of attention and respect for my person. A woman needs that.'

'Rydell gave you that,' her mother said, preparing dinner at the kitchen table. 'He just did it in a different way. He wasn't obvious about it, since he's not the obvious type, and he took it for granted that you'd know and wouldn't worry about it. He's always bin a man involved with his work, but that don't make him neglectful.'

'Oh, *I'm* to blame, right?'

'I didn't say that, Suzy. I'm simply trying to point out that you can't compare Rydell to Wheeler; that one's a married man with two kids and important work, while the other's single, runs a bar in town, and has all the time he needs to be attentive. That's all I'm saying.'

'Joe's busy as well, Mom.'

'Only with his other women.'

'We're not married. He's entitled to play the field.'

'You sure hold yourself cheap that way.'

'I just wanna have some fun. I don't wanna be involved. I've had enough of involvement with Rydell and now I just want my freedom. I can have that with Joe.'

Her mother sighed. 'Here comes your father. Let's change the subject.'

'Yeah, Mom, let's do that.'

Her father came through the door, bringing rays of sunlight with him, looking like a large tree with roots as he kicked his boots off. Then he entered the kitchen, a big man somehow diminished, and wiped the sweat from his face with grubby hands as he took a deep breath.

'It's still hot as hell out there,' he said. 'I just don't believe it.'

He didn't smile at either of them. He'd forgotten how to do that. He just went to the fridge and pulled out a can of beer and cracked it and drank it real quick, like it might be his last. Then he gasped and wiped his lips with his free hand and took a seat by the table. He glanced at the food his wife was making, but his eyes had a dulled look.

'If we don't get rain soon,' he said, 'we're not gonna make it.'

That's all he talked about these days – the state of his crops – and it made him seem less than he had been when Suzy had first come back. Then he'd been just like the country, big and healthy, filled with life; but now, when he complained about the weather, he was somehow diminished.

'Crops is dyin',' he said. 'Too much sunshine, no rain. Ain't never had a summer like this one an' never want one again. It ain't natural, I tell you. There's a plague on this goddamned land. This was once the bread-basket of America and now it's a dustbowl. I don't know what we're headed for.'

Suzy loved him, but he'd changed. The changing landscape had changed him. Now, when Suzy looked out her window, she saw what he was talking about. The golds and yellows had turned to brown, the sun had painted the blue sky white, and the dust, which in the daylight drifted lazily in the breeze, was so dense it even obscured the stars at night and made them less magical.

She could no longer recapture her childhood. What had been would be no more.

'It'll get better,' she said, trying to make her father smile. 'Any day now, you'll hear a clap of thunder and the land will be drenched. It'll all come out right then.'

'If that happens,' her father said without a smile, 'it'll be Noah's flood. The land's cursed. I can tell that.'

The conversations were all like that, filled with gloom and foreboding, and they drove Suzy out of the house and back into Joe's bed. He always welcomed her with open arms and lay beside her, on top of her, below her, every which way, helping her to lose her bad thoughts and feel valued again.

'You're a treasure,' Joe told her. 'Your skin shines in the moonlight. I just have to feel your warm breath to get hard again. I wanna make you breathe quicker and see your pretty tits stiffen. I wanna make you part of me.'

'I believe you,' she replied, ''cause I can feel you. That's why I sound breathless.'

'Jesus, Suzy, let's do it!'

She loved him in heat, when he could hardly stop himself. She liked to spread across the bed like a sheet and let him be her blanket.

'It's so hot there,' she told him. 'My parents' house is

like a furnace. I like it a lot better here, with the
air-conditioning an' all. You can't enjoy this in the heat.
That's why I like it here. It's so cool and you make me
burn. We lie on crisp sheets and roll about and leave 'em
soaked with our sweat. I feel so alive here.'

'What about me? Do I get credit?'

'You're some kinda man, Joe.'

He had his vanity, of course, but she didn't mind that
at all. He was fairly modest with it, just begged now and
then, and she only had to feed him some sugar to make
his tail start to wag again. He was decent, but not too
bright, thoughtful, but not too sensitive, but bright
enough, and with enough sensitivity, to give her more
than his body. He took her out a fair bit – trips along the
river on the *Mississippi Belle*; the Boone and Scenic
Valley Railroad; thrills and spills in Adventureland –
but he also drew her out of herself by letting her talk,
talking back and not acting deaf. He was surprising that
way, as well.

'It's all changed,' she told him. 'It's nothing like I
remember. When I came back, I thought it was the same,
but I only imagined it. Nothing lasts, that's the truth.'

'It *was* the same,' he told her. 'It's all changed since
you got here. This place has changed more in the last
few months than it's done in my lifetime. It's the
weather, honey. We've never had weather like it. The
crops are dying, the land's turning to dust, and the sun
just gets hotter. This summer's lastin' forever.'

'I think my father's farm's in trouble.'

'A lot of farms have already closed.'

'If the farms close, this place will be hell on Earth.'

'You can bet on it,' Joe said.

They sometimes made love in the fields, in the tall,
dust-covered grass. They lay side by side, their clothes a
mess, and drank beer and talked. It was something she
needed.

'I still miss them,' she told him.

'Your kids?'

'Yeah, that's right. When I have you inside me, I feel good, free as air, but when you stop, I think about them again and come over all guilty.'

'You'll go back to them in time.'

'I had my chance and refused. Now, if I try to go back, I think Rydell might stop me.'

'You could be surprised,' Joe said.

'I'm too scared to take the chance. I don't think I could bear the humiliation of being worked over twice.'

'Rydell sure was rough on you. I remember. You were crying.'

'He made me feel that I'd behaved like some kinda whore. Like I'd abused my own kids.'

'He was just angry, Suzy.'

'No excuse.'

'I think it is. When we're angry, or even feeling betrayed, we do all sorts of dumb things.'

'Rydell's not dumb.'

'But he's angry and feels betrayed. That's exactly how you felt when you left him, so you should understand that.'

Suzy sighed and wiped the dust from her skirt and stood up in the dead grass.

'Yeah,' she said. 'I see what you mean . . . but I still can't go back. I won't risk being rejected again. I couldn't take it a second time. Come on, let's get going.'

Joe drove her to Des Moines, where she picked up her own car and headed back to the farm, driving through the afternoon's dazzling light and clouds of fine, drifting dust. The fields rolled away to the horizon and merged with the silvery sky, but the colours of the landscape had been bleached out, leaving it ominous. Suzy who hardly recognized it, kept imagining she was somewhere else, and was glad to see the old, white-walled farmhouse rising out of the approaching fields. She turned into the driveway, parked outside the house, noticed that her father's jeep wasn't there and then went inside. Her mother, wearing her apron, was preparing the dinner.

'Dad still out?' Suzy asked her.

'Yeah,' her mother said. 'But he should be here any minute now. He's always real punctual.'

There was a pitcher of chilled lemonade on the table and Suzy poured herself some.

'Had a good day?' her mother asked.

'Yeah,' Suzy said. 'Terrific. We cooled down by taking the boat along the river, then went for a picnic. Now I feel parched, but healthy.'

She drank some lemonade and it felt good, wetting her dry throat.

'And you?' she asked.

Her mother shrugged. 'Same as always. I just felt the heat a lot more, is all. It must be my age.'

'It's hot,' Suzy said. 'It's hot as hell. Even *I* feel it these days.' She glanced at the TV. The news was showing stormy weather. Europe was being hammered by storms and floods of unprecedented ferocity, with many lives lost. From where Suzy stood, in the kitchen's claustrophobic heat, it didn't seem possible. 'The world's weather's going crazy,' she observed aloud.

'It sure is,' her mother said.

The jeep pulled up outside and Suzy looked at the front door. She was waiting for her father's entrance, that oak-like presence in the sunlight. When he didn't materialize as expected, she went to the open door and looked down through the wire mesh.

Her father had walked away from the jeep and was at the far end of the lawn, kneeling in the shadows by the edge of the cornfield, scooping up the earth in his hand.

Suzy crossed the lawn and reached her father as he

opened his right hand. He let the dry earth fall through his fingers, then turned to look up at her.

She saw in his deeply shadowed eyes the hurt gleam of betrayal.

'You were right,' he said. 'The land sometimes turns on you. We're finished. We're done for.'

Then his eyes filled with tears.

# CHAPTER NINETEEN

When Clare heard the tone of Jack Douglas's voice she knew that something was wrong.

'Please come to my office right away, and I *mean* right away. This subject can't wait.' He dropped his phone before Clare could reply, leaving her stunned.

To get to Jack's office she had to pass the packed, busy offices of the Vice President, Presidential assistants and commissions, and by the time she reached Jack's office, she was breathless. Clare was also filled with the uncomfortable conviction that she was going to see the side of Jack Douglas that Nicola had warned her about.

Douglas was restlessly pacing his office, his face grimmer than she had ever seen it. When she walked in, he stopped and glared at her, then picked a copy of the *Washington Post* from his desk and shoved it brusquely into her hands.

'Have you seen this?' he asked her.

An article was encircled by a black felt marker pen. It had been written by Art Tabori, the same journalist who'd hassled her at the American Geophysical Union in Baltimore, and sensationally entitled, THE GHOST IN THE OZONE HOLE.

She felt sick; a feeling which worsened as she read the article. It was a thorough, reasonable summary of everything she and Rydell now knew and put forward the theory that the complete obliteration of the ozone layer would now take place within five years, instead of decades as previously thought. The only way to prevent this from happening would be to discover what was devouring the ozone and somehow counteract it, but, it concluded, the United States government, concerned only with the immediate cost, was refusing to mount a vitally necessary second Airborne Antarctic Ozone Experiment.

Clare's hands were shaking when she replaced the newspaper on Jack's desk and then faced his angry gaze.

'Did *you* speak to that journalist?' he asked her.

'No,' she replied truthfully.

'Then it had to be that bastard, Rydell. No one else knows about this.'

Clare felt hot with guilt and rage, since she knew that Douglas was correct – it had to be Rydell. She had been angry with him anyway, because of his ungrateful outburst over the phone, made worse by his hanging up on her, but now, knowing what he had done, she felt used and betrayed.

'I'm sorry,' she said. 'I didn't have anything to do with this, but I suppose I'm responsible.'

'Damned right you're responsible! If you hadn't encouraged that little bastard, he wouldn't have done this.'

'I didn't encourage him to do this.'

'You lent your support to his crackpot theory. You encouraged him to think he can do what he likes and now, he's virtually blackmailed our department into financing another Antarctic Ozone Experiment. Thanks very much, Clare!'

'You're going to finance the expedition?' she asked him.

'We don't have a choice. Rydell knew just what he was doing when he blew that story to the *Washington Post*. He's embarrassed the President, as well as this department, and now we either finance his expedition or stand accused of cynical neglect.' His gaze remained cold and furious. 'You think *I'm* ruthless? Then what about your precious Rydell? He's outfoxed us all, the ruthless bastard and now he's got what he wants. Thanks for being so co-operative, Clare. I'm sure Rydell loves you for it.'

'I'm sorry,' she began, shocked and a little bit frightened. 'I didn't think he would . . .'

'Just remember this,' Douglas interjected, jabbing his finger at her. 'I don't know what it is between you and that goddamned physicist, but he's a troublemaker who's caused a furore here and *you're* now implicated with him in this sordid affair. He's won this round, but the President isn't happy – not with him and not with you – and *I'm* certainly not going to forget what he's done with your help. He's got his expedition and you can go along with him, but if nothing beneficial springs from it God help the pair of you! Do you understand, Clare?'

'Yes, Jack, I understand.'

He stared at her, his gaze relentless, then asked bluntly. 'Are you having an affair with this guy?'

'No,' she replied, more urgently than she'd intended.

'Are you going to have an affair with him?'

'Of course not,' she said.

'I don't believe you, so here's some advice for you . . . You've finally let your emotions take precedence over your intellect and already the results have been disastrous. Think about it before you get more seriously involved. Now get out of my office.'

'Jack, please . . .'

'Just get out.'

She did as she was told, shocked and humiliated by Jack's rejection and outraged at Rydell's betrayal, torn between the two men in her life, between her mind and her heart.

Hurrying back to her own office, she gave in to her rage and dwelt with an almost murderous intensity on what Rydell had done. He could not have failed to know that in giving their confidential information to the *Washington Post* he'd be betraying her trust and possibly damaging her career. Yet he'd gone on and done it. Yes, he was ruthless.

Convinced that her doubts about him had been confirmed, she stomped into her own office, determined to have her revenge. Sitting behind her desk, she picked up the phone and dialled his office at NASA–Goddard. His voice rang in her ear.

'Rydell here.'

'Tony, it's Clare.'

There was a nervous pause at the other end of the line, before he said, 'Oh, you read the newspapers?'

'Yes,' she said.

'I had to do it, Clare. I didn't want to, but I had to. This is too big a number to be buried, so there wasn't a choice. Don't get mad at me, Clare.'

'I'm not mad,' she lied, trying to sound as excited as possible. 'I think it was a great idea. And in fact, I'm ringing to tell you that it worked. I've just come from Douglas's office and he told me that the expedition's been approved. He was hopping mad, but clearly didn't have a choice. The expedition's going to be financed and you and I will go with it. I'm so excited, I can hardly wait to go. Congratulations, Tony.'

'Gee, that's terrific news,' he replied. 'Thanks for calling to tell me. And I'm sorry 'bout how I spoke to you the other day. I mean, I wasn't myself that day. I was having some trouble with the kids and . . .'

'Don't apologize,' she said, sounding as pleasant as possible. 'I wasn't at all bothered. I know the kind of strain you must be under. Anyway, why not get together to celebrate your success and maybe talk about what we

167

plan to do once we're in the Antarctic?'

'Oh, sure,' he said. 'That sounds terrific. What do you suggest?'

She thought it typical that he'd ask *her* to arrange something, but in this case it was convenient. 'Are you free this evening?'

'I can get away, I think.'

'Then why not come over to my place, about eight, and we'll have some drinks and ... see where the evening leads us?'

Having deliberately sounded sensual she wasn't surprised when he paused before saying, 'Yeah, that sounds terrific. Where do you live?' When she gave him her address, he said, 'Georgetown! I might have known! Trust you to live with the nobs. Do I have to enter via the servant's quarters?'

'Just ring the front-door bell.'

'OK, then, I'll see you at eight.'

'I look forward to it.'

She put the phone down with a smile and spent the rest of the afternoon at her desk, contemplating her revenge.

That evening she drank a bourbon while she had a bath, then dressed as attractively as possible, wanting to tempt Rydell as much as she could before slapping him down. She had sensed that he was attracted to her, no matter how his aggression hid it, and she was determined to use that against him when he came for his good time. She felt angry, vengeful and *very* feminine. She really wanted to hurt him.

As usual, he did not arrive on time. In fact, he was forty-five minutes late, by which time she had drunk two more glasses of bourbon. Instead of being seduced by the sight of her, he wiped the sweat from his forehead, ran his fingers through his untidy hair, and cast his eyes around the elegant lounge.

'Oh, boy,' he said, 'you really *do* live in style! I mean, this is some joint.'

'You're late,' she said, already starting to lose the seductive poise she had been practising. 'And by forty-five minutes.'

'Yeah,' he said, hardly looking at her as he took in the decor. 'Sorry about that. I had a bit of trouble with the kids, but it's all sorted out now.'

'Trouble? What trouble?'

'Now that their mother's gone, they resent me going out in the evenings. They say they'll get molested or murdered and it'll be on my conscience. A real cute pair I've got there.'

'Can't you get someone to look after them?'

He finally looked at her, focussing on the bourbon in her hand which she hastily placed on the table as he said, 'Well, it's been a bit difficult, you know? I mean I've tried it once or twice, but it doesn't seem to work out. No one's ever returned for a second bout, not even my mother, though I'm hoping she'll change her mind soon. Am I allowed to *sit down*?'

God, he was rude! And his children sounded like little horrors.

'Don't bother,' she said with deep pleasure. 'You'll only have to get up again.'

'*What*? I thought we were having a few drinks and then a meal. Why can't I sit down?'

Clare gazed at him with disgust, wondering why he had obsessed her, since in truth he was too short, slightly overweight, and his brown hair and beard were untidy, whilst his clothes were not in the best of taste. He hadn't even bothered to dress properly. Where had he imagined they were going to eat? In some hamburger joint, no doubt. But he *had* gone to the effort of wearing grey slacks instead of his denims, which at least made his black leather jacket and checkered open-neck shirt look

169

slightly better.

'You're not having a drink, a talk or even a meal,' she informed him. 'I've brought you all this way to tell you exactly what I think of you . . . and that isn't much. I didn't think much of you originally, but I certainly didn't think you'd be as self-centred as you've turned out to be . . .' She paused to take a sip of bourbon before she continued. 'You're a shit, Mr Rydell. A regular little shit. That's the first time I've sworn in my life, so I hope it lends the word extra weight.'

'It does,' Rydell said.

'And *why* are you a shit? Because you don't *give* a shit! Not about me, probably not about your family, and certainly not about too much outside of your work. You only care about what you want, not about how you get it. You don't care about other people's feelings; you don't know they exist. You're a loudmouth, Mr Rydell, unpunctual and inconsiderate; a man with no sense of morality. You're rude, aggressive and ruthless and that makes you a shit.'

'Are you finished? Am I allowed to sit down now?'

His response outraged her all the more.

'No, dammit, I'm *not* finished! And you're not allowed to sit down! You'll stand there like a good little boy until I tell you otherwise. Why? Because I despise you! Because you betrayed my trust! Because apart from being rude and ungrateful and thoughtless, you showed indifference to my position and the damage your ploy might cause when you gave my information to the press to suit your own ends.'

'You've no proof of that, Clare!'

'*What?*'

'You've no proof. Art Tabori didn't say where he got his information – and believe me, he won't say.'

'But you admitted to me that you'd given the interview, when I phoned you today!'

170

'I know, but there are industrial spies, Clare. There are hackers who get into computers and sell on the material. Have you thought of *that*? I'm going to deny it, Clare. I'll deny it to Jack Douglas. After all, it *could* have been a hacker and I *could* be as innocent as a turkey, plucked clean for Thanksgiving. So you didn't have to be embarrassed. You didn't have to take the blame. The fact that Jack Douglas has accused me of doing it, doesn't constitute proof. So I'll keep on denying it. And since no one can blame you without proof, I didn't betray you. All I did was get you what you wanted – that trip to the Antarctic . . . Now do I get to sit down and have that drink or do I get hung unjustly?'

She stared at him, amazed, taken aback by his outrageous cheek, then a bubble of mirth burst inside her.

'Oh, God!' she exclaimed while still laughing. 'I just don't believe this!'

And she reached out to him instinctively, hardly knowing she was doing so, to touch the life that glowed beneath his skin and illuminated his blue eyes. He closed his eyes and she kissed his eyelids, his forehead, his nose and lips, and then felt his hands sliding down her spine as his body pressed into her.

He wasn't ugly to her, then, but someone warm and tender, and she let herself melt into his presence and be consumed by him.

She didn't remember what happened next. Most of the details were vague. She only knew that her clothes were stripped off her on the bed to which, by some magical means, they had painlessly travelled.

'Oh, God, I'm in love!' she whispered breathlessly. 'I just don't believe this.'

He didn't reply – at least, not immediately. He was too busy beside her, above her, inside her, making love as if he knew her instinctively and could make her flesh sing. And while her flesh sang, she purred, stretched herself, coiled about him, and drew from him the response to the statement she had thought she would never make.

'Don't worry about it,' he replied. 'I'm in love with you, too.'

# CHAPTER TWENTY

Rydell and Clare were in Punta Arenas, Chile, for three days before the converted DC-8 air liner had been prepared for its flight. To Rydell's disgust Dwight Collins had refused to let him or Clare take the single-pilot ER-2 research plane, because of Rydell's 'unexplainable behavioural patterns' during his solo flight through the top of the ozone hole. Instead, he and Clare would journey through the bottom of the ozone layer, with a group of other scientists, at an altitude of a mere twelve kilometres while another pilot ventured in the ER-2 through the top of the hole.

'Anyway,' Collins told him, 'if you've finished with your bitching, you might as well know that the DC-8 won't be equipped for another three days, so you and Clare can enjoy the scenery and have a good time. That should settle you down, pal.'

Delighted that Collins had picked up on his new relationship and that he seemed to approve, Rydell took his advice and had a three-day vacation with Clare. Rydell was at ease in the knowledge that his mother had agreed to look after the two boys during his two-week absence, and transported to new heights by the love he felt for Clare. The couple shared a room in the Cabo de Hornos hotel, in the Plaza de Armas in downtown Punta Arenas. During their days together, Rydell showed Clare the magnificent lakes and mountains he knew so well, surprising her by skiing down the snow-covered slopes of the Patagonian Andes and impressing her with his knowledge of

Indian culture.

'You're full of surprises,' she told him later, 'but skiing I still can't believe!'

'I learned it during all those trips to Europe,' he explained, 'which were financed by NASA. I've never skied in America. I'm kind of a different person when I'm away; I wear my old skin back home.'

He was certainly a different person with Clare, less frazzled, more assured, much closer to the self he had lost before he married Suzy. He and Suzy had shared little – he had lived for his work; she had lived for pleasure – but with Clare, he felt he had found his identity. Of course, he couldn't tell her that. It would seem too goddamned *soft*.

Their final day of freedom was spent on a boat cruise to the San Rafael Lagoon, eerily majestic beneath imposing glaciers, the sun flashing off the blocks of broken ice drifting around the boat. Later they returned to the Plaza de Armas, to its vibrancy and colour, where Clare kissed the foot of the statue of Magellan, then got mildly drunk with Rydell at the bar, before finally falling into his arms in their bed. They made love, in between short sleeps, for most of the night.

The next morning, when they returned to the airstrip, they were surprisingly fit.

'Welcome back, boys and girls,' Dwight Collins greeted them. 'Now let's go to the briefing.'

Leaving his office in the prefabricated hut at the edge of the airstrip, he took them into the briefing room. The room was not as full as it had been during the previous mission, with merely half-a-dozen men, wearing bulky flying outfits, scattered on the seats. One of the men looked over his shoulder, gave Rydell a wide, beaming smile, and walked up to him. Rydell was surprised to see that it was his old buddy Rick Polanski.

Rick slapped his large hand down on Rydell's

shoulder and shook him affectionately. 'Collins kept me as a surprise for you,' he said. 'You evil sonofabitch!'

'A surprise? *Evil?* What *is* this?'

Polanski, a big man, looked enormous in his flying suit and actually seemed about to topple over as he chuckled.

'You evil little bastard,' he said, revising his first remark. 'I don't get the *Washington Post* in Phoenix, but I *did* get a visit from some of Jack Douglas's pals, and they kindly brought a copy of the article to help keep me up-to-date. That was some stunt you pulled, kid!'

'I didn't have a thing to do with it,' Rydell lied. 'It was some hacker, believe me.'

'Some hacker, my ass! It was you and we all know it. But Jack Douglas, who wouldn't trust his mother, thought it *might* have been me — something you no doubt intended.'

'Jesus, Rick, would I do that to you?'

'You would and did.' Polanski obviously admired him for it. 'Anyway, Douglas's men insinuated that any further info I picked up should be treated as classified and that any more breaches of security would bring heavy penalties raining upon my tender head. Then they escorted me to Washington DC, where, with Jack Douglas, I discussed the possibility of my coming on this expedition. So, here I am — for reasons which you're about to find out. Let's take a seat.'

'This is Clare Holton,' Rydell said. 'The scientific liaison officer between NASA and the White House, via Douglas's office, but here as a biotechnologist.'

'Pleased to meet you,' Polanski said, glancing admiringly at Clare's lovely face.

They took their seats just as Dwight Collins, wearing corduroy trousers, an open-necked shirt, and a leather flight jacket, walked onto the small stage and stood

175

with his back to a large artist's impression of the hole in the ozone layer. The flight paths of the ER-2 and DC-8 were both marked on the drawing, showing the former's planned flight through the top of the hole, the latter's much lower down at an altitude of twelve kilometres.

'Good morning, ladies and gentlemen,' Collins said smoothly. 'You can all breathe easily this morning, since this particular briefing *will* be brief.'

When his small audience had stopped laughing, Collins touched the large drawing behind him with his pointer, and gave them the same flight information that Rydell had heard during his briefing for the first expedition. Then, when that was clarified, Collins announced, 'The purpose of the previous expedition was to ascertain the rate at which the ozone is depleting around the hole over the Antarctic. You have been brought together, under the supervision of our old friend, Rick Polanski, for a very different purpose altogether.' Here, he paused, grinned at Rydell, then continued, 'According to physicist Tony Rydell's reading of the previous TOMS and SBUV experiment data, the ozone over the Antarctic is being depleted much faster than the CFCs, or chlorofluorocarbons, in the stratosphere can account for. This means in effect that something else, something *unknown* is devouring the ozone at what appears to be a particularly dangerous rate. Since previous expeditions through the ozone hole failed to reveal anything unexpected or unknown in the stratosphere, we can only assume, at this point, that what we are faced with is an unknown organism that may take the shape of cosmic dust, bacterial spores, or charged particles, such as plasmodes or radiobes.'

'Are you talking about an *alien life form?*' Polanski asked, with deliberate, loud emphasis on his last words and a slight, victorious grin on his face.

Collins gazed steadily at him, returning his grin. 'No,' he said carefully, 'I didn't quite say that, though I'm not about to stop anyone here from forming their own opinion.'

'Gee, thanks,' Polanski said.

When the chuckles had subsided, Collins continued unperturbed: 'Our mission is to ascertain if anything organic – or, to please Polanski, *living* – actually exists within the ozone hole. The search for cosmic dust or bacterial spores can only be done with balloons or, more likely, the exo-biology facilities of a space station; so initially you will concentrate on the charged-particle hypothesis and try to discover whether *anything* of an unknown quality, possibly ion-based, is having an effect on the ozone hole.'

'This sounds like something alien to *me*,' Polanski said with another broad grin.

Collins merely smiled slightly, then said, 'Mr Polanski is obviously enjoying himself because this is his field. Indeed, most of you are here at his recommendation. You had to wait three days for the DC-8 to be prepared because the ozone-reading instruments had to be removed from the aircraft and replaced with instruments you know and use when trying to locate unidentified flying objects, because what we're trying to find is certainly unidentified and, if it exists, of an unknown nature. If there's anything up there, whether visible or invisible, we want to hear it, see it, or at least get some kind of reading from it.'

Someone gave a low whistle, which Collins ignored.

'If we don't come back with something,' he said, 'this project will be aborted. If, on the other hand, we get any hint of something unknown, we'll be talking about a whole different ball game.' Saying that, he grinned at Rydell and the beaming Polanski, then added: 'Oh, one last thing. According to certain reports, whatever is up there – if it exists – can have strange effects on human beings, creating hallucinatory states of mind. Should anything like that occur, try to stay calm, remember that you're not alone, and *assess* as much as possible of what you are experiencing. OK, any questions?'

There were no questions as such, but the half dozen scientists glanced at one another in a bewildered manner as if they could not believe their own ears.

'OK,' Collins said, 'let's get going.'

Five of the other six men wearing flying outfits pushed their chairs back, then stood up and left the briefing room. The sixth man approached Collins as he jumped down from the platform, then stopped in front of Rydell, Clare and Polanski.

'You two don't have to look so smug,' Collins said to Rydell and Polanski. Then, offering Clare an easy grin, he said, 'You've got two Cheshire cats on your tail. The best of luck, Clare. Rydell,' he said, indicating the man beside him, 'this is Group-Captain Matthew Horowitz of USAF. He's going to make the same flight you previously made in the ER-2. You two are going to be in radio contact as you fly separately through the hole, so each of you will know what the other is experiencing at any given time. Both conversations will be recorded.'

'Sure,' Rydell said. 'Fine. Nice to meet you Captain.' He introduced Clare and Polanski, then Horowitz said, 'Collins was telling me about your weird experience during your previous flight up there. You got any advice to pass on?'

'Yeah,' Rydell said. 'What you see, or what you feel, could be disorientating to you – it might even frighten the hell out of you – so try to keep your wits about you. Try to distance yourself from the phenomenon and think about it as objectively as possible. Finally, keep reminding yourself that it's not real and can't possibly hurt you. We're gonna be in radio contact anyway, and that might be a help. OK?'

'OK Rydell.'

'Well, let's get going. They're all waiting out there.'

'Yeah, right,' Collins agreed. 'On your way . . . and good luck up there.'

With Clare on one side of him and Polanski on the other Rydell followed the Group Captain out onto the runway. A fierce wind was blowing and the dark clouds threatened rain, so he was glad when they parted from Horowitz and made their way into the relative shelter of the DC-8's fuselage. Its engines were already roaring as Rydell followed Clare up the steps and into the aircraft.

The fear started then.

It was as if, by stepping into the aircraft, he was reminded in detail of just how frightening his previous experience had been. The body of the aircraft, now seemed longer and darker than it normally was because most of the seats had been removed to make way for the mass of scientific instruments. Looking along it he felt oddly trapped, beyond the point of no return. The fear wasn't severe at first – more like a sudden attack of nerves – but although he managed to control it, he still felt badly shaken.

'Where do I sit?' Clare asked him.

'Beside me,' Rydell told her. 'You've got nothing to do here but observe, so you'll sit beside me in the pilot's cabin, while I'm on the radio. Polanski here, he's in charge of these men and all this equipment. At this point we can't check for cosmic dust or bacterial spores, but Polanski's team can take readings of any electronic, orgone, magnetic or gravitational anomalies inside the hole, and also, if we have a miracle, take monochrome, full colour and infra-red photographs and films. Naturally they'll also record any infrasonic sounds, if such exist. Now follow me Clare.'

He squeezed Polanski's broad shoulder, gave him the thumbs-up, then led Clare along the aircraft, past the scientists with their radar and laser systems, magnometers and gravimeters, ambient and parabolic microphones, various recording devices, and the video, motion-picture and still cameras which had been placed in front of various windows on both sides of the fuselage. The doors of the aircraft were closed as he led Clare into the pilot's compartment where he indicated that she should sit beside the pilot before strapping himself in at the other side of her.

When the DC-8 took off a few minutes later, Rydell's throat felt uncomfortably dry. Once more he watched the ground falling away, though not so fast this time, to reveal a vast landscape of lakes, fjords, lagoons and mountains below great swatches of white and grey clouds. The rivers ran towards the sea, the land gradually disappeared, then the sea became a vast bowl of black-shadowed, silvery ripples, filled with rainbow-coloured blocks of ice and glittering glaciers.

'It's fantastic!' Clare shouted against the roaring of the plane. 'It was worth it just to see this!'

Rydell grinned and put up his thumb, but he didn't feel that happy. He kept staring straight ahead, to where the cloudy sky met the sea's concave horizon, thinking about what he was flying into. Ashamed, he chided himself for being stupid, but he couldn't help remembering his hallucination, that ghost, the Suzy who should not have been there, and as more clouds gathered around the aircraft, his fear grew inexorably.

He dreaded seeing the Antarctic, but eventually it glittered on the horizon, its frozen mountain ranges and ice-shelves growing higher and wider as the aircraft crossed the Bellingshausen Sea and approached Ellsworth Land. Then the snowy wastelands were below, the white wilderness spread out around him, and he saw jade icebergs covered with algae and plankton, sheet ice and ice falls, polar plateaus and sheer snow-banks and lakes reflecting towering glaciers – a general whiteness that swept out on all sides to a stunning blue sky.

It filled him with dread. He was inside the ozone hole and that knowledge knotted in his guts, making him reach out for Clare's hand and a touch of reality.

She jerked her hand away. Startled, he looked at her. She was staring straight ahead out of the cockpit at the sky, and the skin on her face was deathly white around her widening, frightened eyes.

Rydell looked out as well but saw only white clouds striated by sunlight, before he glanced back at Clare and saw her trembling, breaking out in a cold sweat. He reached for her again but felt an icy presence. He jerked his hand back as something materialized in front of Clare – a ball of darkness near her feet, spreading out, rising up, taking the shape of a human figure, a ghostly silhouette ... then a silvery-haired man.

Clare watched the man growing. She seemed torn between love and terror. The man smiled and placed his hand on her shoulder and she twitched and then groaned.

'Oh, my God!' Rydell murmured.

A flash of light filled the cockpit and faded away in a second. Rydell looked away from the apparition in front of Clare to see a silvery disc fly towards the east, stop abruptly, hover briefly, then rise vertically at an incredible speed before disappearing, leaving nothing but empty sky.

Rydell blinked, rubbed his eyes and looked out again.

The sky was empty ... No, it wasn't. Something

181

flashed past and was gone. Then there were more flashes that changed into silver discs. They were crossing the DC-8's flight-path, rising and falling, crisscrossing, connected by streams of silvery light and shimmering heat waves.

Clare was sobbing, muttering incoherent words, her knuckles white where she was gripping her chair, her tears falling freely. Rydell saw that the man in front of her, whose hand was on her shoulder, had been joined by a woman of his age, whose gentle smile seemed all wrong.

Then the pilot saw them. His eyes widened in disbelief and he started to say something, but instead glanced down at his own lap. He screamed when he saw the tarantula that was resting between his legs.

'Oh, Christ!' he cried. 'Jesus!'

He swiped at the tarantula, but his hand just went through it, and as he stared down, gibbering, obviously losing his senses, Rydell shouted, 'Don't panic! It's not real! Put the plane on autopilot and get a grip on yourself!'

The pilot shuddered and closed his eyes. '*Do it now!*' Rydell bawled. The pilot opened his eyes as the tarantula disappeared. Then he reached out, turned on the autopilot and sank back into his seat, breathing heavily. When he looked up, he saw the ghosts in front of Clare, so he shuddered, closed his eyes again, and let out a helpless groan.

'Oh, no!' Clare sobbed. 'Please no!'

She was trying to twist sideways in her seat, away from the apparitions, but was being held back by the safety strap and didn't think to unbuckle it. She was trembling, pouring sweat, opening and closing her eyes frantically, and again, when Rydell tried to touch her, an icy cold almost burned his fingers and made him jerk his hand back.

The apparitions remained. The radio was crackling dementedly. When Rydell looked out of the cockpit he still saw the flying saucers, some far away, the size of dimes, some much closer, the size of aircraft, shooting back and forth, with a speed that made a mockery of science.

Then Rydell felt Suzy – even before he saw her. He knew immediately that she was sitting on his lap with her hands on his neck.

His heart raced and he started choking. The light dissolved into darkness. Suzy materialized out of that darkness, giving shape to her substance. She was sitting on his lap, leaning back in a teasing manner, wearing the clothes she had worn when she had visited the house, her smile slightly mocking, seductive, and somehow terrifying.

Yes, Rydell was terrified.

'Suzy?'

She didn't reply. She just smiled in a chilling manner. Then, as if hearing Clare's sobbing, she turned and looked at her. She registered nothing but just stared at her, as if through her, and remained that way, clinging to Rydell's neck.

'Jesus Christ!' Rydell whispered.

The plane continued to fly, guided by the autopilot, heading deeper into the ozone hole. Then someone behind Rydell screamed – someone in the main cabin – as the pilot at the other side of Clare let out a strangled groan.

A snake was sliding up between the pilot's legs and curling over his belly.

He screamed and slapped at it wildly and started kicking his legs while Clare continued sobbing beside him and the main cabin turned into bedlam.

Rydell, trying to keep control, reached down between himself and Suzy, felt her belly against his hand, unbuckled his safety belt and lurched forward, hoping to adjust the radio.

Although he could feel and smell Suzy, he appeared to pass through her.

He tried to contact the ER-2, but got only static. When he tried to contact the Antarctic land-bases the static increased. Cursing, he sat back, pressing his spine into the seat. Suzy immediately reappeared on his lap, leaning back, smiling at him.

That smile chilled his blood.

'Christ!' he whispered. 'Jesus Christ! Don't panic! Stay in control!' But he couldn't take it anymore, so he jumped out of his seat, passing through Clare's apparitions, hurrying back into the main cabin to see what was happening there.

The whole damned place was haunted! The gloom in the long, narrow cabin was filled with streaks of silvery light linked to spinning discs that bobbed magically in thin air and glided gracefully to and fro, particularly around the stunned Rick Polanski. Some of the scientists were weeping, while others were clearly shocked, and all of them were looking at people who should not have been there. The ghosts seemed human, though they wore clothes of different periods, and two of them, kneeling in front of a weeping scientist, were no more than ten years old.

The video, movie and still cameras at the windows were unattended, as was the rest of the scientific equipment.

It was a living nightmare.

Mentally prepared for it and keeping a grip on himself, Rydell realized that the plane, on autopilot, was taking them deeper into the ozone hole – and that the deeper in they went, the more vivid the apparitions became. Hurrying back into the cockpit to get the pilot to turn back, he was blinded by brilliant light. Stopping

184

in the doorway, he rubbed his eyes, adjusting them to the light, before he looked into the cockpit. What he saw horrified him.

The pilot was covered in snakes and spiders, paralysed with fear. Clare was leaning forward slightly, her face hidden in her hands, her body trembling uncontrollably as the two elderly people, now kneeling, embraced her and smiled with a frightening, glacial kindness. And there, beside this tableau, were another Rydell and Suzy.

The ghostly Suzy was still clinging to that other Rydell's neck, smiling as the skin on her face stretched tighter, revealing the bone beneath.

Beyond her was a sky that should not have been there: black as pitch and filled with stars – above and below, all around, offering only eternity.

At that moment time stood still.

# CHAPTER TWENTY-ONE

'Let me go over these facts again,' Collins said softly. 'When you returned to the cockpit, you . . .'

'For Chrissakes, Dwight, we've been over it a dozen times. I'm getting goddamned tired of this shit. Let's just call it a day, right?'

'Please, Tony, just one more time.'

Exasperated, Rydell glanced at Clare, who was staring down at her clasped hands, her face still pale and drawn, her shoulders slumped in defeat. Disturbed to see that, he glanced around the briefing room, which was empty apart from him and Clare. It was decidedly bleak, and too cold for comfort. Sighing, he returned his gaze to Collins and raised his hands as if praying.

'OK,' he said. 'One more time.'

Collins nodded and smiled, then glanced down at his notes and looked up again.

'You returned to the cockpit and . . .'

'The pilot was covered in snakes and spiders. Clare's two apparitions – as she says, her mother and father – were kneeling in front of her, as if consoling her. I saw an apparition of myself, sitting exactly as I'd been sitting when I left the cockpit, with Suzy on its lap, just as she had been, except that the skin on her face was stretching tighter and tighter, revealing the bones beneath, as if about to peel off altogether, or maybe just melt away.'

Clare shuddered beside him, so he reached out to squeeze her shoulder reassuringly. This time he could

186

touch her.

'And outside the plane?' Collins asked him.

'I still can't believe it,' Rydell said honestly. 'Instead of the sheer blue sky over the Antarctic, there was nothing but a great darkness filled with stars. No sign of the Antarctic, no trace of the normal sky. Just this great darkness filled with stars, like being in outer space.'

'And the flying saucers?'

'No sign of them either.'

'And the DC-8 was still on autopilot?'

'Right. And according to the instrument panel we were keeping to our course and should have been, at that point, directly above the Vinson Massif, in Marie Byrd Land, not surrounded by goddamned stars in what seemed like outer space.'

'We lost contact with you long before that,' Collins said. 'Five minutes after you crossed the Antarctic Circle, to be exact. We lost contact with you and the ER-2 at exactly the same time, but at least you returned.'

Clare shuddered again and Rydell knew what was bothering her: according to Collins, shortly after crossing the Antarctic Circle, the pilot of the ER-2 had started screaming dementedly, before he apparently lost control of his aircraft and crashed. Rydell wondered just what the pilot had experienced before going down.

'Yeah,' he said, almost talking to himself, 'at least we returned . . . I guess I was able to control myself better than the others because I'd had my previous experience and was more prepared this time. Anyway, when I saw that according to the instrument panel we *were* still on course – and that what was outside was probably as much an hallucination as what was going on inside – I realized that the deeper we flew into the ozone hole, the more varied and vivid the hallucinations were becoming. So, ignoring what was going on around me in the pilot's cabin, I took the plane off autopilot and turned us back towards the Antarctic Circle. I also tried to make radio contact, first with the ER-2, then with ground control, but failed on both counts.'

'You got nothing but static.'

'Right. But the static was really weird. I was convinced I could hear hundreds of voices, all distant and ghostly, but definitely voices. Then I thought the voices were actually in my head, which made me feel crazy.'

'And you report that they weren't all speaking English.'

'Correct. I'm certain I heard English words mixed in there, but there seemed to be an awful lot of other languages. I recognized bits of French, bits of German. I'm not sure of the others.'

'You don't personally speak any language other than English?'

'Only high school French.'

'OK, Tony, continue.'

'Well, like I said, the closer we got to the Antarctic Circle, the more normal the static began to sound . . .'

'The voices gradually faded away and were replaced by normal static.'

'Right. And I also noticed that the skin that had appeared to be stretched so tight on the apparition of Suzy's face began returning to normal, the apparitions of Clare's mother and father actually stood up to take their previous positions, and the snakes and spiders on the pilot started fading away. Then, just as we approached the Antarctic Circle, they disappeared altogether and the pilot started recovering from the trance he'd been in. As we flew back across the

188

Antarctic Circle, first my own doppelgänger disappeared, then Suzy, and finally the two apparitions in front of Clare . . . and as you know, everything returned to normal at the same time back in the main cabin.'

Collins nodded thoughtfully, glanced at the distraught Clare, then stood up, walked to the window, and looked out at the airstrip as he spoke.

'Well, we know at least one thing,' he said. 'All of the hallucinations were related directly to the most prominent emotions or concerns of the individuals involved. In your case, the major anxiety of the past few months has been the fact that Suzy left you and it was Suzy you saw in both cases. Clare, here, recently lost her father, and lost her mother not too long before that, which may explain why she saw them both in the pilot's cabin. As for the pilot, we checked the psychological profile and learned that while he's in excellent mental health, he has a phobia about snakes and spiders. As for the scientists in the main cabin, one of them saw his two children, who had drowned together eighteen months ago; another saw the fiancée who'd ditched him for another man; the others saw various relatives and friends, alive or dead, and Rick Polanski saw flying saucers – *his* major concern in life.'

'So,' Rydell said, 'the hallucinations are obviously drawn from the individual's subconscious, but once given shape, they become so real that they can be observed by others, as well as giving off human smells and being almost physical.'

'*Almost* physical,' Collins emphasized. 'You could feel Suzy on your lap, and you felt her hands around your neck, yet when instinct made you jump up without thinking, you appeared to pass through her.'

'Christ, yes, that's right.'

'So the extent of their physical reality is, in a sense, dictated by the will of the individual creating them . . .'

189

'Right. And the question is . . .'

'Who, or what, is controlling the mind of the individual?'

'The unknown factor that's feeding off the ozone, whatever it is.'

Collins sighed. 'Jesus!' He looked out of the window as if, by studying the sky over Chile, he would somehow solve the mystery. Rydell placed his hand on Clare's shoulder and let it rest there. She raised her head and smiled at him, but her eyes were filled with grief, and he knew that the apparitions of her parents had severely disturbed her.

'Are you OK?'

'Not too good,' she said, 'but I'm getting over it slowly. I'm just convinced that I'll never forget the experience and I can't bear the thought of that.'

'You'll forget it in time.' Rydell comforted, though he wasn't sure that she would, since he didn't think that *he* would. 'So what happens now?' he asked Collins when he walked back and sat down.

Collins raised his hands in the air, as if praying for clemency. 'Well, something's happening up there – that much is for sure. Your first experience has now been corroborated by the experiences of Clare and all the others, and we know that *something* is affecting those who fly into the hole in the ozone layer. We also know that though your experience wasn't shared by those flying through the bottom of the hole during the first flight, during the *second*, your experience *was* shared by all the others, even though the plane was only flying through the bottom of the hole, while the pilot flying through the top of the hole suffered an experience so dreadful that it made him lose control of his aircraft and crash. So whatever it is that's causing it, it's obviously extended its presence in the hole, from the top to the bottom and is now coming dangerously close to Earth.'

'So what happens now?' Rydell repeated.

'We're preparing a report on what happened to both aeroplanes, which we'll submit to the White House, through Jack Douglas. We're also waiting for the analyses of the readings of the scientific instruments on board – which we hope continued to function throughout the whole event – and the results will be included with the main report. What happens then, depends on what the instrument readings tell us, but clearly, given what happened to you guys, we can't examine that unknown organism – if it *is* an organism – with a manned space station. We can only use payload-carrying balloons, which is what I'm planning to recommend.'

'And when will we have the instrument readings from the DC-8?'

'Tonight,' Collins said. 'I'll call you at the hotel. And meanwhile, pack your bags, since no matter what readings we get, you two, Polanski and the others will be flown back to the States tomorrow morning. You can do nothing else here.'

'Are you staying here?'

'Just to finish my report. I'll fly back in a day or two. Now go and have a good rest.'

Driven back to the hotel in Puntas Arenas by a solemn-faced Chilean Air Force corporal, Rydell and Clare sat close to one another in the jeep but didn't say much. Rydell had his arm around Clare's shoulder, her head resting on his chest. She was leaning against him and he felt her bewilderment, fear and grief as if it was his. He also knew that she would be haunted by what she had seen for the rest of her days.

The dead had returned to her.

For him, it was much easier, since his Suzy was alive and well, yet even he would never forget what he had seen or felt in that aeroplane. Nor would he ever look at the real Suzy as he had done before.

Once in the seven-story hotel in the Plaza de Armas, he and Clare retired to their shared room, went straight to bed, and fell asleep without making love. Rydell had a restless sleep, his dreams based on what he had been through, and was awakened, in the early hours of the evening, by Clare's lips.

She was silently weeping. Her tears dropped onto his chest. She kissed his lips, throat, and chest and then rolled upon him.

'I can't sleep,' she whispered. 'Make me forget. Damn, *I have to forget!*'

Later, satiated, they dressed and went downstairs, had a light meal in the restaurant, drank too much wine in the bar, and walked hand in hand to the shore where, as the sun was sinking, they gazed out over the Strait of Magellan at Tierra del Fuego.

'My father and mother,' Clare said. 'I still can't believe it. They were so real – I could touch them and was touched – now I feel that they're still alive.' The sinking sun set the sea on fire, filled the sky with bloody ink, and a crimson light veiled her wind-blown hair and fine profile.

'I can't live at home anymore,' she said. 'It would remind me of what I saw. I'd be haunted by the expectation of seeing them and the pain and fear that would cause me. I'm going to move out, rent the house, try to put this behind me. And God help me, but I'm in love with Tony Rydell. Do you think he would comfort me?'

'As best he could,' Rydell answered, as if speaking about someone else. 'But bear in mind that he lives for his work and has difficult kids.'

'I need that,' she said, finally smiling. 'It'll give me a challenge. And that's what I'm going to need if I want to forget this.'

'Something different, eh?'

'Yes, something different. A new life with someone new.'

'Move in anytime,' Rydell said.

They waited until the sun had set, then wandered slowly back to the hotel, had another drink in the Winter Garden, then went up to their room. This time, Rydell made the first move, pulling her to him in the darkness, aroused by the image of her in his home. He needed to have her so much, so he made love with deep longing, and when she wept he kissed the tears from her cheeks and then watched her fall asleep. Her sleeping face was like a painting, solemn and mysterious, and he closed his eyes with reluctance, not wanting to lose sight of it. He was just about to drop off to sleep when the telephone rang.

'There's something up there,' Dwight Collins said.

# PART TWO

# CHAPTER TWENTY-TWO

'There's something up there?' the President asked, as if he hadn't heard properly or simply couldn't believe what he had heard.

'Yes, Mr President,' Jack Douglas said, placing Dwight Collins's report on the desk that had been given to the country by England's Queen Victoria. 'The data's all here. There's not too much of it, and what there is isn't great, but it's enough to have convinced NASA's top scientists that something is up there.'

The President glanced left and right, as if frightened of being overheard, then, remembering that he'd already despatched his aide, he leaned forward a little and said, 'Just what are you saying? Do you mean . . .?'

'Something unknown,' Douglas said, trying to avoid the word "alien" and feeling less calm than he looked. 'We don't know what it is – only what it *does* – but we now know that something's definitely there.'

'Where, exactly?' the President asked.

'It originated at the top of the ozone hole over the Antarctic, but since the last air-borne expedition, four months ago, it's spread down to the bottom and is now dangerously close to Earth.'

'*Spread* down to the bottom?'

'Yes, Mr President. It hasn't *moved* down from the top to the bottom. It has *grown* and now extends from the top of the ozone hole to the bottom, practically into Earth's atmosphere.'

'You mean it's some kind of . . . *substance*?'

'We don't know yet, Mr President. Whatever it is, it's invisible. The video, motion-picture and still cameras on board the DC-8 recorded nothing. However, highly irregular fluctuations were recorded on the magnometers, and the helium neon laser system picked up what further analysis may reveal as unique infra-sonic sounds ...'

'Pardon?'

'Sounds below the normal frequency range.'

'Oh, I see.'

'And there were instrumented recordings of what appear to be shock-wave emissions. Naturally, all these readings were taken from the DC-8, which was flying through the bottom of the ozone hole at an altitude of about twelve kilometres, which proves that this ...' Douglas shrugged, feeling inept, 'that whatever affected Rydell during his flight across the top of the same hole – at an altitude of twenty kilometres – had extended down to an altitude of twelve kilometres.'

It was an unusually hot day and Douglas wiped his face with a handkerchief, thinking of the greenhouse effect and wondering if it had started, as Clare had suggested. When he thought of Clare, he thought of her affair with Rydell and quietly raged inside.

'Since the ER-2 crashed without revealing what its payload recorded, how can you be sure that this ...' and here the President groped for a suitable word ... 'this *whatever*, didn't actually *descend* all that way, rather than spread down that far?'

'Naturally,' Douglas said, impatiently, 'since the ER-2 crashed deep in the Antarctic, probably somewhere in the mountains of the Vinson Massif, we're unlikely to ever find it or its instruments. However, I think it's safe to say, from what the land base picked up over the aircraft's radio before contact was lost, that the pilot, one of our best, experienced *something* that was frightening enough to make him lose control of his aeroplane. In other words, a more dramatic version of what Rydell experienced during the first flight.'

'The apparitions.'

'Yes, Mr President.'

'And this ... this *thing* ...' The President was obviously still having difficulty in fitting the word to the situation. 'This, whatever it is, which makes humans hallucinate in an extraordinary, dangerous manner, is also eating away the ozone layer even faster than Earth's chlorofluorocarbons.'

'Yes, Mr President. And at the rate it's doing so, the ozone layer will be depleted within the next five years, which will lead to a hotter Earth, which in turn will lead to flood, famine, and other catastrophes – and that unknown organism, if such it be, might well keep spreading around the globe, with who knows *what* results.'

'Dear God,' the President said. Looking like a man having a bad dream, he studied the Oval Room, as if seeking reassurance, then gazing at the silver-framed photograph of his wife and children, asked, 'And we've no idea what this thing is?'

'No, sir, we don't. According to Clare Holton's report – she is, as you may recall, a biotechnologist by profession – it could be composed of plasmodes or radiobes ...'

'I'm sorry, Jack, I don't ...'

'Electrically charged particles or ions.'

'Ah, I see.'

'However, Miss Holton also postulated the possibility that it could be composed of bacterial spores, possibly transported here in the tail of some meteorite, such as Halley's Comet. She also offers the novel suggestion, gleaned from the former NASA astrophysicist,

Richard Polanski – now a committed UFOlogist, I should warn you – that we could be faced with etherea, or ether, an invisible substance that possibly pervades space and functions as the medium for the transmission of radiant energy, perhaps orgone energy. Electrically charged particles and ether could both account for the unusual magnetic fluctuations recorded during the flight. As for the panspermic hypothesis . . .'

'What?'

'Bacterial spores.'

'Oh, yes, right.'

'The only way to check if this is the case, is to send up relevant recording devices in stratospheric balloons. Either that or we send up a manned space station, but that still leaves the problem of the hallucinations, which would seem to kill that idea. The balloons, then, are clearly the best way of finding out what's up there and discovering an antidote.'

'You make it sound like some kind of virus.'

'It sure seems like one.'

Used to more earthly problems, the President tried not to look bewildered and nodded affirmatively. 'And what do *you* think, Jack?' he finally asked.

'I think we have to tread cautiously, Mr President,' Douglas said, thinking of Clare and Rydell with a clean, icy hatred. 'I think that what we have here *is* something unknown but that those involved, notably Rydell and Polanski – both wishful thinkers regarding UFOs – are convincing themselves, and are trying to convince us, that what's up there is *alien*.'

He had avoided using the word until he could turn it to his own advantage. Now he knew how to do that.

'You mean . . .?' the President started to ask, then stopped, clearly flustered.

'Yes, Mr President. I think that if we're not careful,

they'll have us publicly supporting their view that what's up there is some kind of alien entity. This would not only make us look extremely foolish, but could also lead to public panic.'

'Yes, of course. I can see that.' The President's face was clouded with doubt. 'But if it's *not* something alien, then what the hell *is* it? And if it didn't come here with the cosmic dust of some meteorite, then where did it come from?'

'Mr President,' Douglas said, moving in on his favourite theme, but coating the pill with sugar, 'as you know, I want to believe as much as you do in the sincerity of *glasnost* and *Perestroika*, but CIA reports suggest that they are being used by the KGB – maybe without Gorbachev's knowledge – to penetrate Western intelligence defences more easily.'

'I know this theory of yours Jack, and I have to say I don't necessarily agree with it.'

'I appreciate that Mr President, but you should bear in mind that whatever their intentions, the Soviets have been experimenting for years with cloud-busters and other so-called atmospheric weapons, some of which have been pretty successful at altering weather around the globe, to the disadvantage of the West. And what's up there could be an extension of that particular experimental research.'

The President chuckled indulgently. 'That wouldn't make sense, Jack. If, as you say, the destruction of the ozone is going to lead to a hotter Earth, with widespread famine and the flooding of many cities, including Leningrad, what would the Soviets gain from such a weapon? In fact, their own agricultural crisis is surely ample proof that it's in their own interest to strengthen their commercial ties with the United States rather than sever them. Your theory doesn't hold water.'

'I think it does,' Douglas said. He secretly despised the President's wish to create a lasting bond with the Soviets and was determined to do what he could to prevent it. 'At least it will in the long term. I'm not suggesting that we should resurrect the Cold War with the Soviets, but I have to emphasize that what the world is engaged in, whether consciously or not, is a war for *economic* superiority and that includes the Soviets and Chinese.'

'OK, Jack, I'll buy that.'

'Well, Mr President, accepting that, we have to accept that the only way to reduce our production of CFCs – which will at least slow down the rate of ozone depletion and give us breathing space – would be to dramatically reduce our industrial and agricultural output.'

'That's what's been recommended by Miss Holton and other theorists.'

'Yet to do that would badly effect our economy, aiding our enemies here and abroad, including the Soviets. I therefore feel that Miss Holton's call for a reduction in the use of CFCs would diminish US influence world-wide, with a simultaneous increase in economic power for those countries which quietly ignore their own production of CFCs – there'll be quite a few, no doubt.'

Now it was the President's turn to take out his handkerchief and wipe the sweat from his forehead. He glanced back over his shoulder, squinting against the brilliant light beaming through the French windows, then turned back to Douglas and sighed.

'So you're suggesting that even if we *do* reduce our use of CFCs, countries like the Soviet Union will make promises, but actually do nothing.'

'Yes, Mr President. Their industrial and agricultural output will increase while ours diminishes, eventually making us dependent on *them*.'

The President glanced at his sweat-soaked handkerchief before replacing it in his jacket pocket. 'Well,' he said in a hesitant manner, 'that *could* be true, but it still leaves the problem of the depletion of the ozone layer by CFCs and that other . . . *something* up there. So what are you driving at?'

Douglas knew he now had the President exactly where he wanted him and that while he put a spoke in the spinning wheel of Soviet progress, he could also get Clare and Rydell under his indirect control and ensure that they didn't step out of line in the future. 'It's my belief,' he began, 'that we can *use* the alien element that's depleting the ozone layer. We should *not* reduce our production of CFCs, as we've promised. Instead, we should encourage Clare and Rydell to ascertain what it is up there and then find some way of controlling it, or preventing its growth, and through that knowledge actually create other ozone holes which we could open or close anywhere we desired in the stratosphere. In this way the United States could manipulate the Earth's atmospheric conditions and weather and indirectly, surreptitiously control the whole world. What's up there, Mr President, is a gift and we have to accept and use it.'

The President was lost for words and glanced around in confusion, before standing up and walking to the French windows. There, between the two flags, he looked over the sunlit splendour of the rose garden. He was taking the weight of the world upon his shoulders and wanted Douglas to know it. Eventually, after what seemed like an eternity, he turned back to the Oval Room.

'Can I place you in charge of this?' he asked.

'Yes, Mr President.'

# CHAPTER TWENTY-THREE

'This is Clare,' Rydell said, nervously enough to make Clare feel uneasy. 'She's coming to live with us, as I told you. Clare, this is my mother . . .'

'Howdedoo,' the beady-eyed, grey-haired old woman interjected keenly.

'And my two sons, Don, who's thirteen . . .'

'Practically fourteen,' Don interrupted sourly.

'And Ronnie, who's twelve.'

'Eleven,' Ronnie corrected him. 'You don't even know my age, goddammit. That's 'cause you're never at home.'

'Blasphemy!' Rydell's mother cried. 'That boy needs a good hiding!'

'Right,' Rydell said. '*Eleven*. Ronnie's a bit sensitive about his age because . . .'

'He's so small,' Don informed her.

'I'm not!'

'You are!'

'OK,' Rydell said. 'That's enough. A bit of quiet from you two. Say *hello*, for chrissakes!'

'Hi,' Don said to Clare, bouncing his words off the floor and blowing a bubble of gum.

'Hi,' repeated Ronnie, playing with a yo-yo and studying her with a frank but cold curiosity. 'Do you know my mom?'

'No, she doesn't,' Rydell said hastily. He could see that Clare was disconcerted by the reception she was getting. 'Clare and I work together at NASA,' Rydell continued, 'and that's all *you* need to know.'

'It's nice to meet you all,' Clare said.

'Yeah, right,' Don said sarcastically.

'You must have more spunk than sense to come and live here,' Grandma said. 'The last housekeeper left.'

'I'm not a housekeeper,' Clare said.

'She's living with *me*,' Rydell said tactlessly.

'I hope she can cook,' Ronnie said. 'Grandma's food is like vomit.'

'Tony's told me so much about you,' Clare said desperately to Rydell's mother, tentatively extending her hand. 'It's nice to meet you at last.'

Rydell's mother refused to shake hands and instead clasped her blue-veined hands together, then flexed her fingers. 'Arthritis is a terrible thing,' she said, 'though I'm not the complaining kind. Which room are you sleeping in?'

'She's sleeping in my room,' Rydell said, 'and you damn well know it. Now why don't you make a cup of coffee while I show Clare the house?'

'I was just about to do it,' his mother whined. 'You don't have to boss me.'

While the frail old woman reluctantly stood upright, Clare glanced around the lounge of the tract house and was shocked at how small and cluttered it was. Having lived most of her life in the immaculate elegance of her parents' spacious town house in Georgetown, she already felt slightly claustrophobic in this small, low-ceilinged room and, even worse, was taken aback by its remarkable untidiness. There were books all over the place – on the table, on the chair, piled up on the floor – and, to her distress, many of the albums around the old-fashioned hi-fi were out of their covers, lying on the floor, covered with dust.

'They're mostly my books,' Rydell explained, when he saw her wandering gaze. 'Mostly books on science. I like to have them all within reach, so I keep them around the place.'

That didn't explain the records, the sight of which made Clare's teeth grind, but she didn't think it wise to complain at this early stage.

'Come on,' Rydell said, picking up her suitcases, 'I'll show you the bedroom. Then we'll get organized.'

All the bedrooms were at the back of the house and seemed as small and untidy as the lounge. Rydell hadn't even made his bed that morning.

'Excuse the mess,' he said. 'I was in a hurry to get to work. And my mom's not wildly reliable when it comes to housekeeping.'

'You lost your housekeeper?' Clare asked him.

'More than one,' he replied. 'I'm not sure if it's the boys or my mom, but I know that neither's an easy task. Hey,' he added, seeing the look on her face, 'it's an experience, right? You want something different from what you've had and that's what you're gonna get. Come on, give me a kiss!'

When she kissed him, she felt better, her love for him surging back, but then he led her out of the bedroom, back into the cluttered house, and she saw his peculiar mother and sullen sons and again felt confused.

She had not forgotten the Antarctic, that dreadful experience in the aeroplane, and was still feeling badly shaken by it. Now she had to face Rydell's home, the messy life of the man she loved, and she wondered if her love would sustain her. Her love for Rydell was no guarantee that she would love his children, neither of whom seemed too pleasant.

'I'm hungry,' Don said.

'I'm bored,' Ronnie added.

'Thank God for your health,' Grandmother said, 'which is something I've lost.'

'That's why I'm hungry,' Don said.

'Cause he's healthy,' Ronnie explained. 'We haven't had a thing to eat since breakfast, and that was just cereal.'

'Don't blame me,' Rydell's mother whined. 'I didn't have *any* breakfast. My asthma almost choked me, my arthritis was crippling, and then, when I crawled into the kitchen, I found nothing to eat. This place just isn't organized.'

'*You* were supposed to organize it,' Rydell said. 'That's why we let you out of that funny-farm known as Menopause Manor.'

'It's not a funny-farm. It's a rest-home and you know it. And I had to go back there for a rest after living with you lot.'

'But you returned! You came back, Mom!'

'And I still can't get you organized, since you're all so unhelpful.'

'OK, let's get organized,' Rydell said, beaming brightly at Clare. 'Let's you and I go to the supermarket and bring back the works. We'll have a new life from now on. OK, Clare?'

'OK,' she said, in desperation to get out, not realizing that he would then invite his two sons to keep them happily occupied. They didn't appreciate the gesture, wanting to stay at home with the TV, so when Rydell forced them to come along, they weren't happy and decided to show it. They fought noisily in the car, went wild in the supermarket, and in general made Clare, who wasn't used to shopping anyway, feel that she was shockingly ignorant of the ways of the real world.

'She can't even push the trolley,' Don said. 'You'd think she'd never used one.'

'I never have,' Clare replied.

'Were your servants as dumb as you?' Ronnie asked, 'or did they go to good schools?'

'*Ronnie!*' Rydell snapped.

'What's the matter?'

'Don't be rude!'

'He's just making conversation,' Don explained, 'but she never replies.'

'OK,' Rydell said. 'That's enough. Here, Clare, give me that trolley.'

Rydell pushed the trolley while Clare collected the food, confused by the endless rows of tins and packets, more so because the two boys were so noisy and distracted her terribly. Rydell seemed more at home here, telling her what to collect, but he had a haphazard way of shopping, buying purely on impulse, and by the time they reached the checkout gate, the trolley looked like a mountain.

And Clare was exhausted.

She knew it was purely emotional, a product of disorientation, and tried to fix that firmly in her mind as she stacked their many purchases into boxes in an urgent, haphazard way. Don and Ronnie didn't help – too busy insulting each other – and Rydell was too busy flirting with the girl at the till. Clare felt like screaming then, wanting to run away from it all, but then Rydell slid his arm around her waist and kissed her hot cheek.

'OK,' he said. 'You did really good, Clare. Now let's get back to the house.'

As they drove back to Greenbelt, with the boys hollering in the back seats, Clare looked out at the suburban scenery, the neat rows of tract houses, and thought longingly of her family home in Georgetown, which she had recently rented, with deep regret, to an English diplomat and his family.

She loved the house and all the memories it contained; but since her frightening experience over the Antarctic, she would always feel that the house was haunted by the ghosts of her parents. So she had decided to move in with Rydell because she loved him

208

and needed him, but also because, as he had reminded her, she now needed something different in her life. However, as she studied the sleepy suburbs and their blandly pretty tract houses, deafened by the hollering of Rydell's two undisciplined children, she realized bleakly that she hadn't begun to imagine the extent of the differences between the life she had led and the one she had let herself in for. She could still hardly accept that she had fallen in love with Rydell; now she had to accept that she had inherited his wild boys, possibly crazy mother and untidy, cramped house. It didn't seem real, somehow.

Already secretly yearning for silence and privacy, for the abiding pleasures of the intellect, instead she found herself struggling up the path and into the house, carrying two heavy boxes of groceries while the boys, still hollering, chased one another and kept bumping into her.

'Excuse me,' she said to Don as he started turning on the garden hose, 'but it'd help if you opened the door for me.'

'Just kick it,' he said as water gushed out of the hose and he aimed it at the retreating Ronnie.

'Ronnie!' Rydell admonished as he came up behind Clare, carrying more groceries. Clare managed to kick the door open and stumble into the house, where she immediately placed her two boxes on the nearest table.

'That's it,' Grandma whined from where she was sitting beside the table. 'I've just managed to tidy this place up and already you're dumping that rubbish the first place you see. The kitchen's out back, my girl.'

'I was just resting,' Clare explained, trying to get her breath back, glancing around the room and noticing it was still as messy as before.

'There's no rest for *me*,' Grandma said. 'I'm used here like a nigger servant. I'm too old and fragile for all this work, but no one thinks about that.'

'Stop that, Ma,' Rydell said, carrying his boxes straight to the kitchen. 'We can do without your redneck remarks and moans about overwork. Clare!' he shouted as he disappeared into the kitchen. 'Let's prepare dinner!'

Grateful to get away from Grandma and the two boys shrieking outside, Clare carried her boxes into the kitchen and let Rydell embrace her. She felt good in his arms, as if born to be there, and only wished they could be alone together instead of in this menagerie.

'Don't mind my Mom,' he said. 'Her bark's worse than her bite. As for the boys, they've been unmanageable since Suzy walked out, but I'm pretty sure your presence here will make a difference, given some time.'

'I wonder,' she replied. 'I mean, I think they resent me.'

'Kids forget their resentments pretty quickly, so just play it by ear. Now kick off your shoes and put up your feet and let me cook dinner. I'm the burger king of Greenbelt!'

'That sounds wonderful, but I'll settle for a salad, which I'll make myself.'

'Terrific,' he said. 'You do the salad, I'll do the burgers and French fries, and we'll open a bottle of wine right now and get drunk as we're cooking. Do you think that'll help?'

'It sounds like music to my ears. You pour and I'll drink it!'

Getting drunk helped. When the food was ready, Clare went onto the porch to call the boys in, and when they said they didn't want to eat, she had the courage to challenge them.

'You think we did all this work for nothing? The food's cooked and you'll damned well eat it. Now come in right this minute, wash your hands and comb your hair, then sit down at the table like civilized people and eat with your mouths shut.'

'You can't give us orders,' Don said.

'You're not our Mom,' Ronnie added. 'We only take orders from Mom or Dad and you don't look like either.'

'Would you like a good hiding?'

'What?' Ronnie said, stepping backwards.

'One more word out of you, or you, Don, and I'll take you straight into your bedroom and give you a hiding. Now come in, wash your hands and comb your hair, and sit down at the table. And I mean *right now*!'

They did as they were told. They even ate with their mouths shut. Rydell's French fries looked soggy, his burgers were burnt, but Grandma tucked into Clare's salad with great relish, saying, 'I'll probably suffer for this later, but I'm too polite not to eat.' Rydell opened another bottle and even Grandma had a sip, saying, 'If the Lord Jesus Christ could sip wine, then I don't see why I can't.' Clare had to laugh. She felt drunk and more at home. When she laughed, Grandma gave her a sly smile and, after staring tentatively at one another, the boys also grinned at her.

'Are you a scientist?' Ronnie asked her.

'Yes,' she said, 'just like your Dad.'

'But she was also an astronaut,' Rydell said. 'One of the few female astronauts.'

'An *astronaut*,' Don asked, amazed.

'Yes,' Clare said, 'a few years back.'

'Did you fly to the moon?' Ronnie asked, his eyes wide.

'All the way there and back,' she said.

They were as impressed as hell and suddenly saw her in a different light. Because she was drunk and had started to feel more at home, she answered their

211

many questions, filled them with awe, and won their hearts over that long, drunken, leisurely meal.

'And you've come to live with us?' Don asked her.

'If you don't mind,' she said.

'*I* don't mind,' Ronnie replied. 'Boy, just wait till I get to school and tell my buddies.'

'Yeah,' Don said, just as excited as his younger brother. 'It'll knock them out of their socks!'

They all laughed at that and Rydell poured more wine. Then a voice shouted through the front door: 'Anyone in there?'

'Come on in,' Rydell replied and Dwight Collins entered wearing a gaudy shirt and shorts, carrying a couple of six-packs, and followed by an overweight blonde woman, who was holding up a bottle of champagne and smiling attractively.

'We've come as your new neighbours,' Dwight said to Clare, his grin broad and mischievous; then, indicating the cheerful blonde, added, 'This is my wife, Maggie. Maggie, meet Clare, who used to be a sensible woman before she met Rydell.'

Maggie laughed and shook Clare's hand, then waved the bottle of champagne. 'We live just around the corner, Clare, so if you need anything, drop in. Meanwhile, if one of these so-called men can open this bottle, we'll celebrate your arrival. Here, Dwight,' she said, handing him the bottle. 'You do the honours.'

Clare liked her immediately and liked her even more after a couple of glasses of champagne. Clare's home had been formal, her parents loving but less demonstrative, and in Rydell's small tract house, though it was hot as hell and cluttered, she felt a certain loosening of inhibitions and a lack of constraint. The conversation was loud and careless, argumentative, spontaneous, and in Maggie, – a less sophisticated version of her wealthy, rumbustious friend Nicola – she felt that she had found a shoulder to lean on, a witty and good-natured friend.

'Just look at them,' Maggie said, indicating the two drunken men. 'If they weren't so goddamned intelligent, you'd think they were cowboys. That's 'cause they're NASA men, right? They live for their goddamned *work*. Or, as *they'd* put it, they play as hard as they work, which is pretty much seven days a week, one running into the other. They're not bad, I suppose – they're too *busy* to beat their wives – and a guy who loves his work is less trouble than one who's plain bored. Even Rydell – let's face it, no gentleman! – has a certain, weird charm. Now isn't that right, Rydell?'

'Right!' Rydell said agreeably.

Grandma watched the TV, sipping wine, muttering constantly, and the two boys, Don and Ronnie, having inherited a former *astronaut*, took turns at topping up Clare's glass as an excuse to talk to her. Then she sent them to bed. She was drunk enough to try it on. She said, 'Tomorrow, if you behave, I'll bring back lots of photos from NASA, some of which have been signed by the astronauts, you can sell in the schoolyard. Now how about that?' They were thrilled into obedience, even kissed her goodnight, then followed Grandma's wavering, frail form into the back of the house.

'Gee whiz!' Maggie exclaimed. 'I don't believe what I've just seen! She's got those uncontrollable kids eating out of the palm of her hand!'

'That's why she's a liaison officer,' Collins said. 'I always wondered about that.'

'The more we drink, the more we learn,' Clare responded, then had a fit of the giggles. 'God, I just don't believe this!'

'You're in love,' Maggie told her.

Which was the truth, and the only thing that made sense, the inviolable reality that washed her clean, damned purified her. When Dwight and Maggie had gone she and Rydell went to bed and there, in that small, humid room, they burned against one another in a sensual fever. Clare took confidence from that, shrugged off her fear and breathed, at least briefly forgetting that aeroplane in the Antarctic, the ghosts of the dead, instead regaining her lost faith in the love she gave and received.

Then at last, she slept soundly.

# CHAPTER TWENTY-FOUR

'I don't give a goddamn about the weather,' Suzy's father said, slumped lethargically in a dusty armchair, drinking beer from the bottle. 'I ain't gonna move out. I was born and raised on this farm and here's where I'll die.'

They were all sitting in the living room on a Sunday afternoon, having just finished lunch, having drinks and watching the news on TV, which as usual was not good. It was mostly about catastrophes being caused by the changing weather. Europe was still being devastated by fierce winds and floods, the Antarctic ice was melting at an unprecedented rate, the oceans were rising and many rivers flooding their banks, and while Russia's agricultural wilderness was becoming unexpectedly rich, the American heartland, including Iowa, was turning into a dustbowl.

'No talk of help for the farmers,' Suzy's father said. 'Just this scientific gobbledygook about holes in the atmosphere. What the hell's goin' on here?'

He'd just come back from Des Moines, where he'd been talking to his bank manager, and was looking out of place in his rarely worn, old-fashioned suit with a white shirt and tie. Now he loosened the tie, unbuttoned his shirt-collar and gave a loud sigh. 'Goddammit,' he said, 'who wants science? What about us out here?'

Since he was talking to himself there was no need to reply, but Suzy glanced at him, surprised at how changed he was, aware that never before had he drunk beer from a bottle, uttered a blasphemy, or looked as diminished as he did in that awful grey suit. Then she realized that he was so in tune with the land, he was fading away with it. He had thought that the land would endure forever and now it was failing him.

The shock and grief were destroying him.

'The Lord works in mysterious ways,' Suzy's mother said, doing her knitting and sipping lemonade. 'Praise be, he will shelter us.'

Not sharing the faith that her mother had in abundance, Suzy returned her gaze to the TV in time to learn that the weather was not the year's only bizarre phenomenon.

Not since the 1950s had there been so many reports of UFOs and other unusual phenomenon. The reports, which were world-wide, were believed to be the products of hysteria caused by the uncommon weather. Certainly, so far, no concrete evidence had been produced to support the contention that the reports were based on anything other than emotional and mental disturbances.

But it *was* pretty weird.

'Flying saucers!' Suzy's father exclaimed in disgust. 'I don't believe what I'm hearing! The bread-basket of America – the bread-basket of *the world*! – is being destroyed by the goddamned weather and all *they* can do is try to distract us with news about UFOs and ghosts and other so-called unexplained phenomena. Is this a public service or is it not? We oughta write and complain!'

He had another slug of beer, wiped his lips with his hand, then leaned forward and switched off the TV set.

'I can't stand it,' he said.

'Neither can I,' Suzy said. Glad of an excuse to get out for a while, she stood up and stretched herself. 'I think I'll go in to town. Go and see Joe.'

'It's time you went to see your husband,' her father

said. 'That might be more profitable.'

'I'm sorry, Dad, but I'm not ready for that yet, so let's drop the subject.'

He just shrugged and slugged some more beer. 'Have it your way,' he said.

He didn't really care. He was too concerned with the weather. His crops were dead, he was running out of money and there was no sign of rain. Sorry for him, suddenly seeing the child in the man, Suzy kissed the top of his head, then left the room. She put on a light jacket, climbed into her car and headed for Des Moines.

It was the middle of the afternoon and the sun was a fiery ball, its light dazzling where it fell on the fields that had turned brown and barren. Suzy felt drained just driving, suffocated by lack of air, but luckily the dust churned up by the the car was blown out behind her. She was glad to get to Des Moines, even though, once verdant, it was now as barren as the fields of maize. She drove straight to the Court Avenue District to park near the office towers. From there, she walked through the busy skywalk system and on to Joe's bar, located amongst the restored vintage buildings, art galleries, restaurants and fancy shops of this formerly bustling entertainment district.

Since the drought, people were spending a lot less and the area was already starting to look seedy.

When she entered Joe's cozy, colonial-styled bar, Suzy was glad to feel the cool air-conditioning. Most of the tables were empty, as they usually were these days, but a few men were strung along the bar and Joe was there, cleaning glasses. He looked pretty cool.

He smiled when he saw her, so she smiled back and took a stool at the far end of the bar, well away from the customers. Joe poured her a bourbon on the rocks and brought it along to her.

'You look like a million dollars,' he said. 'The prettiest woman in here. So have one on the house.'

Suzy, the only woman in the bar, smiled and picked up her glass of bourbon and tilted it towards him. 'Here's looking at you,' she said before taking a sip.

'I wasn't expectin' to see you today,' Joe said. 'Anything happening?'

Suzy shrugged. 'No,' she said, lighting a cigarette, 'I just had to get out. My Dad's been to the bank and started drinking beer from the bottle. It's not a good sign.'

'You weren't expectin' good news.'

'But we live in hope, Joe. He's been told that he has to sell the farm, but he swears he won't do it.'

'Give him time to adjust,' Joe advised her. 'He'll face up to it soon enough. It's happenin' all over the damned place – they're sellin' up, moving out. He musta seen a lot've his friends goin', so he isn't alone at least.'

'He's lived there all his life.'

'So did most of the others.'

'I think his heart's broken already.'

'Broken hearts can be mended.'

There was a sudden roaring sound from the TV above the bar and they both looked up and saw torrential rainfall over most of southern Spain. People were sitting on red-tiled roof-tops, on the walls of Moorish villas, looking down at the water sweeping under them, carrying furniture and clothes and other personal belongings, even people spinning slowly on make-shift rafts and rubber dinghys, through streets that had once been dry as bone. Then the scene changed abruptly from howling wind and pouring rain to burning heat and parched farmlands, showing Americans piling their furniture onto trucks and moving out onto the dusty roads. Wiped out by the drought, they were leaving their farms and heading for the cities, desperately hoping to find work.

'Turn that shit off,' a man along the bar said. He was wearing muddy dungarees and had a burnt face and a weathered hat resting beside his beer-glass. 'I came in here to pick myself up,' he said. 'Not to be reminded of why I'm drinking at three o'clock in the afternoon. Turn it off, Joe, goddammit.'

'Sure,' Joe said. 'I'm sorry.' He turned off the TV and no one else complained. 'The farm he worked on's just closed,' Joe explained. 'He'll have to hit the road soon. No family, no more work in this area, and he's fifty-eight years old. Hard times ahead, right?'

'Goddamn!' Suzy said. She finished her bourbon, pushed the glass towards Joe, and said, '*I'm* drinking at three in the afternoon, and now I know why. Fill 'er up, Joe.'

Joe grinned and filled up the glass. She blew smoke rings of different sizes and watched them drifting away.

'Strange times,' Joe said, maybe just to fill the silence. 'Hot places turnin' cold, cold places turnin' hot, and here, in Iowa, the bread-basket of America, the land's turnin' into a dust bowl. Folks are sellin' up and takin' to the road just like they did back in the 'Thirties. We're right back with the Okies.'

'But it ain't the 'Thirties,' Suzy said. 'It seems like it, but it ain't. You know that when you turn on the TV and switch through the channels you'll always come, sure as Jesus, to a programme about the increase in UFO sightings, apparitions and other weird happenings. 'Course, officially they're denied, but the reports can't be stopped and are comin' in from all over the world. You didn't get *that* in the 'Thirties, Joe, and I think it's real weird.'

'Yeah,' Joe said, 'it is.' He gave her that grin that

219

could make her glow inside. 'There's even talk of airline pilots startin' to see things – strange lights in the sky, flying saucers and so on – though most of the reports aren't made official. But I hear things – pick 'em up in this bar – and lotsa folks are havin' lotsa strange experiences. I put it down to this weather, which can drive some folks crazy, and to the fact that the land's bein' wiped out, with all that entails. Folks are under terrific pressure, feelin' haunted, and so they start seein' things.'

'What about you, Joe?'

He shrugged and grinned again. 'I'm suffering a little bit – business ain't as brisk as usual – but so far the only visions I have are of you in my bed. Real pity I'm working right now. You sure do look inviting.'

Suzy glowed inside again. He could always make her do that. In fact, the longer she stayed away from Rydell, the more she needed that feeling. Joe had been good for her, making her feel alive again, and she'd even started thinking of moving in with him and bringing the kids here. He'd be good for them, she felt. He had the kind of strength they needed. He wasn't chaotic and unreliable like Rydell, and he obviously loved her. And now, with the blight on her parents' farm, there were other reasons for staying.

'Hey, Joe,' she said, feeling pretty drunk, 'just how much do you love me?'

'You've had more than one demonstration,' he told her, 'so you've no need to ask.'

'No, I don't mean that. I don't mean sex. I mean, how much do you *love* me?'

'One whole heap, honey,' he said pouring himself a beer.

'What's one whole heap, Joe?'

'You want me, I'm yours.'

'How much?'

'Whatya mean?'

'I sometimes think we should live together, Joe. It's not right, bein' apart like this.'

'You mean married? You're already married.'

'I just mean livin' together, Joe. I mean, just to get closer to each other . . . to give it a try.'

He had another gulp of beer and played with the glass.

'I dunno, Suzy,' he said. 'Why spoil a good thing? I mean, we got a pretty good thing goin' here, so why risk it with that?'

'With what? Livin' together?'

'Yeah, Suzy, I guess. I mean, lovin' is one thing, but livin' together is another. I've been livin' on my own a long time an' I'm kinda fixed in my ways. You know? A man gets like that . . .' He trailed off in an uncertain manner, slugged more beer to cover his confusion, then offered a crooked, nervous grin. 'Besides,' he said, 'sooner or later, you'll go back to Maryland, to your husband and kids. I don't see the point, Suzy.'

Even drunk, Suzy started to feel as nervous as Joe looked. It almost sobered her up.

'That's the *whole* point,' she said. 'I'd only go back for the kids. And instead of doing that, why not bring 'em back here? Then you and I can stay together. You understand what I'm saying, Joe?'

He finished off his beer, then went to pour himself another. When he came back, he didn't look too thrilled and his gaze was evasive.

'Listen, Suzy,' he said.

'Yeah?'

'I love you one whole heap, you know that . . . But this thing, this business with the kids . . . Well, I mean, I don't know . . . I mean, I've never been married, Suzie. That's a whole different ball game. And livin' together, well, that's marriage, no two ways about it. So

221

there's that and the kids. I mean, OK, they might be nice kids . . . But a man like me, never bin married, might find some problems there. You're talkin' responsibility, Suzy. A whole heap of it as well. You're talkin' a really big commitment for kids not my own . . . I dunno, Suzy. I mean, I won't say "No" outright. I'm only sayin' that it needs a lot of thought and a lotta time for the thinkin'. I mean, a man has his ways, you know?'

'You don't want my kids.'

'I didn't say that, Suzy, no.'

'So what if I say, forget about the kids, let's just you and I share things?'

She saw that she really had him rattled and wanted to die. He drank more beer and caressed the glass.

'Gee, Suzie,' he began. He sounded just like a goddamned school kid. 'I love you . . .'

'A whole heap.'

'Right! But lovin' and livin' together are two different things and . . . You know, you've bin married – *are* married – and can deal with certain things; but I've never shared anything with anyone, nor had kids or anything, so, you know, I'm not sure if I could look after them properly or . . .'

'I've got parents as well,' Suzy said. 'You know all about them, don't you? They're gonna lose their farm and everything that gives them dignity and have to do an awful lot of things that they're not used to doing. In short, they're gonna need my help and I'll need yours to help them.'

'Yeah,' he said. 'Right. I mean, I understand that, Suzy. It's just that I don't know that I'm equipped to deal with . . .'

'Yeah,' she said. 'I understand perfectly. Goodbye Joe, and good luck. After I've made my wishes you're going to need that luck. You're going to need it

222

because I'm going to curse you to hell and back. Go fuck yourself, Joe.'

Then she walked from the bar.

She couldn't stop crying and drove the car while blind with tears. She drove across the Des Moines River as the sun was going down, her heart hammering with outrage, the shock making her sweat more, and headed into the dust-wreathed, crimson twilight in a state of dreadful despair. She was angry, disappointed, disgusted and pained, and felt like a victim of her own vain, childish hopes.

Rydell would never have responded that way. You had to give it to him – he wouldn't have done it. Rydell, no matter what his private fears, would have stood up and been counted. He'd have proved his love not eloquently, but with sincerity. He wouldn't have wriggled like a worm on a hook, with his eyes slipping sideways. You had to give it to him: despite his faults, he rose above them. Yes, Rydell, who had almost driven her crazy, had never failed her that much.

And that's why she still loved him.

She cried more when she thought of that. Damned near went off the road. The sun was sinking and the fields of maize were ruined and the crimson light looked unreal. Maybe that explained why she thought she saw her children, Don and Ronnie suddenly standing there in the headlights of her car as she raced straight towards them.

'*God, no!*' she screamed.

There was no time to brake. She was through them in a second. They were there, plain as day, then she shot through them and saw only the road again.

She couldn't believe it, but when she looked in the mirror she saw a disc-shaped light flying over the rolling hills. It was a dazzling, silvery plate, gliding beautifully in the crimson twilight. It flew from the horizon and ascended as it approached, passing over the car like a flickering lightbulb, before it disappeared.

Suzy almost crashed. Afterwards she didn't remember much about it. Screaming brakes and a howling engine. Billowing dust and her own pounding heart as the car groaned and settled down. When it was still, and when the swirling dust had settled, she looked out at the sinking sun.

Nothing there but the parched fields. No Don and Ronnie, no flying saucer. Nothing out there except the rolling plains and sky and a darkening, sinking sun.

Suzy was terrified. *It's just shock*, she thought. She rationalized that she'd been upset, thinking of Rydell and the kids, and that the tension caused by Joe, as well as the news on his TV, had caused her to conjure up that experience as some kind of catharsis.

It didn't stop the pounding of her heart, but she drove on home anyway.

She was concerned for her parents.

224

# CHAPTER TWENTY-FIVE

'Clare seems to be settling in well,' Collins said, as he drove out of his driveway, just around the corner from Rydell's house. 'In fact, she seems to be blossoming. I just couldn't imagine her living here – not in Greenbelt, not in a tract house, and not with you and your mother and kids – after the life she used to lead in Georgetown. Yet it seems to be working.'

'That's 'cause I'm a really swell guy,' Rydell replied, as the car turned into the Greenbelt Road. 'You just never saw it, Dwight.'

Dwight grinned. 'I guess not. But I'm *still* damned surprised.'

'Pleasantly so, I hope.'

'Absolutely. Clare's not only been good for you – she also seems to have tamed your kids and kept Grandma in order. She should get an award.'

That was true enough, Rydell thought. In the month that Clare had been living with him in Greenbelt, she had not only managed to put the house in order – even his records were in their sleeves – but had charmed his two kids into some kind of discipline, as well as winning his mother over. What was most surprising about it all, was that she had brought into his life an order that had never been enforced when he had shared it with Suzy. Now, the house was tidy and clean, the boys were better behaved, and Grandma was so taken in with her new 'daughter' that when Rydell and Clare had to leave home together for a few days she willingly looked after the kids.

'It's still exhausting,' she would say to Rydell, 'but not as bad as it was before. And besides, I don't mind if it's for Clare. She's worth her weight in gold, that one.'

'Why didn't Clare come with us this morning?' Collins asked, as he drove past the fences of the Goddard Space Flight Centre in the rolling Maryland countryside. 'I asked her to come.'

'You asked her too late,' Rydell replied, squinting into the sun and realizing that they were in for another uncomfortably hot day. 'She's already there, Dwight. But she's in the Laboratory for Extraterrestrial Physics, checking on the progress of the balloons that were sent up into the hole from the base at McMurdo Sound.'

'Any results yet?'

'They're analyzing them right now. That's why Clare's there so early. She's like a mother with her new-born baby; she just won't let it go.'

'She's the NASA type,' Collins said with undisguised admiration. 'A woman who loves her work and is relentlessly thorough at what she does. That's why she became one of the first of the female astronauts and ended up liaising between us and the White House – she has the skill *and* the gumption. I just hope that her new domestic situation with you doesn't make her lose that.'

'I don't think it will, Dwight.'

Still, as Collins turned the car through the guarded gates and into the sprawling complex of NASA's Goddard Space Flight Centre, Rydell couldn't help wondering if he was right. Like him, Clare loved her work and could not live without it, and although superficially she appeared to have adjusted to her new life in Greenbelt, he wondered how long it would be before the trials and tribulations of domesticity took their toll on her.

At the moment, she seemed happy, intrigued by the novelty of being a surrogate mother and housekeeper, but right now she was excited about the ozone project. What would happen, Rydell wondered, if that project came to an end and she was given time to dwell on the difference between her past life in swanky Georgetown, Washington DC, and the more humble suburbs of Greenbelt? It made him nervous to think of it.

'Another day, another dollar,' Collins said, parking the car in front of the Institute for Space Studies. 'Let's go, Rydell.'

As he climbed out of the car, Rydell noticed how hot and bright it was.

'Christ, the weather really *is* getting warmer.'

'Right,' Collins replied. 'And if we don't stop that hole in the ozone from growing, it's gonna get warmer and warmer, until . . .' He shrugged his shoulders helplessly.

'The ice-caps start melting,' Rydell completed his sentence for him. 'Which they're *already* doing.'

'You're kidding!'

'No, I'm not. Jack Douglas recently sent Clare a report from the Laboratory of Oceans, which states that their most recent experiment has revealed a slight rise in the sea-level of the South Atlantic Ocean. This is already spreading to other seas and oceans, which explains the rise of many rivers and the dramatic changes of weather around the globe, and it'll get worse as the ice-caps continue to melt.'

'Jesus Christ,' Collins said. 'It's happening quicker than I'd expected.'

'Exactly,' Rydell said, glancing at the people in the offices they passed. 'According to our climatic model's calculations, by the year 2030, we were expecting the equivalent of a two-hundred percent increase in carbon dioxide, inducing a global warming of between 1.5 and 4.5. degrees Centigrade, which would mean a catastrophic drying of the world's chief wheat and corn belts, as well as sea-level rises of between twenty and forty centimetres, eventually leading to the flooding of major land masses. However, with the present, unexpected rate of ozone depletion, all of this has already started and, at the rate it's progressing, should lop about thirty years, or even more, off our estimate.'

'*How* much?'

'You heard me. Based on the hole in the Antarctic alone – in other words, ignoring any other possible areas of depletion – we can expect even more damaging climatic changes within the next decade – say, by the year 2,000.'

Collins stopped walking and stared at him in shock.

'Did you say those calculations hadn't taken into account any other areas of ozone-depletion?'

'Right.'

'Shit!' Collins exclaimed softly, then shook his head from side to side in despair. 'You're in for an interesting morning,' he said as he entered his office. 'You better believe it. Here, take this chair.' He pulled a chair up to his desk, and when Rydell was seated offered him a coffee.

'Sounds like I might need it,' Rydell said.

'With some Valium, old buddy.' Using the intercom on his desk, Collins asked his secretary to bring in Captain Mantell, along with three cups of coffee.

'Who's Captain Mantell?' Rydell asked.

'A USAF pilot from the Wallops Flight Facility in Virginia, recently returned from a tour at our base in Thule, Greenland. He was sent home after ejecting himself from his aircraft during a research flight across the North Pole. I'll let him tell you the rest.'

He was just about to kick his chair back and swing his

feet onto the desk when the telephone rang. Picking it up, he listened a moment, then grinned and said, 'Hi, Clare! Yeah, he's with me right now. Why not speak to me instead of him? I'm a much better listener.' He listened to the response, grinned more widely and passed the phone to Rydell. 'She wants only you, handsome.'

Rydell took the phone. 'Hi,' he said. 'Where are you?'

'Right now I'm in the Science Information Systems Centre,' she told him, her voice business-like, 'assessing the data we received from the balloon payloads in the Antarctic experiment sent up from McMurdo Sound last week. You should see this place,' she continued, as excited as a little girl. 'It has a state-of-the-art Image Analysis Facility that provides access to the ultrafast MPP, or Massively Parallel Processor to ignoramuses like you. The MPP combines the power of 16,384 small processors, which should make you jealous.'

'I am,' Rydell replied honestly. 'So what are you *doing*?'

'Well,' she said, still excited, 'among other things, the MPP is capable of making numerical simulations of complex physical and biological processes. We fed the data received from the Wallops Flight Facility Antarctic Balloon Experiment into it. The balloons' payloads took external readings both at the top and the bottom of the hole in the ozone layer. The data was then interfaced to the Information Processing Division of NASA for processing and evaluation by the Laboratory for High Energy Physics, which concentrated on the origin and structure of any particles, electronic or otherwise; the Laboratory for Atmospheres, which focused on the ozone balance of the stratosphere; and the Laboratory for Extraterrestrial Physics, which looked for charged particles, magnetic and electric fields, and plasmas. The separate findings of those three laboratories were then passed on to the SISC, right here, where the numerical simulations of data produced what may be the answer.'

'Which is?' Rydell couldn't hide his impatience.

'What we appear to be dealing with,' Clare said in a suddenly quiet, deliberately controlled manner, 'is something that isn't organic or carbon-based, but *is* alive in some way or another.'

'Jesus,' Rydell whispered.

'We're talking about plasmodes,' Clare said, ignoring his interjection. 'The analyzed payloads have produced what appears to be some kind of organized motion of plasmodes created by the interaction of electrons and ions. We've defined the plasmodes as being alive in the sense that they appear to have a definite structure, are feeding on the energy of the stratosphere and atmosphere and are constantly reproducing by magnetically converting random particle clusters into non-random ones. In other words, the basic trinity of life – structure, feeding and reproduction. Whatever it is, it's alive, feeding off the ozone layer and other elements in the atmosphere and stratosphere, and constantly reproducing its own kind . . . It's alive and *growing*!'

Rydell couldn't believe his ears unsure of whether he should feel exhilarated or terrified. An alien life-form . . . It was there, above Earth . . . And it was growing as it travelled down through the atmosphere to . . .

'Are you still there or have you fainted?' Clare asked.

'I'm still here,' he replied.

'A bit of a shock, eh?'

'Yeah, Clare, a bit of a shock. I don't know what to say.'

'I don't blame you. We don't yet know if it's conscious or self-aware, though we *are* inclined to believe that it's been dormant for a long time, is gradually coming awake, or back to life, and is responsible for the hallucinations being created inside the ozone hole.'

'How?'

Clare sighed. 'I don't know. No one knows. We only know what we've seen: that it manifests lifelike images from the individual's subconscious. Whether or not it actually *knows* what it's doing, we can't say. We can only say with certainty that it's alive.'

'Christ!' Rydell exclaimed.

At that moment, Connor's secretary ushered into the office a well-muscled man in a short-sleeved white shirt and pants. With his short-cropped brown hair, he looked every inch a pilot, but was oddly tentative in his movements, as if uneasy. He smiled painfully at Collins and took the chair beside Rydell.

'I've got to go now,' Rydell said to Clare, 'but thanks for the phone call. I'm pretty shaken, as you might expect, but it sure was worth hearing. I'll see you tonight.'

'OK. Love you madly.'

He hung up on her sweet voice as Connor's secretary, the good-humoured and efficient Joanne Woods, brought three coffees into the office and set them on the desk.

'Rydell,' Collins said, indicating the man in the other chair, 'this is Captain Joe Mantell, the USAF pilot I mentioned. Joe, this is Tony Rydell, one of our best physicists. I think he'll find your story pretty intriguing. Do you mind repeating it again?'

'No, not at all.' Mantell stood up to shake Rydell's hand. He was tall and very broad, yet oddly lacking in vigour. 'Hi,' he said. 'I've heard a lot about you and it makes me feel better.'

'*Feel* better? Why?'

'Because you're taking this business seriously. When this business happened, I thought I was hallucinating or had gone mad. When it was over, when I was making my report in the debriefing room at the base in Thule, I thought *they* would think I'd gone mad and they probably did. So, you know, it's a relief to know I'm not alone. I mean, it makes me feel better.'

Rydell offered Mantell a coffee but the man said he was too nervous to drink.

'You don't look the nervous type.'

'I wasn't; at least not until this business happened. Now, shit, yes, I'm nervous. Night and day. Every hour. I can't go back in an aeroplane. Jesus, man, it was awful.'

Rydell put his cup back on the desk. 'So what happened?' he asked.

'I've told this story so much, I . . .'

'Just tell me.'

Mantell shrugged forlornly. 'OK,' he said. 'I've been a pilot with the Wallops Flight Facility for years, specializing in payload-carrying flights for upper atmospheric research, most of them across the Arctic Circle from our base in Thule, Greenland. I was good at my job, right? Very experienced. No hassles. Then, last week, when I was flying my customary research version of the ER-2 which I believe you're familiar with —'

'Right,' Rydell said.

Mantell nodded mournfully. 'OK. So when I was flying my ER-2 across the Arctic Circle, passing over Lincoln Sea, heading towards the North Pole, at an altitude of fifteen kilometres, I suddenly felt very strange, disorientated, then saw an unidentified flying object.'

'A flying saucer?'

'Well . . .'

'You can tell me.'

'Well . . . I wouldn't say it was a flying saucer, exactly.

232

More of a brilliant light, a sort of shimmering, pulsating light, that spread out around the aeroplane, filling my cabin until I couldn't see a goddamned thing – not the instrument panel, not my own hands or legs – apart from this dazzling light.'

'Any sound?' Collins prompted him.

'Yeah, right, sound . . .' Mantell grew nervous, just remembering . . . 'Most sounds were cut off when the light appeared, leaving nothing but what seemed like static. I tried to contact Thule and got nothing but more static. The light became so bright, I couldn't see the control panel, and the static seemed to fill my goddamned head until I wanted to scream.'

'It was *static*?' Rydell asked him.

'Sort of,' Mantell replied. 'I mean, it *sounded* like static at first. Then it got louder, too loud to be real, and seemed to be something inside my head . . . a *collision* of sounds, maybe voices . . . I don't know. It was just this godawful, fucking noise that nearly drove me insane . . . So I took the plane down to my lowest recommended altitude of twelve kilometres, hoping for peace and quiet . . .'

Mantell glanced left and right, as if being spied upon, then wiped sweat from his forehead with his hand and took a deep breath. He was dissolving in sunlight.

'I had a brother,' he said. 'We were real competitive as kids. Our Dad was a USAF pilot and we wanted to be the same, but I was the one with the talent, so my brother lost out. When I got my wings, he started drinking. His career and marriage were a disaster. The better my life became, the worse his became, and eventually, when he was still only twenty-eight, he committed suicide.' Mantell took a deep breath before continuing. He seemed like a lost child. 'I was haunted by that for years,' he said. 'I secretly blamed myself. I often dreamed about my brother, was haunted by him . . . and then, in that strange light in the ER-2, my brother materialized . . .'

He stopped talking and stared up at Rydell. He had the gaze of a drowning man.

'Go on,' Rydell said firmly.

Mantell shrugged. 'It was goddamned awful. He was so real I could smell him. He was sweating and I heard his heavy breathing. He even reached out and touched me.' Mantell shuddered. 'I *felt* his touch. There's no doubt about that. I felt him and smelt him and heard him and then lost my self-control. Jesus, yes, I just lost it . . .'

He shuddered again and pressed his fingers to his eyes, as if trying to blind himself.

'I couldn't stand it,' he said. 'I knew that the heavy breathing I was hearing was the sound of his dying breath. He had killed himself over me, and I knew that I was hearing his accusation in the sound of him dying. He died – he dissolved as the aeroplane nosedived – and I nearly went mad . . .' He let out a stricken sob. 'I ejected from the plane,' he said. 'I shouldn't have done it, but I had to. I just couldn't bear staying in that cabin, reliving my brother's death, so I ejected and had to be rescued.' He wiped the tears from his eyes, shook his head, then sniffed and looked up again. 'In that moment,' he said, 'I destroyed my career. I'll never fly again . . . *Never!*'

'Yes, you will,' Rydell lied.

Mantell smiled, grateful for the lie, then stood up wearily and placed a heavy hand on Rydell's shoulder.

'No,' he insisted, looking down. 'I won't fly again and we both know it. But I want you to keep pursuing this thing and find out what's happening. Whatever happened to me, whatever's causing this, it can't be good for the country, the world. There's something up there, Rydell, and it's like nothing else. Please find out what it is.'

'Yes,' Rydell said. 'Thanks.'

Mantell nodded and hurried out, as if running away from a nightmare, then Rydell looked across Collins' desk and met his cautious gaze.

'It didn't happen in the Antarctic,' Collins reminded him. 'This one took place over the Arctic at a very low altitude.'

'Yeah,' Rydell said, sweating though cold. 'As Clare said, it's alive and it's growing. What the hell do we do now?'

'We pray,' Collins said.

# CHAPTER TWENTY-SIX

'I don't want you to go,' Clare insisted as Rydell kissed her goodbye on the doorstop.

'Stop worrying,' Rydell said. 'It's business, pure and simple. I wanna check on her apparition and discuss the divorce. So it's purely business; personal as well as NASA. Besides, she called and insisted on seeing me, so maybe *she* wants a divorce, which would solve a lot of the problems I see looming. So I'm going. OK?'

Clare puffed her cheeks out and sighed. 'OK,' she said. 'But don't linger if she starts coming on to you. Just get out that door again.'

He grinned. 'Goddammit! Clare Holton, the fierce pragmatist, is jealous. I just don't believe it!'

Clare smiled and lowered her head in shame. 'Neither do I,' she said.

Knocked out by her grace and beauty, Rydell kissed her again, before driving off. She waved from the doorstep until he was out of sight.

According to what Suzy had told him when she called, she was still living with her folks in Iowa, they weren't doing too well, and she had flown to Maryland to talk to him about 'something important.' When Rydell had pressed her on exactly what that meant, she had refused to elaborate, saying only that she wanted to talk on neutral territory, rather than the house. She was spending her three days in Maryland at the Annapolis home of her best friend, Caroline Blackwood, but she and Rydell were going to meet in a bar in the town.

Since he was in love with Clare, Rydell was hoping that Suzy was seriously involved with Joe Wheeler and going to ask for the divorce he now believed *he* wanted. However, he sensed that the meeting wasn't going to be that easy, and that he'd be faced with more angry demands about the kids returning with her to Iowa, which he wasn't prepared to allow. Separations were such a messy and exhausting business, and he sighed in anticipation of more unpleasantness.

When he reached Annapolis, he parked his car down by the waterfront. As he walked through the hot, blinding sunlight towards McCarvey's Saloon & Oyster Bar, where he was to meet Suzy, he thought of her ghost, or doppelgänger, and wondered who or *what* to expect when he walked into the restaurant. Perhaps the Suzy he was going to see might not be the real one.

In the event, she was real enough, waving at him from the bar, her blonde hair framing a face still sensually provocative. The loose white T-shirt she was wearing gave a hint of her full breasts beneath. Tight denims and stilettoes emphasized her long legs. She looked, he thought, like a saucy teenager. He had forgotten how cute she could look.

Slightly shaken to find that he still had strong feelings for her, he returned her wave as he approached the bar, aware that more than one set of eyes was studying him enviously. When he reached her, she turned her head aside to blow a thin stream of smoke.

'Still smoking,' he observed.

'My only vice,' she replied. 'Right now, I'm as pure as a nun, which should make you happy.'

Rydell, taking the stool beside her, almost kissed her but changed his mind. 'It doesn't make me anything,' he said, then glanced at her empty glass. 'What are you drinking?'

'Bourbon on the rocks.'

'It's only lunchtime.'

'I'm obviously a born liar,' she said. 'You've just discovered my second vice.'

She looked at him with bright eyes, her smile mocking, as he ordered more drinks: a bourbon on the rocks for her, a beer for him.

'You wanna eat?' he asked her.

'Can we afford it?' she replied.

'There's no "we" anymore, Suzy, just you and me; and at the moment I can afford to buy lunch.'

'You think I called you just to discuss money?'

'Yeah.'

'You're a real bright boy, Tony,' Suzy quipped in a wounded tone which made him ashamed of what he had said. Disconcerted, ambushed by his past, he glanced along the busy bar, and saw business men and sailors rubbing elbows at the counter, eating oysters or eggs Benedict, drinking bourbon or beer.

'A busy joint,' he said, returning his gaze to Suzy's face.

'Yeah,' she replied. 'I like it 'cause it's friendly and informal. We used to come here a lot.'

'Who?'

'You and me, Tony. Remember? We used to come here at least once a month and take a boat out. We both loved to do that.'

'Oh, yeah,' he said with embarrassment.

'I'm staying with Caroline.'

'Yeah.' He knew Caroline well since it was with her and her husband, Ron, that he and Suzy had spent so many weekends here. 'I haven't seen her or Ron for a long time. How are they doing?'

'They're fine. They send their regards. They said you should come see them sometime and not mind about us.'

'Terrific. I'll do that. So what made you decide to stay

in Annapolis?'

'I just wanted a little break . . . Have a friend to talk to . . . See water after the parched plains and rusting tractors of Iowa.'

'Things are bad there, eh?'

'Yeah. Real bad. My folks' farm is done for. The bank's trying to force my Dad to sell but he insists that he won't.'

'He was always a stubborn man.'

'It runs in the family.'

'Yeah,' Rydell said. 'I guess it does, Suzy. Still shacked up with Joe Wheeler, are you?'

He regretted the remark immediately, though she didn't seem too offended.

'I was never *shacked up* with him, Tony. We just met occasionally. It was good while it lasted, but it's finished.'

'Why?'

She shrugged and blew a few smoke rings, watching them drift away from her. 'Something happened that made me think a lot less of him. I was real disappointed.'

'That guy was all muscle and no brains. He never had any class.'

'I've never been very bright when it comes to men,' Suzy admitted. 'After all, I married *you*.'

Rydell had to grin at that. He felt surprisingly affectionate towards her. 'So, do you want to eat or not?' he asked.

'Not really.'

Rydell nodded. 'It's too early for me as well.' The barman brought their drinks and Rydell tipped him well. 'Anyway,' he continued, feeling benevolent, 'it's good to see you. You're looking great, Suzy.'

'You're looking pretty well-looked-after yourself,' she said. 'She must be taking good care of you.'

'Who?'

'The woman you've moved into our home.'

239

'How did you know about that?'

'The kids and I talk on the phone,' she said, 'and they think she's a knock-out, though it chokes me to say that.'

'Don't choke, Suzy. Have a drink instead. Here's to the future.' He held up his glass as he proposed the toast. 'Jesus,' he said, licking his lips, 'I sure do like my beer. So what do you want, Sue?'

'You know I hate being called that.'

'OK, Suzy, I'm here and I'm waiting. What do you want?'

'I want to know if you miss me.'

He was taken aback by that. 'Miss you?' he said. 'Why do you ask me that?'

'Why do you think?'

'You're suddenly bored with your freedom?'

'You really demand your pound of flesh, don't you? Don't look so smug, Tony.'

'I'm not looking smug and I certainly don't feel it. I just want to know why you're suddenly so concerned about whether or not you've been missed.'

'I'm not concerned,' she said. 'I'm just curious. I always felt that *you* were never that concerned, and so, you know, I just wondered. Not that I should have asked. The fact that you've moved some bitch into the house is all the answer I need.'

'She isn't a bitch.'

'She's in my house with my kids.'

'You left both of your own accord,' Rydell said, 'so you can't complain too much.' He quickly changed the subject when he saw her cheeks flush with anger. 'What I wanted to ask you is if you had any *special* reason for suddenly wanting to know if I'd missed you. I mean, apart from the trouble with the farm, are things going OK?'

She shrugged, and sipped her bourbon, keeping her

eyes on the glass. 'Not bad,' she said. 'I mean, I get a bit lonely sometimes. I miss the kids. I even miss you, dammit. So a lotta times I wanted to come back, but couldn't do it, you know? Woman's pride and all.'

'Yeah, Suzy, I know.'

'Anyway, I couldn't do it. I wanted to, but I couldn't. Then Don told me on the 'phone that you had this other woman livin' in the house, and I figured there wasn't a chance of my coming home.'

'No,' Rydell said, 'there isn't.'

Suzy nodded solemnly. 'Yeah, I understand. Anyway, knowing that, I went and got myself a job – I serve in a diner in Des Moines – and that helped me feel better. I mean, it may not be much, but it's something. It helps me and my folks.'

'If I can help you with money . . .'

'No, I didn't come here for that . . .' Her voice trailed off nervously.

'I wanna ask you something,' Rydell said. 'Since you left me, have you ever felt strange in any way? Have you *seen* or *felt* anything strange? Have you had *any* kind of experience that seemed weird or mysterious?'

'Whatd'ya mean?'

'Ever feel . . .?' He hesitated, hardly knowing how to phrase it, searching for the right word. '*Haunted*?' he tried.

She stared solemnly at him for a moment, then burst into laughter. 'Haunted?' she finally said. 'What way do you mean? By the memory of you, or what?'

'No,' he said, realizing how stupid he sounded. 'I'm not suggesting you couldn't forget me. I mean haunted in the proper meaning of the word. Did you *see* or *sense* anything weird or even unusual?'

Suzy stubbed out her cigarette, her brow furrowed in thought. 'You know, there *was* something funny, come to think of it. As you probably know, there *have* been a lot of reports of people in Iowa seeing strange things like flying saucers and ghostly figures.'

'I read about it, yeah.'

'Well . . .' She hesitated, feeling foolish. 'The day I broke up with Joe Wheeler, when I was all upset and driving from his bar in Des Moines back to our farm, I had this sudden vision of Don and Ronnie standing together in the road right in front of my car. It was a real vivid vision. I nearly fainted when I saw them 'cause I didn't have time to brake and had to drive straight into them. I went *through* them, and they disappeared. Shit, I was scared!'

'Anything else?' Rydell asked.

'Yeah,' she said. 'That's what made it even stranger . . . there *was* something else . . .' She had another sip of her bourbon, to steady her nerves. 'Immediately after that I saw what looked like a flying saucer coming at me from the east at a terrific speed. It shot across the car, right above me, then disappeared like the kids. It was so real, I went into a skid and almost shot off the road. When I stopped, my heart was poundin', I can tell you. I was so scared, I couldn't breathe. When I'd recovered, I looked around, but I couldn't see anything unusual, so I just started the car and drove on home. I've seen nothing since then.'

Recalling Clare's contention that the alien virus could be manifesting lifelike images from the subconscious of the individual, Rydell asked, 'And this occurred immediately after you'd broken off with Joe Wheeler?'

'Right. I mean, the word around Des Moines is that a lot of the so-called visions are due to the anxieties and traumas caused by the destruction of the land — troubled people see things . . . Anyway, I'll tell you, that might have been the case with me, 'cause when I broke off with Joe that day, it was over our kids. He'd made it clear that he wasn't interested in looking after them or my folks so I'd been thinking of Don and Ronnie before I had the vision of them.'

'That could make sense,' Rydell said. He was secretly delighted that Wheeler hadn't wanted to look after his kids, disturbed that Suzy had considered the idea. 'But it doesn't explain your sighting of a flying saucer, or UFO.'

'Well, it might,' Suzy said thoughtfully. 'I mean, earlier that same day, when my Dad had returned from the bank with bad news, we were all feeling real low. I sat watching TV, and saw a programme about the increasing incidence of flying saucer sightings and other strange happenings. So, there was that on my mind . . . Then, when I went to see Joe in his bar in Des Moines, we discussed the very same subject before we discussed my kids.'

'Did you ever feel anything odd regarding yourself?'

'What d'ya mean?'

'I mean, did you ever get the feeling that you were somewhere else? Or that there were two of you and *one* of you was somewhere else?'

'Of course not. That's crazy!'

'Are you sure?'

'Absolutely!'

Satisfied that she had been in no way connected to the apparition he had seen in the ER-2 and that it had therefore been released from his subconscious, Rydell decided to steer the subject back to more immediate concerns.

'I'm enjoying this little reunion,' he said, trying to sound more unconcerned than he felt, 'but I'll really have to be going soon, so what did you want?'

'I want my kids,' she told him. 'Since I can't come home again, I want the kids to come with me to Iowa. They'll be better off with me and also good for my

243

parents. And besides, I don't want them being brought up by that woman of yours.'

'You've no right to ask for the kids back when it was you who walked out.'

'I didn't intend leaving them for good. I just had to be alone for a while, to sort myself out. I was feeling sorta bruised, hurt that you'd ignored my threat to leave, and I wanted to think about that before definitely deciding what I should do. Since that woman's in my house, I want you to give the kids to me, to live in Iowa.'

'You've just told me that your folks' farm is finished, so where will my kids live?'

'When we sell the farm to pay the debts, we should have enough left to buy a small house near Des Moines. I've already got a job, my Dad can maybe get something else, and the kids will at least have their real mother.'

'Some mother!' Rydell said.

'*I* was fine,' Suzy retorted. 'The problem was you ignoring me.'

'Iowa's gonna be wiped off the map,' Rydell said. 'I'm not sending my kids there.'

'It's not that bad, Tony. It's only the farms. Des Moines is still OK with good schools and universities and lots for the kids to do.'

'I'm sorry Suzy, you can't have 'em. They're both doing fine here. And besides, you're bound to end up with another boyfriend. Let's not forget that.'

'So what? A woman's entitled to her relationships. It's not gonna do the kids any harm to see me with another man. And after all, you've got that woman in our house!'

'You gotta be joking!' he exclaimed, feeling genuinely affronted.

'What d'ya mean?'

'I pass my kids over to be looked after by you and your goddamned boyfriends? I won't buy that,' he said. 'You must think I'm crazy. You walked out on us, Suzy, leaving nothing but a lot of problems, but now the kids are happy again – they think Clare's great – and you want me to start the disruption all over again? No way, Suzy! No chance! I've got to be going.'

Rydell started walking out of the bar, but she slid off her stool and followed him, catching him just as he stepped outside, into the blinding light.

'Hey, wait a minute,' she said, jerking him around by his shoulder to face her. 'Those are *my* kids, goddammit, and I still love them and want to care for them.'

That took his breath away. He saw the truth in it, but chose to ignore it. 'You're not going to get the kids back, Suzy, and that's all there is to it.'

She looked hurt and angry, which made him feel guilty.

'If I don't,' she said, 'I'll make your life a goddamned misery. I'll file for divorce and I'll fight for money, and if nothing else, I'll bury you in legalities that'll drive you insane.'

'You wanna see the kids?' Rydell taunted. 'Come see them, but you *won't* get them back. I'll see you around, Sue.'

As Rydell drove away, he couldn't resist the urge to look back and saw Suzy, her shoulders slumped forlornly, dissolving in silvery light.

It was as hot as hell out there.

# PART THREE

# CHAPTER TWENTY-SEVEN

'He's only been gone a week and I miss him already,' Clare confessed to Dwight Collins as they had drinks around Rydell's garden table. 'He's more of a nuisance than he's worth, but dammit, I miss him.'

'I don't,' Grandma insisted, sitting beside her in the shade of the umbrella, knitting a pullover as she kept her rheumy eyes on the boys, Don and Ronnie, who were playing in the inflatable pool. 'It's a regular vacation with him gone – no more migraines or headaches. That boy of mine, he'll be the death of me someday, so I'm enjoying this break.'

Maggie threw her head back and laughed in an appealing manner. 'Come on, Grandma,' she said, 'tell us another tall tale! You *dote* on that boy of yours!'

'I do not!'

'Of course you do!'

'Well, *I* dote on her boy,' Clare said, smiling, 'though he doesn't deserve it.'

'That boy of mine has a heart of gold,' Grandma reminded them. 'He's just easily distracted.'

Clare knew that Rydell's latest trip was based on more than restlessness; it was very important. This was their first anniversary; she had been living in Greenbelt for a year. In that time the ozone layer had thinned dramatically in many places, the mean temperature had risen dangerously, and the effects were being felt around the globe in unexpected, frightening ways. Now Rydell was in the Amazon – one of the worst affected regions – to check out the more bizarre results of the ozone depletion while having a break from the recent outburst of legal warfare with his wife. He was dealing with a public and *private* crisis, and Clare wanted to be with him.

'I appreciate you dropping in like this,' she said to Collins and Maggie. 'It's nice to have a bit of extra company when Tony's not here.'

'Anything for a free drink,' Collins grinned. 'It's all in a day's work.'

The remark made Clare smile, but she did feel grateful to both of them. Sitting here in the backyard, in the dazzling heat of an unnatural summer, she was reminded of the fact that her year with Rydell had been the strangest year of her life, for more reasons than one.

Having come from a society of pragmatic, ambitious and powerful people, in Washington, she had been forced to dramatically adjust her way of thinking in order to settle into this more commonplace environment. As she had soon come to realize, it was an insular colony of NASA scientists, technicians, computer operatives, test-pilots and administrators, most of whom were employed either by NASA–Goddard Space Flight Centre, right here in Greenbelt, or by the Navy's Surface Weapons Centre in nearby Whiteoak. Most of them were heavily involved in their work and could play just as hard, but few seemed to have outside interests. Thus, whereas Clare had formerly socialized mainly with politicians, journalists and high-ranking military personnel she now spent most of her spare time with 'cowboy' test-pilots, eccentric scientists and technologists like Rydell, hard-drinking men and their women, at boozy parties and barbecues, or in noisy bars. To her amazement she liked it and enjoyed the informality. The transition had been made a lot easier because of the unobtrusive support of Collins and

Maggie, who lived just around the corner from Rydell and were clearly his best friends. Now they were her best friends too.

'I swear you've blossomed,' Collins said casually, gazing steadily at her. 'You look younger than you did a year ago. This new life must be good for you.'

'Love and passion,' Maggie explained, her smile broad and mischievous.

Clare felt herself blushing. 'Stop it, Maggie. You're just trying to embarrass me. I know you love doing that.'

'I hope you have a strong bed,' Collins said.

'We can hear the noise in our house,' Maggie added.

'You two have always had the filthiest tongues,' Rydell's mother said, glancing up from her knitting, 'but this gal's looking healthy because she's found a healthier way of life – looking after her man and his children and taking pride in the home. That's a woman's place, after all.'

'A woman's *place*!' Clare exclaimed.

'Oh, my God!' Maggie added.

'That's it,' Grandma said. 'Make fun of me, the pair of you. But a woman's place is in the home, always was, always will be. And that's why Clare's blossoming. She's found that there are more important things in life than independence and money. Go on, Clare, admit it!'

'Definitely not!' Clare retorted, though aware that she had done what she had sworn she would never do – give up her independence for the dubious pleasures of a lasting relationship. Those pleasures had been bought at a high price. She had given up most of her luxuries, turned her back on security, in exchange for several burdens – Rydell's children, loopy mother, and ostracized wife, who, over the past few months, had displayed a genuine talent for making life hell on Earth. Clare had not had the dubious pleasure of

251

meeting Suzy, but felt that she knew her. At least through her solicitors.

'I'm tired,' Grandma said. 'I can't take this heat. I'll go inside and check how lunch is progressing and give you a call when it's ready.'

'Thanks, Mother,' Clare said.

'No need for thanks,' Rydell's mother replied. 'I'm not the kind to accept favours. As long as I'm here, I'll earn my keep.'

'Let me help you,' Maggie said.

'No need, I'm perfectly capable.'

'I know you are,' Maggie said diplomatically, 'but I want to help anyway. I need something to do.'

The boys whooped and ran back into the pool, while Rydell's mother and Maggie retreated into the kitchen to prepare a late lunch.

Clare had a sip of her orange juice and looked across the table at Collins.

'What exactly is Tony doing in the Amazon?' he asked her. 'Checking on more ghosts?'

'That's it, Dwight. That's exactly what he's doing. Since the hallucinations started materializing on the Earth, the Amazon's been one of the most strongly affected areas and Rydell and others have gone to check it out.'

*And not just there*, she thought, feeling deprived. In fact, over the past three months, with members of British, European, Canadian and Indian government-sponsored research teams, all cooperating to solve the mystery of the alien virus, Rydell had been to the Arctic and Antarctic, New Zealand, Bali, Great Britain, and even Arizona. Clare missed him and envied him, but had to stay in Maryland or, more specifically, Washington DC, to deal with Jack Douglas and the President.

'Rydell has all the fun,' she said.

Collins smiled. 'He's a busy boy, all right. And at the rate that thing's spreading around the Earth, he's going to get even busier. That virus, for want of a better word, is starting to cause chaos on a world-wide scale. It's frightening.'

Clare agreed. The unknown, alien 'virus' was spreading around the globe and eating its way through the thinning atmosphere in many locations. Even before reaching the lower atmosphere, it had started altering the face of the Earth, melting ice-caps, raising sea-levels, blighting crops, increasing skin cancer in humans and numerous related diseases in animals, affecting food and other resources.

Also, during the past three months, when the virus had seeped down through the thinning atmosphere, aircraft pilots had started reporting that during their flights they were being tracked by UFOs, and harassed by hallucinations or ghosts. Such reports had been submitted with increasing frequency all over the world, causing alarm and growing concern, until eventually what had been feared actually occurred: pilots started either ejecting in terror from their aircraft or actually crashing.

Luckily, no commercial flight had been affected yet but the governments of many nations were now secretly concerned that sooner or later they would, with dire consequences. What would happen should the virus spread to other forms of transport, defence installations, or the populace?

Wide-scale destruction and death.

Already, in certain parts of the world, for reasons of safety, commercial airline services had been cancelled and the citizens reduced to travelling by boat or overland. The possibility of that happening in the United States was not too far away.

'Yes,' Clare said to Collins, 'it's frightening. That's

why we've got to stop it. We have to find out more about it and then neutralize it.'

'What do you have so far?'

'Very little, Dwight. We're still analyzing it. We only know that it's some kind of plasmode life-form – based on the interaction of electrons and ions – and that it's constantly reproducing itself, or growing, by feeding off the ozone in the atmosphere. We believe it was transported here from elsewhere in the galaxy, most likely in the cosmic dust of a meteorite, such as Halley's Comet, and that it's been dormant for a long time, probably brought back to life by the heat generated by the depletion of the ozone layer.'

'A depletion actually started by us.'

'Right,' Clare said. 'We started the depletion of the ozone layer with our irresponsible use of CFCs, then, once we had awakened the virus, it began eating the ozone layer even faster than the CFCs had been and now it's spreading all over the damned place, gobbling ozone wherever it goes. *That's* all we know about it at the moment, but it's enough to cause sleepless nights.'

'It's causing *me* sleepless nights,' Collins said, 'that's for damned sure. From what I hear, there's been a sudden spate of so-called "ghost" reports from as close as Andrews AFB, with one case of a pilot ejection prior to crashing, and that means the virus has seeped down over this area.'

'No one's going to admit it,' Clare told him, 'just as there's been no official mention of the virus anywhere in the world. It's the world's best-kept secret.'

'They're frightened of panic,' Collins said. 'I secretly panic when I think of the virus seeping down over here.' He waved his hand to take in the whole of Maryland, Washington DC, Virginia . . . 'This area's filled with air-force bases, national-defence establishments, and numerous research facilities, including

NASA, many of which come under my command. I lie awake at night, with Maggie complaining beside me, wondering when the first materialization is going to appear to a NASA employee engaged in highly sensitive or dangerous work. I keep imagining the man going crazy, and doing something dangerous. That's my new nightmare, Clare.'

'Lunch is on the table, so get yourselves indoors!' Maggie called out from the kitchen.

'We hear you loud and clear,' Clare called back. 'Kids, get out of that pool!'

The boys did as they were told and Clare helped them to dress. Then the four of them trooped into the house to sit down to lunch. Grace was not said in this house, but when Clare glanced around her, at Dwight, Maggie, Grandma and the two boys, she thought of the invisible virus spreading out above Maryland and wanted, for the first time in her life, to offer a simple prayer.

She would pray for salvation.

# CHAPTER TWENTY-EIGHT

It was raining in the Amazon jungle, a torrential downpour, as Rydell huddled with the others beneath the high canopy of the trees, boots buried in mud.

'Shit!' Polanski complained, huddled beside him in his rubber cape, like a rock in a waterfall. 'Constant humidity, goddamned gloom and mud, spiders and bugs the size of your fist and now this goddamned rain! It's a real bitch, I tell you.'

'Yeah,' Rydell replied, wiping the rain from his eyes and squinting into the dripping forest, 'I feel like a worm wriggling through slime. I'd like to go home right now.'

'How much longer?' Polanski asked their guide, a handsome Brazilian, Antonio Bozzano, who was squatting beside them, unconcerned.

'Not much longer,' Antonio replied, then shrugged, as if time was irrelevant. 'Once the rain stops, perhaps thirty or forty minutes. It depends on whether or not the Indians have moved again – since this started, they've moved a lot.'

The systematic, ruthless destruction of the Amazonian rain forests by the Brazilian government had made it one of the areas where the depletion of the ozone in the atmosphere was greatest. Because of this, there had been more reports of 'virus hallucinations' made here than anywhere else, with an attendant, dramatically high incidence of accidents involving aeroplanes, trains and even road transport. All were due to a loss of control on the part of crew or drivers, reportedly caused by the sudden appearance of 'ghosts', 'doppelgängers' and other bizarre materializations.

The majority of reports had come from the rain forest's most devastated areas and according to reports submitted to the authorities in Manaus, the Indian tribe Rydell and his team were meeting had been most severely affected by unexplained phenomena, to the degree where it was threatening to destroy the tribe's whole way of life. Rydell, Polanski and his two paranormal specialists were here to try to record as much as they could of the disturbing phenomena.

The two other scientists in the team, Larry Curtis and Ray Maneer, were sitting under a tree facing Rydell and Polanski, surrounded by their equipment and three of Antonio's Indian bearers, covered in mud, as drenched as river rats, and looking as miserable as Rydell felt.

Rydell was not used to the wild and as he sat in the mud of the Amazon jungle, listening to the relentlessly heavy drumming of the rainfall, he thought longingly of his warm, cozy tract house in Greenbelt, and of Clare, who would be in bed right now, hopefully yearning for him.

'Shit!' Polanski exclaimed again. 'Even Manaus, when I think of it, is starting to seem almost civilized, certainly appealing. Just put me back in that sleazy hotel with a hot bath and clean sheets, and I'll never complain again.'

The remark made Rydell grin. The journey to the rain forest hadn't been comfortable. Now, he found himself yearning for their first few days spent in exotic Rio de Janeiro. They had stayed in a suite in the Copacabana Palace, overlooking the famous beach, and were given a guided-tour by the charming Antonio Bozzano. After a few pleasurable days they had taken an aeroplane to Belem. There the hotel was less luxurious, but they were charmed by the place – its Portuguese colonial homes, *Belle Epoque* houses, its streets lined with mango trees, leading to elegant squares, parks and busy markets. Then another flight to Manaus, the chief inland port of the Amazon basin, a seedy but exotic town on the bank of the Rio Negro, just above the confluence of the Amazon. Their hotel had been downtown, a decaying, ramshackle place, its rooms uncomfortable, its lobby filled with pimps and whores.

They had been there only one night, but that was one too many for Rydell, who'd been relieved the next day, when they boarded a paddle-steamer for their journey to the confluence of the Amazon. There the coffee-brown Amazon met the inky-black Rio Negro though they seemed not to mingle, the line between them visible for miles. Travelling another fifty miles upriver they had disembarked at a wooden jetty, overshadowed by soaring trees, where they were met by three Indian bearers. Since then they had been marching north into the rain forest, for what seemed like an eternity.

In fact, they had only been marching for two hours, but Rydell felt drained and disorientated, as if on that alien planet he had so often dreamt about.

'I think the rain is stopping,' Antonio said, holding out his upturned palm to catch some drops. 'We can start off again.'

'I don't think I can do that,' Rydell said. 'I'm too numb to move.'

'Get your ass out of the mud,' Polanski said as he made the first move to go. 'Just pretend you're a boy scout.'

'Another day, another dollar,' joked Curtis. 'And we're earning it!'

'Aye, aye,' Rydell murmured, rearranging the straps of the rucksack on his back as the Indian bearers picked up the rest of the equipment and started into the jungle. They were followed by the two scientists, who were swallowed up by the trees before Antonio motioned Rydell and Polanski forward and fell in beside them.

Rydell hated the rain forest. It overwhelmed and confused him. As they marched deeper into it, he felt more oppressed and nervous. He had imagined it as beautiful – the greenery lush in brilliant sunlight, the flowers blooming in a profusion that would dazzle the eyes – but the sunlight rarely penetrated as far as the forest floor as the enormous trees prevented all but a strange and forbidding light to enter, the constant dampness and humidity encouraged claustrophobia, and the pervading silence felt threatening.

'It's like a fucking bad dream,' Polanski said, breathing heavily beside him. 'I can't wait to get out of here.'

'Are we close?' Rydell asked Antonio.

'Yes,' the guide replied. 'We're practically there. And if what I hear is true, if the tribe is breaking up, we should find them scattered throughout this area, so be careful.'

'Careful?' Polanski asked. 'Why careful?'

'If it is true that the manifestations have caused the tribe to break up, the Indians could be unpredictable – and possibly dangerous. There's also the chance that we could experience what they have, which could also be dangerous.'

'Yeah, we have to watch out for that,' Rydell said. 'We have to try to keep a grip on ourselves, no matter what happens.'

'Right,' Polanski said. 'You got it.'

Rydell rubbed the sweat from his eyes to see a

machete rising and falling as the native bearers up ahead whipped back the foliage, creating a path.

Green, it was all green, now deepening in the gloom, and Rydell had to look carefully to see the other forest colours. Against the shadowy brown of the tree trunks he could distinguish pale dangling lianas, yellowish-white fungi that covered the entangled branches, dark clusters of Cannon-Ball fruit, and the red flowers of the heisteria which occasionally lent colour to the gloom.

Rydell hadn't expected this – he had expected a riot of colours – but now he knew that most of the colour was high up in the forest canopy near the sun. That was where the true wealth of forest wildlife could be found: the insects, monkeys, snakes, and great variety of birds. Down in the gloom there was damp mud and silence, stinging flies, poisonous spiders and eighteen-inch rodents, brown moths and sloths, large cats and man-eating snakes. Down where he stumbled and sweated, was a world to make the flesh creep.

And even as he thought it, feeling dizzy and unreal, he heard, between the hacking sounds of the machete, a noise nearby that made his flesh creep. It was a high-pitched, ghastly wailing.

'What the fuck?' Polanski whispered.

'It's an Indian woman,' Antonio said. 'I know that sound – it's the wail of someone mourning. They must be here, all around us.'

The woman's wailing continued, echoing eerily through the gloom before another sound – the whip and slap of parting foliage – heralded the arrival of a shadowy, painted figure.

The Indian, almost naked, his body as brown as a berry but painted in gaudy colours, stopped when he saw the white men. He stared at them through mad eyes, looking back over his shoulder as his double appeared and stopped, exactly as he had done before. The first Indian let out a cry of fear, then plunged into the forest and was lost in the foliage. The second Indian disappeared instantly as if by a conjuring trick.

The three Indian bearers, their equipment on the ground, started gibbering amongst themselves, their eyes wide with dread, then raced back the way they had come. Antonio bawled at them but they ignored him and kept running.

'Jesus Christ!' Polanski whispered. 'It's enough to freeze your blood. Did you see what that Indian was running from?'

'Yes,' Rydell said. 'His double.'

'Like you in that airplane, right, Rydell?'

'Yes, Polanski, the same.'

'And they're creating those doubles from their own minds, right?'

'You're a bright boy, Polanski.'

'The flying saucers,' Polanski said, 'the ones I saw in that airplane . . .'

'You created them out of your own mind because you wanted to see them.'

'And what the others saw – the dead relatives and snakes and spiders – they were also created out of the minds of the individuals present?'

'Yeah,' Rydell said, not wanting to discuss this, remembering Clare's stricken face as she stared at her dead parents and the airplane travelled on into infinity, 'I think you've got it, Polanski.'

The distant ghastly wailing continued.

'What happens now?' Larry Curtis asked, looking excited. 'Do we go on or not?'

'I didn't come all this way just to turn back,' said the other scientist, Ray Maneer, looking challengingly at each of them in turn, 'so let's divide up the equipment between us and head for that woman.'

'Right,' Rydell said. 'Let's do that.'

They marched on into the forest, aiming towards the dreadful wailing. When they found the woman she was squatting cross-legged in the mud, besides a gravelike mound, rocking a baby in her arms. She was sobbing and hugging the baby like someone demented and when Antonio knelt beside her, held her shoulder, and spoke to her in Portuguese, she spat out a stream of words which he translated for the group.

'It's her dead child,' he explained. 'That's its grave she's sitting beside. The child died a month ago and was buried right there, but a few days ago, while others were also being haunted, she awakened from a normal sleep to find the child kicking in her arms. She came here immediately, expecting to find the grave disturbed but seeing that the grave was untouched, could not bear to leave. So she sits here with the child, going crazy, and refuses to move. She told me that the village is haunted and that most of those who lived there have either fled or are mad. Come on, let's get going.'

After that it became a nightmare. As they moved deeper into the rain forest and approached the Indian village, they repeatedly came across Indians, men, women and children, all of whom had obviously run away in the hope of escaping their individual demons, which sprung from their subconscious.

Most often their demons took the shape of people, but frequently they were manifested out of fears and phobias, taking the shape of spiders, snakes, alligators, piranha fish – fearful creatures from bad dreams.

Indians, male and female, writhed moaning on the ground, scratching and slapping themselves. Others clung to their ghostly loved ones, or cowered from their ghostly enemies, or simply stared, rendered helpless by their terror, at their equally terrified doppelgängers who, not knowing that they were unreal, did not know who the real ones were.

The rain forest was dark and humid, a dream of shadow and shifting light, and at the base of the enormous tree trunks, beneath the giant lianas, the Indians, isolated from one another, sobbed, smiled, sang, screamed, and were destined either to starve to death or succumb to insanity.

Their own thoughts were destroying them.

Rydell stumbled into the village clearing with the feeling that he was escaping from a nightmare. He focused on a patch of cloudy sky high above the soaring trees; the sight was his hold on reality. Then he noticed that Polanski was looking around him intently, as if, if he stared hard enough, the horrors would disappear.

'Did we see that?' he asked Rydell. 'Or did we just fucking dream it?'

'I don't know,' Rydell said.

'Lord have mercy on all of us.' Antonio was now clearly rattled. 'May His light shine upon us.'

'This is sensational,' Larry Curtis cried with excitement as he quickly unpacked his instruments. 'This is the greatest paranormal event in history and *we're* here to capture it.'

'Damn right,' said his partner, the heavily built Ray Maneer. 'It's the opportunity of a lifetime. I can't believe what's going down here. I think my fucking head's burning.'

'It may not be UFOs, but it's hot,' Polanski added as he helped set up the portable magnometer, ambient and parabolic microphones, and video- and motion-picture-cameras. 'It's *fanfuckingtastic*!'

He was just fixing the video-camera to its tripod, when, as if in answer to his subconscious desires, a pulsating, disc-shaped light materialized in the sky above the clearing.

263

'Holy shit!' Polanski exclaimed softly. 'What the hell's *that*?'

'A UFO,' Rydell said. 'A flying saucer, Polanski. What you've been searching for all your life – you and half of the world. The virus is feeding off your mind, ingesting your subconscious thoughts and deepest desires, re-creating them right before your eyes. What is willed, will be done.'

Polanski squinted up at the brilliant light, watching it bobbing and weaving, and shook his head in denial.

'We've been searching the skies for years for these things,' he said, 'and they were all in our minds. There it is – a goddamned flying saucer – and without us, it can't exist.'

'You got it,' Rydell said, jerked out of his mesmerized state by the sound of his own voice.

He glanced up at the flying saucer, but was almost blinded by it, so lowering his gaze he looked at the men around him. They were shading their eyes to squint above them, trying to see the flying saucer in detail, but like Rydell, they lowered their gaze to glance about them.

At that moment, Rydell heard Clare's voice whispering his name. She was squatting by the doorway of a thatched hut, wearing the shirt and slacks she had worn when they said goodbye, looking up at him with a warm smile.

The warm smile chilled his blood.

'Oh, no!' Rydell heard himself whispering. 'Please, God, I can't bear this!'

He had to look away to try to keep a grip on reality. The sun was burning down through the clearing, turning the rain to steam, which coiled and spiralled over the earth to form a silvery mist. An Indian, spitting foam, his eyes mad, drew from his belly his poisoned entrails, which he started to eat.

264

Larry Curtis stared at him, too stunned to work his camera, while beside him, Maneer, caught in his dead mother's embrace, wept the tears he had been unable to shed when she was buried six years before.

'Clare?' Polanski whispered. 'Am I seeing right? Is that *Clare* over there?' He was staring at the thatched hut. Clare ignored him, but smiled at Rydell.

'Control!' Rydell yelled, feeling insane. 'Keep control! Stand outside it and see it and treat it for what it really is! Bear in mind that it's not real!'

Polanski looked down at his feet, which were buried in green slime. He shuddered and gasped. The slime coiled around his legs, developing tentacles as it slithered up towards his groin. With icy eyes and slobbering mouth it dragged him down to the ground.

Polanski screamed as he fell, but Maneer and Curtis ignored him. The former wept helplessly, hugging his mother, while the latter, still too stunned to work his camera, dissolved in the pulsating, silver light that beamed down from above.

'*No!*' he screamed suddenly.

Nothing was happening to him – he was just denying what he was seeing – but the sound of his voice whipped Rydell raw and made him turn back to Clare. A flying saucer passed overhead, casting its brilliant light on her. She was walking towards him, past the Indian with the dripping entrails, and she held out her hands and smiled as if she wanted to drink his blood.

Rydell's heart broke.

'Lord have mercy!' he heard Antonio exclaim. 'We must flee from here! *Now!*'

Antonio grabbed his shoulder and slapped his face. Stunned, Rydell looked above him and saw the pulsating light; looking down he saw Polanski being swallowed by a green mass with many tentacles and icy eyes.

265

Polanski had often joked about his greatest fears, making light of his nightmares: his belief that an alien life-form, if highly advanced, could have transcended the physical body to become a protoplasmic and pitiless intelligence. He was now being devoured by the physical manifestation of his most deeply rooted fear.

'Oh, Christ!' he sobbed. 'Jesus!'

'It's not real, Polanski!' Rydell suddenly bawled, keeping his eyes away from Clare's double. Then he reached down and grabbed hold of his friend and jerked him up from the mud. *Let's get the hell out of here!*

That did the trick. They broke loose from their imprisoning dreams: Polanski cursed and jumped upright, grabbing Rydell by the shoulders, kicking at the nightmare below him, which disappeared as he did so. He screamed at Maneer and Curtis, who also broke free from their creations and with Rydell and the others ran away from the village and its terrible hauntings.

'The equipment!' Curtis shouted.

'To hell with it!' Antonio responded as he ran. *We must get away from here!*

Rydell didn't have to be told and kept running, refusing to look back past the many Indians who were scattered throughout the forest, writhing, groaning, clawing bloodily at themselves, some smiling beautifully and waiting to die to join the dead they had brought back through love. He ran past them all, past the dying and the demented, away from the flying saucers and Polanski's mother and his monstrous Clare, thinking of what was here: that invisible presence from the stratosphere, the mysterious, alien offspring from the hole in the ozone layer – How, he wondered, could they ever defeat it while it did these things to them?

Clambering over the giant lianas, Rydell fell in the mud but got up again and kept running. He ran until there were no more haunted Indians, no flying saucers, no ghostly loved ones, and a breeze from a lake in a nearby clearing cooled his hot, sweating skin. *Then* he fell down – they all fell down as one – and gasped for breath in anguish.

'We left the equipment,' Curtis gasped.

'We got nothing,' Maneer said shamefully.

'We got out with our sanity,' Polanski said, 'which is more than we might have done.'

'We failed,' Rydell said.

No one replied to that. There was nothing to say. They just lay there in silence, gradually getting their breath back, sinking into the mud, surrendering to the forest gloom in their dread and despair. Finally, they all climbed reluctantly to their feet and, though weary, they started the long trek back to the river.

Rydell thought of Clare's double smiling at him and was chilled to the bone.

She had smiled like the living dead.

# CHAPTER TWENTY-NINE

The way it happened, you couldn't believe it because it didn't seem possible. Suzy thought she knew when it had started – that vision of Don and Ronnie and the flying saucer shortly after – but then she decided that it had begun before that, when she'd lain awake all those nights, brooding about whether or not she was guilty of deserting her children, and had betrayed Rydell or not with Joe Wheeler. She'd had lots of visions, then, those awful dreams, lying in bed, but whether or not that was the start of it, she still couldn't say.

Certainly the kids on the road. Now *that* hadn't been a dream. It might've been an hallucination, or just vivid wishful thinking, but certainly, with that flying-saucer shaped light, it had been *some* kind of experience.

You just never knew.

Well, you did.

She knew now.

The first time she knew that the visions were for real was the evening her father didn't come in to dinner. He'd gone out to check his crops, as he did so often these days, trying to convince himself that they would somehow get better; that the rain might eventually fall. So, Suzy looked through the window, wondering why he hadn't come back, and saw him kneeling at the far end of the lawn, looking up at another man in dungarees. The other man was her father's age and looked a bit like him. He was standing there as still as a rock, just gazing down, smiling. Suzy saw him clearly, illuminated in the crimson twilight, and didn't for a second think that he wasn't real, though something about him seemed strange. Then, with a shock, she realized what it was: the man had no shadow.

Hardly able to believe her own eyes, Suzy turned cold in the heat, then burned up with a flush of panic.

No shadow.

No movement.

That was strange as well. The man was too still to be real. He looked almost like her father who was kneeling there crying, wiping the tears from his eyes with the back of his hand.

With her heart racing, Suzy left the house and hurried across the lawn. Though terrified, in a kind of dream, she managed to cross the lawn and, before reaching her father, called out his name.

When her father jerked his head around to look at her, the other man vanished. Just like that; into thin air.

Shocked almost witless, Suzy froze where she stood, blinking repeatedly and looking around her, until she got her senses back. Then she noticed that her father too was glancing about him, as if trying to find the missing man. He was sobbing, which he had never done before.

'It was my father!' he cried out.

For days after the event, her father talked obsessively about the vision, saying that his father had been as real as night and day; that he'd even heard his breathing, and that he'd looked exactly as he'd done ten years ago, just before he died. He talked himself to exhaustion, then became listless, and would spend hours on the porch, just looking over the brown, barren fields, obviously waiting for his father to return and maybe give him a sign.

Nothing else happened out there. It took place in the house the next time. It happened a couple of days later, when Suzy's mother was preparing dinner. Suzy heard her loud gasp, then the clattering of the pan, dropped in shock.

'Oh, dear God!' Suzy's mother whispered.

Looking up from the sofa, Suzy saw her mother framed in the kitchen doorway, her hands across her mouth, her lovely brown eyes widening as they focused on the big kitchen table ... Then Suzy saw the three people at the table ... Her father, the man he'd claimed was his father, and a woman who looked the same age. They were sitting facing her father, both with their hands at the table, smiling silently at him.

Her father, who was staring at them, mesmerized, had tears on his cheeks.

Suzy thought she could see faintly through both people, but she couldn't be sure of that.

They filled her with terror.

Her mother broke into tears, breaking the dreadful silence, and her father, jerked out of his reverie, looked up. When he did so, the people sitting opposite became vaporous, transparent, before gradually fading away, just like smoke rings.

Suzy's father and mother clung to one another, both weeping profoundly, while Suzy sank into a chair, feeling weak, shaking badly.

She was seeing her father's hallucinations and so was her mother. She was seeing inside his thoughts.

'Yeah,' her father told her, 'I'd been thinkin' about them a lot. As I watched the farm die, when the bank said I had to sell, I started thinkin' more and more of the good ol' days, when my folks ran the farm and we ate well an' had a good life. I was yearning for that, see? I wanted it back. And so I thought a lot about that, about my younger days, my folks, and so musta willed them back into existence. Praise the Lord, it's a miracle!'

'It's the devil's work,' Suzy's mother said fearfully. 'We have to get outa here. It's a sign that we got to sell up and move somewhere else. This place is haunted, I'm sure of it.'

'I ain't movin', darlin'. No way. I was born and raised on this land and I'm gonna die here. It's a miracle, I tell you. A *good* sign. The Lord be praised, we'll be saved!'

But they wouldn't be. Suzy knew that for a fact. The land had died and their debts were piling up and the bank was growing impatient. Half of the county had been forced to move, selling up, hitting the road, and Suzy knew it was just a matter of time before her father would be forced to face the facts and do exactly the same. She dreaded that day, the heartbreak it would cause, and maybe that's why she also started seeing things, like she had that first dreadful night, after breaking it off with Joe Wheeler.

An awful lot of people were seeing things.

The whole damned county was haunted.

Suzy saw her dreams come true. Her troubled thoughts were given life. She hadn't been quite the same since her last meeting with Rydell and now, on top of the worries she was having about her parents, and after the disappointment she'd had with Joe Wheeler, she was pining to be back home where she belonged, with Rydell and the kids. So, she thought about them, too much for her own good, and started to see them by the side of the road, in her bedroom, and out there in the ruined fields.

When she saw them, she was filled with a combination of terror and longing.

A lot of folks in this particular, blighted area were

reporting similar visions. At first they were shy of talking, but then too many things happened and gradually, when it all became too much, the word got around. People confided in one another, saw psychiatrists, took sedatives, but soon even the most reliable of witnesses were reporting strange visions. The visions were discussed at home, from the pulpits in the churches, and in the revivalist tents that soon sprang up all over the place to deal with the newly converted. A lot thought it was the Second Coming, that the visions were signs from God, and every kind of religion was given a new lease of life.

'When I see my folks,' Suzy's mother said, 'I simply get down on my knees and pray. Seeing them sometimes breaks my heart – it's as painful as the day they died – but other times I feel a rush of love that washes me clean. I used to think it was the devil's work, but now I say praise the lord, 'cause I know, as sure as they're in front of me, that we'll meet again soon.'

Others claimed it was the changing weather and the destruction of local agriculture and commerce – just folks driven mad by debt and the loss of their farms – but there were also whispers about the atmosphere, the pollution and thinning ozone layer, affecting people's brains and making them hallucinate . . .

'I wouldn't praise the Lord too soon.' Suzy's father was slugging beer. 'They had that case on TV: the local farmer who killed his family. They'd bin known as a happy family, no problems at all, then he picks up his shotgun and slaughters his wife and four children, before sticking the barrel of the gun in his mouth and blowing his head off. Was losin' his farm, of course – that could've been part of it – but they say he most likely saw somethin' and was driven insane. I'm inclined to believe that.'

The local media picked it up, then the national

media, and although other parts of the country were similarly affected, Iowa was clearly the worst hit so far.

After a few weeks, you took the hauntings for granted, even if frightened by them.

'You have to will them away,' Suzy told her folks, 'but that can take time. Sometimes you see them too suddenly and at the wrong time. When that happens, *anything* can happen and that's how you get tragedies.'

Being awake was like dreaming, which was dangerous. It was easy to crash your car when you suddenly saw something; easy to run over a pedestrian; easy to have a heart attack or burn your house down by accident. Folks were doing it more and more though it was officially denied. And there was the cancer. No one talked loudly about diseases, but whispering carried a long way, and besides, you just had to look around you and you couldn't deny it. It wasn't just the crops – though Lord knows, they'd surely died – but also the animals dying in the fields before your eyes, from infections of the skin caused by parasites, which were caused by the sunshine.

'The Earth's atmosphere's getting thinner,' Suzy explained to her Dad when he slumped deeper in his chair in front of the TV after yet another ecological program. 'We've polluted the atmosphere with all our sprayin' and dust-croppin' and supersonic aircraft and so on, and now the atmosphere around the Earth is getting thinner, even disappearing some places, and leavin' us unprotected from the sun's rays.'

'The sun's *good* for you,' her father retorted.

'Only when it's filtered by Earth's atmosphere,' Suzy explained. 'There are these rays, you know? They contain something called UV-B. We're all exposed to UV-B, like when we get a suntan, but now we're getting too much of it and it's causing real problems. Cattle suffer from ailments such as eye cancer and pink-eye, which lead to blindness; fish and other forms of marine life will die out for lack of larvae and phytoplankton . . . '

'What's that?'

'Some kind of food, I guess. Human beings will suffer from an increase in all kinds of diseases, including herpes, hepatitis, cataracts, infections of the skin caused by parasites, and two forms of skin cancer: one can be cured by surgery, but the other – malignant melanoma – which is apparently incurable.'

'You mean fatal?'

'Yes, Dad.'

'So we have to get out of here,' her mother said, looking twice her age, sipping lemonade and repeatedly wiping sweat from her face with the sleeve of her blouse. 'Go somewhere not so bad. Iowa seems to be worse than most other places in America – at least so far – and since we can't keep the farm going anyway, we might as well move on.'

'Move on where?' her husband asked, crumpled deep in his seat, looking diminished, and slugging beer from the bottle. 'We ain't *got* nowhere, honey.'

'Yes, we have,' Suzy said. 'We can go to Maryland. The problem isn't near as bad there. In fact, so far it hardly exists. And I've got good friends there and Rydell, even though he won't have me back, will certainly help us. So let's go to Maryland.'

'You mean sell up,' her father said.

'Yeah, Dad, that's what I mean. We're gonna have to do it sooner or later, so let's do it now.'

'I ain't movin' until they throw me off,' her father said. 'Take that as a fact, gal.'

Suzy lit a cigarette. She smoked an awful lot these days. She knew she wasn't helping the Earth's atmosphere, but she just couldn't help herself.

'Why wait till they throw you out? Why suffer that

indignity? When they decide to do it, they'll come here with state troops and you'll just have to go. So why not go now?'

'Because I won't have it said I cut and ran. I wanna make my protest.'

Suzy sighed in frustration. 'We may not get out then,' she said. 'That may be too late. These visions have caused a lot of accidents and there's talk that if a passenger 'plane crashes, the commercial airlines will be closed down. If that happens, we'll revert to bein' a nation on wheels and the roads are gonna be crammed with refugees. Yeah, Dad, the roads'll be packed with *Okies* – 'cause that's what we'll become.'

'This ain't the Third World, Suzy. It's the United States of America!'

'It was the same America in 1934 – but they still had the dust bowl and Okies. So if we wanna get out as best we can, we've got to go now.'

'I ain't shiftin',' her father said.

In despair, Suzy went to bed early, feeling older than her years, and feeling the need to be a child again, she cuddled up with a teddy bear. She cried herself to sleep, during which she dreamed about the house in Greenbelt where she was about to prepare breakfast for Don and Ronnie. Then Suzy realized that it wasn't a dream; that her eyes were wide open.

They weren't sitting across the table in the kitchen–diner in the house in Greenbelt, but in the moonlight coming in through the window at the end of her bed. The boys were wearing their normal school clothes and staring at her unnaturally. She swelled up with love and fear.

'Go away!' she hissed.

Their unnatural smiles broadened.

'Go away!' she repeated. 'You're not real! Goddammit, you're just my imagination. You don't exist. *Go away!*'

Though terrified of the apparitions, they made her yearn for the real thing, and Don, as if sensing this, turned his head to give Ronnie a ghastly smile and place his hand on his shoulder. Ronnie, with the deathly grace of a somnambulist, stood up and stepped forward.

Suzy sucked in her breath.

Ronnie stopped when she did that, as if whiplashed by the sound. His smile wavered, as her yearning for him – for the real child – was obscured by her fear. She remembered that she'd created him, and slid out of the bed.

'Don't come near me,' she said.

It was a ridiculous thing to say – they couldn't hear her, after all – but it made her feel a little more sane and in control. She tried to will them away, to shut them out of her mind, but since they remained there, she opened the bedroom door and stepped into the hall.

She walked down to the kitchen where the lights were still on. Her father and mother were sitting at the table, holding hands, silently weeping at the ghosts of themselves.

They had created what they wanted back – the better past that had sustained them – and were looking at selves who were ten years younger. When they trembled, the others did; when they wept, the others wept. When they laughed hysterically the others mimicked them perfectly. But you could tell they were apparitions because the light went straight through them, leaving no shadow at all, faintly revealing what was beyond them.

At least it *seemed* that you could see what was beyond them, though you couldn't be sure of that.

Suzy held her breath. She wasn't too sure what she should do. She knew that if she interrupted – made a noise or walked up to them – the illusion created by her yearning parents would be broken and the apparitions would disappear. She was going to do that, but felt immediately, oddly guilty, sensing that her parents, in their despair, were having a moment of bliss.

It was in the nature of the hauntings: they brought either bliss or dread and since in this case, they brought bliss, Suzy returned to her room.

Don and Ronnie, or the apparitions she had created, had gone when she left, leaving everything as normal. The moonlight beaming obliquely through the window fell on an empty floor. Suzy knelt there. She felt as if she was at an altar. She closed her eyes to the light, bowed her head and clasped her hands, then whispered the prayers she had uttered every night since her childhood.

Afterwards she asked for forgiveness and mercy.

She begged for release.

'Please let me go home,' she said.

# CHAPTER THIRTY

'I thought I'd meet you here for lunch,' Jack Douglas said, 'to remind you of the world you gave up for life with Rydell.'

Raising her eyes from her crab-cakes and glancing around at the wealthy politicians dining in the Jockey Club, Clare understood what he meant, but didn't respect him for bringing up the subject.

'I'm not denying that I'm enjoying this unexpected lunch,' she said, 'but frankly, I'd be happy enough without it, and have been for some time.'

'Is that true, Clare?'

'Absolutely.'

'I just can't imagine it. You out there in Greenbelt, acting like an obedient housewife, dining on hamburgers and beer on his lawn with the neighbours. You belong here, not there.'

'I belong where Rydell is,' she said firmly, 'which means Greenbelt is home to me.'

The remark made him flinch, but he controlled himself, finished the last of his crab-cakes, and said spitefully, 'You said you'd never surrender your individuality for the love of a man.'

'Maybe that remark was made because of the calibre of man I knew at the time, Jack.' His cheeks reddened with suppressed anger, but she pressed on regardless. 'In fact, I feel that I've *discovered* my individuality by moving in with Rydell, and that what I was before was not the real me, just some kind of pretender. As for being an obedient housewife, that's not remotely true.

I'd remind you that I'm still working as a physicist and liaison officer between NASA, the Pentagon and the White House. I'm not *just* a housewife.'

He sat back and stared at her without warmth. 'No,' he said, 'not just a housewife. A hot little mistress too.'

'I certainly hope so, Jack.'

His cheeks turned red again. He was about to make a retort, but decided to smile instead.

'And does your common-law husband know you're having lunch with me today?'

'Of course.'

'And he doesn't mind?'

'Why should he mind? He knows I have to meet gentlemen like you as part of my liaison work for NASA and, more importantly recently, as part of my campaign to protect the ozone layer. He knows that I'll return safe and sound.'

'I can't even steal an hour, then?'

'No, I'm afraid not.'

'Just think, Clare, it would almost be adultery, with all the excitement that holds.'

'I'm not interested in that kind of excitement, so put it out of your mind, Jack.'

'*I* committed adultery for you.'

'That was *your* choice. *I* didn't commit adultery. I simply had an affair with a married man who had recently left his wife. Of all else I am innocent.'

'I'll never forgive you for dropping me for Rydell.'

'I know. It shows.'

'God, Clare, you're still one tough bitch.'

'Not with Rydell, I'm not.'

His eyes flashed when she said that, his clenched knuckles turning white, but he soon regained his composure and charm.

'Do you mind if I smoke?' he asked.

'I'd rather you didn't,' she replied.

'You've joined the anti-smoking lobby, have you?'

'I can't let people smoke in my presence, given what I'm involved with. I won't encourage further contributions to our current rate of CFC production.'

Jack smiled but his eyes were icy and she wondered how she could ever have lain beside him, her naked skin touching his. He had been her lover, certainly, but never someone she could have loved.

'Well,' he said, 'since, as you believe, an *alien* presence is devouring the ozone, why the hell should we worry about our minor contribution to the depletion?'

'Because, Jack, it's also true that our continued use of CFCs isn't helping us to slow down the rate of depletion. In fact, as long as the West continues producing CFCs it stands guilty of *aiding* that unknown entity. To discover the nature of that thing and find a way of stopping its growth, we need all the time we can get and smokers don't help us. Not that your office is helping much either, but then who would expect it to?'

Douglas noted her sarcasm, but refused to be rattled by it. 'What *do* you expect?' he said. 'You ask us to believe that something alien is in the atmosphere, but even you and your friends don't know what it is.'

'We know that it's some form of plasmode or radiobe life-form that organizes itself, and communicates with itself, by means of electromagnetic forces. We just don't know exactly where it came from or how to stop it from spreading.'

'That's not much to go on. The Soviets could have created it in a laboratory.'

'It's true that scientists have created primitive plasmoids and radiobes in laboratory experiments, proving that they *could* exist under certain conditions, but we've a hell of a long way to go before we can create anything capable of surviving for more than a few seconds in normal atmospheric conditions. So your Soviet theory is nonsense.'

'In the meantime,' Douglas continued, as if he hadn't heard her, 'any dramatic reduction in the use of CFCs would dramatically weaken us economically and therefore politically, which would delight our Soviet friends, irrespective of *glasnost*.'

'But you *know* that something different has entered our atmosphere, causing chaos. Why do you refuse to face up to the fact that we have to do something to prevent it?'

'The President and I are in agreement that something has to be done, which is why we're financing your work with Rydell. However, it *is* our belief that this new presence in our atmosphere is more likely to be some kind of new atmospheric weapon produced by the Soviets. They have, after all, previously used cloud-busters to alter the weather where it suited them so this new element could be no more than an extension of that work. After all, we haven't had any reports of similar hauntings taking place in the Soviet Union, which suggests that the virus hasn't reached them yet – which tends to imply that *they* are controlling it.'

'That's nonsense, Jack.'

'That's what was said about cloud-busters, but they caused the first droughts in the United States since the war.'

'You can't be certain of that.'

'We're almost certain. At least we know for a fact that the Soviets possess cloud-busters that actually work.'

'Is that why you're now committed to supporting the agricultural and industrial lobbyists in the White House?'

'Correct,' Douglas said without shame, perhaps even with pride.

281

Hoping to wipe the smug smile off his face, Clare said, 'And that's also how you've managed to convince the President that this whole thing is a Soviet plot, based on their well known parapsychological research, to weaken the economy of the Free World?'

Douglas stopped smiling. 'Who are you to say what the Soviets are or aren't doing?'

'Come off it, Jack!'

'It's my duty to tell the President what I honestly believe, particularly regarding matters relating to the national and international economy. I certainly believe what I've just told you.'

'That sounds like a pretty pompous mouthful.'

'You always *were* a lady with a sharp tongue!'

'Why don't you just tell the truth, Jack? You don't for one second believe the Soviets are behind this. You're using them as scapegoats because, as I've recently learnt, you have strong financial ties with many of the companies responsible for the CFCs, notably oil and airline companies. The truth is that you'll switch the blame onto the Russians rather than threaten your own interests.'

'Who told you that?'

'An old friend. A *Washington Post* journalist.'

'His name?'

'That's my business.'

'An old friend of Rydell's, most likely. The same old friend who blew this whole story in the first place.'

Clare smiled. 'Are you going to deny your personal and financial interests?'

'Naturally. Would you care for dessert?'

'Since it's free, I'll have the cheesecake.'

'An excellent choice,' Douglas said.

He ordered cheesecake for both of them which they ate in silence, uncomfortable with each other in this intimate dining room. Occasionally Clare glanced at

Douglas, aware of how much he had changed. She realized that he resented her affair with Rydell much more than she had imagined, and was letting it cloud his judgement. He had changed in other ways too: his normal anti-communism had become more strident and, as he had great influence with an ailing President, it was positively dangerous.

'What you're telling me,' she said, 'and what you're implying to the President, is based on the most pitiful form of self-deception.'

'I think I'll get the check and pass on the brandy,' he replied and, without waiting for her reply, nodded at the waiter. Then he smiled thinly at her.

'The fact that the Soviets haven't reported any manifestations doesn't mean a damned thing,' she said, holding his gaze. 'The Chinese haven't yet reported any manifestations either, but then the Chinese, like the Soviets, aren't as free as the Western World with that kind of news.'

'I think I get your drift, Clare.'

'I'm sure you do, but I'll make it clearer anyway. What I'm suggesting is that the Soviets, or the Chinese for that matter, wouldn't necessarily report such a phenomenon, even if they were experiencing it. The fact that they haven't officially announced it doesn't mean it's not happening.'

'If it was happening, we'd know about it, Clare. We do have good intelligence.'

'It's good, but it's gossip. I have it on gossip picked up in Clyde's restaurant at Tyson's Corner, Virginia – a favourite CIA hangout – that since the Arctic and Antarctic ice-caps are already melting; the process that will eventually lead to the flooding of Leningrad has begun. The Soviets certainly wouldn't be engineering that themselves. In fact, as you well know, in 1985 Gorbachev and Reagan signed an agreement to co-operate in the protection of the environment and the USSR and US have been working together for several years on global-warming problems.'

'Scientific cooperation doesn't necessarily go hand-in-hand with politics,' Douglas insisted as he hastily signed his credit slip and stood up. 'And since global warming will dramatically increase agricultural productivity in the central region of the USSR, as well as Europe, while it dramatically decreases in the US, their scientific co-operation in this case could be superficial.'

'Nonsense!' Clare snapped. 'The Soviets are well aware of the fact that the increased agricultural productivity in the regions around Moscow are hardly likely to compensate for the flooding of cities such as Leningrad. In fact, if anything, they've good reason to have doubts about *us*, since either accidentally or by design, the US may have altered the atmosphere by use of satellites. And even those Soviets who do not believe we've a political motive, suspect that we may have started this business on a purely experimental basis and have since lost control. In that sense, they believe it's our fault.'

'Bullshit,' Douglas said as the waiter pulled Clare's chair back. 'I haven't heard a damned thing about this. You've invented it!'

'You've heard about it, all right,' Clare said, walking out of the restaurant with him. 'You've known about it for a long time, but you're trying to blame the Soviets in order to unburden Western multi-nationals of their responsibilities and enable them to keep up production and line your pockets. Isn't that true?'

'This conversation is finished, Clare.'

They parted on the sidewalk and walked off in opposite directions, no longer friends. Clare drove back to Greenbelt with a feeling of great sadness, as well as trepidation. She sensed that Douglas would now turn more resolutely against her, Rydell and the many others who were working to solve the problem. Bearing in mind what Nicola had told her about his ruthlessness, it wasn't a heartening thought, but at least she had Rydell.

He had returned from the Amazon a few days ago, not as jocular as he had been, haunted by his experience there. He had told her about that experience, shivering helplessly in her arms. Now such phantoms were everywhere, regardless of time and place, materializing out of the ether, causing panic and madness.

As she drove along Greenbelt Road, past the familiar fences of the Goddard Space Flight Centre and the houses of those who worked there, she became aware of the sunlight, too bright for this early afternoon and felt slightly suffocated in a heat that should have gone by this time of year. Though bright, the light was hazy; an ever-shifting, silvery mist, in which the houses of Greenbelt seemed unreal. The weather was changing and she wondered just how long it would take for the alarms to ring world-wide.

She turned off the main road into the neat, suburban streets, and thought of how the world was being changed beneath a great shroud of silence. It was the silence of secrecy, the blindness of officialdom, and she knew that until the world was informed of what was happening speculation and unfounded suspicions would run rife. Widespread ignorance, encouraged by those with vested interests like Jack Douglas and his business associates, could eventually lead to increasingly extreme forms of nationalism. Clare shuddered to think of it.

She drove up to Rydell's house and saw him standing on the porch, shading his eyes with his hands. As she stopped the car and got out, she was surprised to see him hurrying towards her. When he reached her, he took hold of her shoulders and squeezed gently but urgently, his good-natured face grim.

'There's just been an item on TV,' he said. 'A packed PAN AM 747 en route to London crashed into the Atlantic shortly after take off from Kennedy Airport. So far there's no reason to believe it was malfunction. According to ground control, everything seemed perfectly normal – until suddenly, without reason, the flight crew started screaming hysterically. The 747 went out of control and crashed into the sea. There were no survivors.'

Clare stared at him, too shocked to speak, then fell into his arms.

'It was the virus,' she whispered.

# CHAPTER THIRTY-ONE

The man who climbed out of the car in the silvery light of the afternoon wore a finely-cut grey suit, an immaculate white shirt and tie, and expensive black patent-leather Italian shoes that were already covered in dust.

Suzy's father was sitting beside her in his rocking chair on the porch, his shotgun resting across his knees, his gaze steady on the man who stood beside the squad car, patting down his wind-blown silvery hair with a nervous smile. The driver's door opened and the county sheriff, Jack Baker, got out, adjusted his stetson, tugged at the holster belt around his heavy hips, then nodded at the nervous man.

They both walked towards the house.

Suzy's father gently kicked his booted heel against the floor, starting his chair gently rocking, and ran his fingers lightly along his shotgun. He seemed very relaxed.

When Sheriff Baker and the city guy reached the steps of the porch, Suzy's father, still rocking gently in his chair, said in a neutral tone, 'Put one foot on that porch step, Jack Baker, and I'll blow you to Kingdom Come.'

The Sheriff stopped and raised his hands as if surrendering to the enemy. He glanced at the man beside him, grinned nervously, then said, 'OK, Abe, we don't want no quarrel. We just came to deliver.'

'I figured that.'

Relieved, the man in the suit put one foot on the

porch and started withdrawing a paper from his jacket pocket. Suzy's father lifted the shotgun off his knees and the man immediately stepped back again.

'Suzy,' her father said, 'what do you see in front of you?'

'I see a man with a paper in his hand, Dad. Some kinda document.'

'That's right,' her father replied, stroking his shotgun. 'That's just what I see. What you got there, Mister?'

'What we've brought, Abe,' Sheriff Baker began, 'is . . .'

'I asked the city gentleman,' Suzy's father replied. 'I'm sure he can answer.'

'You know what I've got, Mr Winger. You know I'm from the bank. You refused to sell your farm and you've run out of funds and now we're gonna ask you to move. This farm belongs to us, Sir.'

'No, it doesn't,' Suzy said. 'We don't owe you that much.'

'If he won't sell, M'am, we'll have to sell for him and take what we're owed.'

'You'll sell real cheap, right?'

'No demand these days, M'am. Just look at the weather, at the fields, and you'll know what I'm saying. We don't want this, M'am, no more than you do, but facts are facts and business is business, so this farm has to go.'

'The only one's gonna go is you,' Suzy's father said, 'if you place one goddamn foot on my porch. And that goes for you, too, Jack.'

The Sheriff, an old friend, remained right where he was, toying with the pistol on his hip to hide his embarrassment.

'Listen, Abe,' he said, 'we gotta deliver these papers. If you don't take 'em, we'll just drop 'em on the ground and that makes it legal. You've gotta go, Abe. The law's the law, after all. The farm's dead and you got a lotta debts an' someone's gotta collect. That's the bank, Abe. That's what banks are for these days. Mr Peters, here, he's just like you and me; he just does what he has to do. It's all over here, Abe. Everyone's movin' out. You just gotta cut your losses and go and try somethin' else, somewhere else. That's it, Abe. I'm sorry.'

'I ain't givin' my house to no goddamned bank. The farm – yes. Not the house.'

'The house is part of the farm, Sir,' the city gent said. 'Right now, it's the most valuable part. It's the house and the land the bank wants. And if they want it, they'll get it.'

'Think you're smart, don't you?'

'No, Mr Winger, I don't. I'm just a man that has to do a dirty job 'cause I can't afford otherwise. You should understand that.'

Suzy glanced at her father. His handsome face was like granite. It was only the way he stroked the shotgun that made you realize how mad he was, though he was hurting real bad.

'Get off my land,' he said. 'Get off or I'll blow you off. They'll be pickin' the pieces up in Des Moines and I won't give a damn. You're trespassin' an' that gives me the right and this is still America. Go to hell. Goodbye, gentlemen.'

Sheriff Baker sighed and raised his hands even higher. 'When we come tomorrow,' he said, 'we'll come with a lot of help. That means shotguns and dogs, even bulldozers, to raze this place to the ground if we meet with resistance. Don't be crazy, Abe. You can't fight this so just pack up and go.'

'I'll think about it, Jack. I'm thinking about it. I've thought about it. Get going.'

'Abe . . .'

Suzy's father, a deeply religious man, turned the shotgun in his hands until it was aimed at his old friend, Sheriff Baker.

'You better get going, Jack.'

The Sheriff dropped his hands to his sides and shrugged in defeat.

'OK, you win. At least for today. Harry,' he said to the man in the neat suit, 'just drop those papers on the ground at your feet. This is still Abe's land, so by dropping 'em you've delivered 'em legally. OK?'

'OK,' the city gent said and dropped the papers. They lay in the dirt and everyone stared at them. 'If you're not gone by tomorrow morning,' the man said, 'it's gonna turn nasty. I'm sorry, but that's all I can tell you. Now you folks have a good day.'

He got back into the car. Sheriff Baker shrugged and followed him. The car backed out of the driveway and disappeared in a cloud of dust.

Suzy looked across the land, at what had once been golden plains, and saw the brown desolation of the blight and the clouds' shifting shadows. These days you often saw other things – flying saucers, ghostly lights, all the things that you'd dreamed about – but what you never saw in the sky were real-life planes. There'd been too many crashes of airliners and private planes, so now the only people allowed to fly were those in the Air Force. Iowa had gone back to the wheel, to the long dusty roads, and other states were gradually going the same way, one after the other. It was like the Third World: blighted crops and primitive transport. The country had changed virtually overnight and gone back to the past.

'Sun's goin' down,' her father said.

'Yeah,' Suzy said.

'It looks different when you see it through all that dust.'

'It doesn't seem real, Dad.'

The door behind Suzy squeaked open and her mother came out. She'd just been doing the dishes inside and was drying her hands with the dishcloth. She looked awfully old these days.

'We got the order to move, right?'

'Yeah,' Suzy's father said. 'The papers are lyin' there on the lawn if you wanna dirty your hands.'

'I just cleaned them, Abe.'

Abe chuckled. 'Good woman.'

'We've gotta go, Dad,' Suzy said. 'We can't fight the law.'

'You don't think so?'

'No.'

Her father sighed. 'I guess you're right. It's just that I won't give them the house. It's mine and I'm keeping it.'

'It's mine as well,' Suzy's mother said.

'I know that, Gladys. I ain't forgettin' that. When I say somethin's mine, I mean it's ours, and darn well you know it.'

'Stop rocking that ol' chair of yours, Abe. Sit still when I talk to you.'

'OK, Gladys. I'm listening.'

Suzy felt a hand lightly brush her cheek as her mother passed to sit in front of her father, on the porch steps. You could tell she was gazing down at the papers on the lawn, but she didn't move to fetch them, wouldn't dirty her fingers, and instead just cupped her chin in her hands and gazed out at the dead fields.

'I can't take it no more,' she said. 'There's no reason for this, Abe. The land's dead and gone and it ain't comin' back and we're haunted so much we can't sleep, so we might as well go. We get these visitations – that's a biblical word, honey – and I say they're a sign from God that we've got to go. We can't live with the past.

The visitations are from the past, 'cause we're yearning for a past that was killed by the weather. Suzy knows all about that.'

'I know she does. I'm still listenin'.'

There was a moment of silence. Suzy watched the sun go down. The very mention of her mother's grandchildren, her children, had made her go weak at the knees and feel lonely as hell and she knew that if she let that feeling grow, the kids would appear right in front of her. That could be heaven or hell and you never knew which, so it was best avoided, most times.

'What I'm sayin',' her mother continued, having gathered her thoughts together, 'is that we've held out as long as we can and reached the end of the line. I *know* you love the farm, Abe – dammit, I love it too – but when land dies, it's just like a human bein'; it rots and gits buried. Let's bury it, Abe. We got no reason to stay here. As Suzy says, an' has said for so long, you can't fight it forever. They're gonna come tomorrow for sure. They'll have the weight of the law behind them. We can leave on our own or get thrown off, and I say, let's have dignity. I say let's leave tonight.'

'And everything inside the house? You wanna leave that as well?'

'I don't want it, Abe. These visitations are enough. All that's inside the house is the past and the visitations are enough of the past to last for our lifetime. Let's take what we can carry. Pile it up on the truck. Anything that don't fit, don't go, which is a good way of doin' it. We gotta take the truck anyway. There's no planes flyin'. Like the TV said, the whole country's back on wheels, so we ain't got the choice. We take what we can take and then we go. Don't let pride make you blind, Abe.'

'A man has his dignity.'

'There's a way to keep that, Abe.'

'If I let 'em take the house, I'll be lettin' 'em kill me.'

'You just have to leave, Abe.'

'And the house?'

'I'm just walkin' away. What I don't see, I don't know.'

'OK, Gladys. Let's do it.'

Suzy couldn't believe what she was hearing. These were her parents – decent, law-abiding folk -- but they had their own language, a morality carved in rock, and if they couldn't keep their dignity one way, they'd do it another. She knew what they were talking about, what would happen, what it meant, and while it shocked her, made her feel like a criminal, she was also exultant.

'They'll be here as soon as sun comes up,' she said, 'so let's start straight away.'

Her mother stood up in front of her. She glanced down at the piece of paper on the lawn, but made no move to touch it.

'It's bin a long time,' she said.

'Yeah,' Suzy's father replied. He stopped rocking in the chair, laid the shotgun on the floor, then stood behind his wife and embraced her like a sixteen-year-old. 'A long time,' he repeated.

Suzy looked at them standing there, silhouetted by the sinking sun. She wanted to see the golden fields, the brilliant sky, the crystal stars, but her folks were posed against a background of parched earth and dust-darkened twilight, facing the world's end.

'Praise the Lord, we had a good time.'

'What we had, He took from us.'

'I'll wash your mouth with iodine, Abe Winger, if you say one more word.'

'I feel broken, Gladys.'

'You won't when you say goodbye.'

'I'm not stealin'. I'm just refusing to let *them* steal.'

'That's why I'm lettin' you, Abe.'

It took a long time to pack. It took half the damned night. First they had to make choices – do we take this or that? – then they had to load the truck and choose what to discard and then, when even the suitcases were bulging, they had to discard more. Suzy worked hard to help them, but also watched, learning a lot about the dignity of silence and the pain it could hide. She never heard them crying but saw the glint of tears on their cheeks. When the pain increased, becoming close to unbearable, it released what they needed to help them endure: they packed their things in a house filled with the ghosts of the loved ones they'd lost. The house was filled with the dead.

Suzy saw her grandparents. She'd last seen them as a child. They were sitting around the kitchen, in the gloom of sunset, and they glowed with an almost imperceptible light. They were apparitions – she knew that – but you could see them and hear them breathing . . . and when you reached out to touch them your hand passed through them. They were there, yet not there. Real, yet not real. You could have called them reflections, but they didn't do what you did, though they sometimes did what you *wanted* them to do.

They could fill you up with love or terrify you.

They could drive you insane.

Suzy's folks were healthy people who'd received and given love. What they and Suzy saw, only strengthened that love: They saw God in the walking dead.

When you saw Him you cried as her parents cried a lot, but they wept out of love and were renewed and did what they had to do. They loaded their best things on the truck, packed the suitcases to bulging, and then, before dawn, when the stars were caught in webs of pink light, they fell to their knees in front of their relatives and old friends and clung to one another, weeping profusely as they reached out to touch the dead.

But the dead could not be touched. And invariably when that happened, they disappeared, as if violated. Suzy's parents had broken their own spell. They touched their relatives and let them go. Then, wiping tears from their eyes, they both looked at Suzy.

'You OK?' her father asked.

'Yeah,' she replied.

'Then let's git going,' her mother said. 'We got a long road ahead of us.'

They walked down to the truck beside the lawn. Suzy glanced up at the sky, at the stars obscured by dust, then across the dead fields lit by the dawn and in the shadow of passing clouds. It wasn't what she had known – that magical place of her childhood – and so she climbed up into the truck with a sense of relief. Her mother climbed up the other side and then slid in beside her.

It was real quiet at dawn.

Suzy stared at the old frame house, its walls white in the pre-dawn darkness, the lights from inside beaming out onto the porch. Her father wasn't on the porch – he was inside the house – and sometimes his silhouette was framed by the windows. He was in there a long time, doing what he had to do, but eventually he backed out of the house and down the porch steps. He was shaking a can up and down; a man who knew what he was doing. He'd obviously used more than one can and left the rest stacked inside. He kept backing towards the truck, splashing the porch, then the steps, and eventually threw the empty can aside, straightened up and spread his hands in the air.

No, he wasn't praying. He was just stretching himself. He walked up to Suzy, smiling, and said, 'You know what I'm doin'?'

'Yes, Dad. And you do it.'

His smile broadened like the dawn. 'I won't give 'em

the house,' he said. 'I won't let 'em sell it off in return for dimes and then ask for my thanks. I'll retain what's my own.'

'If they don't get it,' Suzy's mother said, 'then it's always your own.'

'Right,' Abe Winger said with pleasure. 'You're a woman worth knowin'.'

That was his name – Abe Winger – and the name made her think of him as someone as strong as a redwood tree. Suzy had thought of her father that way for years, ever since she was a child, and had only changed her mind in recent months, when the dying land had diminished him. Now he showed her what he was made of – yes, dammit, he broke the law – when he lit a match and threw it onto the kerosene he'd emptied onto the lawn, all the way from the house.

The morning's darkness was filled with flames.

Yellow flames and black smoke. The flames moved with the speed of light. They raced away towards the house, eating up the kerosene, before dancing up the steps of the porch and straight through the front door. There was a rushing, roaring sound. God was taking a deep breath. Then God let out his breath with a mighty roar and set the whole house afire. It was so fast, it was shocking. First a white house, then a furnace. A ball of fire, white, yellow and red, ballooned up to the starlit sky. The stars disappeared. The flames ate away the darkness. The house crumpled as the sun started rising beyond the dead fields.

The fire became a great spectacle.

'Goddammit,' Abe Winger said.

'You did right,' his wife responded. 'It's OK to cry, it don't matter. We kept what was ours. OK, Suzy, start drivin'.'

Suzy wiped the tears from her own eyes and drove into the dawn light. She saw a column of dust not far ahead and knew what it meant ... more people in flight.

'Lord have mercy,' her mother said.

# CHAPTER THIRTY-TWO

'The other night I woke up to find my dead parents by my bedside. I am the President of the United States, Mr Douglas, and that's what I experienced. We must put an end to this.'

Douglas knew what he meant. In the few months since he'd had his unpleasant lunch with Clare, everything he had tried to keep hidden had dramatically surfaced. Now gazing hopelessly at the ailing President, he thought it a bitter irony that the accident which had unlocked Pandora's box had occurred even as he and Clare were having that lunch – the crash of the PAN AM 747 en route from New York to London.

The plane had crashed while in full contact with Ground Control, ensuring that their experience did not remain a secret and was eventually leaked to the media through pirated tapes. Within days the whole world had confirmation that something strange was happening in the atmosphere, caused by something that was rumoured to be an alien 'virus' but which no government had so far officially acknowledged. This had increased world wide criticism of political leaders and the President was worried.

'I agree that we must put an end to it, Mr President, but that isn't as easy as it sounds.'

'I haven't suggested it's easy,' the President responded, 'but I want to know what's been happening. You said earlier that those physicists, Tony Rydell and Clare Holton, who've been investigating the phenomenon for the past year or so, have finally completed their work and submitted a report through NASA's Space and Earth Science Directorate. Have you brought the report?'

'No, Mr President. The report is being edited . . . '

'I *beg* your pardon?'

'Not censored, Mr President,' Douglas said too quickly. 'The report, which is written in very scientific language, is being edited into a more comprehensible format and will be on your desk tomorrow morning.'

'Well, since it will probably be as incomprehensible as its predecessor, perhaps you could tell me, right now, in simple language, just what it says. I mean, what *is* this alien entity we're all being haunted by?'

Douglas glanced down at his notes. 'According to the report by Rydell and Miss Holton . . . ' he began.

'You mean, they're not officially representing NASA with this report?' the President interjected in a short-tempered manner.

'Well, of course they are, Mr President. I'm merely suggesting that this is *their* opinion . . . '

'An opinion officially endorsed by NASA? I mean, it *is* an official NASA report?'

'Well, of course, Mr President!'

'Then we must accept the report as valid, must we not?'

'Yes, Mr President.'

'Good. Let me hear it.'

Humiliated, Douglas glanced down again at the notes, which he could hardly bear to look at.

'According to the final NASA analyses of the international research material collated by Rydell and Holton, the so-called 'virus' is formed from two alien life-forms; plasmodes and radiobes. They were picked up in interstellar space and transported in the tail of Halley's Comet as part of its Orionid and Eta Aquarid meteor showers. The alien life-form was left behind by the comet during its flight of 1910 in the shape of a cosmic dust, when Earth actually passed through the comet's tail. The cosmic dust is an inorganic intelligence which organizes itself, and communicates with itself, by means of electromagnetic forces.'

The President asked weakly, 'Did you say . . . *intelligence*?'

'Yes, sir. And that intelligence is growing stronger in the increasing global warmth as it takes strength from the most intense human thoughts.'

The President leaned forward on his desk, his look anxious. 'Let me get this straight. Having devoured most of the ozone layer the virus is somehow feeding off the more intense thoughts of individual human beings and materializing as the physical embodiment of those thoughts? Is this what we have here?'

Douglas took a deep breath, humiliated as he thought of how he had sneered at Clare and Rydell when they had been right. 'I fear so, Mr President. And now Earth is becoming populated with ghosts and doppelgängers as well as other apparitions, such as flying saucers.'

'Why would they see flying saucers?'

'Wishful thinking. Since the manifestations are created from the minds of the witnesses they're obviously seeing what they'd like to see: the spacecraft of superior beings who've come to protect them. Another theory, first propounded by Jung, is that flying saucers are the manifestations of the racial memory of primitive mankind, who believed that all the gods came from the sky. So, for one reason or the other, that's what people are seeing now.'

'And these various manifestations, these so-called *hauntings*, are causing increasing worldwide havoc by haunting, at the most unfortunate moments, astronauts and pilots, train, bus and automobile drivers, vital computer operators, and the controllers of national defence systems – not to mention causing fear and derangement in normally sane citizens.'

Douglas sighed, unable to answer, then nodded affirmatively.

'So the world's falling apart,' the President said.

'Yes, sir, it is. In some places, it is worse than others. And right here, in the United States, we're suffering more than most. No commercial airlines are running, some states are already cancelling all train-services for reasons of safety, and most of the country is suffering from severe drought and in some places, famine. The US is like some Third World country. The Midwest has been devastated and thousands of people are on the move, most of them heading for the cities, where they hope to find work. And because of that, gangs of scavengers are forming and the general crime-rate is rising. It's one hell of a mess.'

The President stared steadily at him, as if trying to look into his mind and pluck out the truth.

'So all this is happening, but you still don't accept that it's being caused by an *alien* virus.'

'There's no proof that it's an alien virus,' Douglas said, thinking of his vested interests in the chemical and oil industries, since the banning of commercial airline flights had made his shares in airline companies plummet to rock bottom. 'NASA only has proof that it exists – so it *could* have been man-made.'

'I have to say, Jack, that the Russians are blaming us; the Israelis are blaming the Arab States and vice versa; South East Asia is blaming Japan, which is blaming the Chinese; and the Chinese are blaming everyone not massacred in Tiananmen Square a few years ago! Most of those laying the blame are politicians, of course. According to my FBI reports, the scientists are reluctant to support our claims and are leaning more towards the theory of an unnatural, or alien, phenomenon. So given these contradictory theories, I'm not sure *what* to think.' He paused, as if contemplating his own confusion, then asked: 'What else do we have to deal with? Please leave nothing out.'

'I think you know the rest, Mr President,' Douglas said with a sinking heart. 'The depletion of the ozone layer is dramatically changing Earth's atmosphere and climate. Once fertile areas are suffering from famine; deserts are being flooded by torrential rainfall and rising tides caused by the melting ice-caps. The increasing lack of protection from the sun's ultraviolet radiation has led to widespread skin cancer including malignant melanoma, as well as a dramatic rise in herpes, hepatitis, cataracts, and skin infections caused by parasites.'

'Mostly white people.'

'Yes, Mr President, which is leading to unpleasant social developments, including those I've already mentioned in regard to the US.'

'Of course,' the President said drily.

'And apart from the agricultural devastation,' Douglas continued, wanting to get it over and done with, 'we face economic ruin because of the destruction of our livestock, fish, and uncultivated vegetation that otherwise could have replaced the crops destroyed by the droughts.'

'An unprecedented catastrophe,' the President said.

Douglas sighed. 'I'm afraid so.'

'Dare I ask about the political implications?'

'Another disaster for us,' Douglas said. 'While we suffer from drought, the central agricultural region of the USSR, around Moscow, is having more rain than ever and is enjoying a consequent fourteen per cent increase in grain produce. Longer growing seasons and faster growth rates are also increasing agricultural production in most of northern Europe; even Japan is having a massive agricultural boom. Now those nations are wealthier than we are, and that makes them dangerous. Already, Europe and the Soviets have put their heads together and are raising the price for the grain imports we now require. They're going to suck us dry, Mr President, if we don't do something about it.'

'What do you propose, Jack?'

Douglas knew what he was going to propose and why. He'd always been a pragmatist. He'd thought he despised Clare for surrendering to emotion, but had since learned his real rage was caused by jealousy – she'd given him up for another man and worse, for *Rydell*, the man who'd gone on to make a fool of him with the story he'd cunningly leaked to the *Washington Post*. Douglas had thought Rydell was a fool; now he knew that he wasn't.

Worse than that, he'd been forced to accept that the most challenging woman he'd known had given him up for someone else; a sloppy individual from a tract house in Greenbelt. Now Douglas knew that he wasn't as pragmatic as he'd thought, that he was just as emotional and petty as other men, and that his need for revenge against Clare and Rydell was as strong, if not stronger, than his desire to cast his shadow across the world. It was as strong as his greed.

Douglas didn't give a damn for his former wife and children, could muster little emotion for his brothers and sisters, had no feelings for those who had helped or hindered him in his ruthless climb to the top, but burned with a passion as hot as his ambition to make Clare and Rydell pay the price for what they had done to him.

Obviously, it was senseless, more senseless, to his mind, than Clare's love for Rydell; yet with all the will

303

in the world, he couldn't rise above his pettiness. So, when he spoke to his President, he chose his words with considerable care.

'We sit tight, Mr President. There's not much else we can do. Whether or not this thing is alien or man-made, sooner or later Tony Rydell and Clare Holton will find a way to stop its growth and, by so doing, maybe find a way of controlling it and actually *using* it. And when they do, no matter who originally created it, we can turn it to our benefit.'

'Oh? How?'

'We'll be able to control the weather and atmosphere to our own advantage.'

'Our advantage?'

'Right now, Mr President, the Soviet Union, Europe, and Japan are enjoying an unprecedented agricultural boom, while we slide into a pit – drought and accumulating debt – which makes us increasingly dependent upon them. This *must* be and *can* be reversed. If we can control the alien virus and actually learn to use it to change weather conditions wherever and whenever we choose, we can become the Super Power that we once were. As I see it, Mr President, this isn't political aggression, but the ultimate responsibility for which this great nation was destined.'

'I have doubts about that, Mr Douglas.'

'I *don't*, Mr President.'

'I'll have to take your word for it,' the President said, too ill to argue. 'OK, Jack, we'll sit tight.'

'I think that's wise, Mr President.'

# CHAPTER THIRTY-THREE

Driving home in the early evening from the Old Executive Office Building in Washington DC, Clare found herself glancing nervously at the other cars on the Baltimore–Washington Parkway, fully expecting some driver to go crazy and cause a murderous pile-up. It was not a paranoid fear, but one based on a new reality. The virus had seeped down over Virginia, Washington DC, Maryland – the whole damned country – and for the past few months had been causing havoc. The hauntings, now so-called, drove a lot of people crazy – and were making daily life increasingly dangerous.

Recently, for reasons of safety, following the practice in those states affected earlier by the alien virus, all flights of the last operating commercial airlines in the United States had been banned, and it was rumoured that soon even train and bus services would be cancelled.

Pretty soon, Clare thought, we'll be back to travelling by wagon-train, just like the pioneers.

She recalled what she'd seen recently on TV . . . all those farmers from Oklahoma and Iowa and Illinois, moving in their hundreds, in automobiles and trucks and trailers, all piled high with belongings, from their farms and onto the dusty roads that led to the cities . . . exactly like the Okies in the Thirties, dispossessed overnight.

It was a whole different world these days.

She took the Greenbelt turn-off, squinting against

305

the silvery twilight. The sun was that much hotter, and the light stung the eyes. Yes, it was a new world, unprecedented, inexplicable . . . Parched crops here, unexpected floods elsewhere; strange diseases in animals and humans, as well as sorrow and madness . . . Clare died a little just thinking about it, wondering if it would ever end.

She and Rydell were working on it and knew more or less what it was; what they didn't yet know was whether or not the alien virus, which undoubtedly was conscious, was capable of reasoning, self-awareness or motive. Rydell was convinced that it was conscious, but had no self-awareness, and that it was essentially some kind of etherea, which is why he had just finished another week with Rick Polanski, involved with the UFO organization's Project Skywatch International, in the burning hell of Phoenix, Arizona.

Rydell and Polanski had recently discovered that the areas with the highest incidence of hauntings were those with the greatest magnetic deviation – the same areas where previously many UFOs had been witnessed – and they now believed that the alien virus, a plasmoid life form, was also a form of orgone energy, acting through the medium of magnetic current.

In the desert heat of Phoenix, which had greatly increased in the past year, they had a lot of phenomena to examine. Rydell was due back later that evening and Clare, who missed him terribly when he was gone, looked forward to seeing him.

Darkness was falling as she parked the car in the drive. The lights were on inside, shining over the lawn, and she looked up automatically at the sky, but saw nothing unusual. She locked the car and walked inside, looking forward to having a shower, dressing herself up for Rydell's return and settling down with a drink.

When she stepped inside, she heard both boys

sobbing. The sound chilled her blood. She stopped just inside the front door, in the bright light of the lounge. Seeing that the pleasantly cluttered room was empty, she took another step forward.

The front room and the kitchen were divided by a short hallway which was bathed in the pale light beaming in from the kitchen.

The boys were sobbing like demented creatures. There was no other sound. Clare looked left and right, hoping in vain to see Grandma, then crossed the front room, practically on tip-toe, and nervously entered the hallway that led to the kitchen. She stopped again in the hallway, terrified by the unseen. She could see the lamp on the kitchen table, the back windows beyond it, not the boys. Clare wanted to call out their names, but was too frightened to do so. Instead, after taking a deep breath, she walked through the hallway and stopped, where the light became much brighter, to look into the kitchen.

The boys were, as she had suspected, sitting at their normal places, facing Grandma. They had obviously started dinner but the food was untouched. Something had happened to stop them eating and they were frozen with fear.

According to Rydell, both boys had always had a phobia about spiders, and now that phobia had been released from their subconscious and given a hideous reality.

The spiders covered the table in front of them, as well as the floor around them, too large to be real, yet vivid. Silky-furred tarantulas, black widows and other monsters formed a seething mass around the boys, who were close to hysteria. And because the boys were too frightened to move, the spiders just watched them.

Clare felt her flesh crawling.

Grandma was oblivious to the seething mass of

spiders, staring upwards, in a trance of delight, at a man wearing coveralls. He was grey, rather distracted, and looked just like an older Rydell.

Then Clare remembered the photograph of Rydell's father which Grandma always kept in her room and realized that the man in coveralls was her much loved, dead husband.

She started screaming. She *thought* she had started screaming. In fact, she just sucked her breath in.

'Dear God!' she murmured.

The boys saw her and took heart, their eyes widening with relief. The spiders closed in on them in a seething mass, as if about to devour them.

Grandma was oblivious. She was smiling up at her dead husband. There were tears on her cheeks and she wiped them away, trying to sniff others back. Her dead husband returned her smile.

Clare thought she was suffocating. She saw Rydell in that dead man. She understood that the dead man, though real, was *not* real, and that although he could have touched her and she could have felt him, she would, if she tried to take hold of him, simply pass through him. She understood that, yes, but it didn't help too much because in him she saw the ageing of her beloved Rydell. She didn't want to face that.

'He's not real!' she said aloud. 'Nor are the spiders. *Grandma!* Look at me!'

Grandma looked at her, smiling. 'Hi, sweetie,' she said.

'Grandma . . .'

'Yes, honey?'

'Are you all right?'

'I'm in heaven. I always knew Sam and me would be reunited, and here we are, bless the Lord!'

'He's not real, Grandma.'

'Don't be a bitch, Clare. I swear, child, you're sound-

'They weren't real! Now be quiet!'

She ran even faster, desperate to put it all behind her and was relieved to reach the Collins' house, around the corner from Rydell's. Clare frantically rang the bell, then tried to compose herself, but when a surprised Maggie opened the door, she heard herself blurting out like a demented person, 'Is everything OK in here?'

'Clare!' Maggie exclaimed, squinting into the evening's darkness at her and the boys. 'What? Sure, everything's OK in here! Why? What's up, Clare? Has something . . . ?'

'It's OK. No one's hurt,' Clare said, pushing the boys past Maggie and into the house, then following them in. 'God, I'm so glad you're home,' she said. 'OK, kids, settle down now!'

The boys had managed to stop their crying and were now merely sniffing as they stood undecidedly near the living room door. Dwight appeared in the doorway as Maggie slammed the front door shut. He glanced down at the boys, motioned them inside, and said, 'Take a seat, kids.' When they did, facing the flickering TV, he asked, 'What's going on, Clare?'

'I need a drink real bad, Dwight,' she told him.

'Bourbon?'

'Right. On the rocks.' As he poured her the drink, she told Maggie and him what had occurred in Rydell's house.

'Obviously,' she concluded, taking the drink from Collins, 'Grandma conjured up her dead husband and then the boys, terrified by seeing that, unwittingly conjured up what symbolized their terror – the creatures they secretly dreaded the most – spiders. In other words, they created their worst nightmare out of their terror.'

'Christ!' Maggie whispered, glancing down at the

311

boys, who, though still frightened, had calmed down a bit.

'The virus is here,' Collins said. 'We already know that. There have been other hauntings in Greenbelt, as well as illness and even death caused by virus-induced diseases, including skin cancer! Goddammit, it's here!'

'You boys want a drink?' Maggie asked.

They both replied with a nod.

'The cat got your tongues?' Maggie asked them in her winning, mock-stern way.

'No,' Don replied.

'I'll have a coke,' Ronnie added.

'You want a coke as well, Don?'

'Yes, please.'

'OK, then.'

Maggie went into the kitchen while Clare sipped gratefully at her bourbon, then walked to the living-room window and looked across the darkened gardens to the back of Rydell's house. She could see the light beaming in the kitchen, though she couldn't see Grandma. Shivering, she turned back to Collins and said, 'I can't take the kids back there for at least a day or two. They'll be too scared to go back there. Can you put them up for a few days?'

'Of course,' Collins replied. 'We can do with the company. Is that OK with you kids?'

They both smiled and nodded their assent.

'OK,' Collins said, 'that's settled. The boys are staying here for a couple of days,' he told Maggie when she returned with the iced cokes. 'Is that OK with you, Maggie?'

'My pleasure,' Maggie said, smiling reassuringly at them as she gave them the drinks. 'I could do with some new men in my life. Things are looking up, kids.'

The boys smiled gratefully again, sipped their drinks, looked at the TV, and Collins unobtrusively led Clare and Maggie back into the kitchen.

'So,' he said, 'the boys are taken care of. Now what about Grandma?'

'I'll have to go back,' Clare said, shivering just to think about it. 'Her haunting won't last forever; it'll probably disappear when she gets tired or falls asleep. And if she shows no signs of doing either, I can probably make it disappear by slapping her out of her reverie.'

'But according to you,' Collins said, 'she *wasn't* in a reverie. In fact, according to you, she became aggressive, particularly when you tried to suggest that her dead husband hadn't really returned.'

'Dammit, yes,' Clare said, remembering with a spasm of dread. 'I forgot about that.'

'She could be dangerous,' Maggie said. 'There's been a lot of cases like that recently. As the virus spreads, it seems to grow in strength. The materializations are becoming more real, and in a lot of recent cases the victims of the hauntings have turned violent, rather than let themselves be awakened — if that's the right word — to the degree when their ghosts or doppelgängers can be dematerialized. If it's a ghost of someone they love, as it is with Grandma, they'll fight to keep the goddamned thing with them. And by the sound of it, Grandma's close to that condition — so you better be careful.'

'Where's Rydell?' Collins asked abruptly. 'Is he still in Phoenix?'

'Oh, my God,' Clare said, thinking of Grandma and her ghost, dreading how it would affect Rydell if he entered the house and suddenly saw his dead father. 'He's due back any minute! We can't let him enter the house without preparing him first. I've got to get back there and wait for him and tell him what's inside. *I've got to go back right now!*'

313

'I'll come with you,' Collins said as Clare placed her empty glass on the table.

'I'll stay here and look after the boys,' Maggie said. 'Now you better get going.'

Clare kissed her on the cheek, then left the house with Collins and hurried back across the darkened lawns towards the end of the street. Her heart was racing, her blood pounding, as she turned right at the end of the street and looked towards Rydell's house.

'Oh, shit!' she whispered, stopping automatically when she saw Rydell's car parked in the driveway. 'Oh, God, we're too late!'

'Let's go,' Collins said, taking hold of her shoulders and starting to run again, over the lawns, towards the house. 'He must be inside already!'

Clare couldn't bear to think about it, yet her head was filled with it, forcing herself to imagine what Rydell would be feeling as he stared at the father who had been dead for eight years. She felt his shock, his disbelief and heartache, and almost wept as she raced into the house, close behind Collins.

She called out Rydell's name even as she hurried through the living-room and into the hallway, where Collins, stopping abruptly, let her pass into the kitchen.

Rydell's back was turned towards her. He had not heard her call. He was breathing harshly as he stared across the table at his mother and father.

His mother was still in her chair, looking up at her dead husband, holding his hand as he smiled down upon her with a deadly warmth.

'Oh, God!' Rydell said, his voice breaking, his body shivering in spasms. 'Oh, Jesus! Oh, no!'

Clare placed her hand on his shoulder and he stared at her, his eyes tearful, then looked back at his father and mother and shivered again.

314

'No!' he bawled at his mother. 'He's not alive! *Stop thinking about him!*'

His mother turned her head, stared at him in surprise, then said sweetly, 'Your Dad's returned to us, Tony. I prayed to God and He answered.'

'No!' Rydell bawled. '*No!*'

And even as he denied the existence of his father, that ghostly figure seemed to quiver. Then, as Rydell's mother looked up in shock and grief, it began to dematerialize magically, fading and shrinking.

'No!' Grandma cried out in terrible grief, her hand clawing desperately at the air where the ghost had stood. 'Don't go, Sam. Come back!'

'Go!' Rydell bawled. '*Go!*'

As if obeying him, his dead father faded and shrank simultaneously, until he was no more than a cloudy shape the size of a child.

Rydell's mother wept. Clare was filled with grief and fear. She kept staring at that childlike shadow, an amorphous spectre . . . To her horror, as she watched she saw it changing again, gaining shape and definition. Then Rydell cried 'Oh, Jesus!' as the cloudy substance became a small boy.

The boy was about ten years old and looked just like Rydell. He had dishevelled brown hair, a gravely intelligent face and was staring at Rydell as if bewildered by what he was seeing. Rydell knew he was staring at himself.

'Oh, my child!' Grandma exclaimed, her face radiant with joy. She rose from her chair, her hands reaching out to embrace the boy, her face flushed. 'Oh, please let me hold you!'

'*No!*' Rydell exploded, hurling himself forward, propelled by fear and outrage. He clawed at the boy and passed through him, crashing into the wall behind.

The boy vanished abruptly. Grandma cried out and

fell. She was clutching her heart and writhing on the floor as Rydell and Clare knelt beside her. Grandma groaned in agony, and as Clare's hair fell on her face she shuddered and died.

'Oh, God, no!' Rydell sobbed, cradling her grey head in his arms, rocking her gently back and forth, his tears wetting her face.

Clare looked on, feeling helpless.

# CHAPTER THIRTY-FOUR

The fires were burning in the darkness of America. All over the land there were camps just like this one; sprawling collections of tents, sleeping bags, automobiles and trailers, with the people huddled together under the stars, around open fires, boiling coffee and baking potatoes while they traded experiences.

It wasn't safe to travel by night, since gangs of scavengers were all around, and the camps were usually formed outside of the towns because the townsfolk didn't want the new 'Okies' cluttering up their environment. So the Okies huddled together for safety, not wanting to travel by night, though even being together didn't necessarily guarantee their safety.

Apart from the outlaw scavengers, there were the vigilantes to deal with, recently formed by gangs of locals who despised the new Okies, didn't want them near their towns, and came out in darkness, wearing masks and carrying weapons, to harass and abuse them. Often they fired upon them, wanting them to pack up and move on, which they usually did.

The camps formed anyway, being better than nothing, and at night their fires burned all over the land, illuminating the new, disordered America with the eerie glow of the lost.

'Who'd a thought,' Suzy's father said, 'that we'd end up like this? Livin' off the land like hobos and bein' treated like bums. It sure makes you think some . . . '

He was kneeling in front of a fire in a field outside

317

Clarksburg, West Virginia, resting up with Suzy and her mother before starting the final leg of their journey to Greenbelt, where they hoped that Rydell would help them. Looking at her mother, who seemed older every day, Suzy hoped they would make it, since they'd already been on the road too long and were starting to feel it.

The journey this far, which by plane would have taken about an hour, and by road, under normal circumstances, a couple of days, had taken them three arduous, hellish weeks.

'If we'd known it was goin' to be like this,' Suzy's mother said, 'I don't think we'd have started.'

'Nope,' her father replied. 'I guess not. But we can't turn back now.'

He said it with quiet pride and Suzy understood why; when she thought of what they'd been through these past few weeks, she could scarcely believe it.

You never really thought of how big the country was until you had to do without planes and take to the road. Their progress was further blocked and harassed at every turn by townsfolk who couldn't bear the sight of the Okies.

She and her folks had started this journey, thinking they'd just drive straight to Maryland, not knowing that thousands like them had already clotted the roads. When they'd been turned back, they'd tried another route, cutting across country or making great, looping detours, and while that worked, while it helped them advance that much further, it took a hell of a lot longer and didn't save them from running into more trouble.

They'd travelled by day and camped out at night, but their progress during the day (because of the constant harassment and having to turn back so often) had been made at a snail's pace. Nevertheless, they'd been lucky managing to get even this far. Now, when

Suzy thought about it, the journey seemed like a bad dream.

They'd joined the first weary travellers just outside Des Moines, latched on to the tail of that great, dust-wreathed column of automobiles and trailers and trucks piled high with furniture, and stayed with it until they were stopped that first evening, outside Davenport, by a gang of townsfolk carrying shotguns and clubs and insisting that they couldn't even rest up inside the city boundaries. A fight broke out and shots were fired. People were screaming, so Suzy burned out of there and headed south, towards St Louis, even though it was in the wrong direction.

She managed to head east again when she passed around Fort Madison, but ran into another convoy of Okies on the road to Peoria. They saw their first camp there – a great sprawl of automobiles, caravans, trucks, tents and sleeping bags – and because it was nightfall, they were forced by the police to camp there for the night. In fact, they were kept there for two days, treated like prisoners, and only let out in rotation, as part of a group of about a hundred – one group at a time.

They hit the road again, but didn't get very far, being turned back at Bloomington, forced to go all the way to Springfield, and only managing to cut across Illinois after spending a couple of days in another camp.

There was a long tail-back at La Fayette, Indiana, and it was attacked by a gang of scavengers; about twenty men and women who swarmed out of the woods on either side of the road, wearing ragged clothing, firing pistols and swinging machetes, to grab what they could from whoever was closest and, if they weren't shot or wounded themselves, run back into the woods with their booty. There was a lot of firing and screaming, but it was all over quickly, though by then a lot of Okies had been killed or hurt badly, while one of the scavengers had been wounded and captured. Some of the Okies, enraged, beat him to death with sticks and rifle-butts, then left his battered body at the side of the road and continued their slow progress towards whichever city they had set their minds on, whether or not it would welcome them.

At Kokomo, Indiana, the police arrived in force to arrest those responsible for the killing of the scavenger at La Fayette. When no one would admit to the killing, the police used it as an excuse to imprison the whole group in a makeshift camp just outside town. That evening, a local vigilante group, many of them drunk and hollering, drove wildly around the circular barbed-wire fence in their cars, firing indiscriminately into the camp, killing and wounding many men, women and children. The police, who'd been guarding the camp, had mysteriously disappeared. When the vigilantes had gone and the Okies had buried their dead and loaded up their wounded onto the trucks, they smashed through the gate and drove off, scattering into small groups that headed into the darkness in all directions.

You only travelled at night if you had to – and that night, they had to.

Near Dayton, Ohio, they were in another long convoy of Okies that was attacked by more scavengers who swept by in open-topped automobiles and on motorbikes, firing pistols, grabbing valuables from the Okie trucks, and even snatching up a couple of teenage girls and racing away with them.

The girls were not seen again and everyone knew why.

By the time they reached Springfield, Ohio, Suzy and her folks had learned that they belonged to a despised group – the dispossessed – and that people more fortunate than themselves, less affected by the changing weather, feared and loathed them as they might some other kind of species.

They also realized that they had been passing through a dramatically changed United States, with barren fields, empty granaries, closed factories and silent skies, in which rising unemployment and a breakdown in communications – all mail was now delivered overland and the mail service was overburdened – was leading to increasing lawlessness and localized, vigilante justice.

A more dangerous country.

In another camp in Clarksburg, West Virginia, their thoughts set on Baltimore, which they'd heard was the least dangerous route, Suzy and her folks were just three amongst thousands, dispossessed and looking for somewhere to lay down their weary heads.

Suzy wanted to lay her head on Rydell's pillow, but she didn't think that would happen.

She bent forward towards the fire, spreading her hands, feeling the heat, and sniffed to take in the smell of smoke and baking potatoes.

Her mother, who could not lose the habits of her kitchen, was holding the potatoes over the flames on a long, blackened fork.

She looked awfully old.

'I can't wait,' she said to Suzy. 'I keep thinkin' of your kids. When you git old, you look to the kids to give you the strength to go on. That's all that's kept me goin', Suzy. When it got rough, I thought of them. I willed them to appear and they appeared and became the raft I could float on. The visitations are good that way. They frighten some, but not me. I see them as affirmations of life and it gives me my strength. The visitations are blessings.'

Damned right, the world had changed, Suzy thought by the fire. She recalled the journey they'd made from Iowa and realized that the hallucinations, or visitations, had become commonplace.

Even now, by the camp fire, glancing up at the night sky, Suzy saw flying saucers, lights that dazzled and tormented, faint images of faces and events through which the light of the stars shone. Others saw the same things and reacted in their own ways, some dropping to their knees and praying to what they witnessed, some screaming and falling down in fits of panic, and some simply sighing or shrugging and lowering their gaze.

It was dealt with on an individual basis, and you couldn't predict that. What you could predict was what it had done in a general sense: created a lot of lunatics and bizarre religious cults; made the real world and the world of dreams merge; made daytime like night.

'We've gotta go,' Suzy's father said. 'We can't hang around here. I've got a feeling about this place and the feeling ain't good and what it tells me is that the people runnin' this place don't know truth from bullshit. Excuse me, Mother, I'm sorry.'

'It's OK,' Suzy's mother said.

She was on her knees, leaning forward, turning the potatoes in the flames, refusing to give up her kitchen, even here, in the open air. There were flying saucers streaking across the sky above her, but she didn't look up. She was too busy cooking.

'What I mean,' Suzy's father said, 'is that this place don't smell good. Those policemen at the gate and that Sheriff who put us in here, they seemed nice enough, they acted decent, but they smiled like dead animals. We ain't here as guests, I tell you. We're here as prisoners, sure as dammit. Come tomorrow, when we try to drive out, we're gonna find those gates locked. That or somethin' worse. Those people, they don't have farms, they haven't lost, and they fear those that have. I don't know – I could be wrong, I know that – but I just have this feelin'.'

'So do I,' Suzy said.

She had lots of feelings these days. They were all wrapped up inside her: feelings about Rydell and the kids and the love they'd shared. When too intense the feelings became visions that had a life of their own. She'd lived with them night and day, taking succour from them, frightened by them, and now she just wanted to get her family back and know the real from the unreal. That was the good in the visitations – they could remind you of what you valued – but in the end, what you wanted was the real to protect you from the ghosts.

As for this camp . . . yeah, her Dad was no fool . . . it had the feel of a prison.

'You both have these bad feelin's,' her mother said, forking the potatoes and pulling them from the flames and placing them, nicely blackened and blistered, on the cloth by her knees, 'but what do we do? We can't sneak out tonight – the gates are heavily guarded – and even if we *did* manage to get out, we'd be helpless alone. You know what those scavengers do – they rob and rape and kill – and if we didn't git picked off by them, the vigilantes would git us. I say we stay put. I say we've got no choice. These folks is all we've got now. We can only move out when they move on, and that's a hard fact of life.'

Suzy glanced around her. There were lots of fires burning. The flames flickered in the American night and made the starry sky smoky. Not the country she knew – no golden fields of maize, no blue skies, no green hills – but another country, a foreign land, an

323

alien terrain, where the dust of blight was the norm. These fields weren't farmers' fields, but the barren soil of imprisonment, made up of automobiles, trailers, trucks piled high with possessions, tents that had originally been bought for pleasure and, inside and around the tents, people stripped of their dignity. They still had their pride – you couldn't take that from people – but the changing weather had changed their lives, destroying their livelihood, and overnight they'd become the pariahs of the country.

No wonder they accepted the hauntings as commonplace. It was the *real* world that frightened them.

Right now, for instance, there were real people and apparitions, and unless you were experienced, and looked carefully, you couldn't tell which was which. Of course, you could if you checked them out: the apparitions had no shadows, seemed a little transparent (you had to look real hard to see that) and moved little and slowly, like puppets on a string, while the real people, the ones creating them, were either gibbering like fools, shedding tears or smiling.

The world of dreams had become real.

'OK,' her father said. 'We stay. I guess we've got to. I'm just sayin' that I don't know what will happen come the dawn and it's time to go. I'm not too sure we'll be going. There's somethin' brewin', I'm tellin' you.'

'Here,' Suzy's mother said, 'have a potato. It's the best I can do.'

'Your baked potatoes are the best in the country, even when they're charred black.'

'You never *were* good with compliments.'

Suzy had to smile at that. It did you good to see love shining. She picked up a baked potato, which smelt of earth and ash, and bounced it from one hand to the other because it was so hot.

'I feel like a kid again,' she said. 'Like we're all

camping out.'

'You remember that?' her father asked.

'Yeah,' she said, 'of course I do. You and Mom and I, we'd all go out on a Sunday and have us a picnic.'

'You were real cute in those days.'

'I'm not now?'

'Now you're beautiful.'

'I take back what I said,' Suzy's mother said. 'He *is* good with compliments!'

'I know my women,' Suzy's father said.

'You learnt the easy route, Abe.'

'It takes a man with sense to take that route, Gladys, and you sure look good on it.'

Suzy loved it when they talked that way, bantering easy, their words lingering, but she didn't think her mother looked good. Even kind words had limits. In three weeks, her mother had aged thirty years. It scared Suzy to look at her.

Scared her more when the shots rang out.

She would never be able to piece together exactly what happened, except that at first she thought it was outlaw scavengers, then realized, when she saw the masks and decent clothes, that it was a group of vigilantes from the town, hell-bent on getting rid of the Okies or having some vicious fun.

They'd surrounded the camp quietly, driving without lights, but they all switched on their lights at the same time and started firing their weapons.

The sudden roar of the guns was shocking and followed immediately by people screaming, then the cars outside the fence roared into life and started racing around the perimeter with the vigilantes still firing.

The apparitions vanished the instant the guns fired, when those creating them were jerked from their own thoughts by the god-awful noise.

325

The Okies scattered for cover, women sweeping up their children, but a lot of them fell in the stampede, sometimes right on the fires. Sparks showered into the air, the cars' headlights were blinding, and some of the vigilantes started letting off fireworks which hissed and whined into the sky to add to the chaos.

Suzy jumped up, dropping her baked potato. She grabbed her mother's hand and jerked her to her feet, crying, 'Come on! Let's go!'

Her father was already moving, holding his shotgun across his chest, and together they ran to their truck and clambered inside. There was a loud crashing sound, then the shrieking of twisting metal, and Suzy saw a vigilante truck smashing into the main gate, tearing the posts from the ground, bringing the whole gate down and bouncing over it. The truck just kept coming, racing into the camp, and the men in the back were firing rifles and hollering like crazy.

More fireworks were let off, exploding into the night sky, the sparks and coloured streamers arching back down to blend with the smoke.

Suzy pressed her foot on the accelerator and headed straight for the fallen gate.

People were running every which way, ducking bullets, falling down, as more vigilante trucks came bouncing over the smashed gate, the men in the back hollering and firing as if at a funfair. The police had conveniently vanished as they did every time, and it was clear that these particular townsfolk were going all out, no limit. Men were spilling off the trucks, swinging clubs, grabbing women, and as Suzy gunned the engine and raced towards the fallen fence, Abe stuck his shotgun out the window like a man who meant business.

'Sonsofbitches!' he said.

He fired the shotgun at someone and Suzy kept

driving. She had to swerve out of the way of an oncoming truck, and as she passed it she glimpsed sweaty faces and hot, hungry eyes. Gun-barrels spat fire, bullets richocheted off the truck. Suzy gripped the wheel tightly as the truck hit the fallen gate, bounced up and rattled its way across it. She heard women screaming, kids crying, men laughing evilly, then an explosion – probably a petrol bomb – as she turned right and headed along the road, away from the bedlam.

'Lord have mercy,' her mother whispered to herself. 'These are terrible times.'

Her father was slumped in the seat beside her, taking deep, faltering breaths. He laid the shotgun across his knees and pressed his hands to his belly.

'God, it hurts,' he said quietly.

He removed his hands and held them up. They were covered in blood. Satisfied, he placed them back on his stomach and said, 'Keep drivin', Suzy.'

She felt a great, swooping fear, but kept her voice calm. 'We're gonna have to stop and bandage that wound, Dad.'

Her mother's head jerked around, her eyes widening in terror. 'What . . . ?'

'It's all right, Gladys,' Abe said, 'It's not as bad as it looks. Keep drivin', Suzy, until we're well away from that camp and those crazy townsfolk. Don't worry 'bout me none.'

'We stop now!' Suzy's mother said.

'No, we don't,' Abe replied. 'We don't stop till we've put a lot of miles between us and Clarksburg. It's too dangerous for you two.'

'Pull over, Suzy!' her mother snapped.

'Keep goin',' her father insisted.

'You pull over right this minute, Suzy!'

'OK, Mom,' Suzy said.

327

She pulled over to the side of the road and cut the engine when the truck was under the trees. Her father turned to open his door, then gasped and sat back, pressing his hands tighter to his stomach, starting to sweat.

'Someone's gonna have to help me down,' he said, sounding hoarse and shaken.

'Oh, dear God!' Suzy's mother said as she opened the other door and clambered down. Suzy put on the hand-brake and stared at her father; he was sweating and biting his lower lip, trying to smile.

His breathing was laboured.

Suzy's mother opened the other door and reached up to Abe. 'OK, Abe,' she said, 'take a deep breath and then turn towards me. You'll just have to bear it.'

Abe did as his wife had said. He shuddered, as if whiplashed, so Suzy took hold of his shoulders, steadying him, wanting to hug him as he edged off the seat. He took another deep breath, held it in and then slid to the ground.

He groaned aloud as he slipped out of the cabin and into his wife's arms. She held him for a moment, supporting him, kissing him, before helping him down to the ground. He sat there, propped up against a tree, with his hands on his belly. When he removed them, the blood squirted out and splashed on his legs.

'Oh, my Lord!' Suzy's mother said.

She tore his shirt away and looked at his belly, then closed her eyes briefly.

'Suzy,' she said, as Suzy dropped onto the grass, 'get a towel from that bag in the truck. Make sure it's a clean one.'

Suzy did as she was told. Fear was flapping its wings around her. When she handed over the towel, her mother ripped Abe's shirt away, then wrapped the towel around his belly and tied it real tight.

Abe groaned aloud again.

'I'm sorry, Abe,' Gladys said, 'but it's got to be tight. It might stop the blood till we get help, though I don't guarantee it.'

'We ain't gonna get help,' Abe said. 'You can't move me again.'

'You'll be all right.'

'No, I won't, Gladys. My insides are all torn up.'

Gladys bit her knuckles, but couldn't stop her tears. 'Don't you go and take that attitude, Abe Winger. You'll be all right. You know you will.'

'Hold my hand, Gladys.' She did as she was told. 'Suzy,' he said, 'kneel down behind your mother and put your arms round her.' Suzy knelt on the grass and put her arms around her mother. 'Let's just stay awhile like this,' her father said, 'and stop all this snifflin'.'

But Gladys kept crying and Suzy soon joined her, feeling the bird of fear settle upon her to blot out the stars. She held on to her mother. Gladys held her husband's hand. The breeze crooned through the trees, making the brown leaves dance and rustle, as Abe closed his eyes and whispered, 'Glory Road! I see a light in the distance. All the way down the line, there.'

His breathing became heavier. He coughed and spat up blood. When he shuddered, Gladys tightened her grip and Suzy pressed closer to her.

Gladys murmured the Lord's Prayer. Abe muttered something and then was silent. Gladys finished her praying as Abe opened his eyes.

He whispered, 'What the hell, I don't know . . . ' and then closed his eyes again. He shuddered and gave a light sigh, then passed on to Glory Road.

Gladys fell against him, embracing him, sobbing with grief, but Suzy just knelt there on the grass, looking at them in disbelief.

Her heart was breaking. Her whole body constricted.

She heard another noise, something besides her mother's sobbing, and glanced back the way they had come, to see what it was. The distant lights were blurred by her tears, but approaching at a good speed. She thought it was probably the vigilantes, but she just didn't give a damn.

The sound of her mother's weeping filled the night and that's all that concerned her.

# CHAPTER THIRTY-FIVE

Rydell awoke in the dawn with a dreadful sense of foreboding. He had dreamt about his mother's funeral which had taken place three months before, as well as suffering visions of Suzy and what she'd been through.

He hadn't been himself since the funeral. He had felt constantly haunted by death and now, when he lay in the bed beside Clare, staring up at the streaks of sunlight that were fanning across the ceiling, he felt oddly dislocated from the real world, as if dreaming himself.

He remembered seeing the child that was himself the day his mother had died. The child had never returned and so far, at least, Rydell hadn't been haunted by his dead parents. Yet others were being haunted, all over the world now, and he knew that any day he could awaken to find someone standing there. The thought filled him with dread.

To distract himself he rolled towards Clare's naked body. He awakened her, exploring her with his hands and took pleasure from her smile, but didn't make love to her. He wanted to, but this morning he felt too guilty, so he gave her just a hug before he slid out of bed.

'Can you take the kids to school?' he asked her, when he had showered and was getting dressed. 'I have to have an early meeting with Dwight and then go to meet Suzy.'

Clare rolled over in the bed. 'Sure,' she said. 'That's no problem.'

'You really don't mind me seeing Suzy?'

'No, Tony. I think you *should* see her. She's obviously been through one hell of a time, so it's the least you can do.'

'Yeah,' he said, 'I guess so.'

But he felt pretty bad, torn between love and duty, filled with guilt because he knew that his seeing Suzy would hurt Clare, while his refusal to do so would hurt Suzy, for whom he still had deep feelings. He'd never thought too much about feelings until his marriage broke up; now his feelings were very confused and threatened to swamp him.

Christ, it was awful!

'Thing is,' he began.

'You don't have to say it, Tony.'

'Yes, I do. I've gotta say it. She came through hell to get here and while I'm pretty sure of what she's gonna ask for, I've still got to go. I owe her that, at least. It's a simple matter of respect. Her father's dead and she's got a sick mother and she's in Annapolis, so I've just got to go.'

'I know all that already,' Clare said. 'You don't have to repeat it.'

She wasn't angry, but he knew she was exhausted and that could be the reason.

'She was in Annapolis six weeks,' he said, 'before she even picked up the phone. She came from Iowa by road and lost her Dad and now her mother's sick and she still didn't phone! She said she just didn't have the nerve, but that now she needs help.'

'I know,' Clare said. 'You told me.'

'So you're angry.'

'No, I'm not. You're feeling guilty, but I'm not angry. I just wish you'd accept the situation without getting so emotionally confused. You owe her a lot, Tony, you really do, and I don't resent that. It's *you* who feels

332

guilty.'

'Yeah,' he said, feeling pretty damned foolish, 'I guess that's what's bugging me.'

'Go and see her and you'll feel better.'

'You don't have to worry . . .'

'I'm not worried about that at all. I'm just awfully tired, Tony.'

He leaned over the bed, kissed her, straightened up and asked, 'Are you going to work today? You should take a day off.'

'I think I will,' she replied. 'I feel like giving myself a break. I've worked every damned weekend for the past month and now I'm exhausted.'

'You *look* exhausted,' he told her. 'You've looked exhausted for weeks now. I've told you before, you shouldn't let this project obsess you. You're working too hard.'

'We have to crack it, Tony.'

'A *lot* of people are trying to crack it, but they're not all working themselves to death as you seem to be doing.'

'I'm OK.'

'You're exhausted. You fall asleep in front of the TV. You can hardly get out of bed in the mornings and when you do, you're still tired. Yeah, take the day off. At least one a week. My woman needs *some* rest.'

She smiled at him. 'OK, Tony, I'll try. Now you'd better get going.'

'Yeah,' he said. 'I guess so.'

Sitting in his car during the short drive to NASA he hoped that Clare would take him seriously and try to rest up. She *had* been very tired recently, not her usual self at all, and he was convinced that it was a combination of the shock of his mother's death and her growing obsession with the alien virus that was changing the face of the Earth.

Her exhaustion was clearly caused by overwork, which was something he knew about. Suzy had left him because he'd worked too much and spent too much time away from home. He'd ignored her resentment, or at least treated it lightly, and in the end, she'd felt neglected and looked elsewhere for recognition. In a sense he was guilty of having driven her out; and he'd done so because of his obsession with nothing other than work. No mistresses. No one-night stands. Just goddamned work . . . And now Clare was obsessed as he had been and was becoming exhausted. He'd have to keep his eye on her.

When he had settled into his office in the NASA–Goddard Space Flight Centre, he put a call through to Dwight Collins.

'Rise and shine, sleepy head! Here I am, bright and bushy-tailed.'

Collins laughed and said, 'Get your ass down here and let's have our talk. Then you can go and see Suzy.'

'I'm really looking forward to that,' Rydell said.

'I bet you are,' Collins said.

Rydell grinned and put down the phone, then went to see his friend in the Institute for Space Studies. The windowless walls of the office had formerly been covered in charts and maps relating to atmospheric phenomena and world-wide pollution; now they were related solely to the hauntings caused by the alien virus, and Rydell noticed that the numerous coloured pins now covered the whole world.

'It's no longer just America, is it?' he said, glancing up at the charts and maps.

'Nope,' Collins replied from the other side of the desk upon which rested a small, gold-framed sign announcing: *Dwight Collins, Energy and Environment Program Director*. 'It's now a global phenomenon. And even the people Jack Douglas said were responsible for it are now suffering, which should have left him with egg on his face.'

'*Should* have?' Rydell asked, pulling a chair up and sitting down, facing Collins.

Collins grinned laconically. 'Douglas is a consummate politician who just thunders ahead.'

'And how's the great man doing that?'

'By responding to each new development with a brand new political philosophy that blatantly contradicts the one that's gone before. And the President, now pretty ill, is too tired to do more than nod when his string's pulled.'

Rydell chuckled at that, but Collins leaned forward, his elbows on the desk and, chin resting on his hands, suddenly looked serious.

'I wanted to see you,' he said, 'because I want to know why you think Douglas is being so generous to us.'

'You mean in financing our ozone research?'

'Exactly.'

Rydell shrugged. 'Search me. I can only assume that he's after the glory he can steal if we manage to crack this.'

Collins nodded. 'Maybe . . . and then again, maybe not. I think he has bigger fish to fry and that *you* should be careful.'

'*Me?*'

'You stole his girl, Rydell, and he's known as a vengeful man.'

'I don't think he's a schoolboy,' Rydell said, 'and that's what you're suggesting. He's hardly likely to use this extraordinary business to pursue a personal vendetta.'

'You don't think so?'

'No. He's a mature man, not an idiot.'

'There are no mature men in love or war and we're dealing with both.'

'It's been a few years, Dwight.'

'Vindictive men have long memories. And if Douglas can pay you back *and* profit by it, I think he'll try to.'

Thinking of Clare and what they had shared together, Rydell welled up with love. But when he thought of her with Douglas, sharing his bed, he couldn't help feeling resentment.

Shocked, he said, 'Yeah, maybe you're right, but what can he do?'

Collins sighed. 'I'm not sure, Tony. I only know that for the past few years the whole world's been in conflict over the virus, each country thinking it was the other's secret weapon, and assholes like Douglas used it as anti-Soviet propaganda. Now, since the Soviets, and the Chinese for that matter, are also suffering from the climatic changes and virus-hauntings, we know it isn't a secret weapon created by a foreign power, but a real phenomenon of a dangerous, alien nature. Yet . . . ' and here Collins shrugged and raised his hands as if appealing to God, 'human nature being what it is, instead of uniting the world the presence of the alien virus has simply changed the balance of power and now the United States is practically a Third World country. We've had a crippling drought, our exports have been halved, and given the speed of the rise in the world's mean temperature, I think it's safe to assume that New York will be flooded within five years, in which case, we might as well pack up and go to live in Calcutta.'

'All of this I know,' Rydell said. 'So what about Douglas?'

'This is off the record,' Collins said.

'For chrissakes, Dwight . . . '

Paranoia was in the air. You inhaled it. Rydell knew exactly how his friend felt, since he felt the same way: frightened by the changing world and how that was affecting global politics as well as frightened of being

336

haunted by the demons locked up in his mind; frightened of giving his thoughts to the virus and becoming its victim. It was himself he was frightened of.

'Shit,' he said, 'let's get it over and done with. Just spit it out, Dwight.'

But Dwight didn't spit it out. He took a deep breath and spoke with deliberation.

'As you know, two weeks ago the European Economic Community and the Soviet Union signed a formal agreement designed to combat the devastation caused by the changing climate through the opening of doors to free exchange of commerce and scientific ideas. They're now exchanging crops, industrial and chemical products, and any research material they've so far found on the alien virus, but they're not including us in this brave new form of *glasnost* – they've left us out in the cold.'

'Right,' Rydell said. 'I know that.'

'Douglas loves it,' Collins informed him. 'It's right up his street. He's been trying to gain the President's support for his economic plans and now, given the fact that the United States had been isolated, he's been able to convince the President – no bright spark, as we know – that the Soviet–European alliance is using the ecological disasters and hauntings to further degrade US influence in the international business community. In other words, we grow weak while they grow strong.'

'I believe you,' Rydell said. 'Douglas likes to play power games. But where the hell do I fit into this? Even Douglas can't . . . '

'Off the record, right?'

'For chrissakes, Dwight . . . '

'OK.' Dwight took a deep breath before he spoke. 'There are whispers that Douglas has convinced the President that in doing so much work on weather engineering with foreign scientists, including some in Europe and what used to be East Berlin, you were instrumental in making conditions worse here than they are anywhere else. In short, you're a traitor.'

'What bullshit!' Rydell felt his heart racing.

'Not according to Douglas,' Dwight replied. 'According to him you've spent half of your professional life in Europe, have worked closely with European and Soviet scientists, and in your *own* country have done nothing but antagonize those with whom you work, with your theories about UFOs and other paranormal subjects. Then, of course, when your beloved Soviets, in cooperation with European scientists, advanced from simple cloud-busting to more advanced weather engineering, you, Tony Rydell, were there helping them. According to Douglas, even if you're not totally responsible, you certainly helped create the weather conditions now destroying the United States, and he's about to use that story with the President to turn him against you.'

'Jesus,' Rydell said, hardly believing what he was hearing. 'So what do I do?'

'Well, it'll be a few months yet before Douglas makes his move. He'll have to prepare his case against you with a great deal of care. In the meantime, since I think his plan is to get you drummed out of NASA, you'd better double your efforts to stop the spread of the alien virus, and remember to mind your back and get ready to duck.'

Rydell sighed and stood up. 'Thanks, Dwight,' he said.

'Remember: this is all *off the record*.'

'No sweat. And now I'm going from one problem to another.'

'Suzy?'

'You got it.'

'Best of luck.'

'Thanks. I'll see you.'

Driving to Annapolis, he had to squint against the heat haze, scanning the sky for flying saucers created by the virus and giving careful attention to the other drivers, in case one was 'haunted' while driving and lost control of their vehicle in their panic. It happened a lot these days, as could be seen by the many wrecks scattered along the roadside – now too many to be towed away by the local authorities.

The psychologist, Carl Jung, had been correct in his belief that certain UFOs were psychic projections resulting from man's need to believe in the existence of a higher power. Because the virus created reality from men's minds, it was creating small flying saucers that harassed aircraft, automobiles and even pedestrians, and caused accidents. So Rydell drove with care, checking every passing car, and was relieved to reach Annapolis without incident and walk unharmed into the bar, where Suzy was waiting.

'Why am I always the first?' she asked him with a nervous smile. 'Do you arrive late on principle?'

'You're living in Annapolis,' he replied, feeling distinctly uncomfortable, 'but I had to drive here.'

'I hate driving these days,' she replied. 'It's become so damned dangerous. Last time I drove to Washington these flying saucers crossed the road and caused a god-almighty pile-up. I was lucky. Real lucky. Can I get you a beer?'

'Yeah, Suzy. Thanks.'

She was looking surprisingly well, considering her recent experience, and was wearing formal clothes, which made her seem more mature. She looked really attractive.

Feeling guilty that he should even think that way about her, Rydell waited until she'd ordered his beer, then said, 'I'm really sorry about what happened to your

Dad. It must have been pretty rough.'

'It's always rough, Tony.'

'If you'd told me I'd have gone to the funeral. I felt bad, being left out.'

She glanced down at the floor. 'I should have told you. I know that. It's just that I couldn't bear to face you at that particular time. I wasn't ready for that. So there was just me and Mom, Caroline and Ron – they took us in when we got out of the hospital in Annapolis.'

'You ended up in a *naval* hospital?' Rydell asked her.

Suzy chuckled and shook her head, as if she didn't believe it herself. 'Yeah,' she said. 'We were real lucky. A few moments after Dad died we saw headlights coming towards us and thought it was some of the vigilantes who'd attacked the camp we'd escaped from. In fact, it was a bunch of cadets on their way back to the Naval Academy at Annapolis – real nice kids – who helped load Dad back up onto the truck, then stayed with us until we reached Annapolis, where they took us straight to the naval hospital. Dad's body was taken away and we were looked after for the night. Next day, I phoned Caroline and she and Ron came to collect us. They took care of Dad's funeral an' all. Me and Mom, we were too shocked and exhausted to even think straight.'

'You're still staying with Caroline and Ron?'

'No. We only stayed there at first because we had no cash. The farm was wiped out completely. That's why we were originally comin' here to see you. I was hoping you'd help us out for a time and, more important, help Dad's wounded pride by finding him some decent work to do.'

'I'd've done that. I really would, Suzy.'

'Yeah, Tony, I know you would've. Now, of course, Dad doesn't need a job and Caroline got me fixed up as a waitress in a friend's restaurant near the waterfront. It's nice and it pays well and now Mom and me are in our own apartment so, you know, we're OK.'

'Your Mom's recovering?'

'She took it real hard, but she's OK. A lot older lookin' these days, but she's out and about.'

'Listen, if there's anything I can do to help . . .'

'I just want my kids back.'

Rydell sighed in exasperation. They were back to it again. He really sympathized with her and felt guilty as hell about her, but he still wouldn't let her have the kids, no matter how much she tormented him through her solicitors.

'I'm getting exhausted with all this legal business, Suzy. I wish you'd give it a break.'

'I can't,' she replied in a matter-of-fact way with no sign of animosity. 'I want my kids back and I'm going to get them and that's all there is to it.'

'You won't get them, Suzy. You left *us*, after all. And besides, they're perfectly happy where they are. Clare looks after them well.'

'I'm not arguing against that – I mean, I've nothing against Clare – but no matter how nice she is to them, she isn't their mother.'

'You're making my life hell on Earth, Suzy.'

'I told you I would.'

'Aren't you ever going to stop?'

'Not until I get my kids back.'

'It must be costing you every goddamned cent you earn.'

'It is, but it's worth it.'

A mother's love, he thought. You can't fight it. It knows no limits. And then, maybe in frustration, he said something he hadn't planned to say. The words just blurted out.

'I want a divorce, Suzy.'

341

His words seemed to cleave the air. She stared at him with widening eyes, so visibly shocked that it made him feel like a louse.

'You want a . . . *divorce*?'

'I think it's time, Suzy.'

'Gee, I only want my kids back; I never dreamed of *divorcing* you.'

'But we don't live together! It's been nearly two years, Suzy! And since then, you've had boyfriends, so why stay married?'

'*You're* living with another woman. I've just had some boyfriends. I've never let one of them move in, like you let Clare. And now you want a divorce!'

She turned her head away, sniffing a little as she sipped her drink, making him more ashamed of himself.

'Goddammit, Suzy!' he exclaimed, glancing along the crowded bar, inhaling a lungful of smoke from the big guy smoking beside him. 'We haven't lived together for two years! Why *not* get a divorce?'

She looked back at him again, her green eyes threatening tears. 'I left you, sure, 'cause I thought you'd come after me. When you didn't, I was even more hurt, but I couldn't crawl back. So I stayed with my folks. I had boyfriends, but that was all. I lived that way, goddamn you, 'cause I couldn't believe that you wouldn't come and drag me home sooner or later. But you didn't, Tony! *You didn't*! Instead, you got another woman. And even then, I kept thinking it would end and then you'd want me back. You understand, Tony? It's something called love. I always had it for you and damned well proved it, but you didn't do the same. Instead, you neglected me, let me go without a fight, then rearranged your goddamned life without looking back once. A divorce? I *don't believe* in divorce! I believe in our marriage. Goddammit, I loved you and still do!

342

Are you that blind, you bastard?'

She didn't wait for a reply, but quickly slid off the stool and hurried out of the bar without paying the check. Too stunned to think clearly, his cheeks burning with shame, Rydell started after her, was called back by the barman, paid and then hurried out, into the afternoon's blinding light.

He looked left and right, but he couldn't see Suzy. He walked up and down the street, looking into the side-streets, but he still couldn't see any sign of her. Realizing that she must have shot off in a taxi while he was still paying the bill, he wandered down to the waterfront and looked out, beyond the anchored sail-boats, at Chesapeake Bay.

He wanted to drown himself, but instead, he sat on a bench, let his racing heart settle down, and realized that Suzy had filled him with shame for the way he had treated her. He was now in love with Clare, so there could be no turning back, but Suzy had reminded him of the love he'd once shared with her and of how – and this he now accepted – his neglect was the cause of their break-up. His children had lost their mother and Suzy was now alone, but throughout it she'd continued to love him and want him back, while he, as usual too blind to see, had built himself a new life.

Though he was in love with Clare, he felt responsible for Suzy's suffering and knew that he still loved her. Certainly not the kind of love he felt for Clare, but love, all the same.

Confused and badly shaken, he drove back to NASA–Goddard and put in an unsatisfactory afternoon's work. However, he couldn't concentrate properly; kept drifting off into painful and tormenting thoughts about Suzy, Clare and the plot that Jack Douglas was hatching against him. The forebodings of the morning returned to haunt his afternoon. He lost track of time and stayed on a lot longer than usual.

Since the 'hauntings' most people tried to avoid driving at night . . . but now he had no choice. Cursing to himself, he hurriedly locked his office, left the building and climbed into his car to start the drive home. He pulled out of the car-park, drove between the guarded gates, then started the short drive along Greenbelt Road. The stars in the sky were brilliant, the moon was a mottled cheese, and he noticed that the road was deserted, which made it less dangerous.

Then he saw the woman standing far down the road in the beam of his headlights.

Instantly filled with dread, he put his foot on the brakes, slowed the car down, and started to flash his headlights to warn the woman to move.

She didn't take any notice. She didn't move at all. She was wearing a familiar black dress that fluttered in the breeze, and she stared directly at him, into his headlights, as the car raced towards her.

'Goddammit!' he muttered, pressing harder on the brakes. He felt a sick lurching of his stomach because the ghostly figure standing in his headlights was somehow familiar. 'Oh, Jesus, not . . . !'

It was Clare.

He slammed on the brakes and went into a skid, just missed her and came to a shuddering halt.

Shocked, frightened, he gazed out the window and noticed that she hadn't moved an inch and was facing in the same direction, her back now turned towards him, the breeze rippling her black dress.

He opened his door, calling her name as he did so, and practically fell out of the car. She turned towards him. He was just about to ask her what the hell she was doing there, when he saw the deathly smile on her face, illuminated by moonlight.

'Oh, no!' he whispered.

It wasn't Clare. It was her double. She had Clare's smile, but a deathly one. Rydell shivered and glanced left and right, desperately wanting the real Clare. Then he looked back at her double. She was walking towards him, smiling, her hands raised in the air as she tried to embrace him.

She passed through him and vanished.

Rydell was briefly paralysed, then suddenly he felt nauseous, and hurried to the side of the road where he vomited on to the tarmac. When he had finished and was straightening up again, he *knew* that something was wrong. *Something to do with Clare.*

In a sudden panic, he jumped back into his car and drove home as quickly as he dared. The lights in the house were on, but in this case gave no comfort, and as he hurried up the path to the front door, he felt frightened and feverish. He opened the door with his key, filled with dread at what he might find, but when he stepped inside the kids were in the living-room, watching TV. His *kids*, not their doubles.

'Where's Clare?' he asked.

Don jerked his thumb in the direction of the kitchen, but kept his eyes on the TV.

'Thanks,' Rydell said and hurried into the kitchen to find Clare, the real Clare, but wearing the same black dress he had just seen on the road and sipping a mug of coffee in a strange manner.

When he walked up to the table and smiled at her, his smile was returned, though in a weary, pained way.

'I saw your double on the Greenbelt Road,' he said, 'and knew that something was wrong. What is it, Clare?'

'You'd better sit down,' she said.

He took the chair facing her and looked directly at her, tremendously relieved that it *was* her, but still shaken with fear.

'Well,' he said, 'here I am, so what's wrong, sweetheart?'

She reached out and took his hand. There were tears in her eyes as she raised his hand and kissed it, her lips lingering over it, before lowering it again. She kept holding it, squeezing it.

'This morning I lied to you,' she said. 'I didn't take a day's rest. I've been feeling so bad lately, much worse than I told you, so this morning I went to the hospital to have myself checked out. I've since become another statistic on the growing list of diseases caused by the virus. I'm suffering from malignant melanoma. Yes,' she clarified. 'Cancer.'

# CHAPTER THIRTY-SIX

'Until this happened,' a distraught Rydell said a week later to Clare, 'I desperately wanted to make contact with the virus in some way or another – learn about it and maybe communicate with it – but now I hate it and want to destroy it. That's all I can feel.'

Clare was lying in a hospital bed, looking surprisingly healthy and rested, waiting to have the radiation treatment though she didn't think it would help at all. She was being brave about it, really cool, and that made him hurt more.

'You shouldn't feel that way,' she said, squeezing his hand reassuringly. 'As a scientist, you should disregard what's happened to me. The virus, after all, though alive in some way, doesn't actually know what it's doing to us, if indeed it knows anything at all, so you have to keep me out of the picture and retain your scientific objectivity.'

'That's impossible,' Rydell said, feeling bitter and unable to hide it.

She smiled at him and squeezed his hand again. 'No, it's not,' she said. 'Difficult, but not impossible. And it's your duty as a scientist, as a father, as my lover, to find a bridge between us and the virus – between the known and the unknown – just as you and I've found a bridge between us. If *we* can build a bridge between us, Tony, then *nothing's* impossible.'

It was a joke with serious undertones and got a smile out of him, but when he looked at her lovely face and thought of how quickly its light would fade, he was filled with unutterable rage and fathomless grief.

He had suffered the grief all week, often numb with shock, and at times as if in a nightmare that he couldn't shake off. The virus had done for his mother and now it was killing Clare, giving her the cancer it had given to thousands of others. Clare had noted sardonically that this hardly made her a special case.

Maybe not in global terms, but she had certainly been special to him and it filled him with grief to think that she would die. He felt hopeless anger and a burgeoning hatred for the growing alien virus – now seeing it as a great darkness covering the Earth and creating out of its mysterious depths a world peopled with only the living dead or those doomed to die. It made him shudder to think of it.

'I don't know how you can adopt that benevolent attitude towards it,' he told her. 'I've tried, but I can't.'

'Maybe because you take for granted what I only received as a gift: our life together, your children.'

'Some people would call that a penance.'

Clare smiled at that. 'It was a gift for me,' she said. 'I never had to give that much before so never knew just how much I could get back in return. And what I got back from you and the kids was a hell of a lot.'

'I don't understand that. I thought you had loving parents.'

'Yes, I did. I was lucky that way. My parents were loving, but not in the way you'd know it, so what they gave me, more than love, was respect and belief in myself. They didn't teach me to *feel*; they taught me to *think*; for years I was ruled by my head and not by my heart . . .'

'Very sensible,' Rydell cracked.

'No,' Clare said, 'it's not sensible. It's a form of denial, a rejection of part of yourself in the hope that life will be simpler. I didn't want to accept the responsibilities that love could bring, but all the time I was feeling guilty because of what I recognized as my cowardice. Then I met you, fell in love against my will, and in accepting the differences between us, I conquered that cowardice. I also learned to love your kids, and that still makes me feel good. But I'm concerned for the future they'll have if we don't manage to stop the virus spreading. That's why you've got to try to, Tony. It's something you owe them.'

He knew what she meant when he tried to visualize Earth's future. He saw a world of fire and flood, of drought and famine and phantasms, cancer and death. He saw the dead returning, materializing out of thin air, to torment those they had recently left behind in a literal hell on Earth. He saw a world in which the line between life and death, between the dream and the reality, would no longer be definable to the living; a world in which the dead would be as real as those who perceived them.

It was the world his children would inherit if he didn't try to prevent it.

'Right,' he said, feeling more determined. 'I'll give it a try, at least.'

'That's m'boy,' Clare said, smiling. 'You do it for all of us but particularly for the kids. I'll feel a lot better, no matter what I have to go through. And do it as quickly as possible, before Douglas goes too far.'

'Too far? I know he's out to get me, but what do *you* mean?'

'Two years have passed since we became involved with the hole in the ozone layer, the greenhouse effect and the alien virus. Thankfully, during that time, most of the developed countries have stopped thinking of the virus and its effects as a rival nation's secret weapon and have instead accepted it for what it is: an *alien* entity.'

349

'Yeah, right,' Rydell said, thinking of that other alien entity inside her, the tumor already spreading to her lymph nodes and liver, and hiding his urge to weep with a wry grin. 'I already know that, Clare.'

'But human nature being what it is,' she continued with admirable equanimity, 'instead of uniting the world against it, the virus has simply changed the global balance of power.'

'With all that implies for foreigners' political clout when it comes to dealing with us,' Rydell interjected. 'And your old boyfriend, Jack Douglas, is naturally paranoid about that.'

'Yes,' Clare replied, unembarrassed by his jibe and possibly pleased by his show of jealousy. 'And according to what I heard on the grapevine, he's convinced that if these climatic trends continue, the US will be forced to take dramatic steps to keep the wolves from its door.'

'What steps?'

'It's Douglas's belief that Northern Europe and the Soviets, now united in their economic strategy and becoming more arrogant as their wealth and power increase, will try to starve the United States of the imported agricultural produce it now needs, reducing it to a state of total dependence upon them. If that happens, Douglas believes that the United States should, if necessary, take over at least some of the territories of northern Europe by force.'

Shocked, Rydell gave a low whistle, then shook his head from side to side and said, 'Politicians!'

'I also picked up a rumour,' Clare continued, 'that although Douglas was, in a sense, forced into backing our project, he's also hoping that our research will lead not only to a way of stopping the growth of the virus, but to a way of actually controlling it, as well as the ozone depletion, which would give the United States control over the world's weather, and thus indirect control over the whole world's economy. Jack's no Good Samaritan.'

'Goddammit,' Rydell said, 'I don't believe it. That guy has no scruples!'

'No,' Clare said, 'he doesn't. That's why we've got to stop the spread of the virus and return the Earth's climate to normal, before Douglas finds a way of using it to his own sordid ends. So you have to stop hating the virus, Tony, find out what it is and then find either a bridge of communication between it and Earth or a way of getting rid of it altogether. And you have to do it before Jack Douglas or someone like him does something politically catastrophic.'

'I agree,' Rydell said. 'I just find it difficult when you're here in this hospital.'

'The virus is conscious in some way we can't imagine and appears to want only one thing. It wants to live as *I* want to live. Why should that be a crime?'

Rydell sighed. 'Well, I guess in that sense it's not a crime, but I *still* hate the virus.'

'You shouldn't,' Clare said. 'We shouldn't even be calling it a *virus*. A lot of people now call it "Dream Maker" and I think it's a much better name. It reproduces our dreams and nightmares and makes them seem real. That's a gift or a penance, depending on what you see, but it's certainly what Dream Maker does.'

Rydell nodded, then glanced out of the window. He saw silvery lights flying across the white sheet of the sky, given life by the minds of wishful thinkers all over the land. The flying saucers *were* beautiful, the products of romanticism, but dark dreams and horrors were also created out there and could lead to heartbreak, tragedy and all kinds of madness.

The world had become a hall of mirrors where the

images were the hopes, enchantments and furies of the unlocked subconscious. It was a world of bizarre splendours, of demons and ghosts, and you had to keep your wits about you at all times to judge what you were seeing. You could learn to control it, at least most of the time. You could learn to sense them coming, to feel your mood creating them, and to blot them out of your thoughts before they took shape. You could do that *sometimes*, but not always, so you could never relax.

Now strangely moved by his thoughts, Rydell leaned across the bed, raised Clare's hand to his lips, kissed it and lay his head upon her breasts, listening to her heartbeat.

It was beating for him.

She ran her fingers through his hair and kissing the top of his head, whispered, 'It's all right. I'll be all right,' and then, her body trembling with emotion, held him passionately, longingly.

'Oh, Christ,' he whispered.

He was thinking of how much he loved her, but it was all wrapped up with Suzy. When he thought of Suzy, on the verge of creating her image right there in the room, he became so confused about his feelings that he felt torn apart.

He loved Clare, as sure as God, but he also loved Suzy. The strength of his guilt told him that and could not be denied. He had to blot her out, to keep her away, to prevent Clare from seeing what he was thinking. The thought of that made his heart race.

The door behind him opened and he knew without looking that the nurses had come to take Clare for her treatment.

He straightened up reluctantly and tried to look composed, but felt his heart breaking with love when he saw her slight, tender smile.

'I'll be here, waiting,' he said. 'Don't you worry about that.'

'I'm not worried. I'll let you do all the worrying. You'll worry enough for both of us.'

He kissed her smiling lips. They weren't as warm as they should have been. He stood up and nodded at the white-uniformed nurses, then gave a quick wave of his hand and fled from the room.

He waited outside the hospital, in blinding sunlight, torn between pain and rage.

His love and grief knew no bounds.

# CHAPTER THIRTY-SEVEN

Leaving his ailing President in the decaying Oval Office, Douglas didn't know whether to laugh or cry. He wiped the sweat from his face and silently cursed the fierce heat. He noticed the cracks in the dried-out walls of the corridors of the West Wing and was reminded that the walls of the Oval Office had not been much better. The heat was destroying the walls, plaster insets and window-frames quicker than they could be repainted, and the White House, once immaculate, was running to seed.

Just like the President. The man Douglas had just left was a sad reflection of his former self; humiliated by the steep decline in United States' economic and political influence; shattered by the recent death of one of his daughters from cancer, caused by the depleted ozone layer; and haunted by her repeated appearance he was gradually, wearily, surrendering his authority to Douglas and his economic administrators.

Douglas wanted to weep when he thought of how the mighty had fallen; but felt like laughing when he thought of how easily, how surreptitiously, he had taken command of the White House. He had succeeded by convincing the increasingly distracted President that Europe and the Soviet Union were exploiting the ecological disasters that had beset America during the past two years and by so doing, were waging a successful economic war against the

United States. Because of this, Douglas had told him it was imperative that the White House decision-making apparatus be shifted away from the Department of Defence and instead placed under the authority of the Department of Management and Budget, headed conveniently by himself. The President, rendered impotent and increasingly humiliated by the economic decline of the country, had let this come to pass and now Douglas was in command; more powerful than the President.

For the purposes of intimidation he had deliberately arranged for NASA's Energy and Environment Programme Director, Dwight Collins, to wait for him in the lonely splendour of the West-Wing Reception Room rather than his own office. As he opened the door and walked in he expected to find a nervous victim awaiting him in awe.

'You're late,' was Collins' acidulous greeting. He was sitting on an antique sofa, under a mid-nineteenth-century American landscape painting, beside a late-eighteenth-century English bookcase filled with porcelain birds, but the opulence hadn't intimidated him.

'I've been burning my ass here for twenty minutes and I'm not amused, Douglas.'

'I'm sorry,' Douglas said, taken aback by Collins' lack of humility. 'I've just come from the President and . . .'

'I'm a busy man,' Collins said, obviously unimpressed by the mention of the President, 'and when the person I'm meeting suggests the time, I expect them to stick to it.'

'OK,' Douglas said, feeling flustered. 'I'm sorry. I didn't mean to be late.'

'No,' Collins said sarcastically, 'I'm sure you didn't. Now what do you want?'

Studying Collins, who was large-boned and handsome, Douglas realized that he could not easily bluff or frighten him. The man was a former astronaut and Clare's friend, and when Douglas realized that, he thought of Rydell and filled up with hatred.

Douglas hadn't given up his marriage for Clare – they had met after his separation – but his affair with Clare had certainly encouraged him to turn his back on his family. Then Clare had fallen for Rydell, that sloppily egocentric physicist, and Douglas had been left out in the cold. Not thrilled with his bachelor life, had tried to get back in with his wife and family but they had rejected him so he had turned towards his work, growing ever more powerful as his hatred for Clare and Rydell became a ruling obsession. He was aware of this obsession, loathed its grip on him, but couldn't resist it. *He had to have his revenge.*

'What I want,' he informed Collins with pleasure, 'is for you to drop Tony Rydell from the National Ozone Programme.'

'Why?'

'That's not your concern.'

'I'm the Energy and Environment Program Director and Rydell happens to be my best man so it *is* my concern. Now why should I drop him?'

'Rydell's a notoriously controversial character whose public statements have been an embarrassment to this administration and have politically damaged NASA in particular. That's reason enough, I think.'

'No, it's not,' Collins said. 'Rydell first got into trouble for stating publicly that the UFO phenomenon should be officially investigated – he didn't even claim that they existed – but since millions of people are now being haunted by flying saucers, I think it's safe to say that his stand has been vindicated. He got into trouble again when someone informed the press of the existence of the alien virus in the atmosphere, but since

356

there's no actual proof that he's the one who blew the cover, I can't officially use that as grounds for his dismissal.' Collins spread his hands out in the air in a mocking gesture and shrugged his broad shoulders. 'So why should I dismiss him?'

'Because your President wants you to.'

'Then my President has to give me a reason that I can convey to the press. And so far, through you, he hasn't even come close to doing so.'

Douglas forced a smile, even though he was enraged, and sat down in the white chair opposite Collins.

'Can I get you a drink?' he asked.

'No,' Collins said. 'I'm working.'

'And honourable NASA-men don't drink while they work.'

'No, Sir. They might get dismissed. It's always best to be safe, right?'

'You're an arrogant shit,' Douglas tried for a reaction.

'I'm the product of my training,' Collins replied. 'And *you people* financed that.'

Douglas knew then, without doubt, that this man was Rydell's friend and would do everything in his power to protect him. He envied Rydell that and it made him despise him more.

Trying to hide what he was feeling and instead act like a man driven by more serious concerns, he said, 'OK, let's forget Rydell. Let's not be so personal. Let me put it to you plain and simple, no matter how much it hurts.'

'Please do,' Collins said.

Douglas could have strangled him, but instead just smiled bleakly and said, 'Rydell was just our excuse because, as you've just confirmed, he's your best man. In fact, what we really want is to drop the National

Ozone Programme completely'.

He had thought it an inspired lie, but again it didn't work, since Collins simply leaned forward and calmly repeated the one word that Douglas couldn't bear to hear:

'Why?'

'Pardon?'

'Why should we drop the programme?'

'Because it's costing a fortune,' Douglas said, 'and hasn't produced a damned thing. It's a complete waste of time.'

'I don't think so,' Collins said. 'In fact, I think we've solved the mystery of the virus and can stop it, thanks to Rydell and Clare. Am I allowed to continue?'

Collins' smile was like a razor-blade, cutting cleanly through Douglas, making him realize that he was the victim of a carefully planned coup. This bastard, Collins, in cahoots with Rydell and Clare, had set him up, and now, no matter how hot was his rage, he had to look cool.

'Of course,' he said. 'Why not? By the way,' he added, unable to resist retaliation, 'how's Clare these days? I believe she isn't feeling too well and has been off work a lot.'

'She's got virus-induced malignant melanoma,' Collins said.

Douglas suddenly felt sick. 'Cancer?' he asked stupidly, his heart racing.

'Yes,' Collins said. 'You heard me. A skin cancer caused by the virus *you* don't want to stop.'

'Malignant?'

'What do you think?'

'Oh, Christ!' Douglas said. He felt a spasm of anguish, a brief flickering of real compassion, before surrendering to self-concern, wondering fearfully when the virus would encircle *him* in its invisible claws.

He was terrified of it, as were most sensible people, but he feared anonymity even more and the virus that was haunting the world was giving him power.

'Unbelievable,' he said, sighing. 'Even Clare, for God's sake! Well,' and he nodded judiciously, as if forced to be brave, 'we owe it to Clare and all the others to defeat this damned virus, and contrary to what you've just said, I *do* want to defeat it. So continue. I'm listening.'

'The research programme headed by Rydell and Clare has proved conclusively that the alien virus takes its energy and consciousness from heat and is invading the Earth for that very purpose: to feed off its warmth. So, the way to stop the virus is to *freeze* it back to sleep and then somehow replace the ozone that's been destroyed.'

'And how do you intend to do that?' Douglas asked.

'The virus has spread over most of the globe and is feeding off its atmosphere *and* the energy of human brainwaves, reproducing human consciousness in lifelike form but it's still a *single* entity or, more precisely, one giant brain, or consciousness.'

'I'm following you,' Douglas said impatiently, nodding to indicate that Collins should continue.

'So,' Collins explained, 'if we could somehow perform a lobotomy on the virus's "brain", we believe that the rest of it, scattered around the globe, would gradually die off, or at least return to its former dormant state . . . its long sleep.'

'A neat theory,' Douglas said with slight sarcasm, 'though it *does* raise the question of how you perform a so-called lobotomy on such a virus. Have you solved that one too?'

'Yes,' Collins replied without hesitation, unable to resist another sharp smile. 'Tests undertaken by the Laboratory for Extraterrestrial Physics at the

NASA–Goddard Space Flight Centre, in Green-belt . . . '

'Under Clare's supervision.'

'Correct. As I was saying, the results of those laboratory tests have led us to believe that we should fly a plane through the major hole over the Antarctic and spray it with liquid oxygen cooled to at least minus two hundred degrees centigrade; just below the so-called 'safe' point for cryonic preservation. This should make the virus retreat from the ozone-hole, back into the relative warmth of the unfiltered sunlight just above the stratosphere, before freezing the bacterial spores of the virus back into insensibility. The spray will have been mixed with an artificial gaseous matter composed of water, carbon dioxide, ammonia and hydrogen cyanide, a combination which forms the molecules essential to chemical evolution and to the creation of *ozone*. We hope that this way the depleted ozone will be replaced and again act as a shield between the Earth and the Sun and, more importantly, protect us from the sleeping alien virus, letting the world's climate gradually return to normal. We think it'll work.'

Douglas thought he might be right, but took no pleasure from the fact, since he had personally profited from the misfortunes created by the virus. The threat of the destruction of the US economy had transferred power from the Oval Office to Douglas' department and despite the long-term danger to the Earth, he could not bear to lose that power. On the other hand, faced with this *fait accompli*, he could hardly say no.

'Well,' he said, trying to buy time and think of a way out, 'you've certainly given me something to think about. Obviously, if you think it'll work, we have to try it. On the other hand, it's not the kind of decision I can make alone, and I think that any foreseen dangers should be discussed.'

'There *is* one obvious danger,' Collins said.

'Oh, what's that?'

'The hauntings,' Collins said. 'Anyone attempting to fly into the ozone-hole over the Antarctic, where the virus has its strongest influence, could go insane through exposure to the most extreme form of the hauntings. The pilot might be forced to relive his whole life; an experience that could possibly destroy his sanity, no matter how objective he tried to be. That's Rydell's greatest fear.'

'*Rydell's* greatest fear? You mean Rydell is the chosen pilot?'

'Of course,' Collins said. 'What better choice is there? Rydell knows more about the virus than anyone else and he also has a personal commitment that could help him to combat the virus's hauntings, if that's possible.'

'Do *you* think it is?'

Collins lowered his gaze, studied his hands, then shrugged and raised his eyes again.

'I don't know,' he said.

Douglas thought of the bizarre hauntings that were causing chaos, destruction and madness on a worldwide scale and having himself experienced their awesome reality, he could imagine the hell that would be created in the very heart of the virus. No, he did not think that Rydell or anyone else could defeat that, but if he did, he would bring back with him the secret of control over the virus and the ozone itself, which is what Douglas wanted.

So, on the assumption that Rydell either wouldn't return or would return with the means to control the holes in the ozone layer, Douglas decided that he couldn't lose either way.

'Well,' he said, trying to sound as neutral as possible, 'if Rydell wants to try, we'll have to let him. I'll set the wheels in motion immediately and pray that it's worth it.'

'Thanks,' Collins said drily.

# CHAPTER THIRTY-EIGHT

Suzy saw the fires burning in the American night. They were burning across the land to let the people know that the new dispossessed were on the move, looking for a place to lay their weary heads. The smoke from the thousands of fires billowed up from the dark fields and mingled with the clouds and then formed a hole in the atmosphere that now was even bigger than the United States. There was something living in that hole, growing bigger every day, and Suzy knew in her dream that it was called the Dream Maker and was feeding off her dreams and the dreams of others to make those dreams real.

Suzy dreamed that she was inside the Dream Maker, making real what was unreal. She somehow knew she was dreaming.

The bedroom was in darkness. She knew that without looking. She opened her eyes, awakening, to see that she was right. Recalling the dreadful journey from Iowa to Maryland she let the eerie pale glow at the end of her bed take shape.

Her dead father came back to life.

He was staring right at her. He seemed to be in a chair. At first he was motionless, then he smiled a little, but there was something odd about the smile, as if it wasn't quite making it. She could see him and hear him breathing, watched his hands open and close, but his eyes, which had always been filled with kindness, had an uncertain, blind look.

'Hi, Dad,' she whispered. 'Can you hear me?'

But he didn't reply.

You always wondered what they experienced; if they saw or heard anything. Although if he sat beside her, she'd be able to feel him, she knew that if she actually tried to touch him, her hand would go through him and, most times, make him disappear again.

At first the apparitions had been frightening, like you expected a ghost to be, but after a while you got used to them, learned to take them as you pleased, and even learned to call them up or blot them out with the power of your mind.

Suzy had learned to do that – she had a special facility for it – and it made her feel more in control of the bizarre world outside.

'I've been invited,' she told her dead father. 'That makes this day somethin' special.'

But he didn't reply.

The pain of losing him filled her up, like a mournful bell inside her, and she threw the sheets back and crawled forward to reach out and touch him. When she reached him, she saw through him – the faint shape of the cupboard behind him – and his eyes, when you saw them up close, were looking right through her. She shivered and tried gripping his shoulder, but her hand slid through space.

He dissolved into nothing.

Suzy slid off the bed, stood where her father had been, observing that it was colder than elsewhere in the room. She walked to the window. The apartment was high in the hills, with a view of Chesapeake Bay, and the rising sun was laying its light on the water and making it glitter.

Most of the town was still asleep and the dawn was filled with peoples' dreams: Suzy saw disc-shaped lights gliding gracefully across the bay, rising and falling in silent motion, hovering over the roof-tops of Annapolis.

364

as if protecting those sleeping.

She saw other visions as well: a white-robed man walking on water, a flower becoming a tree, houses bathed in the imagined light of God, a lawn covered in stars.

She saw what people were dreaming, what they yearned for in sleep, and although there were nightmares as well, she deliberately shut them out. She had learned that she could do that. She would feel them coming and stop them. When she felt the fear trickling up from the dark depths, she just closed her mind.

She had that facility.

Turning away from the window, she left the bedroom and went into the one next door. Her mother was in the bed, studying the brightening light in the window, a dreamy, introspective smile on her face, which now seemed old and wise. When she saw Suzy standing there, she looked up and smiled even more lovingly.

'The kids are sleepin' soundly in their beds,' she said. 'I just saw them clear as day.'

'That's good,' Suzy said.

'Why?'

'I've been invited.'

'Yeah, Suzy, you told me. You were in a bit of a daze when you told me, but you told me last night.'

'Dad's alive and well,' Suzy said. 'He just passed over, but he's there all right. He came to the foot of my bed this morning, and I knew he was OK.'

'Yeah,' her mother said. 'I often see him myself. I see him and my folks an' they're all OK. I might soon be joinin' 'em.'

'Don't talk that way, Mom.'

'It's the truth and you know it, Suzy. I've got that illness the Dream Maker gives to a lot of people – skin cancer – but now I know there's nothin' to fear, that it's just passin' over. What did Abe call it? Glory Road! And that's what it is. It's just a road to the other side.'

'I haven't told Rydell.'

'You did right in that. In your circumstances, it wouldn't be fair to tell him. You'd git him back the wrong way.'

'You mean he'd feel more guilty.'

'He's that kinda man, Suzy. He feels a lot more than he shows. He loves you, but he's blind as a bat and too distracted for reasonin'. So, no, you can't tell 'im yet.'

'You want breakfast, Mom?'

'I wanna dream. I guess I'll go back to sleep. When's it all gonna happen?'

'This morning. Ten o'clock this morning.'

'I'll be awake when you git back.'

Suzy left the room, went into the kitchen and made some breakfast. When she'd finished, she had a shower, dressed and then left the apartment. The sun had risen fully and flooded the bay with light: the hills around it, once verdant, now parched and brown, the many boats seeming to float in the heat haze above the water's flat surface. It was an illusion – the boats were actually in the water – but the heat haze could fool you.

The apparitions could fool you too. You had to drive carefully, as Suzy did when she drove away from her apartment down the hill to Annapolis. The town tumbled around the bay, looking as pretty as a movie set, and the silvery saucers gliding over the water were serene in their beauty. They never looked quite real – the clouds sometimes showed through them – but they glided silently to and fro, rising and falling, sometimes hovering, and a lot of people had already gathered around the bay to spend hours looking at them.

Some people worshipped them.

Suzy turned away from the town and took the road

to Washington DC, keeping a close eye on the other drivers. Being on the road was dangerous, as the many wrecks testified; drivers would lose their concentration and let Dream Maker get to them and suddenly find themselves with ghosts and apparitions inside the car, then panic and lose control and crash into other cars. They would see the ghosts of the dead or the manifestations of their own phobias – snakes and spiders, giant ants and cockroaches – and unprepared, they'd go crazy behind the wheel and that was the end of it.

It was those or things outside their vehicle – the apparitions of loved ones suddenly standing in the road ahead; flying saucers suddenly flying across and blotting out your vision; the road seeming to split open or bridges falling down – and those, also, would make them do the wrong thing and cause terrible accidents.

That's why you had to learn control, concentrate on feeling them coming, blot them out of your mind before they took shape and still handle the car.

Suzy could do that now, though a lot of others couldn't, and that's why, as she drove along at a safe speed, she passed the many wrecked vehicles, too many to drag away, that now littered the roadsides and fields.

Wrecked cars were now commonplace.

Suzy felt more nervous about the invitation than she did about the apparitions, but she still kept firm control of her thoughts and a keen eye on what others were creating.

Just before she got to Greenbelt, she saw an enormous flying saucer racing out of the east, shooting right across the freeway, causing a driver ahead to swerve across the road, into the oncoming traffic, ending up in a tangle of shrieking metal; horns screaming and hooting.

Suzy didn't stop. There was nothing she could do. As she passed the collision she felt a wave of pain and terror, sensed something in the car beside her, blocked it out of her mind with her will and managed to lose it. She was so glad she could do that. Not that it was easy with the things she had on her mind. She kept thinking about the kids, Rydell and Clare, and those thoughts kept crowding in upon her threatening to make her weak. She could be thinking about them and maybe forget about everything else and then the apparitions would take her by surprise and make her do something stupid.

As she took the turn-off to Greenbelt, she became even more nervous.

'I've been invited,' she said aloud.

Suddenly, she had a flash of Don and Ronnie standing in the road right in front of her. She almost slammed on her brakes, but she checked herself just in time and shot on through her ghostly kids. When she glanced in her rear-view mirror she saw nothing but the car on her tail.

Thank God, she hadn't braked.

She was on the long road that took her straight to their house. Driving past the endless fence of the NASA–Goddard Space Flight Centre she suddenly filled up with emotion over all she had lost.

She kept her eyes on the other drivers, bracing herself for the flying saucers, but thought of her kids and Rydell, of her neighbours, Dwight and Maggie Collins, of the good times they'd had and the troubles they'd shared before she and Rydell lost touch. Don and Ronnie flashed up ahead, but she closed her mind and willed them away, and gripped the steering-wheel so tight she almost lost control and went off the road. Then she thought of Iowa, the land's beauty, its destruction, and remembered that hellish journey to

Maryland, during which she had grown up. Yeah, she had matured, learnt about life and death, and knew that even her father's death had taught her to live again.

'Glory Road!' her father had whispered.

In death there was new life.

Her tears came straight from her heart, brimming up in her eyes, and she felt the pain and love and despair and wondered where it would lead. She turned off the Greenbelt Road, drove between the tidy houses, looked at all the dried-out, dead lawns, then welled up with yearning. Stopping in front of her own house, she cut the engine and sniffed back her tears. She was nervous as hell and all confused, but she wouldn't show that.

She was here for a very good reason.

She had been invited.

# CHAPTER THIRTY-NINE

The radiation treatment hadn't worked, the surgery had also failed, and now Clare felt like an old woman, her inner-light dimming. Sitting in the rocking chair by the window in the front-room of Rydell's house, looking out at the silvery mid-morning, she yearned to join her father and mother in death, where pain and humiliation couldn't reach her.

Yes, humiliation; she touched the wig on her bald head, then ran her fingers down her browning skin and gave a faint shudder, wondering when it would end.

*Please let it be soon*, she thought.

She was alone in the house. The children were at school. Rydell was at NASA–Goddard, clearing his desk before his trip, and Suzy should be arriving any minute for the meeting that Clare had arranged without Rydell's knowledge.

She felt compelled to sort this matter out before facing the other thing. It was a form of repayment.

Gazing out of the window, waiting to see Suzy's car, she thought of how much she owed Rydell for what he had given her: his love and the love of his children, a less lonely life, the knowledge that she was better than she had thought and had a meaning beyond work. He had helped her break loose from her constraints and become a free woman. She owed him for that.

Looking out at the silvery haze, which represented a changing world, she realized that it was the virus, that the virus was *in* it, and that it could manifest itself at any moment through even her thoughts. She would see her father and mother, talk to them, *touch* them, as she had done so many times since that first time in the aeroplane over the South Pole. She hadn't told Rydell about it – she hadn't wanted to disturb him – but now, with her initial fears laid to rest, she actually wanted to see them. Since the cancer, she wanted to join them and escape from this hell on Earth.

It would all come in good time . . .

A car drove out of the heat haze and stopped just outside the house; a woman climbed out, blonde and slim, sedately dressed, and squinted across the lawn at the house, then walked up the path. Clare sighed and stood up, reaching the door as the bell rang. When she opened it, she saw the face of a sad, world-weary, lovely child . . . and a tentative, green-eyed gaze.

'Suzy?'

'Yeah, right. You're Clare, I suppose.'

'Yes.'

'Gee, I still can't get over this; a call from my husband's live-in woman! I feel really weird, you know?'

'Yes,' Clare said, liking her immediately. 'I know what you mean. I feel foolish inviting you into your own home, but please, Suzy, come in.'

She stepped aside to let Suzy in, watching her standing uncertainly in what had once been her own living-room, then closed the front door behind her and said, 'Relax. Sit wherever you like. Can I get you a drink?'

Suzy stared wonderingly around the room, as if reliving old memories. 'Yeah, thanks. You got a beer?'

'Sure.'

'A beer would be OK.'

Clare went into the kitchen as Suzy sank into an armchair. She returned with a beer, handed it to her, then took the chair facing her. Suzy stroked the wet rim of her glass, then licked her finger.

'It must feel pretty strange with me here,' Clare said.

'Yeah, it does.' Suzy sipped at her beer and her artfully painted, sensual lips broke into a smile. 'I thought you'd be younger,' she said innocently, without malice. 'I mean, you look a bit older than I'd ... Whoops, sorry!' And she covered her mouth with her hand as her cheeks burned bright red.

Amused, Clare said, 'Don't be embarrassed. I know what you mean. In fact, I'm not as old as I look. I'm just pretty ill. Which is why I called you.'

' 'Cause you're ill?'

'Yes, Suzy.'

Suzy glanced around the house again, then sipped more beer. Resting the glass in her lap, she sighed and said, 'Well, here I am. What do you want?'

It was a simple, direct question, compelling Clare to compose herself, to control her confused thoughts and troubled emotions.

'You still love Tony, don't you?' she asked, feeling a little embarrassed.

'Yeah,' Suzy replied, rolling her big green eyes and offering a sigh. 'I guess that's my problem.'

'You've been giving him hell over his application for a divorce. You're not going to agree to a thing, are you? You won't ever let him go.'

A flush brightened Suzy's cheeks and her gaze was resentful. 'Why should I? They are *my* kids you're looking after! And besides, I *belong* here!'

'But you walked out,' Clare reminded her to test the water.

'Yeah, right, I walked out. That doesn't mean I didn't want to come back. I walked out 'cause I thought he'd *drag* me back, but he didn't, the bastard. Instead, he met you and moved you in and wiped the slate on his past.

He broke my heart when he did that.'

'He didn't mean to do that.'

'But he sure as hell did it.'

'He thought you really wanted to leave him and that hurt him badly.'

Suzy shrugged, glancing longingly around the room, then studied her glass of beer. 'Well, I guess it's all over now ... but he can't keep my kids.' She looked up again, her gaze angry, her lips pursed defiantly. 'And I suppose that's why you wanted this private talk? To persuade me to stop my legal claims and let *you* have my kids!'

'No, Suzy, that's not why I brought you here. I know you won't give the kids up and I don't want you to.' She wasn't too sure how she should continue, so just came out with it. 'I'm very ill, Suzy. That's why I wanted to see you. In fact, I don't have too much longer to live: a few days, a few weeks.'

'Oh, Jesus!' Suzy whispered, turning red in confusion, as most people did when confronted with the same statement. 'Oh, hell! I mean, I don't . . . I . . . ' Eventually she regained her composure and asked simply, 'Does Tony know?'

'He knows, but he thinks I've still got a lot of time. He doesn't know it's going to happen so soon, and I don't want him to know.'

'So why tell me?' Suzy asked.

'Because I love Tony *and* your children and I know they love me . . . '

'Yeah,' Suzy interjected bitterly. 'Right!'

'But they also love you more deeply than me and they're going to need you back when I'm no longer here.'

'Are you kidding me?'

'No. Rydell still loves you.'

'And you?'

'What he feels for me is something entirely different, partly based on his need for company and having a woman in his life, but I know that deep down he's always felt guilty for letting you go without trying to get you back. He feels deeply for me, yes, but I could never replace you, and when I'm gone, he and the kids are going to need you. I love them enough to want you to come back to them, and now I'm glad to know just how badly you want to.'

Finding it hard to take in what she heard, Suzy clasped her delicate hands together and studied them distractedly. 'Gee,' she whispered, 'I don't know what to say. I mean, I don't know if it's right that we're discussin' this now, you being so . . . '

'It's *right*, Suzy. It's *fitting*. Now I want you to promise that when I'm gone, you'll get in touch with Rydell. I'm sure you'll find him responsive.'

Suzy turned her hands in her lap, then sighed and nodded. 'OK, I promise.' She sucked in her breath, then exhaled slowly. 'Is that all?'

'Yes, that's all.'

'OK.' She stood up and glanced around her. 'I guess I'd better be goin' then, before they all come home.'

'I think that's best.'

Suzy nodded distractedly, moving from one foot to the other. Eventually, after reluctantly opening the front door, she turned back for a moment.

'I want you to know,' she said, 'that I think you're a fine lady. My kids told me how nice you were and you've looked after them better than I did, and I think I've learned a few things from that. I was pretty immature and didn't know what I was doin', but if I get 'em back, I'll do better than I did before. As for Tony . . . God knows, he's not the easiest, but that don't excuse me. He owes me some, but I owe him some as well, and we'll just have to work it out. I'm sorry, but I

374

don't know what else to say. I'm not good at this kinda thing.'

'Neither am I.'

Suzy smiled, then looked embarrassed again. 'You got skin cancer from the hole in the atmosphere?'

'Yes, Suzy.'

'My mom's got it as well, but don't tell Tony; he'd just be bothered. An awful lot of people are getting it these days.'

'I know I'm not alone, Suzy.'

'I didn't mean it like that.'

'It's commonplace, but we can't discuss it. No matter what words we use, they always seem the wrong ones.'

'My mom discusses it. I think she almost welcomes it. She says the virus is beneficial, that the diseases it gives have their purpose, and that dyin' is just a simple passin' over to where all our loved ones are. That's why we see dead folks a lot these days. Dream Maker's lettin' us see them as a form of welcome. At least that's what my Mom says.'

'It's an interesting theory,' Clare said, feeling slightly better. 'Have you heard of Ethereans?'

'Yeah. A lotta folks are calling the apparitions Ethereans. The name's entered the language.'

'There's a reason for it. According to one scientific hypothesis, Etherea's a parallel world composed of ether, an invisible substance believed to pervade space as a medium that transmits radiant energy. Some physicists believe that the flying saucers and other UFOs being seen in increasing numbers are living aeroforms, propelled and sustained by orgone energy. Normally existing in the invisible world of Etherea, they're made visible to us by the virus, or Dream Maker.'

'So the apparitions of people could actually exist in Etherea.'

375

'That's right, Suzy. When you die, you simply pass on to the other side, which could be the world of Etherea.'

'That's kinda like what my Mom says.'

'Let's hope she's right, Suzy. It's a comfort to think so.'

Suzy scuffled her feet and looked at the floor. 'Well,' she said, 'it's been nice to meet you.'

'Nice to meet you as well.'

'Goodbye, Clare.'

'Goodbye. And good luck.'

Suzy smiled in a hesitant manner, then nodded and walked out, closing the door quietly behind her. Clare watched her through the window, feeling relieved to have talked to her. She sat on until Suzy had driven away, then got out of her chair. Going into the bedroom, she lay on the bed, and exhausted, instantly fell into a deep sleep.

Clare was awakened by the sound of the boys in the kitchen, and opened her eyes to see Rydell staring at her, his eyes filled with concern.

'Hi, honey,' he said. 'You OK?'

'Yes, I'm fine.' She sat up and rubbed the sleep from her eyes. 'Just resting, that's all.'

'Can I get you a coffee?'

'No. Just hold my hand.' When he had done so she asked, 'Have you told the boys they're moving in with Maggie while you and Dwight are away and I'm in the hospital?'

'Yeah. They're delighted. I think they treat Maggie's house as a summer camp. I packed their bags this morning and Maggie'll take them when she comes to say goodbye to you. Then I'm gonna take you to hospital and drive to the airport. Dwight left this morning.'

'Back to the Antarctic for your greatest adventure,' Clare said, managing a smile.

'Let's hope it's a *successful* adventure.'

'I'm sure it will be,' Clare said with more confidence

than she felt, well aware of what Rydell was going to and what could happen to him. She thought of that great hole in the ozone layer, of the mysterious heart of the alien virus, and was filled with a terrible dread which she had to conceal. Rydell would have to fly into the unknown and might never return, and even if he did survive his great adventure, she would be dead before he returned home.

This was their final farewell, though Rydell didn't know it.

'Dammit,' he said, squeezing her hand, 'I just wish it wasn't happening right now. I don't like being away when you're having that treatment.'

'Stop worrying,' she told him. 'Maggie's going to visit me every day, so I won't feel too lonely.'

'That's something,' he said, as the front door opened with a bang and Maggie called out their names. 'In here!' Rydell called back and Maggie entered the bedroom, her plump face, surrounded by blonde hair, filled with good cheer.

'Hi,' she said, standing in the doorway. 'I've come to say goodbye and take the boys. How are you feeling Clare?'

'I'm fine. A bit tired, that's all, but it's probably emotional.'

'All these farewells, eh?'

'I guess so, Maggie. First the boys, then Rydell here. It's one of those days.'

Maggie walked across to her, leaned down and kissed her cheek. 'We'll both feel ten years younger,' she said, straightening up again, 'by just getting rid of these guys for a few days. We'll have us a lazy time.'

'Right,' Clare said.

'Shame on the pair of you,' Rydell added.

'So, Rydell's taking you to the hospital . . .'

'Right.'

'And I'll drop in tomorrow afternoon, after the treatment.'

'Thanks, Maggie.'

'And right now I'll take the boys away and let you both have some peace.'

'A real sweetheart,' Rydell said.

Maggie ran her fingers through his hair, then walked back to the door and bawled for the boys to come and say goodbye. They appeared almost immediately, and walked across to stand by the bed, where Rydell was sitting. They knew that Clare was ill, but had been told it wasn't serious; nevertheless, they were both a bit shy when they looked at her drawn face.

'All set?' Rydell asked them.

'Yeah,' Don said.

'Clare's going into hospital this afternoon, I'll be flying off a few hours later, and both of us should be back the same time – about ten days from now. In the meantime, I want both of you to behave yourselves and not drive Maggie crazy. OK?'

'OK,' both boys said simultaneously, looking uncomfortable.

'Give me a kiss,' Clare said, 'and then you can go.'

She knew she wouldn't see them again and that knowledge made her brim over with an emotion she didn't dare show. She embraced each of them in turn, holding them too tightly, kissed them and maintained her composure with gentle sarcasm.

'OK, you pair of trouble-makers,' she said, 'you can now torment Maggie. Take your baggage and *go*!'

'See you, Dad!' Don said, embracing him.

'In a week,' Ronnie said.

'Right,' Rydell said. 'In a week. And meanwhile, *behave* yourselves.'

'OK,' they both said at the same time, then hurried out of the room.

Maggie kissed Clare again, patted Rydell on the head, and said as she left, 'Give that man of mine my regards when you get to Antarctica. And I'll see you tomorrow, Clare.'

'Right,' Clare said. 'Tomorrow.'

Maggie waved one last time and disappeared through the doorway, leaving Clare and Rydell alone, still holding hands.

Clare took a deep breath, trying to still her racing heart, hoping Rydell wouldn't notice the grief she was feeling. On an impulse she said to him, 'I want you to do me a favour.'

'Oh? What's that?'

'I want you to leave now and go straight to the airport. I don't want us to say goodbye in the hospital. I want us to say goodbye in this house, where we've shared so much together.'

'You wanna go to the hospital *alone*?'

'Yes. I'll take a cab.'

'I'd feel lousy if I let you do that, so don't ask me, Clare.'

'Please,' she insisted. 'I'd prefer it this way. I want to say goodbye here and now, in this room we both loved so much.'

'You make it sound so *final*, Clare. I'll be coming back, I promise you. That virus won't make *me* insane. I'll fly in and out again.'

'I don't know about that,' she said. 'What you're doing is really dangerous. Jack Douglas has only given you permission because he's convinced you won't make it back. He has no other motive.'

'I don't give a goddamn about Jack Douglas. I'll come back, believe me.'

'I still want you to leave now. I won't say goodbye in a hospital. I want to say goodbye here, where we shared so much, and I want to do it right now. I don't want it dragged out.'

He gazed steadily at her, then squeezed her hand. Finally, he kissed her on the forehead and whispered, 'OK.'

'I'll come and see you to the door.'

'Man and wife,' he replied.

She thought of Suzy, but didn't say anything; instead, she got dressed properly while he called for a cab, joined him in the living-room until the cab arrived, then clung to him until he opened the door.

When he did so, he was weeping.

She had never seen him cry before and the shock ripped through her, tearing at her heart, making her cry as well, forcing her back into his embrace for one last, desperate moment. They kissed repeatedly, clinging to one another, before he dried his tears and walked out, refusing to look back.

She watched his departure through the window, her tears falling silently.

The cab turned the corner at the end of the street, taking Rydell out of her life for all time, but she stood on, staring into the silvery heat haze, as if inside her own dream.

Then she sat down in the silence of the empty room and contemplated her own demise.

# CHAPTER FORTY

Rydell was flown out that November, which was the austral summer, on an ancient Military Air Command C141 cargo plane from Point Mugu Air Force Base in California on a sixteen-hour flight to Christchurch, New Zealand, with stops in Honolulu and Pago Pago in American Samoa, en route. After losing a day crossing the International Date-line, he landed at the Christchurch International Airport, then flew on a New Zealand Air Force cargo plane for another eight hours towards the American base at McMurdo Sound, on Ross Island, Antarctica.

Strapped into his seat in the rear of the ever reliable four-motor propellor plane, with nothing to look at but the huge stacks of freight chained to the deck, he couldn't help remembering his last flight over Antarctica, when the aeroplane had been harassed by UFOs. Such hauntings were now part of everyday life, a commonplace terror, but nowhere more powerfully alive than in the Antarctic, over which the heart of the alien virus mysteriously beat. And so, as the aeroplane flew above the black peaks and vast white plains of Cape Adare, then across the Ross Sea, he was not surprised to see the extraordinarily graceful flying saucers. He was convinced that the saucers were no more than the creations of the common, subconscious yearning of Man for something beyond his grasp.

Rydell thought they were wonderful.

He willed them out of his consciousness as the plane descended over the Ross Ice-Shelf and had managed to lose them completely before the plane landed on the ice runway of McMurdo Sound.

He had not been personally haunted on the plane, for which he was grateful.

Dwight Collins was there to greet him and drive him back through the ramshackle complex of buildings, storage yards, muddy streets, and rubbish dumps, which made up McMurdo Station, situated on the southern extremity of Ross Island, surrounded by ice-filled grey water and gleaming white glaciers.

'About a mile from here,' Collins told him, 'is Observation Hill, where the New Zealanders erected a cross in memory of Scott and his buddies who died on their return from the Pole. If you fail I'll erect one to you, right here on Cape Armitage.'

Rydell grinned. 'When do I make the flight?' he asked.

'The day after tomorrow,' Collins told him. 'When you've caught up on your sleep.'

'Good thinking old buddy.'

Rydell caught up on his sleep that same evening, but awakened in his bunk bed to find the room which he was sharing with Collins filled with an unearthly light in which faint figures quivered. Collins was still sleeping, though tossing and turning restlessly. Rydell guessed that the faceless figures in that ghostly white light were the people in his dreams made manifest. It was a strange experience, but one he had become used to; sharing the subconscious of one's fellow human beings. When he slid out of his bed and shook Collins awake, the light receded back through the walls and the faceless figures disappeared.

When Rydell told Collins what he had seen, Collins grinned ruefully, and admitted that he had been dreaming he was dying and his bed was surrounded by grieving relatives, then added, 'It's just another taste of what you're going to be in for when you fly into the ozone hole. Best brace yourself, old pal.'

'I'm already braced,' Rydell replied. 'I saw a lot of flying saucers when we flew in; then this business in here. I've heard reports that the Antarctic has become a huge fantasy land, with more apparitions per square mile than anywhere else on Earth. Is that true?'

'Hell, yes, it's true. It's just too bizarre, man. If you want to work here you have to accept magic as the norm, which is another reason you're not flying until tomorrow: just being here will form a kind of preparation for what you'll find in the hole. Whether or not it'll be enough, we can't say, but at least it'll help.'

What Collins told him proved to be true. That morning, Rydell saw many small flying saucers gliding serenely across the glittering ice peaks under the azure sky, as well as many human apparitions who constantly haunted the hundreds of administration, mainte- nance, transportation and communication personnel of McMurdo Base. Most of the men treated the hauntings with indifference or idle curiosity, though occasionally someone would break down in tears and have to be comforted. It was a world of flying saucers, visionary lights and spirits, co-existing with the real world of the base, with its rusty buildings, muddy streets and snow-covered surroundings. It was very bizarre.

To fill in Rydell's time that afternoon, Collins took him on a visit, first to Shackleton's hut at Cape Royds, twenty-five miles farther north on Ross Island, then to Scott's hut at Cape Evans.

Nothing happened at the first stop, but when they were outside Scott's hut, studying the surviving bales of hay for Scott's ponies and the pony harnesses still hanging in the open stalls adjoining the hut, Rydell thought of the great explorer and suddenly saw him materializing, initially as a dark shape rising out of the snow, then as a clearly defined man, wrapped up in his Antarctic clothing, with frost on his beard, standing clearly in front of the empty kennel, near which lay the mummified remains of a dog, its leather collar with a rusted chain still fastened around its shrivelled neck.

The skin of the dog's head had shrunk away, exposing the skull and the white teeth in a frozen snarl, but the ghostly Scott, as if not seeing this, knelt down to stroke the animal, then turned away and walked into the hut.

Intrigued, Rydell and Collins followed him in. In the gloomy interior of the hut, they found Scott's ghostly companions lying on the two-tier bunks in their original sealskin, fur-lined sleeping bags. Their breathing was audible. Scott, or his apparition, had gone to the far end of the large room and was standing motionless, with a bewildered expression on his bearded, frost-covered face.

Glancing at Rydell and Collins, as if not sure what he was seeing, Scott went to the table in front of the window, examined its assortment of chemical equipment – alcohol burners, glass-stoppered reagent bottles, test tubes and stands – then went to the other table to study the corroding components of a primitive wireless set. When he reached down to touch it, his hand went right through it, so he frowned and glanced across at the framed photograph of King George V and Queen Mary, which hung against the partition near the centre of the room, but was beginning to fade. As Scott gazed at that fading photograph, he also started to fade away. When an aeroplane passed overhead breaking Rydell's concentration, Scott suddenly disappeared altogether, as did the men lying in the sleeping bags, which now were all empty.

'Jesus Christ!' Rydell whispered.

'Get used to it,' Collins told him. 'You'll get a lot more tomorrow.'

Whether a dream or an hallucination, Rydell couldn't be too sure, but that night as he was sleeping he vividly saw Clare having her radiation treatment in the hospital. She looked distressed.

He opened his eyes, feeling as distressed as Clare had looked and saw only the room's gloom. He thought he might have glimpsed a fading light, but he couldn't be sure of that.

The next morning, feeling more tired than he should have been, he prepared for take-off.

In the early hours of the morning, Collins drove him in a pick-up truck to Williams Field, an airport on the Ross Ice Shelf, five miles from McMurdo Base. The artfully redesigned ER-2 was waiting on the airstrip, dwarfed by the soaring ice-cliffs, its new payload packaged in different pods, one under each wing.

Escorting Rydell from the pick-up truck to the aeroplane, Collins said, 'Please be really careful, Rydell. Try to keep control of yourself. What you've seen here so far isn't a tenth of what you *will* see and once you enter the heart of the alien virus at the top of the hole you'll probably lose radio contact.'

'I'm aware of that,' Rydell said.

'And another thing. I'm particularly bothered by that last experience you had when you looked out of the cockpit and saw nothing but a great darkness filled with stars, like being in outer space or some other galaxy, when you should have been directly above the Vinson Massif in Marie Byrd Land. We don't know what that was, but it certainly proved that the deeper into the ozone hole you fly, the more varied and vivid the hallucinations are likely to be.'

'But I did make it back,' Rydell pointed out.

'Yeah, you made it back, but you hadn't gone as far as you intend going today and what we *don't* know is what you'll experience if you keep on flying after seeing that same phenomenon. What I'm saying in effect is that if the hallucinations don't get you, that starry darkness, whatever it represented might get you instead. You understand?'

'Yeah.'

They stopped by the ER-2, studied the white pods containing the cooled liquid-oxygen, then faced one another and shook hands.

'Good luck,' Collins said.

'I was *born* lucky,' Rydell replied, trying to smile, but instead choking up as he looked at Dwight and thought of his wife, Maggie. He was so grateful to them both for looking after Don and Ronnie, as well as visiting Clare on a daily basis during her confinement in hospital.

The hospital.

Radiation treatment . . .

The hope of remission . . .

Hope Clare did not share.

Rydell was shaken suddenly. When he dwelt on Clare, he thought of death. And in thinking of death he was led back to the alien virus, which could bring the dead back to life and make dark dreams come true. Then he thought of Clare's double on the Greenbelt Road that evening and his love for her turned into a fear that made his heart lurch. Clare's double had smiled like the living dead. He knew then that there would be no remission for her, and that the treatment she was receiving back in Maryland would serve no real purpose. She was dying, knew that this was so, and had hidden it from him.

Rydell filled up with grief.

'If I don't come back, Dwight . . . '

'Don't say that, Tony.'

386

'If I don't come back, tell Clare, Suzy and the kids that I was thinking about them today.'

'They all know that, Tony.'

'But tell them I *said* it.'

'OK, Tony, I'll tell them you said it. Though you're definitely coming back so stop all this bullshit.'

This dismissive remark was good for Rydell, making him pull himself together, but he couldn't help thinking that this could be his last trip, his final day on Earth, and it made him well up with emotions that tugged him first this way, then that. He was filled with grief for Clare, but also with love for Suzy, and those feelings only led to a mire of guilt over how he had treated them. He'd cut Suzy out of his life, driving her away from home, and had brought Clare into his life while still loving Suzy. God, he was an idiot! Sometimes he could be so dumb! And now he loved both of them, though he felt for them in different ways. He was torn between the grief he was feeling for Clare and the guilt he felt over what he'd done to Suzy and the kids. He was shattered by the knowledge of the pain his thoughtlessness had caused, and realized that he wasn't yet a man, but still a callow, self-centred boy. Which brought him right back to Clare.

'Clare's dying, isn't she?'

'Nonsense,' Collins said.

'She's dying, and you and Maggie know it and want to protect me.'

'Jesus, Tony . . . '

'Don't let her die alone.'

'Maggie's right on her case, Tony. And don't even ask me about the boys. . . . I'm their godfather and guardian.'

'You're also the best friend I've got, Collins.'

'Just get in the aeroplane.'

They embraced emotionally, then Rydell climbed

into the aeroplane, and a few minutes later he was in the air, back in control of himself.

There was no going back now.

Suzy was watching him, protecting him with her will and saw him in the dimming light of her mother's eyes as he flew into the unknown.

Her mother was on her bed in the small apartment in Annapolis, fading away into death's darkness, her eyes fixed on that distant light. It was a long road into darkness – Glory Road, as Abe had called it – and the light shone brightly at the far end like a beacon at sea. Suzy could see that light, the flicker of hope in her mother's eyes which illuminated her twin reflection and drew her into herself.

'There's nothin' to fear,' her mother said. 'It's no distance at all. I feel Abe waiting for me.'

Suzy used her facility to see what there was to see, and fell into the bottomless well of her mother's gaze to find what she most wanted. Her father was there; Don and Ronnie, even Rydell's mother, all doing whatever they had to do in the world she knew well. The kids were playing on the lawn, Rydell's mother was watching TV and Abe was on the porch in the house in Iowa, his steady gaze fixed on the sunset as he rocked in that old chair. Then Suzy saw Rydell, in the cockpit of an aeroplane, his face covered with an oxygen mask, his eyes filled with confusion. She saw what he was thinking as his thoughts were there in the cockpit with him: Ronnie and herself, Clare, Don and the lines of light binding them together.

She could see they were bound together by love and pain and the need for commitment.

Rydell saw them as well.

Suzy's heart went out to him, her love wrapping itself around him. Exhausted, she lay on her mother's breast to hear the last of her heartbeat.

'Glory Road!' she heard her mother whisper as her dimming eyes widened. 'As God is my witness!'

Then, as her mother quietly passed on, Suzy reached out to Rydell.

He flew over the Ross Ice-Shelf, then the Beardsmore Glacier, and an hour and a half after taking off, the frozen peaks of the Transantarctic Mountains came into view. He flew farther and higher, above dark peaks embedded in white and blue ice, cascading ice-falls, then smaller, more scattered peaks, glistening expanses of virgin snow before finally seeing the awesome, featureless, seemingly endless Antarctic ice-sheet.

It was farther south than he had ever flown before, yet nothing had happened.

During the flight he had been keeping contact with McMurdo Base, but suddenly, just as he was wondering why nothing had occurred as he checked the illuminated digital display of the navigation computer, radio contact was lost and replaced with static.

Rydell checked the control panel. He was at latitude 89S. He began his steep ascent into the heart of the ozone depletion, where the alien virus thrived most healthily at an altitude of twenty kilometres and as he did so, the static's volume increased and the control panel blinked out.

He was travelling blind.

'*Don't worry*,' Clare said.

She had spoken out of the static, but her voice was loud and clear, and Rydell nearly lost control of the aeroplane, so great was his shock. He looked left and right, fully expecting to see her, but saw only blue sky and endless white plains curving across the horizon.

He felt his heart racing, but kept ascending, flying

blind, and cursed that he didn't know how high he was nor when to release the cooled liquid oxygen into the atmosphere.

'Yes, Tony, I'm dying.'

He saw Suzy's face, but it was Clare he heard speaking, and she added, 'I'm doing this for you. I won't let it drag out.' She was right there in front of him, speaking out of Suzy's lips, and he almost screamed when Clare's face emerged, superimposed over Suzy's vanishing image. The last he saw of Suzy were her green eyes wreathed in smoke rings, which vapourized, leaving nothing but stars in space.

Rydell didn't make a sound, but he plunged down through himself, retreating from Clare's dying by seeking his essence, and emerging at that place in his subconscious, where time and space had no meaning. He was in the past and the future, Here and There simultaneously, and when he tried to break free by looking out of the cockpit, he saw only a vast inky darkness filled with stars and strange moons. . . . A vertiginous cosmos.

He tried to release the liquid oxygen, but couldn't find the control, and groped blindly across the dead control panel, wondering where it had gone. Then Clare impressed herself upon him, writhing against him, melting into him, and the living heat of her alien body set a torch to his senses. He heard the scream of his breaking heart, a palpable sound, before the darkness of the cockpit was filled with light that beamed down from above. Looking up, he saw an enormous flying saucer, descending upon him.

'No, damn you!' he cried aloud, and tried to will it out of existence, to squeeze it out of his mind, but this only drained him of energy and set free his spinning thoughts.

He was in the heart of the virus, in a cosmos created

by it, and felt the aeroplane diving (or was it actually ascending). Then the great flying saucer above (or below) multiplied and divided and became many smaller saucers, glowing, spinning particles which, interacting, formed the magical, dazzling consciousness of Dream Maker.

Rydell found himself racing towards himself in the creation of matter.

Passing through himself, he went back through his past, through his life, to his origins: first Clare, then Suzy, then his boys, Don and Ronnie, then his mother and father.

The dominion of the dead spread out around him. The myriad ghosts of his subconscious: his loved ones, his heroes, his closest friends and bitterest enemies, his dreams (those great leaps through the mind) and his most secret nightmares – giant spiders and centipedes, entrails writhing like intertwined worms or snakes, his fear of drowning, of being buried alive, decapitated or burned to death – he lived them all until eventually he was sucked back into his mother's womb, then ejaculated in water and blood to the thunderous noise of the living world.

His mother heard his first cry. His umbilical cord was cut. He was dangling upside-down, kicking furiously in God's strong grip, then tumbled through an unfamiliar radiance and fell upon soft flesh. He gargled and sucked, demanded and was fed, was nurtured and grew into a child, forgetting what he had been. Remembering only his recent past, he looked forward to the overlapping, hopeful futures that might never be, existing only in dreams. He glimpsed a timeless vision of himself in the heart of the virus, and having glimpsed it he tried fighting it.

While the spinning, pulsating lights swept past on either side, he knew only that he was either plunging towards Earth or ascending towards the stratospheric heights were the alien virus's heart beat. He realized that this was so, was aware that he was himself, but even as he groped again for the control to release the liquid oxygen, the alien virus filled his mind, drank from it, recreated it, and hurled him beyond his precarious present and its fears into that future which had haunted his dreams ever since his childhood.

Rydell saw it coming.

At first it was just a pinprick in a vast sheet of darkness, then a gleaming white eye, but then it expanded, flaring out in all directions, and raced at him, exploding around him, obliterating the real world.

He was sucked through time and space, hurled into another dimension, spiralled down through the cascading voices of history and returned to his constant dream.

Space folded in upon itself. The sudden silence was stunning. He looked up from Europa, across the valleys and frozen mountains, and saw the great golden globe of Jupiter. It hung above the white mountains of frozen ice, streaked with yellow and gold, its Great Red Spot a bloody wound. Around it were the satellites – thirteen, maybe more – and all of them, the enormous apple and its seedlings, were drenched in stars.

Rydell knew where he was – close to the Jupiter of his dreams – and realized that the dream had been telling him about this moment in time. Throughout his life he had dreamed about the future that had now come to be.

Understanding this, he also understood the alien virus; it encompassed the past, present and future simultaneously, consuming them as one, regurgitating them at will, taking its sustenance and sense of reality from the collective mind of humanity, which had become, since the alien's awakening in Earth's stratosphere, its sole source of self-knowledge, its only known past and future.

The collective humanity of Earth was the alien's God. Without Earth, it could not be.

'Yes,' Clare said, loud and clear, repeating the words she had spoken to him, 'the virus is conscious in some way we can't imagine and appears to want only one thing. It wants to live, as *I* want to live and you *want* me to live. Why should that be a crime?'

And when he heard her, he saw her.

Clare was looking right at him. He grew strong as she grew weak. He emerged out of the ether, that oddly glowing white light, and took shape at the end of her bed until he seemed almost solid. He looked a little confused, as if not sure of what he was seeing, but she sensed that in some way he could perceive and would know what was happening. That made it easier.

She had planned it meticulously, to save him and the children pain, and there in the hospital, on her bed in the private ward, where the nurses would find her and deal with her, she followed her father's example and swallowed some pills.

'I won't be humiliated,' she said, speaking to Rydell's double, 'and I refuse to make you or the children suffer by letting it drag on. I do this for love, Rydell.'

And then, while Rydell's double looked on, she washed the pills down with water.

After that, it was easy.

He was there, after all – in the aeroplane over the South Pole – but he was also right here in the ward, standing beside her father and mother, between Don and Ronnie, to share their love and concern as she faded away.

She knew they would stay with her during the journey she had to make along the dark road to the light that led to the other side . . . perhaps to the living heart of Dream Maker, also known as Etherea.

There she would find resurrection.

It was easy, fading away. You went just like an apparition. You focused on those you loved and their smiles were like the sun as you dissolved into the light of the spheres and drifted out of your pain.

She knew just who she was. She was Clare, whom Rydell loved. She loved Rydell and his children and her parents, where they stood in her radiant dreams.

The children were at home with Maggie. Her parents were waiting for her. Rydell was in the aeroplane over the frozen wilderness, exploring the heart of the virus, his own heart, the world's centre, and he would venture forth into the great unknown, but always return to her. She was Clare and she was dying . . . yet she could not die because Rydell loved her.

You were Clare.

*I am Clare.*

When Clare died, she joined . . .

Rydell survived the hole, doing so through his love, taking the faith and courage he needed from what others gave to him: Clare's selfless sacrifice, Suzy's abiding love and loyalty, Don and Ronnie's dependence upon him. The lines of light that bound them all together were the feelings that saved him.

Taking the aeroplane up as high as it would go into the mysterious heart of Dream Maker, above the vast and desolate beauty of the Antarctic wastelands, he suddenly sensed Clare's death, shared the experience with her and gave himself to Clare and Suzy as he had never done before. He cared more for their feelings than he did for his own fate. . . . Which is why he survived.

His ascent into the heart of the ozone hole was a journey into the light-flecked mind of the alien virus and, since the alien had soaked up his thoughts like a sponge, also a journey into his own forgotten self. He was sucked down through his centre, through the labyrinth of his inner being, and travelled into the boundless cosmos of his subconscious to find the source of himself. There he discovered his past and future, both at one with his present, in the shape of his father and mother, Suzy, Don and Ronnie, then found himself face-to-face with Clare, whom he touched and made whole.

At that moment, she was as real as he felt.

And at that moment, she died.

He knew she had just died. The alien virus told him so. And even as it did it told him that the love he was losing would always be with him.

Clare wasn't dead. She was only sleeping. She was here, like him, in an eternal present, and would always exist for him.

And in knowing this, he knew that the alien virus was not an enemy. It was destroying the world through innocence, and had no awareness of original sin or the pain it had caused. The alien virus was male and female, Man and Woman, in the Garden of Eden, an innocent babe, naked and crying, hungry only for life.

Rydell survived his countless hauntings and the terrors and splendours of a world beyond him. He was hurled into a bizarre voyage through time and space, beyond the finite world, into the infinite, where nothing was what it seemed and all things were possible.

He had no sense of direction, no idea of where he was but felt that he was tumbling down through an immense well of dream-haunted darkness. First the darkness was flecked with lights, silvery pinpricks on a black sheet. Then the lights enlarged to become saucer-shaped craft and immense, glowing moons. They shot upwards, out of sight, and were replaced by glittering stars, which rose silently in great waves, curving over him, sweeping him through pools of fire. He was cast through spinning space, a kaleidoscope of light and sound, living the events of history, hearing the voices of lost humanity, before racing along a darkening tunnel with a light at its far end.

He thought it was death's door.

The light expanded and flared up, becoming a radiant, blinding sun, and he went through it and was scorched and consumed, then was spat out the other side into the ultimate darkness.

He heard a silence so complete it was terrifying and he broke it by screaming.

That scream, reverberating throughout the universe, was the beginning and end of life.

Rydell died, was reborn and burst back into time and space, crying out in exultation and dread before becoming a full-grown man once again.

He was in the cockpit of the aeroplane, the sky above, the land below. Finally back in the real world, given strength by his love and faith, he released the gas created by Clare, who had found eternal life.

He was starting the process that would make the alien virus retreat to above the stratosphere, letting the ozone layer renew itself and return the earth to normal. Flying back and forth, inviolate, given strength by his love and faith, he sprayed the heart of the ozone-hole, which was also the heart of the alien virus, defying his doppelgänger and the phantasms of the dead. He responded to Clare's and Suzy's doubles with love instead of fear, refusing to let spinning moons and voluptuous suns intimidate him, ignoring the flying saucers and cascading stars of God's pure light. He kept going until the tanks beneath the aeroplane's wings had been emptied and he could head back to base.

He turned the aeroplane around, and in the dazzling sun, caught sight of Clare disappearing, followed by Suzy and all the others, until only the clean sky remained above the boundless, white wilderness.

He thanked God for His mercy.

And having done that, he flew back to the base of McMurdo Sound, where Dwight, pale-faced and distraught, welcomed him home. Maggie had just phoned Collins to inform him of the deaths of Suzy's mother and Clare.

Rydell wept like a child.

# CHAPTER FORTY-ONE

Clare was buried in the parched fields of Maryland in the heat of the afternoon. As her coffin was lowered into the earth the love and grief of those gathered around her was made manifest in the shape of the flying saucers flying serenely overhead, under a silver-streaked azure sky.

Those flying saucers, Douglas knew, would gradually disappear as the Earth, now freed from the alien virus and its attendant apparitions, returned to what it had been a few years before, when he and Clare had been lovers.

He had lost her before she died, as he had lost his wife and children, and now he had nothing left but ambition and the power it would give him. He would use that power to get at the man who had made him lose all the rest; that shit, Rydell.

Rydell was being comforted by Dwight and Maggie Collins while his two sons, dressed neatly in dark suits, clung to their mother.

Suzy Rydell was dressed demurely in a dark skirt and jacket, but Douglas, who had heard a few stories, wasn't fooled for a minute. Apparently she was as common as muck, just like Rydell, which is why Clare had liked him. Taking satisfaction from that thought, Douglas waited patiently for things to end. Still smarting from Rydell's success he was biding his time, looking forward to the chance to crush him. He watched the coffin being lowered into a hole in the ground and felt a twitch of guilt and pain, which he instantly disowned. Douglas played his part well in the subsequent rituals of mourning, shaking a hand here, patting a shoulder there, nodding coolly at Dwight Collins and Maggie.

Then Douglas walked up to Rydell who stood, now dry-eyed but clearly shaken, with his two sons and Suzy.

Rydell stared at him, startled.

'Hello, Rydell,' Douglas said.

Rydell sighed. 'Hi, Douglas. I'm sorry if I look a bit surprised. I didn't expect to find you here.'

'Why not? I was one of her oldest friends. Surely *you* should know that!'

'Yeah, right,' Rydell said.

Douglas studied him carefully. He was bowed, but not broken. He had obviously taken a certain amount of strength from his wife's return.

Now that Douglas examined Suzy closely, he found her very attractive. She was holding hands with her two sons and studying him with candid, green eyes.

Douglas introduced himself. 'I'm the President's aide,' he said.

'Before or after he fell to pieces?' Suzy replied. 'Did you help him with that?'

Douglas was taken aback by the remark, felt humiliated and outraged, and realized that the little slut was not the fool she seemed. He refused to commit himself to a reply and instead turned back to Rydell.

'I'm really sorry about Clare,' he said.

'Sure,' Rydell replied doubtfully.

'She would have been proud of what you did in the Antarctic, I mean, you've practically saved the world.'

'Thanks,' Rydell said. 'Though that's not strictly true. A lot of people around the world contributed to solving the problem; Clare and me, we just collated their work and supervised the analyses. Of course,

Clare's the one who found out *how* to control the virus; I just did what was necessary.'

'And succeeded,' Douglas said, remembering how humiliated he had been when Rydell had returned, though Rydell's success had benefitted Douglas.

'From what I heard,' Rydell said in his customarily blunt manner, 'you *didn't want* me to succeed, since the problems being caused by the alien virus were actually advancing your career.'

Douglas, smiling, barely able to conceal his pleasure, moved in for the kill. 'Well,' he said, 'it's certainly true that the problems caused by the ozone depletion changed the country's political priorities and placed my economic considerations ahead of those of the Department of Defence.'

'I dig,' Rydell said with soft sarcasm.

'On the other hand,' Douglas continued unperturbed, bearing down with all his might, 'the destruction of the alien virus . . . '

'It's just asleep,' Rydell corrected him.

' . . . will eventually return our climate to normal,' Douglas continued enthusiastically, 'thus returning economic power to agricultural and industrial America. It's *also* true that the method you used to put the alien virus to sleep could be used in reverse, I believe, to awaken it whenever, or wherever, we desire. In other words,' he continued, expressing his fondest hope, 'the gas Clare created has shown the government how to *control* the hole in the ozone layer, opening or closing it at will, thereby also controlling Earth's atmosphere. In short, you've given this government unprecedented control over the Earth's weather which means we can control the success or failure of world-wide agriculture and thus the world's economy. I'm back in business, Rydell, and it's all thanks to you and Clare.'

He felt victorious as he spoke, flushed with pride, excited by vengeance.

Rydell stared steadily at him, a glint of mockery in his eyes, then shook his head at Douglas saying, 'You're daydreaming. We wouldn't have given you that opportunity. We knew damned well you were trying to use us and ensured that you couldn't.'

'But I can!'

'*No, you can't!*' As he spoke Rydell grinned broadly, finding pleasure in his adversary's pain. 'The opening of an ozone hole anywhere in the world,' he said, his gaze as steady as a rock, 'would reawaken the dormant virus – as I told you, it's not dead; it's only sleeping – and let it back in through the thinning atmosphere. And once in, it would spread again in an unpredictable manner, which means *you* wouldn't be able to control it anymore than the Soviets, the Europeans or Chinese. No, you *can't* control the ozone layer or the alien virus, you can only leave them alone. I'm afraid you're fucked, Mr Douglas.'

The obscenity was offered like a slap in the face and Douglas flinched. Without a word he turned away and walked to the limousine and let it take him back to a future he could not bear to face. He had been foiled by Clare and her lover, Rydell, and now his future was empty.

When Clare's double materialized eerily beside him, her smile like ice and fire, her dead eyes hypnotizing, he knew he was damned and would certainly be haunted, with or without the virus, for the rest of his life.

# CHAPTER FORTY-TWO

Clare was dead in body, but not in spirit. Her spirit lived on through the rebirth of the Earth.

In a matter of months the final report of an alien 'haunting' had been filed, the world's mean temperature had returned to normal and the ice-caps had stopped melting. The crops and animals had become healthy again and most importantly, at least to those who had personally suffered, the increased incidence of skin cancer and other ailments caused by the sun's unchecked ultraviolet rays had dropped to an acceptable level.

Suzy's mother had been buried, returning to the earth she loved, and Suzy had moved back with Rydell to start a new life. She knew that she'd changed – she was more mature, aware of suffering – and the love she felt for Rydell was somehow more meaningful. Without him and the kids, she'd been empty, incomplete, but once home with the comforts of the familiar, she felt like someone redeemed.

Rydell, he was still dishevelled and obsessed with his work, but now he thought enough to glance occasionally over his shoulder and check what was happening to his wife and children. He'd changed in other ways too and was more considerate of Suzy's feelings. When he touched her in bed it was like being drawn back to adolescence. They were both like kids again, making love tenderly, slow and easy, and they slept arm-in-arm as real lovers do. It was like being reborn.

What relieved Suzy the most was that Clare didn't intrude. Her presence was in the house but that just helped them both to accept that it was OK for Rydell to think about her without feeling embarrassed.

She usually appeared around the house when Rydell was open to his grief; sometimes on the moonlit lawn, wearing that black dress, her hair windblown; other times at the table in the kitchen, just smiling at them. She never came when the kids were there – Rydell wouldn't have let that happen – but she materialized when he let his guilt or grief pour out to create her. He sometimes wept when he saw her, his tears falling against his will, and when that happened, Suzy would take him in her arms and rock him just like a child.

'It's all right,' she'd always say. 'It don't matter. It's doin' you good. That's what she's here for.'

You could share life with the dead the way you couldn't with the living; their impermanence made it easier to trust them and hold them in good stead.

Clare never materialized in the bedroom, which Suzy took for a good sign, and gradually as the weeks passed into months, she came less and less and eventually faded away altogether, never to return.

The apparitions were disappearing all over the world. As the hole in the ozone layer shrank and Earth's temperature returned to normal, the hauntings tapered off and gradually became few and far between. A lot of people no longer saw them even when they were present, and only those with a special facility, like Suzy, could still summon them up at will.

For as long as possible, she clung to her folks that way, seeing her father in his rocking chair, her mother right there in the kitchen, sometimes even seeing herself as a child in the old white house . . . but gradually even they faded away and failed to return.

*

'Are you happy, sweetheart?' Suzy asked Rydell.

'I have my moments,' he replied. 'If you mean, am I happy being back with you, the answer is yes.'

'You love me, don't you?'

'I always did, Suzy. I just have a forgetful disposition, though I'm trying to fix that.'

'You're never gonna fix that, Rydell, but now I know how to handle it. You and me, we're a team for life.'

'Amen,' Rydell said.

He took her hand and squeezed it and she glanced through the window and saw a white light with a tail streaking across the vast, starry sky. At first she thought it was an apparition, something wrought from her beating heart, but realizing that it couldn't be that, she sank back into her chair.

Shooting stars had a life of their own, even though they looked magical.

That thought, though neither new nor original, filled Suzy with wonder.

She might stay young forever.


One evening, a few years after his great experience over Antarctica, Rydell climbed into his car and drove to the long road that ran between the suburbs of Greenbelt and the high fences of the NASA–Goddard Space Flight Centre.

He stopped halfway along the road where he had once seen Clare's double, then got out to stand all alone in that still, moon-lit darkness.

There, in the night, in that vast silence, he thought about life and love, about marriage and children; about how Suzy had returned to him – a different person, as he was – and about how Clare had left a note saying that Don and Ronnie needed their real mother. Love has many faces, he thought, and is filled with surprises.

The three of them, he, Clare and Suzy, had been touched by the virus, and had all been redeemed by it.

He thought of Clare with the pain of loss, brimmed over with love for Suzy, and gazed up at the lustrous, star-bright sky, at the pale eye of the moon, remembering that the alien virus was not dead but simply sleeping, and that some day, some way, it might reawaken and return to the Earth.

To do what?

*As* what?

Overawed by that knowledge, but also uplifted, he held the image of his loved ones up before him like a beacon as he drove back to his modest, untidy home in the dead of the night.

# RAMA II

## *Arthur C. Clarke & Gentry Lee*

RENDEZVOUS WITH RAMA is one of the bestselling
science fiction novels of all time. In this brilliantly
imaginative sequel, another Raman spacecraft approaches
Earth, in the year 2200. Once again, an expedition is
mounted to explore the spacecraft, determined this time
to unveil some of the mysteries which remained when
RAMA left the solar system seventy years previously.
Clarke and Lee build a persuasive picture of Earth two
hundred years in the future, and give a stunning
exposition of the spacecraft that is ... RAMA II.

0 7088 4833 8
SCIENCE FICTION

# VOICE OF THE WHIRLWIND

## *Walter Jon Williams*

Steward is a clone. Fifteen years are missing from his life, because his 'alpha' never got around to having a brain-scan update. And in those fifteen years, everything has changed . . .

Two hundred years on from the events of HARDWIRED, the Orbitals have become independent feudal states, each with its own private army. The Orbital Policecorp which held Steward's allegiance has collapsed in his fifteen-year blackout; First Contact with an alien race has taken place; he has been married twice; and he has been murdered. Steward returns to the planet Sheol, where he fought a war and where the answers to his questions about the past can be found . . . if he can stay alive long enough.

In this return to the universe of HARDWIRED, Walter Jon Williams proves that he is a master of action, character and galaxy-spanning plot.

0 7088 8349 4
SCIENCE FICTION

# THE DIVIDE

## *Robert Charles Wilson*

He was designed to be the perfect man. And at first the experiment seemed a success. John Shaw – the product of secret government research into enhanced intelligence – was from birth far beyond anything human. Brilliant and charismatic, John could have been anything he wanted – except that which he longed for more than anything. To be normal.

So John created Benjamin: an alternative persona, a way of coping with people who hated what they could not understand. He was everything that John wasn't – but now those very differences are killing him. Benjamin has become the dominant personality, more and more often in control. John's altered body has left his mind at risk – and unless he can discover the truth that will fuse both parts together, both he and Benjamin will die.

Robert Charles Wilson spins one of his most stirring, tightly woven tales with THE DIVIDE. Reminiscent of FLOWERS FOR ALGERNON, it is at once an adventure story and a sensitive look at the consequences of man's actions – and of one man's quite literal search for himself.

0 7088 4841 9
SCIENCE FICTION

# interzone

## SCIENCE FICTION AND FANTASY

Bimonthly                                                          £1.95

- *Interzone* is the leading British magazine which specializes in SF and new fantastic writing. We have published:

| | |
|---|---|
| BRIAN ALDISS | GARRY KILWORTH |
| J.G. BALLARD | DAVID LANGFORD |
| IAIN BANKS | MICHAEL MOORCOCK |
| BARRINGTON BAYLEY | RACHEL POLLACK |
| GREGORY BENFORD | KEITH ROBERTS |
| MICHAEL BISHOP | GEOFF RYMAN |
| DAVID BRIN | JOSEPHINE SAXTON |
| RAMSEY CAMPBELL | BOB SHAW |
| ANGELA CARTER | JOHN SHIRLEY |
| RICHARD COWPER | JOHN SLADEK |
| JOHN CROWLEY | BRIAN STABLEFORD |
| PHILIP K. DICK | BRUCE STERLING |
| THOMAS M. DISCH | LISA TUTTLE |
| MARY GENTLE | IAN WATSON |
| WILLIAM GIBSON | CHERRY WILDER |
| M. JOHN HARRISON | GENE WOLFE |

- *Interzone* has also published many excellent new writers; graphics by JIM BURNS, ROGER DEAN, IAN MILLER and others; book reviews, news, etc.

- *Interzone* is available from good bookshops, or by subscription. For six issues, send £11 (outside UK, £12.50) to: **124 Osborne Road, Brighton BN1 6LU, UK.** Single copies: £1.95 inc p&p (outside UK, £2.50).

- American subscribers may send $22 ($26 if you want delivery by air mail) to our British address, above. All cheques should be made payable to *Interzone*.

------------------------------------------------

To: **interzone** 124 Osborne Road, Brighton, BN1 6LU, UK.

Please send me six issues of *Interzone*, beginning with the current issue. I enclose a cheque/p.o. for £11 (outside UK, £12.50; US subscribers, $22 or $26 air), made payable to *Interzone*.

Name _____

Address _____

_____